Estella's Revenge

Barbara Havelocke is an international bestselling author, whose psychological thrillers have topped Amazon and Kobo.

Her writing career started in journalism, interviewing the real victims of crime - and the perpetrators. The realistic, complex characters who populate her fiction reflect this deep understanding. When not writing, Barbara is found walking her two dogs, Scamp and Buddy, or taking photos of wildlife.

BARBARA
HAVELOCKE

Estella's Revenge

hera

First published in the United Kingdom in 2024 by

Hera Books
Unit 9 (Canelo), 5th Floor
Cargo Works, 1–2 Hatfields
London SE1 9PG
United Kingdom

A CIP catalogue record for this book is available from the British Library.

Print ISBN 978 1 80436 704 9
Ebook ISBN 978 1 80436 701 8

This book is a work of fiction. Names, characters, businesses, organizations, places and events are either the product of the author's imagination or are used fictitiously. Any resemblance to actual persons, living or dead, events or locales is entirely coincidental.

Zallman-Caps used for drop caps by D. Rakowski

Look for more great books at www.herabooks.com

Printed and bound in Great Britain by Clays Ltd, Elcograf S.p.A.

I

For Hilda Price, my nan.

You always had a better ending for every story.

Man for the field and woman for the hearth:
Man for the sword and for the needle she:
Man with the head and woman with the heart:
Man to command and woman to obey;
All else confusion.

'The Princess', Tennyson, 1847

Prologue

It is dark, so dark, as dark as my soul, but still there is just enough light down this dank alley for me to see that my hands are stained with something sticky. My blood. In this half-light they look slate-grey but I imagine them as the colour of the half-finished shawl I have been knitting, the vibrant wool lying unspooled somewhere nearby, across the filthy cobbles.

Beneath the blood veneer are cuts and open wounds where my knuckles have split on impact. An experimental try at gently opening and closing my hands makes me suck in my breath, short and sharp, and a smell reminiscent of a butcher's shop hits my nostrils, mixed with the rank tang of urine, and the freshness of petrichor.

In that first surge of action the pain was blotted out. Now it is rushing in, along with...

I need to stop these ridiculous thoughts and try to find out where all the blood is coming from.

I hold my hands out and take a little shuffle backwards, trying to get away from them and the truth they spell out in violent vermillion. My stomach heaves. I hurriedly wipe my hands on my clothes – and they find something unexpected. My fingers explore. There is something protruding from my bodice. Something long and thin and cold to touch and... realisation dawns.

It is a knitting needle. My own knitting needle.

My heart, which had been slowing, speeds up painfully again, and as I pull the homely weapon out my breathing comes in gasping huffs that refuse to be controlled.

Murder, I think. *How did it come to this?*

Terror, anger, regret, guilt...

They aren't the emotions singing through me. No, it is joy. Absently, I lick my lips. A metallic tang of blood spreads across my tongue as my thoughts start to shout.

Murder! It was always going to come to this!

Tears fall: happiness and relief forming a river down my cheeks. Slowly, I fold down onto the damp cobbles and curl up, red hands over my head, trying to quiet myself when all I want to do is scream my elation at finally accepting my fate.

The sound of footsteps running grows fainter. And beside me the dead body starts to cool.

Chapter One

NOW

LONDON, 1835

We do not have a history of good weddings in my family. The opposite, in fact. This has been at the forefront of my mind while organising my own nuptials, and one obvious way to ring the changes has been the dress. I was determined mine should be totally different from my adoptive mother's, thus guaranteeing the day be nothing like her disaster. Not for me the slim, elongated silhouette, with no hint of a waist, which was so popular back in 1813. I have gone for the totally modern: a gown the colour of the sky over the marshes of my home on a cold spring day, the damask silk material so heavy it weighs me down. It has the widest sleeves to be found – the modiste assured me during the fittings that no one had bigger sleeves than I. A glittering silver and diamond buckle on my belt accentuates my waist, and the bell skirt hem touches the floor and hides shoes that are beautifully bejewelled and embroidered with the sun, moon and stars, even though, satisfyingly, only I will ever know it.

Mother won't be here today to see the outfit, though, or my triumph over London society. She'll be sitting at home, in the dark, brooding. Her chin resting on hands folded atop her walking cane, as she gazes into the fire, wearing her own wedding dress, once white but now yellow as old bone. I invited her, of course, but had already known the answer would be an emphatic *no*.

The man I've chosen to wed is not a good man. He isn't kind or charitable; if asked to give alms to the poor, he would ask what the poor had ever done for him. He hasn't a dizzying intellect that makes me want to listen to him extol for hours on a subject, convinced he will change the world with his ideas. He isn't a sharp businessman who will earn a fortune and so guarantee us a comfortable life. Nor is he that most sought after of creatures: the handsome man, who dazzles people into forgetting and forgiving all those shortcomings. I'm even happier to report that he is no smooth-talking charmer; instead, he is more often than not monosyllabic, and has a curious way of skulking in the corner of rooms, spreading a cloud of sullenness that slowly sours the atmosphere and causes people to make excuses and leave.

In short, he is perfect for me.

What you see is what you get with Bentley Drummle: ambitious, determined, persistent, patient as a toad waiting under a stone. He won't disappoint. There is no pedestal of false adoration from which he can tumble. So often I hear married women complaining about their husbands. 'He used to make sweeping declarations of undying love, and gaze at me as if I were the only item in the entire world worth seeing. Now he doesn't acknowledge me when I walk into the room,' they complain – or words to that effect. I have no such high expectations of Bentley and so he will never injure my feelings this way.

Our marriage is practical, not lofty, and with this comforting thought I step through the church entrance. At the rustle of my voluminous skirts, everyone turns in the pews to look. There isn't a single person gazing down the white rose-lined aisle that I care about. No friends, no family apart from those I abhor, no childhood acquaintances. The stares in my direction are not dewy-eyed, they are a mix of hard, cold, envious, curious. This is the wedding of the year, all the ton are here, the polished gems of society, just as Bentley promised when he asked for my hand:

'*We will be the talk of the town. We will hold all of London in our thrall, Estella. Everyone will want to be like us. And then – then it will be the whole damned country who will be in our power. Lord, together, nothing can stop us.*'

No chattering of love from him, just facts. Together we will conquer, but I am the one in control. Bentley needs my cleverness to guide him and my charm to win allies. I will be the power behind my husband, and his triumphs will be mine in a world where a woman cannot achieve for herself.

Beside me, Mr Jaggers proffers his arm.

'Time to enter the spider's web. There can be no turning back once the vows are made, you understand?' he says.

Those clever obsidian eyes impale me from beneath spiky black eyebrows. They would make my heart beat faster, if I had one capable of feeling. My gaze moves from them to the querulous vicar at the altar, who is peering around the broad back of my husband-to-be and the equally tall but far more delicate form of Startop. Startop, the one person who could be described as Bentley's friend. Only last month Bentley spent an entire night laughing that he owes Startop £100, and delighting that he is too afraid to ask him to pay it back. The memory makes me smile. I know the very worst of Bentley Drummle, and by knowing the truth I am secure.

With a regal nod, I silently take Mr Jaggers' arm and together we sweep through the church towards my new life; the whisper of petticoats and congregation members are the only sounds. By the time I reach the altar, and Bentley turns to smile at me and take my small hand in his huge paw, I'm as aglow as any other bride.

There is quite the crowd at our wedding reception, the bright colours of their outfits an ever-shifting kaleidoscope against the white of the great hall. Sunlight streams through the huge windows as well as the glass dome in the ceiling, dazzling when it hits the crystal and glass of the tableware and chandeliers. Gigantic displays of white roses are barely noticeable against the decorative white stucco on the walls, but I know they are there, and that is enough. On tables are bowls containing white rose petals, held aloft by brass cherubs.

Bentley and I work our way through the room, stopping here and there to make connections with any guest of influence, or sweeping past those we invited only for the amusement of belittling. We make a beeline for Sir John, Bentley's godfather, a man with monumental wealth, whose teeth and eyes are a matching saffron.

'Congratulations!' he booms. 'With your baronetcy-in-waiting, Bentley, and the youthful beauty of your charming new wife, you are the perfect match for one another.'

He takes hold of both my hands and rubs his thumbs over my skin in a way that makes me want to knock his stupid, old-fashioned white wig off his ugly head. Of course, he thinks the only thing I can bring to the marriage is my looks – he is echoing society's opinion. Galling as it is, I am not naïve enough to be ungrateful for the advantages my beauty gives me, though, nor those my husband's station affords us.

My husband. How strange it is to even think the phrase.

Bentley is close enough to peerage that many friends and relatives spread their compliments over him thicker than jam on a piece of toast. In this particular case, though, we will be the ones laying it on thick, as Sir John has a great fortune and even greater influence.

'You are too, too kind,' says Bentley. 'How wonderful to see you here, despite your terrible loss. I was sorry to hear about your wife.'

'Yes, yes, it was a shame. It's been three months now, though, and one must get on with life.'

There is a look in the wily old dog's jaundiced eye that emboldens me. 'Sir John, if I could have but one wish it would be that everyone could share happiness like ours. Soon, I'm certain, you'll enter married bliss once more.'

'What's that? Yes, yes, another wife. I would like more sons. You can never have enough of them, you know. Of course, you'll be discovering this yourself.' He gives a barking laugh that sends a cloud of malodorous breath at my face, and leans in conspiratorially. I lean back – and as I do so, catch the conversation immediately behind us.

'—its cover. You know who her adoptive mother is, don't you? You haven't heard the story? It was quite the scandal! The brewery heiress, Miss Havisham – a recluse, you know, over Kent way, or is it Essex, I forget; some godforsaken backwater, anyway—'

I recognise the voice of that pernicious witch, Mariella Featherstonehaugh, who hasn't managed to bag a husband yet despite two years of her best efforts. It isn't a surprise to hear the gossiping, and it cannot be allowed to distract me, so I incline my head closer to Sir John's again as he speaks.

'Do you happen to know of any young ladies of good standing who are from thoroughbred breeding stock?' he asks.

'Mmm,' I manage. It is no use, I'm going to have to breathe, so put my hand over my mouth and nose momentarily, as if thinking. 'I will put my mind to that question, though I am sure that any woman you set your cap at would feel honoured.'

I feel safe enough to say that because I am no longer in danger of encouraging the attentions of men such as this. There is safety and security in marriage that simply isn't available to the unattached woman, which is one of the reasons why I decided to shackle my own leg. Also, Bentley and I have already discussed how grateful Sir John will be if we find his new wife, and have someone in mind. The backing of such an influential man could make a huge difference to our future political ambitions. In the elections at the start of the year, he was the power behind several of the MPs who were elected for the Tories. Today will be the perfect day for introductions…

As if on cue – exactly as if, because it *is* on cue – I reach out and tap the shoulder of a young woman gliding past us.

'Elizabeth, how wonderful to see you here. Are you well? And how are little Grace and Jane – ah, you are so good with your younger siblings; you'll make such a wonderful mother one day. But I am forgetting my manners, forgive me. Sir John Taykall, may I introduce Miss Elizabeth Cleaver.' I add into his ear, ignoring the hair sprouting from it: 'Someone who, it suddenly occurs to me, may be relevant to our conversation.'

I became acquainted with Miss Elizabeth over the course of the season, talking to her sometimes at the various balls, gatherings and promenades in the park. Her family has a title but no money, and seven daughters but not one son, of which she is ranked around the middle in age, and bottom in beauty. All of which means she is desperate enough to marry someone whose breath can shrivel leaves.

Elizabeth has braced herself for this introduction, and it's pleasing to see how she flirts demurely by fluttering her fan – a convenient way of distributing the halitosis.

Bentley and I stay long enough to ensure conversation is flowing between them and then slip away to talk with more of our guests.

In the centre of the room is a feast with all manner of delicious food, from asparagus pie to salmon, and even two pineapples, that rarest and most expensive of fruits, which only those of highest status can afford. They are causing quite the sensation; even Sir John looks impressed by them. Towering above it all is the wedding cake, taller than a man.

As I look upon my triumph, I suddenly see black mould at the bottom. The blackness spreads, consuming and devouring and ruining.

Spiders with bloated bodies scuttle across the whole, until it is entirely shrouded in its own silk wedding gown of webs. The long white scar on my right thigh gives a deep dull throb.

I gasp, blink, and the vision disappears. Everything is pristine again.

Bentley gives my arm a squeeze and we continue, stopping to lord it over envious creatures or charm those who could be useful to us. Although we are predators used to acting alone, my husband and I are learning rapidly how to go for the jugular together.

Only a handful of our guests are not part of the fashionable set, among them my relatives in family if not in blood, the Pockets. Over in a corner is Matthew Pocket, once close to my mother but no more, along with his wife and the countless children they share between them. They have attended not in order to curry favour, but because they genuinely and unfathomably hold Bentley and me in affection. Seeing them here almost pierces my armour and makes me feel happiness. I am about to head their way when I notice three other relatives whom I recognise instantly, even with their backs to me. Sarah, Camilla and Raymond are also Pockets but, unlike Matthew, they hate me. The feeling is deliciously mutual. Today they are dressed almost as if in mourning at my success, in tired greys and browns, looking suitably out of place as they glare around the dazzling room.

With a nudge and nod in their direction, Bentley and I change course towards them.

'—obscene amount of money. So vulgar.'

'It is a sad fact that money cannot buy taste.'

'Indeed – the very idea!'

'And those pineapples cannot be real. Imagine the cost if they were.'

'If they are real, then they – no, I cannot bring myself to say it, it is such an abhorrent idea. All I will say is that it is always commendable to keep up appearances, especially to uphold the family name, but such wanton waste, such falseness and fakery, it does no one any good. No, I shall go further: I believe the pineapples are *rented*.'

'No! Is that possible? I have heard they cost fifty pounds each to buy, but to stoop so low as to rent—'

'Oh, yes, I believe there is quite the business to be had in renting them to make them more affordable to those of less than profligate tendencies. Although goodness knows that girl has always—'

'Cousins, how wonderful to see you here,' I announce loudly, having heard enough. Those hypocrites are accusing me of being simultaneously cheap and wasteful; I really cannot do right for doing wrong in their eyes. All three jump – how satisfying – and Sarah gives a tiny shriek from her wooden countenance as she spins and sees me.

Chapter Two

NOW

LONDON 1835

Sarah recovers quickly and tries to turn her shriek of shock into a squeal of delight that is so far removed from her usual character that I feel Bentley, whose arm is through mine, juddering with barely contained amusement.

'Dear Estella, Bentley, how charming everything is,' she says. 'What a terrible shame it is that Miss Havisham could not be here with us.'

Beside her, Camilla gives a great sigh, and when she is certain she has my attention, a quiver appears through her lips and she dabs at her eyes with a handkerchief with such enthusiasm I fear for her sight.

'It is a tragedy that she is not among us, though no surprise given all she suffers. And I have suffered at the thought of how she must have struggled and pained herself with the thought of not being able to join her family...' She flounders for a moment, realising she has used a word both she and Sarah avoid in connection with me. '...that is to say, to be with us, while watching her ward's marriage. The *idea*! Raymond is a witness to the sleepless nights I have suffered while I wonder about how poor Miss Havisham would feel. Indeed, we almost did not come ourselves, in order to be at Satis House and support her, but in the end we decided to come here instead.'

'Camilla's digestion has been terribly afflicted,' Raymond confirms. 'She's been at the ginger almost constantly.'

'It is inspiring to see how well you have rallied and disguised your discomfort,' I say. 'The way you are forcing yourself to eat and drink with such rigour is truly brave.'

'We are so grateful you are here,' adds Bentley, giving a bow.

Sarah seems to be trying to work out if we are mocking them or not. Given the almost-but-not-quite baronetcy, she gives us the benefit of the doubt.

'Are you going on a wedding tour?' she asks.

'Paris. I've a house there, though it's rarely used, and some relatives I wish to introduce to my bride,' Bentley replies.

Envy pales Sarah's complexion, but Camilla rallies, enveloping me in an embrace that takes me so by surprise I find myself reciprocating. Perhaps because of Bentley's standing and the protection this affords me, she is finally calling a truce between us.

When her lips are close to my ear she turns slightly and whispers.

'How very well you look, Estella. Is that how you have managed to land such a catch?'

Shocked, I pull away and stare at her, breathing rapidly at the insult. I could swing for that woman – and once, many years ago, her plan for me to do just that came terrifyingly close.

'Bentley, come, we have other guests to attend to,' I manage.

'Indeed.' He gives another bow. 'Camilla, as your digestion is so delicate, I won't insult you by offering you a slice of the pineapples we have bought for this occasion. Nor will I put you, Sarah, Raymond, in the awkward position of having to refuse in solidarity.'

The knowledge that they will never again have the opportunity to taste that exotic jewel has all of them reddening at the ears and neck.

Bentley starts to lead me away, but I turn back.

'Camilla, dear, have you lost a button? You look like you have.'

Seeing the redness of all three of them spread from ears to entire countenance is deeply satisfying. Bentley and I stroll on, and though he asks me what I meant by my comment, I shake my head and promise one day I will share the story with him but now is not the time. He grunts, like a bull snorting.

'You were right about them being a bitter bunch; particularly Camilla,' he says. 'Someone with such a chip on their shoulder generally has something to hide.'

'There's no great mystery. She hates me because I am the sole heir to the Havisham fortune, and she thinks it should go to blood relatives not an adopted child. In her head I'm a thief; I've stolen her inheritance.'

He shrugs those vast shoulders. 'Forget her, then.'

But he's got me thinking. Over the years she has hidden many things, and I'm no longer able to ferret them out using my old methods. Perhaps Bentley can help me find something that would finally free me from the Pocket family. No more being on edge, no more watching my back.

'You believe she has secrets?'

'Everyone has. Although I prefer the simplicity of fists, knowledge can be a useful club to batter people with. One of my servants, Joseph, is particularly useful for this sort of labour; have a word with him and he'll scent it out like a bloodhound. He can work on it when we're away.'

'He sounds useful. While he's at it, have him look into Mariella Featherstonehaugh.'

'Ah, now I was told something very interesting about her that she wouldn't want people to know…'

The wedding feast is a total success, but it is time to leave for Satis House, where we will spend the evening with Mother before going on to Paris. Bentley has disappeared to a corner with his friends from the gentlemen's club, The Finches of the Grove, and although I can't see them I can hear them – and they're becoming more and more raucous. There's a sound of glass shattering, and cheering follows. From the same corner of the room as the noise, there is a knot of young men, and for some reason a chair is being held aloft and waved around. Some of the other guests are starting to look worried and disperse, so I ask Startop to calm things down and find Bentley.

He is younger than my husband and far more delicate in both looks and manner. He takes a step away to do my bidding, then hesitates and turns.

'I wish you every happiness, Estella. You deserve so much, and I hope that you and Bentley have all your dreams come true.'

The ridiculous sentimentality makes me want to laugh, but sincerity shines from him. In some ways Startop reminds me of Pip, my friend since childhood; my only friend. Both always leave me feeling confused.

'If deserving does come into it, be grateful that you did not win my hand, for you could never deserve me – no, no, I mean it as a compliment, for you could never be happy with someone such as I. When you realised your friend wanted me for himself, you bowed out, didn't you? You say nothing, but I know. Bentley would never do the same for you, you know. He sees what he wants and sweeps all obstacles from his path, including you. We are similar in that respect, he and I. You are too kind, too considerate for us.'

From the corner of my eye I see Bentley watching us, throwing back a glass of champagne and wiping his mouth with the frill of his shirt which hangs over his hand. One of his Finches friends whispers in his ear and they guffaw loudly, slapping each other on the back.

The Finches are a loud, annoying, but necessary evil, as far as I am concerned. I cannot pretend to like how they act. They are overbearing public school boys who have refused to grow up, and continue their appalling behaviour in this private club, The Finches. They like nothing better than to not only drink expensive champagne but throw it all over the walls of whatever unfortunate building they have chosen to patronise. They wreck the place, destroying furniture and furnishings, pulling paintings from the walls, smashing everything they can get their hands on. You will never hear of them getting into trouble for this; the law would never prosecute them, nor any proprietor press charges, because the members are all too influential and too rich, buying silence with a wedge of cash and a condescending air of entitlement. They are mostly lords and barons, or will be when they inherit. A handful are new money – and incredibly rich. Each one can help Bentley to climb the ladder of political office all the way to the very top. For our ambitions won't rest until he is the leader of the Tory party, and then prime minister. After that, all manner of lucrative opportunities will open up.

Bentley leaves his twittering friend and swaggers over. His cheeks are flushed as he puts his arm around my shoulders, knocking my shawl off then bending to hand it to me.

'It's time for us to leave,' I say.

'You say, do you? Lord!' His eyes are glassy and he knocks against me as he sways a little.

Startop laughs. 'Come on, old chap, let's get you sent on your way. You can drink with the Finches any time, but you only get one wedding night.'

More shouting and cheering, more tinkling as glass breaks. I wince.

'Don't cause a fuss, I'll pay for the breakages plus a bit more for compensation. Eh? Will that shut you up?' someone is shouting.

'Startop, would you be so kind as to deal with that? We really had better be on our way,' I say.

Bentley stands straighter. 'I'll say when we go.' He stares at the increasing melee, and gives a small belch. 'We can go now.'

Moments later we climb into the waiting coach and head east out of London. As the city falls away into Kent countryside I find myself wondering what it would have been like if I had accepted Pip's declaration of love. Our wedding probably would have been a modest affair, and certainly no Finches or pineapples. Perhaps it would have taken place back in the village we are both from. I'm smiling, I realise.

But that is just a silly daydream, because I don't love Pip.

Then again, I don't love Bentley.

There was someone I loved once. That is a mistake I'll never repeat.

Chapter Three

THEN

SATIS HOUSE, 1821

The brilliant summer sun behind me cast a long shadow that danced and bounced as I skipped across the top of caskets of ale that had been hammered shut for as long as I could remember.

Outside was where I most loved to play, particularly around the brewery buildings, which stood empty, their doors always open as if waiting hopefully for the workers to return. Some of the wooden doors were becoming listless in their rejection, though, sagging on their hinges and rotting along the edges.

Beyond the high enclosing wall that surrounded the grounds, and through the ever-locked wrought-iron gates of Satis House, coaches could be heard going past every now and again, or the conversation of people walking by on their way into town, which was a quarter-hour's walk away. Yet from inside the courtyard came no sound except the hypnotic stridulation of grasshoppers, invisible in the long grasses that had overtaken the house's grounds many years ago. That and hollow thuds as I played my version of hopscotch. The great clock neither ticked nor tocked, stopped eternally at twenty minutes to nine, as were all the clocks inside.

The heat made the air shimmer and smell baked. Soon my movements became heavy and I grew cross. Frustrated and in need of company, I headed inside to search for Mother. The second I stepped over the threshold the cool instantly welcomed me, and the darkness, too, for even on the brightest of days the house was as black as the bottom of a plague pit. In the whole of my nine-year life I'd never seen any curtains or shutters opened.

Giving a little shiver, I picked up a candle and pattered along the corridor and up the stairs, accompanied only by my shadow and the comforting buttery glow cast by the candle.

I found Mother in one of her most frequently-haunted spots – I would never use the term 'favourite' as she was always so full of sadness. She was sitting before a dressing table, one elbow resting on it and her head cupped in her hand as she gazed at herself in the gilded looking glass.

As I watched silently from just inside the door, she idly picked up one of the many sparkling jewels that lay frozen in time on the dressing table, leaving a silhouette in the thick dust. She held it against her yellowing skin and once-white dress. A sigh. Then she put it back in the exact place it had come from.

I had learned from an early age to always put things back exactly where they had come from, for even the smallest of errors right or left would send Mother into a rage that was rapidly followed by sorrow so deep it took her days to climb from it. Once, when I was about four, I had dared to touch one of the flowers that made up what must have once been a pretty bouquet, by then so dried up that the gentle brush of my finger against a petal had turned it to dust. As punishment, I had been sent to bed and given only bread and butter, and water – until I realised that Mother had no real idea of how long I was to be punished for, in this house without day or night or other markers of time. And so I had crept from my room and gone about my business as usual, without comment from her.

Watching Mother made me sad both for her but also myself, because I wasn't allowed to play with all the enticing items lying about the place. I itched to dress up like a princess from a fairy tale in the splendid pastel gowns that lay scattered across the room over furniture and in half-packed trunks. There were exquisitely trimmed cloaks and fur-lined pelisses left draped across chairs, never to be worn. Gloves of the softest kid leather, fine lace handkerchiefs, a gold watch and chain (stopped at twenty minutes to nine, like all timepieces in Satis House), and satin shoes covered in delicate embroidered flowers and hearts, or the entwined initials P and E; all lay where they had been abandoned that fateful day when Mother's heart had been irreparably broken so many years ago.

She had never recovered from it. The most important thing in my life was making Mother happy. I lived for the moments she stroked my hair or laughed at a silly comment I made, and lifted herself from her more sombre moods.

Mother was reaching towards either the prayer book or some more jewels as I announced my presence with a 'Hello'.

'Ah, Estella, come. Would you like to try some of my jewellery?'

I rushed forward, smiling wide. 'Oh, yes! Do you mean it?' For she had never before allowed this.

She scowled at my question. 'What have I told you about believing what people say? It is deeds, not words, that matter. Never forget that.'

'Of course. I'm sorry, Mother.'

She twitched her fingers, beckoning me closer, then held an emerald first against her silver hair, then against my brown. It glittered so that I gasped in delight. Replacing it, she next picked a necklace and put it around my neck.

'It's heavy, isn't it? Great beauty is a weighty burden. You're growing older, child, and turning into a pretty little thing; watch that you learn quickly the lesson I was taught so harshly.'

'Great beauty is a weighty burden,' I repeated, dutifully, wondering if she meant that the necklace was so pretty people might try to steal it. Or if she simply meant the necklace was heavy, because, as she explained, it was made from gold and diamonds. Somehow neither explanation seemed to fit with her melancholy glances.

'I was beautiful once,' Mother said, stirring again suddenly. 'Though it is hard to see now that I have rotted away to this shell, once I was like you. Pretty and light-hearted, without a care in the world. Don't believe me? Come, let me show you something.'

She leaned on her walking stick to stand with a groan, then moved across the floor with the uneven gait that was so familiar to me, because she wore only one shoe. Its counterpart sat on the dressing table, unworn and pristine apart from its decoration of thick dust and spiderwebs.

Along the corridor we went, to one of the rooms that we never used. No candles burned in here, no fire was lit – for even though it was summer outside, the constant darkness made the house permanently chilly, and so fires always burned in the handful of rooms we frequented. Stepping into the room, I gave a little gasp of shock as fine, sticky strands trailed across my face, but I did not cry because, although unexpected, it was far from unusual to walk through spiderwebs.

Mother placed her hand on my shoulder and guided me across the floor. Here and there were signs that once the wooden boards had been highly polished, and the great silk rug that was rotting away and curled at the edges must at one time have been vibrantly magnificent. We reached a large fireplace with ornate mantel, then Mother lifted the candle high above her head and illuminated the likeness of a child on the edge of womanhood.

'This was me as a young girl of thirteen, with no idea of the cruelty life had in store for me. There were no clues that the moment of its hanging would be the first time the rot at the core of my home would be exposed, and my innocent heart cleaved in two for the first time.'

Chapter Four

THEN

SATIS HOUSE, *1821*

As I stared up at the life-sized oil painting with fresh fear in my heart at Mother's words, the candle flame reared up in a sudden draft and I fancied the young girl above me – large-eyed, imperious but fresh-faced – seemed to lean closer. Her commanding hand reached towards us. It almost beckoned, inviting me into her world of pain where the wound was fresh and clean.

Then the flame danced again and the painting was only a painting once more.

'My mother had died when I was a babe, but that gave me no real sadness as I had no memory of her,' Mother said. 'Father doted on me, and so I never felt there was a shortfall of love. As such, my childhood was idyllic. I was cosseted and indulged, and generally made to feel as if I was the most important person in Father's world.'

Even then she had the self-assurance of one used to having her own way. And why not? At that moment Pandora Havisham had been rich, beautiful and clever, with all the magical possibilities of her future lying before her.

That this young woman could have turned into the person beside me didn't seem possible. I looked from one to the other and, yes, the full mouth, though turned permanently in a line of disappointment now, was the same; the eyes, even larger in her shrunken face, were an identical shade of dove-grey with flecks of hazel; even the cheekbones, more prominent since her once-plumped rosy cheeks had become ashen and sunken, were still the same if I looked hard. And the expression was certainly familiar: haughty, imperious, used to being obeyed. But I saw the softness, too, which hid behind all of that.

I let Mother lean on me, and pressed into her as we both gazed at the youthful version of her. She squeezed my shoulder and started to talk again.

'You should have seen this house then. Everything crisp and clean and sharp and airy and light and bright and beautiful.'

She was almost smiling as she turned about her, looking into the past and seeing the room as it was, not the mildewed reality where panels of gilded duck-egg blue and white striped wallpaper peeled from the walls, morosely mottled with black. Behind the closed shutters, the vast windows reached almost from floor to ceiling.

'This parlour was a favourite of mine and Father's. It is a south-facing room, and the sunshine would stream in all day long. Often I would play the pianoforte you see over there, at Father's request. So many happy hours. He adored hearing me sing as I played – oh, yes, my singing voice was considered clear and sweet, though now if I tried to give voice it would more resemble a cracked bell – or I'd sit on the chaise longue embroidering or reading.'

The chaise and chairs were covered in material that matched the wallpaper.

'It must have looked splendid indeed in here,' I said.

'There was so much light. But the light is dishonest; it casts shadows, and in those shadows hide lies. The coddling I received as a child was all fakery that left me soft and ripe to be plucked by those who wanted to consume me.' Her smile had dropped away. 'This painting,' Mother lifted her hand to point, almost seeming to shake her fist at it, 'captured the last of my innocence, though I had no idea at the time. Father chose the moment of this painting being hung to break my heart. Even as we smiled in delight together, he took my hand and informed me that he had been living a double life. He was married. That was shocking enough, after so many years of it being only the two of us. But there was more. He had been married for a long time and kept it secret from everyone – even me, his own flesh and blood, the supposed centre of his world – because he was ashamed of tying himself to nothing but a servant. A cook! Can you imagine, a Havisham working in service, even a Havisham in name only? Unthinkable!

'Though other men came after and struck their blows, Father was the first to break my heart. He had lied to me for so long that it left me bereft. How could he have kept something so huge from me? All those years of half-truths and downright lies he had told me to explain why he was away from home so often. The fond way he would speak of Mama to me, as though her loss had pained him – and how could it, when he had satisfied himself with such an inferior replacement? It made me question everything I knew about him.

'Still, after a few short days I forgave him because he told me he was full of regret at hurting me, and promised to spend the rest of his life making amends. After my sheltered life I was ill-prepared for someone letting me down. I had built no armour around myself in protection because I had never needed any, you see? So I promised to forgive him. The cook, he told me, was dead, and so there was no point in holding a grudge.

'There was another blow to come, though, for Papa had a reason for making his revelation. Once he knew I had accepted the first part, he imparted the next – for tricksters often deliver their poisonous lies in drops rather than one big gulp, to make them easier to swallow.

'This former cook had given him a son. No doubt that was how she had tricked him; trapped him by—' Her fingers stopped moving, clenched into a fist. 'So Father had a son, who was brought to live here because his mother was dead, and I was given no choice but to accept him. And I did, Estella. I tried. You may well ask what my payment was for such kindness? Arthur was several years younger than I, and had inherited his mother's weak disposition – blood will out, Estella, always – he was a feckless, weak fool of a man. And what he did to me—'

Her hand trembled with the strength of her anger. She lifted her walking cane and thumped it on the floor, the hollow thud echoing in the almost-empty room.

'He and others struck at me with their deceit, each puncturing my innocence, each deception tearing another part of me away, peck, peck, peck – *I love you, Pandora; keep it as our special secret, Pandora; you will always be safe, Pandora; you're imagining things, Pandora*. They hollowed me out like carrion crow at a corpse, until there was nothing left but these bones you see before you.'

Her fingers rose to gently pluck at her chest cloth as she spoke, as if she, too, were trying to scratch something from her sparse flesh. She pulled at the chain about her neck, from which hung a small notebook and pen. Finally, Mother's eyes seemed to focus away from the past and back to the present. She looked down at me.

'There is no kindness in sheltering people from the harsh realities of life, Estella. To live is to suffer. That is what I prepare you for. I will not leave you soft and exposed, I will harden you so that you can survive, nay, thrive. That is true love, not words that caress you into vulnerability only to make it easier to rip your trembling heart from you. Do you understand?'

Though my own heart did hammer against my ribs, I kept my face staunch as I nodded. 'Oh, Mother, I'm so sorry everyone let you down,' I cried. 'I'll always be here for you, I promise. I will never betray you.'

'In this place there is no time,' she replied, 'yet time will tell the truth of your words.'

I wrapped my arms around her waist and hugged her, trying to give her comfort. She squeezed me, then patted me on the back while pulling away to take my hand.

'The memories have chilled me, let us return to the dressing room and sit by the fire. We can play cards; would you like that?'

With a nod, we walked back through the darkness. I was happier being with her beside the fire than playing in the high summer sunshine.

Chapter Five

THEN

SATIS HOUSE, 1821

The following day we had visitors. The little group of Mother's relatives generally appeared together in the same way there is rarely a single cloud, and were referred to collectively as the Pockets. Like clouds, they also made life duller, for they would put Mother in a terrible mood with their creeping conversation and heavy-handed compliments, but as they sometimes gave me sweets I still looked forward to seeing them. Usually, they tarried with a listless air, waiting always in the same room to be called for an audience with Mother, but on this occasion Camilla jumped up and greeted me with a smile the moment I wandered in.

'Shall we play a game?' she asked. Although her face was as expressive as dough sitting neatly in a loaf tin, she had an explosive manner of speech, as if she spoke aloud every thought the moment it arrived. She had never before struck me as the playful type – anything but – however, she clapped her hands together with such glee she almost hit herself in the face.

'I really don't think we should,' replied Sarah. She gave a wooden smile through firmly locked teeth.

'Estella, don't listen to these spoilsports. Come, come, let's away!'

With an airy laugh that brooked no argument, Camilla took my hand and bustled from the room, leaving me to hurry to keep up or be dragged. As we stepped outside, she gabbled.

'This place was wonderful once. So busy! Everyone in the county and beyond drank Havisham beer and liquors. It was a byword for quality. And the money it brought in! Ah, let's play indoors – it's rather hot out here, isn't it?'

She pushed open the door of one of the great barns. The light softened but stayed bright, for there were many long, thin windows through which sun streamed, and at one end of the building was a set of double doors high up in the wall, which always gaped open, as if in surprise at what had happened to this once-mighty place.

'Let's go up here, where we won't be disturbed by those fuddy-duddies,' prattled Camilla. Up we went, climbing the stairs to the platform in front of those high doors, each step accompanied by a rasp or squeak from the wood. 'What game shall we play? What's The Time, Mr Wolf? Or how about Blind Man's Buff?'

'You choose.' The games were unfamiliar, but I was not going to admit that.

'Blind Man's Buff it is – we can use my scarf. You can be "It" first. I'll blindfold you, spin you round three times, and then you have to try to catch me. Once you do, we'll swap over and I shall be "It".'

A simple game indeed. The thought of being blindfolded held no fear for me, accustomed as I was to navigating Satis House in darkness, often without even a candle. Yet as soon as the soft fabric of Camilla's scarf went over my eyes and the light disappeared, my heart started to race. It felt very different from the house.

'I'm not sure—' I began.

'Not sure that it's tight enough?' Camilla gave the material a hard tug, making me gasp. 'We don't want any cheating, do we? The *idea!*' Her chuckle tinkled in my ear. I laughed, too – it was silly to feel uneasy.

I couldn't see anything, not so much as a vague shape. She grabbed my shoulders, her pudgy fingers stronger than expected, and spun me like a top, surely many more than three times. By the time she let go I couldn't walk straight.

Camilla's voice danced around me from all directions. I turned this way and that, my fingers grasping nothing but air. All sense of location disappeared. Disorientated, I didn't know left from right, front from back, up from down on this high platform as I stumbled giddily on, always following Camilla's calls, her laughter. My eyes darted blindly and my head tilted this way and that, listening.

Mother's voice whispered in my ear, telling her tale from yesterday.

'*Though other men came after and struck their blows, Father was the first to break my heart…*'

I was used to the darkness of the house, knew every step, every feel of the ground beneath my feet, every twist of corridor. Everything in the barn smelled different, the air moved and stirred with breezes, strands of my hair tickling my face, while in the house the air lay stagnant.

'Over here!'

I turned, ran, stumbled.

'He and others struck at me with their deceit, each puncturing my innocence, each deception tearing another part of me away...'

'Over here!'

How had she got behind me?

I didn't like this game, not one bit. My new friend was always just out of reach, as if teasing me. Breath panted – mine or Camilla's, it took a moment to work it out, before I gave chase. Coarse cotton slid over the back of my hand then was gone. Missed her!

The floorboards creaked beneath me at the movement. I concentrated. The floorboards! They held the clue. They seemed to give and bounce with our steps, like keys on a piano.

'Tricksters often deliver their poisonous lies in drops rather than one big gulp, to make them easier to swallow...'

'Oh, nearly!' giggled Camilla. She sounded out of breath – and something else. There was an unrecognisable tone to her voice.

A creak. The floorboard beneath my right foot went down slightly. My head twisted as I turned, trying to catch a sound. Was that breath to the right of me? I was about to move towards it when a clatter came from my left. Confident at last, I stepped forward.

Into nothing.

One leg plummeted down through the rotting wood, the other folding beneath me until my whole body slammed to the floor. At the same time something sliced through the soft flesh of my inner thigh. I screamed long and loud. Utterly blind – what was happening?

Flinging my body from side to side, I begged for Camilla to come and help me, but there was no reply except the tortuous creak and moan of rotten wood. I clawed at the floor, trying to pull myself up. My nails sank into wood as soft as butter. I scrabbled at the blindfold, trying to tear it from me. It was tied too tightly.

'Help me!' I cried.

Another groan from the floor, a splintering sound, and then I was flying down, down, down, my skirts lifting around me, air rushing over my skin…

Then pain. Nothing but flames of white-hot pain burning away all else.

Starbursts of sound broke through the darkness. They grew stronger, louder, longer, until finally my eyes decided they weren't too heavy to open, after all. Someone was sitting beside my bed.

'Mother,' I whispered.

Another blink and my eyes focused. It was Lydia, Mother's most trusted servant.

'There you are, sleepyhead. You gave us quite the scare for a few hours, Miss Estella.' Her face was pale with soot-dark semi-circles beneath her eyes. 'Here, take a sip of this.'

The water tasted sweet on my dry lips. As she spoke, someone stepped forward. Dr Hawkins was a pudding-faced gentleman of kindly demeanour and grey pallor, who sometimes checked on Mother.

'Ah-hum, you've been very ill. You lost a lot of blood – we had to give you a blood transfusion. I don't hold with such newfangled, experimental treatments but Miss Havisham was adamant that everything be done that was possible. Quite a state she was—'

'All's well that ends well, I say.' Lydia's mouth smiled but her eyes glared at him.

'Oh! Yes, ah-hum, no need for details, eh? No, no. You were lucky you landed on the soft straw when you fell through that rotten flooring, it would have been the death of—'

'Are you hungry, Miss Estella? Some chicken broth?'

I nodded. 'Mother?' My voice cracked midway.

'I'll fetch her once you've eaten. The doctor's given her something to help her rest at the moment.'

'Yes, yes, it will be a few hours before… well, least said, soonest mended.'

I nodded, but my heart was heavy. Why wasn't Mother waiting by my side like Lydia and the doctor? Was she going to break my heart as her father had shattered hers?

Chapter Six

NOW

SATIS HOUSE, 1835

Bentley may have been drunk at the beginning of the journey from our reception, but by the time we reach Satis House almost five hours later he's sobered up.

He has only been here once before, when he stayed for dinner and asked Mother for my hand in marriage. He is subdued here, that familiar sulky expression back on his face as he looks around; he is intimidated by our surroundings but trying not to be.

It's hard for me to understand why this house, my home, has this effect on people, but it always does. So I try to see it with a newcomer's eyes, which is easier coming as we do straight from our light, bright white wedding.

Twenty-five years ago, Satis House was a manor so grand that people would come by to be shown around by servants and wonder at its finery, provided the master and mistress were not home. Now, the fine architecture is crumbling; the courtyard is an overgrown jungle; paint peels from the window frames, which are starting to rot. Even the impressive black wrought-iron gates are rusting to brown, including the two chains festooned across them to bar them from ever being used – instead everyone, including Bentley and I, use the former tradesmen's and servants' entrance around the side, which is also locked, though this lock is well oiled.

Inside the ruin continues, and it is forever darkness. We do not open windows to let in fresh air, nor even open curtains to let in the sunlight. Bentley looks around the room he will be sleeping in and his posture is like a dog with his tail tucked between his legs as he stares at a patch of mould that darkens one corner of it. His eyes travel across to the threadbare velvet counterpane that once was opulent.

'We should stay at the hotel in town, instead. The Blue Boar, I think it's called.'

'I want to be here with Mother.'

'This is a small bed,' he says finally.

'It's big enough for you. And if you draw the curtains around the bed, it's quite cosy.' Cosy as a tomb. I haven't drawn the curtains on my four-poster since I was a child. 'My room is just opposite, if you need anything. Staying overnight here is…' I hesitate, unsure of how to put it delicately. 'I know you've had dinner here, when you asked for Mother's permission to marry me, but overnighting is different. There are things you need to know. Mother doesn't sleep, not really. You may hear her roaming the corridors in the small hours. Do not be afraid of the sound of footsteps. Also—'

'Afraid? Oh, Lord! It will take more than womanish talk of wandering mothers who act like ghosts to make this man afraid.'

He pulls me to him and tries to kiss me but I turn my head in time, so that he slobbers on my cheek. Gasping, I push him away, and he laughs.

'It's damn cold in this house, Estella; are you sure you wouldn't like me to warm you in bed tonight?'

'Has the drink made you forget yourself, Bentley? You know the terms I set when I accepted your proposal: we are husband and wife in name only. There will be no children. Ours is a business arrangement; with my brains and your connections we will be a great success together.'

He sits heavily on the bed. 'Those were your terms.'

'Thank you. Now, come on, get up, it's time to see Mother.'

'What time is it, anyway? My damned pocket watch has stopped.'

As he nods, still glaring at his pocket watch and giving it a little shake, I look at him intently to check there is no misunderstanding about our marital arrangements. Bentley's momentary feistiness, brought on no doubt by an excess of alcohol, has passed. I'm glad we understand each other.

I'm keen to show off my new husband to Mother; after all, I have given over my life to her whims, and at her behest cut myself off from all feelings in order to carry out her plan. Perhaps, even in this act of wedlock rebellion, she might against all odds finally approve of my actions. It is foolish to hope… and yet I do.

I pick up the single candle and we start once more down the corridor. The air is stale and familiar, heavy with damp and the dust that plumes up with every step we take. Our shadows loom large over us, stalking silently behind, curious to see why we are here in this place where no one ever comes and nothing ever happens. The familiar scratching behind the wood panels tells me old friends are present, though I will not be acknowledging them in front of my husband. He would think me quite insane.

'And then I rode an elephant, like an Indian queen, and everyone cheered,' I say.

Mother stares into the fire, nodding. Bentley and I exchange looks in the dim light thrown by a couple of candles. Like me, she wears her wedding gown. She has been wearing hers for more than a score of years, and the Regency-style gown created for the gentle curves of a young woman now hangs off her shrunken frame. The delicate lace overdress has been repaired so many times it is becoming impossible to keep up. Her veil trails down onto the floor, only half on, as always.

How bizarre she must seem to those unaccustomed to her. Yet I know every stitch, every jewel, every pleat by heart, and usually find comfort in her constancy.

'Are you quite well, Miss Havisham?' my husband asks.

'Of course she is,' I reply, lightly. 'She's brooding and unhappy, which is when she's at her happiest.'

She finally looks up at this, and thumps her walking cane on the floor. Dust clouds into the air, hangs for a moment, scintillating in the candlelight, before settling again. 'I heard every word you uttered. Who do you think you are, child, to question me?'

'I think I am no longer a child. In any case, you may claim to be listening, yet you made no reaction at all to that tall tale about the elephant, which was clearly a fabrication.'

'Ah, you think I am an old fool suddenly, and would dare test me?' Her voice begins to rise, but she checks herself and swallows. She looks from me to Bentley. 'Would you do an old lady the courtesy of fetching a glass of water?'

He stands and bows with a nod, listening as I explain where the kitchen is. As he leaves the room he pauses at the door to throw a smirk my way. It is a good feeling, knowing we are thinking the same thing, totally harmonious. He knows exactly what is going on. It's disappointing Mother won't let herself be proud of me for what I've achieved, but it was foolish of me to hope. When he steps out into the enveloping darkness and closes the door behind him, I speak.

'What is it you want to say that can't be said in front of my husband? Please,' I hold my hand up, 'do not protest innocence. In all the years of my life neither I nor anyone else has ever seen you either eat or drink, though we know you must. Let us be honest with each other. For once, let us be honest. Generally, you devour every detail of my triumphs, but today you don't seem at all interested in my greatest victory: my wedding day.'

'Your greatest victory is marrying that man?'

'For business.' It's my fresh start, my chance to be a woman of enterprise and finally have my freedom of thought and expression, no longer having to be Mother's puppet. At last, I can be unapologetically myself.

'Business?' She repeats the word, a hollow echo of me.

Her hand is bony and fragile as it takes mine, her skin so paper dry I can almost feel my own flesh desiccating at its touch; yet there is steel in her grip as she squeezes as if she dare not let go of me. It makes me feel trapped. Still, I try again to reason with her.

'We've come all this way to share our day with you; we had to leave the wedding celebrations early in order to be here at a reasonable hour. Why don't you care? Is it because it brings back memories of your own wedding day or—?'

'Estella, what have I done?' she interrupts. 'You are a clever girl, you can surely see what Bentley is? It is all my fault. You should have married Pip; he loves you the way I had dreamed of being loved but never thought possible, and given—'

'I don't understand why you keep going back to this. I told both Pip and you at the time: I do not love him. I am incapable of feeling love

– and it is thanks to your endeavours that I am so. Whatever I am, you wrought me. You took me on as a malleable child, and scorched away all feelings of tenderness, reworking me in the furnace of your hatred, constantly stoking those flames for years and years, until you had forged the thing you most desired in the world: a woman with no capacity for gentle emotions. You should be celebrating.'

'I didn't realise… I didn't mean—'

I wrench free of her. 'You did, and what is more, I accept that you did. My entire life I have given myself over to your wishes and done exactly as you wanted, and yet you are still disappointed in me. You gave me no choice but to find my own path – I warned you I had tired of the old life.'

'Estella, my daughter, my love—'

'Love? What do you know of love?'

'Now you are a married woman there are things you should know; things I've kept from you. Secrets. You must listen to me—'

'I'm not interested in anything you have to say. Not unless it's "congratulations". I have done everything you've ever asked of me, even when—'

'No, no,' Mother moans. She beats at her breast with a fist, and shakes her head in a frenzy of denial. 'Listen to me, Estella. You don't know—'

The sound of the door opening pauses us both.

Chapter Seven

NOW

SATIS HOUSE, 1835

Despite my heart thumping, I try to regain my composure, and incline my head to Bentley as he strides over with the glass carafe of water and a tumbler, and sets them down on the floor in front of Mother. He knows better than to try to use any of the furniture, or move anything on any surface, for she will not countenance that. Sitting beside me, he and I both reach to pour the water and laugh, while Mother groans. At least she has let go of me and calmed down since Bentley's interruption.

'As I said,' I continue, 'I had grown tired of the old life. My husband and I are making plans now for the future, and while I hope you will approve, they will go ahead regardless. I am no longer your marionette, capable only of doing as you bid, Mother; the ties have been cut, and now it is time for me to make my own choices, which is long overdue.'

'We have grand plans, Miss Havisham. We would love to share them with you,' adds Bentley.

'You will approve, Mother; some involve taking revenge on people familiar to you.'

She moves her fingers impatiently, as if swatting at something annoying, but her face remains set and her sunken eyes, their whites as yellowed with age as her gown, never leave mine.

'I must speak with you alone, Estella.'

'Mother, anything you say can be said in front of my husband.'

'Not this, never this.' She starts to shake her head again. It takes some effort on her part to pull herself from the past, where she often gets lost in well-trodden paths of bitterness and regret. 'Listen to me, just one more time if never again after that. You're making the same mistake I did, throwing your life away on a worthless man, and that is my fault, all my fault, but if you will only listen to me now then I will start trying to make up for all the damage I've done to you.'

'Well, really—' Bentley starts to bluster but I speak over him calmly.

'It is too late for apologies or second thoughts.'

'If you leave him before the marriage is consummated then it will be a simple job to annul—'

'Madam, you go too far!' my husband roars, leaping to his feet. 'Do you expect me to stand by and say nothing to these gross insults?'

I too have stood. I will not let myself be overcome with common emotion, so take a breath, plump my sleeves, as if to emphasise the difference between we two brides, then turn to Bentley. 'Would you leave us, please? I feel it is perhaps time to retire after our long day. You know where you are sleeping?'

For a moment he glowers, looking as if he has plenty more to say. Then he does something totally unexpected: he throws his head back and laughs.

'Oh, Lord! There is no logic to women. I shall leave you to your sparring.'

For several moments after we have been left alone neither of us speaks, and the only sound is the coals on the fire shifting slightly as they burn away to ashes. Miss Havisham continues to stare at me as if she can somehow place her thoughts, and thereby her influence, inside my mind through force of will alone. Idly, I reach out a finger and break a spiderweb that stretches from the side table to the chaise, twirling the sticky strands around my fingers as I had as a child.

It is I who breaks the silence at last.

'There was something you wanted to say, yet you refuse to speak. Well and good, you can listen. You made your thoughts on my marriage perfectly plain before the wedding, and clearly you have not changed your mind. Neither have I. We are at an impasse, and must find a way for you to accept the reality of the situation, which is not something you are good at, if history is anything to go by. As I said earlier, I am what I am, and I am what you created, so enjoy it; enjoy watching my success where you have failed: for I have a man and I can control him, yet he will never control me. You would prefer me to stay in the darkness, here with you, but I intend to step permanently into the light. What you do is your own decision. Good night.'

My voice is calm but inside I am trembling with anger, fear, unhappiness, I know not what.

'Estella, I do not know how to say what needs to be said. There are things I have hidden in my heart and you must give me some moments at least to try to uncover them to myself fully before I can reveal them to you.' She gives a great sigh.

And so I wait. Mother says not another word, though. Not even as I finally leave the room. Yet even with my back turned I can sense her eyes following me across the room and to the door; and as I close the door behind me I glance briefly at her and see her sinking her chin to her hands, which rest across the cane once more, and still she glares longingly at me.

It is with a sense of gratitude that I reach my bedroom and undress. As I throw back the counterpane and see with relief a warming pan, a gentle tap on the door makes me groan. The day has been long and I am exhausted; will I never get some rest?

Bentley is waiting when I open the door.

'I wanted to check you were all right.'

'Oh! That's kind of you. You have no need to worry, bickering with my mother does me no harm. I'm just sorry you didn't receive a warmer welcome.'

'Talking of which, it's blasted cold in this house. It's full of draughts and damp...' He licks his lips and leans against the doorjamb, staring at me.

'Is there no warming pan in the bed?'

'Eh? Oh, yes, there is.'

'Then I suggest you embrace that. Good night, Bentley.'

I shut the door, stare at it, and start to hum happily. I've got him right where I want him.

Even so, I turn the key in the lock.

Chapter Eight

THEN

SATIS HOUSE, 1821

'No, Jeremy, you're supposed to be defending the castle,' I called. My friend raced across the wooden floor of the dining room as fast as his little legs could carry him – and it was a constant source of amazement just how quickly he could go when he was so tiny. He skulked by the food on the table but didn't show any interest in eating anything.

'Come back!' I begged. Jeremy scratched behind his ear. Turning to Delilah, I shrugged. 'Clearly he doesn't want to pretend to be a knight. But you're still a beautiful princess. See, this is your mighty castle.'

The joy of being a child is the gift of a good imagination. The 'castle' was in reality a long table that stood in the middle of the room, covered in what had once been a brilliant white tablecloth of the finest linen and scalloped lace, now jaundiced with age and smeared with black dust where mould stole across it, trying to escape food that had long rotted to indistinguishable piles.

Once, long ago, a great banquet had been laid out and then abandoned, when the old house had been full of light and life. The centrepiece of the feast had been a great wedding cake that now crouched over all the ruin, a magnificently rotting hulk so covered in cobwebs that it was almost impossible to see it. Yet such was my imagination there was no doubt in my mind that when Delilah looked to where I was pointing, she saw a drawbridge, turrets, pennants fluttering in the wind... Jeremy spoiled the illusion by launching himself forward to grab a blotchy, bloated spider that was scurrying across the tablecloth. He squeaked with excitement when he caught it.

Another squeak – or should that be shriek – rent the air.

'What on earth are you doing, child? The idea! What would Miss Havisham say if she knew?'

'My dear, who would tell her but us, and that would never happen, now, would it?'

The voices were recognisable even before I turned. Camilla Pocket, and her shadow Sarah Pocket. Since my accident Camilla had shown confusing extremes of either ignoring me or showering me with concerned affection – the latter always in front of Mother, I noticed. How all the Pockets adored Mother! Although even at that tender age I was starting to sense that their words and thoughts didn't always go hand in hand. Their feelings about me appeared even more complex; certainly too complicated for a child of nine to be able to interpret. All I knew was that despite honeyed words and generous gifts, of late I had noticed their looks were more bitter than sweet. The sight of me playing in the dust of the dining room floor appeared to have pushed them over the edge into apoplexy.

It had been six months since I plunged through the floorboards, and to my shame I was still clinging to the manor house and mostly avoiding the other buildings. Despite the doctor's fears of my being left with a permanent limp, I had recovered so swiftly and fully that he was often heard commenting on what 'stern stuff' I was made of. For several weeks I had thought this meant my survival depended upon my being stern, until Lydia explained it meant I was strong, and that smiling would not make me ill. Playing with Jeremy, Delilah, et al, always made me happy... but the shriek from Camilla stopped me short – was I in danger again?

Sarah's hands were on me, pulling me to my feet. Camilla, meanwhile, was fanning herself, while propped against the wall as if fighting a fainting fit.

'To think that someone raised up by someone so high could sink so low. The very idea!' said Camilla.

'I was just playing with my friends,' I explained.

'Friends? Friends!' If she had exchanged 'friends' for 'murder' it could not have been said with greater hysteria.

'That's Jeremy, and over there is Delilah. Oh! And disappearing into that crack is Sir Walter, who is easy to spot as he has only half a tail.'

'You disgusting little changeling, playing with mice. Mice! Miss Havisham should send you back—'

Sarah's hand on Camilla's arm brought the latter to a halt. 'Come, come, Camilla. It isn't the child's fault. After all, today is Christmas Day, a time of celebration, yet I am sure Miss Havisham hasn't given you a single gift, has she, Estella? She is too wrapped up in her own tragedy – such a terrible tragedy for sure, and one that haunts me. Still, it is none of it your fault, and you should not suffer. And, Camilla,' she added, turning to her relative, 'she clearly does suffer, reduced as she is to playing with rodents and vermin.'

'They are my friends. What is Christmas Day?' I asked.

Neither answered. Camilla glared at Sarah. Sarah glared back and twisted her head to one side while bulging her eyes in a way that seemed to convey something to Camilla, for suddenly she said a quiet, 'Oh...'

Righting her head, Sarah continued to address me. 'It pains me to see you without presents, without treats, without friends.'

'It pains us,' said Camilla, her voice going up slightly at the end, almost as if she were questioning.

'Ah, dear cousin, can't you see it is because poor Miss Havisham is suffering so much herself that she cannot recognise what this unfortunate child needs is her own parents. But I have said too much!' Sarah's hand flew to her mouth, and the way she turned to me reminded me of the wooden marionettes I sometimes played with, making them act out parts in stories I made up. 'Ignore what I said, I should never have mentioned your real parents.'

'Mother is my parent.'

'Of course she is. In every way that counts. Forget what I said, for no good will come from you asking questions about parentage, I'm sure. It would get us all into terrible trouble.'

Camilla shook her head. 'She is a clever child, Cousin Sarah. How long before she starts to ask why it is her mother has the name *Miss* Havisham, and is therefore clearly unmarried.'

'As always your wisdom is breathtaking,' said Sarah.

The house was always cold, even in the handful of rooms where fires were lit; but the cold that seeped into my bones and heart at that moment was nothing to do with the damp surroundings.

'What do you mean by all this?' I demanded. For even though I was young, I had been raised by Mother to be confident.

'Perhaps you should ask Miss Havisham, or seek out your parents and ask them. It isn't my place, not my place at all,' said Sarah.

'No, indeed. It isn't our place,' echoed Camilla, who seemed all sorrow now. Her lips twitched as she looked at me, as if some inner struggle were taking place, before adding: 'Poor child.'

My hand rested on my hips and my chin jutted out. 'Stop being so silly and tell me what you're talking about,' I ordered.

'We couldn't possibly—' said Sarah.

'The idea!' said Camilla.

'Although if you were to push us—'

'Only if pushed. Who are we to deny, when pushed?'

'I suppose...' began Sarah. And then she started to talk, saying things that made my head whirl and my heart pound. Things that turned my entire world upon its head. I felt stupid, and deceived.

I wasn't a Havisham by birth, only by adoption. Mother had taken me on when I was three.

'It shouldn't have been down to us to tell you, though, Estella,' said Camilla.

'We're so very sorry you had to hear this way.' Sarah nodded.

'But the truth always comes out, doesn't it?'

'And you're such a brave girl. I know you won't do anything so silly as running away.'

'Oh, no! The *idea*! You mustn't do anything like *running away*.'

'I would never,' I said, frowning.

'Although,' Sarah pondered, 'I could understand it if it were to go in search of your parents. Your real parents, who must be so very upset that they have lost the beautiful child they adored. How would they feel, I wonder, if they saw you playing in the dirt, with mice and spiders, beside a pile of rotted food, instead of being in their honest bosom?'

'Searching for loving parents does seem a good reason to run away. To London. It's the best place to start your search, I'm sure. And it's such a brave thing to do.'

'And you're such a very brave girl that it's just what someone such as you *might* do.'

'But no, you must never, we would never suggest such a thing.'

'Am I interrupting a gallows confession? It has the air of one,' came a voice. All three of us whipped our head in its direction. Leaning against the door frame, gnawing on his forefinger, stood Mr Jaggers.

He stopped long enough to throw the finger in our direction. 'Shall I play prosecution or defence?'

At the sight of him Sarah and Camilla scattered excuses and scurried from the room, just like my friends the mice. Mr Jaggers was Mother's solicitor and man of business, and sometimes stayed over in the guest wing of the house, where the few servants who remained also slept. Recently, I had noticed that while he was always kind to me, he seemed to make others nervous. He smiled as he watched Sarah and Camilla's backs disappear, then he came towards me.

'What was that about? Come, come, there's no need to be coy.'

'It… they… we were just playing,' I stuttered, and did the only thing I could think of, and ran away, too, before he could ask any more questions.

Chapter Nine

THEN

SATIS HOUSE, 1821

For the rest of the day I thought about what Sarah and Camilla had told me. According to them, Mother had lied to me, even though she said she hated people lying and that she had been destroyed by them.

Sarah had hinted that Mother was mad.

That I wasn't treated as other children were.

That somewhere out there were my real parents. Missing me. Longing to see me.

She and Camilla had even sought me out after I left Mr Jaggers, and they had given me a whole guinea to help me on my journey – although they still insisted I must *not* run away and had been strangely reluctant to let go of the coin as they proffered it.

Eager to prove the Pockets wrong, I had slipped away into town and wandered along the curiously empty streets. Against the dimness of the winter's day, many had already lit candles and lamps, the glow spilling from windows onto the pavement. Curious to see what other families were like, I peered in through the windows. Almost every home was decorated with evergreen boughs, along with mistletoe and holly; some even had small trees displayed inside, bedecked with colourful paper chains and the like. Families had gathered together and were exchanging gifts and feasting. There was so much laughter. Outside, I wrapped my arms about myself to hold together the aching chasm that had opened inside me, created by confusion, betrayal and anger.

The Pockets had been telling the truth about Christmas. Which surely meant everything else they had said was the truth, too. Somewhere, my real parents waited for me.

Perhaps they were right about something else: that I should seek my blood family out.

My first memory was a vague affair, like most people's; more like a dream than reality. There was shouting. My little fists so blackened with grime that they resembled lumps of coal as they pounded on the floor, determined to be heard above the commotion.

Who was shouting? I could not fathom it. Given the news of my adoption I could only conclude someone had been shouting at my birth parents; someone awful who stole me from them.

My next memory was even shorter. The smell of soap, so strong that my nostrils tickled into a sneeze. My hands, still filthy despite the soap aroma, clung to a velvet lapel. Huge adult hands with skin gnawed around the nails, unwrapping my own small, clinging fingers in a gentle but firm fashion, then the sensation of me being lifted away even as I reached to go back to my safe haven. Fear, I felt. And then the memory disappeared.

There was nothing helpful for me.

Back at home, I mulled over those memories and the Pockets' words, even as Mother tucked me in. Everything had changed. I looked around my home with fresh eyes and did not like what I saw.

My bedroom, previously loved, seemed suddenly sinister. It was dark but for the light thrown by a single candle on my bedside table, the flame from which danced in the many draughts of the old house. I pulled a stiff sheet closer around me, listening not to Mother's voice telling me a bedtime story, but to the noises further out in the darkness. Scratching came from inside the walls themselves. Could Mother not hear them? She did not stumble or hesitate in her speech once as the insistent scrabbling came again; instead, she continued on in her deep voice, telling the tale she had chosen to send me to my dreams.

Why was she not afraid of the mice, like Sarah and Camilla? Were they right that our home was bizarre, or was my mother correct? My mind tumbled like a stone in a river, helpless against the current, never allowed to rest. I no longer knew how to think or feel about anything, and the things I had accepted without question the day before filled my mind with fear and turmoil. Rather than sleep enveloping me as Mother spoke, I felt increasingly on edge. Mr Jaggers' face haunted me, too: why had hearing about my conversation with the Pockets caused him such consternation? And why had they scattered at the sight of him?

Trying to find peace, my eyes roamed what little of my bedroom I could see. The curtains on my four-poster bed were pulled across on three sides, and halfway across on the fourth, in order to keep the cold and damp out. Beyond them, deep shadows were thrown across the wood panelling on the walls, making monsters of the innocuous. A giant spider clung to my bedroom door. Only after several minutes of terrified staring did I realise it was the coat hook, given strange new life by the candle. A humpbacked man stretched his arm towards me across the wall, his hands twitching with eagerness to snatch me from my covers. It was the heaped shadow of my dressing gown carelessly cast across the back of a chair, and the movement of his eager hands was caused only by the undulation of the single flame – yet the knowledge did not lessen my fear. Instead I burrowed further beneath the sheets, attempting to hide, and tried to listen to the story.

I knew it by heart, for it was one often told to me at bedtime as if it were a cautionary Gothic fairy tale from *Children's and Household Tales*, by the Brothers Grimm, Jacob and Wilhelm.

'This monster named Compeyson hid his terrible cruelty behind a handsome face and impeccable manners,' said Mother. 'Always beware the man who is handsome on the outside, for he will be ugly on the inside. I was so young, so innocent, that it was easy for him to steal my heart. He promised to keep it safely with him always, locked away with his own, for he said he could not live without me. Like all fairy tales, we planned our wedding so that we could live happily ever after.'

Her voice came from just outside the candle-cast circle of illumination. I thought of the painting she had shown me in summer of her as a girl of about thirteen, and as I listened I morphed her into a princess, a queen even.

'On the morning of the wedding, at twenty minutes to nine, I put the finishing touches to my attire while servants packed clothes for our marriage tour. It was then I received a letter from my husband-to-be. It revealed his deception: there would be no marriage. He didn't love me, he never had. He and Arthur had come up with the plan together, to take my money and humiliate me.'

She had ordered everyone from her room, from the house, and fell ill for some time before she finally recovered enough to live her life forever frozen at twenty minutes to nine on her would-be wedding day.

There was a soft thump, a sound all too familiar as Mother beat her chest with her fist. 'They broke my heart!' she cried.

Claws scraped against wood as my former friends played. I flinched, letting out a squeak.

'You cry, but this is not the worst wrong in this sorry tale,' said my mother, misunderstanding.

She leaned forward. The candle threw her features into relief of black and rotting yellow, her eyes staring from deep holes. Her white dress was the colour of old bones, the material threadbare, and there was a tear in the delicate lace of her bridal veil, which cascaded down her back in funereal splendour. Strands of her silver-white hair stirred in the same draught that made the candle gutter, as she reached forward and clasped her white-gloved hand over my sheet-shrouded arm and I tried not to shriek again in terror, tried not to shrink from her touch.

'Never love. Never trust. Hurt men before they hurt you. Steal their hearts and break them,' she hissed. Even through the sheet I could feel her violent fervour through the tremble of her hand.

I nodded.

'True love is the stuff of fairy tales, Estella, for it casts a spell that makes women give themselves so completely that all control over self is lost. So blind will your devotion be that you will gladly humiliate yourself, be utterly servile, trust someone else's word over your own, submit to their whims, and offer up not only your heart but your very soul. I did. You must never do this. You will take everything they have and offer nothing in return. You will smite their souls and grind them to dust.' She beat the pillow with her fist. 'Swear it. Say the words.'

'I swear. I'll never love anyone. I'll never trust.'

It was how we always ended this story. Satisfied, Mother leaned closer still, planting a kiss as soft as the touch of a beetle running across my forehead. Then she leaned back and took the candle with her. I bit my lip to hold in the whimper, but she noticed despite my best efforts.

'You're suddenly afraid of the dark, Estella? This must be a difficult place for you to live, but you must grow used to it.' She paused. 'Still, I don't think it will make you too soft to keep the candle here. You must blow it out when you feel yourself grow drowsy; we don't want a fire to break out. Do you understand?'

'What about you? Aren't you afraid of the dark?'

'I am the dark.' She smiled as she said it. Instead of reassuring me, it made me even more afraid.

She set the candle back on the bedside table, and gazed down at me again. This time her face was soft, a tenderness in her eyes as she tucked the sheet a little tighter around me and then pulled the curtain around my four-poster bed fully across apart from a tiny crack, so that only the faintest hint of light showed beyond the heavy fabric.

'Sweet dreams, Estella,' said she. 'Dream of everything that makes you happy.'

Her progress to the door was in her usual uneven gait, a soft tread of her stockinged foot followed by a click of her single shoe upon the floor. Why, when everyone else wore two shoes, did she insist on only wearing one? It only added to the weird, nightmarish aspect that surrounded both her and this place that I called home.

She walked past the grasping man and toward the monstrous spider. They held no fear for her.

After she had closed the door behind her, I heard her strange, lopsided progress down the corridor. Finally, I slid from beneath the covers. It took a few minutes only to dress in the boys' clothing I had stolen from a washing line earlier, while in the village. The idea for my disguise was taken from an adventure-story book in our library, and seemed a perfect way for me to go unrecognised. Stealing clothes from the poor villagers was my only option, for nothing could be moved at the manor without it immediately being noticed. My long hair was stuffed under a cap; the thick-soled boots I wore felt heavy in comparison to my usual delicate slippers. The boots had been a particularly lucky find, having been set beside the door of a cottage, presumably in preparation for cleaning.

Taking up the candle, I stepped out into the corridor. Hope soared in my heart, for I was going on a mighty quest: I was going to find my parents.

Chapter Ten

THEN

KENT SEA MARSHES, 1821

I had been afraid as I crept through the house but now I was on the marsh it was as if I had been reborn. There were no fetid walls to block the wind rushing along beside me. The village was behind me, and all that lay ahead was marshland criss-crossed with ditches and meandering creeks until they reached the sea. Even the darkness, which would have scared most people, held no fear for me: it was my world.

There had been but one moment when I had momentarily been afraid. It had seemed to me that footsteps followed me along the High Street, and all through the village. No matter if I slowed or went faster, they always kept pace with me, until my heart had beaten so hard that I feared it must surely be heard and give me away. Once out in the open expanse of the marsh, though, there had been no one behind me.

Why had I chosen that particular route? No reason at all. I had barely ever been past the confines of Satis House, and had never gone further than the village, so had no idea of the world beyond what could be gleaned from books. The marsh was surprising, but keeping off the roads seemed a good idea in case my absence was discovered and Mother sent servants to pursue me. The sense of freedom loosed a laugh from me. With no idea of which direction to go, I followed the wind. My thick-soled boots made a satisfying slapping sound on the clay mud as I trotted over the marshes, past the occasional field.

Something moved ahead of me, halting my headlong rush. What was it? Instinctively, I hunkered down, eyes straining to make out the shape... as a long, low sound came. It was only a cow, in a field with her fellows. Relieved, I started to stand – just as a cannon boomed. My hands covered my ears and I sank down again, my heart hammering until I regained control over my fear, for it was a familiar noise heard many times over the years, though always previously muffled by walls and distance. I knew what it meant. The cannons were fired from the prison boats, the Hulks, to warn locals that a prisoner had escaped.

An offender so desperate and violent they had been labelled for deportation to Australia was out there somewhere with me.

I thought of the footsteps that had followed me.

For a moment I turned back towards the warm glow of the village lights, so far away. Their sparkle seemed to call to me, to sing of how easy it would be to go home; for home was what Satis House was. For all its strangeness and darkness, it was all I had ever known; and for all Mother's idiosyncrasies, she took care of me and I loved her, even while knowing it was against her rules. The lure of adventure, of finding my true parents, was too strong, however, for me to return. The marshes were vast, and the chances of me seeing this escaped convict were slim, I reasoned. So I pulled my flat cap lower and continued.

The wind rushed with me, growing in strength, its cold knives slicing through my thin woollen jacket and breeches to enter my bones. Even that didn't slow me. I did keep checking around me for the escapee or his pursuers, though. I was doing just that, Janus-faced as I tried to look constantly behind and before me, when suddenly one foot went jarringly further down than expected and water filled my boot – I had stepped into a deep puddle. The sucking mud held me tightly and we struggled against each other until it finally released me with such speed that I tumbled onto my back.

Damp and covered in mud from head to toe, I needed a place to sit so that I could at least empty my boot of water. A scrubby bush, battle-weary from its war against the wind, seemed the perfect place, so I limped toward it. As I upended the boot, enough water poured from it to surely fill the Thames… and a man's voice sounded beside me.

'What's a pretty little thing like you doing out here all alone?'

The words were polite, the voice smooth and cultured, yet a quality in it made me shiver. It belonged to a tall man with a proud bearing. Beneath a large-brimmed hat was a face that would have been handsome if not marred by a sizeable bruise on one cheek. He wore the rough clothing of a convict as if it were cut from the finest silks and softest velvets, and reached down a hand to me as though I were a princess and he a knight about to lift me onto his white charger.

'That disguise wouldn't fool anyone, fair heart,' he added. 'Even the most cunning garb would not hide your quality. Are you all alone? A runaway?'

I nodded despite myself. In spite of his clothing and my initial suspicion, I found the honey of his voice soothing me in the same way that the Pied Piper's music must have drawn out the trusting children of the fairy tale.

'Come, dear child.' The fingers of his outstretched hand twitched to beckon. Just like the grasping shadow man from my bedroom. 'Let me escort you to safety. Once upon a time I was intimate with this part of the world.'

'I go my own way.' Clinging to the tattered ruse, I made my voice sound gruffer than it truly was.

'That can't be allowed. I couldn't possibly have you tell others you have seen me – and what gentleman would I be if I didn't ensure no danger befell you?' He grabbed me by the shirt and pulled me upright until my toes dangled just above the ground. His handsome mouth split into a dazzling smile. 'Think how easily you could drown in one of the creeks and your body never found. Or be buried alive in sinking mud. And there are some fates, I am told, even worse than death, that can await pretty girls such as you.'

He bit his bottom lip as if imagining eating something juicy. I had sense enough to know that whatever he was thinking it boded ill for me, and began to struggle. My heavy-booted kick connected with his shin bone. *Thwack!*

He let go of me with one hand and slapped me. Stars exploded in my eyes.

A shout rang out. 'Oy! I'm a-coming for you, do you hear me?'

My captor turned, allowing the moonlight to highlight the bruise across his cheekbone. His eyes widened. The ground rushed to meet me as I was dropped and I curled up in a whimpering ball as my Pied Piper ran. His footsteps hurried away, but others hurried towards me. Rough hands were on me. I screamed.

'Did he hurt yer? Did he?' Voice rougher than hands. I looked up in terror to a face covered in mud. White eyes bulged from it. 'Come on, boy – girl? Are yer injured?'

'No, s-s-sir. Please, don't hurt me.'

'I'll get him. I'll make him pay!' Then the second convict was off, running gamely after his quarry who was slowed by shackles, unlike him. 'Yer won't get away! I'd rather hang than let yer get away! I'll have yer liver. I'll have yer eyes.'

He swiftly caught his prey, tackling him to the floor. The two grubby convicts fought the clenching clay as much as each other, dealing blow after blow. Their sounds of shouting and fighting drifted after me even as I ran in terror back towards the village as fast as my little legs would go. My adventure was at an end, my search for blood relatives over before it had begun in earnest. I'd let myself down. I'd let my parents down. But I couldn't help it – I had to get back to safety. Life outside Satis House was far more terrifying than it could ever be inside. I longed for the shelter of those impregnable walls again, and for solace in the arms of Mother.

Chapter Eleven

THEN

SATIS HOUSE, 1821

My heavy boots stirred the dust of the corridors, the motes clinging to me like a 'welcome home' hug as I wearily stumbled towards my bedroom, eager to put my adventurous night behind me. There was much to think about, but for now sleep was beckoning far harder than the shadow man on the walls who once again accompanied me and my lone candle. There was no nose-tinglingly sharp smell of cold, fresh air, only the familiar aroma of mildew and fires burning low in grates. No wind tugging at me, only stillness. My mind was so full of visions of climbing into bed and pulling the counterpane over my head that I felt I was there already, breathing in the warmth created by my own exhaled breath. I turned the corner – and walked straight into someone.

The smell of soap enveloped me, as massive hands grabbed my shoulders with such weight I sagged at the knees.

'Boy! What are you doing here?' a voice boomed out.

My eyes reluctantly travelled up the smart black cutaway coat, over the huge gold chain attached to a gold repeater watch, taking in the velvet lapels, the impressive white cravat, and finally coming to rest on Mr Jaggers' face. His bushy black eyebrows drew together momentarily over deep-set eyes, but that was the only hint he gave of astonishment as he realised I was not a small stranger roaming the corridors of the great house, but its youngest resident.

'Hmm. Clearly we need to talk,' he decided.

'Please, sir, could it wait until morning?'

He stopped me with a look. I was so tired I was swaying, but had no choice but to follow him and the cloud of soap scent that always hung about him – and as we did so I realised something. Earlier, when trying to recall my first memories, I had remembered the aroma of soap. And chewed fingers. And a velvet collar.

Everything in my young mind slotted together. It was Jaggers who had taken me from my parents and handed me to Miss Havisham so that she could become my mother. Had he forced them to give me up?

At the revelation I gave a small gasp, just as we reached the dining room. His heavy hand dropped on my shoulder at the sound, steering me towards the dying fire still glowing fitfully in the grate, taking the edge off the damp air. As ever, the dining table was covered with the rotting wedding feast. Before that day I wouldn't have given it a thought, it seemed so normal to me, something that had been there my entire life. Now it turned my stomach to think of it. I deliberately placed myself between the putrescence and Mr Jaggers, my back to it.

One great hand lifted to scratch at the strong black dots of beard showing on his cheeks and chin, then he bit his forefinger as he studied me.

'Child, I put it to you that you have a secret. Do you deny it?' he said at last.

'You have one, too,' I said boldly.

'Oh-ho! So that is how you wish to play this game. Where is your evidence of the charge you lay against me? My evidence is clear as day.' He gestured to my clothes. 'Where have you been?'

'Just playing about the rooms here. Boys' clothes are so much more comfortable than girls'.'

Jaggers pointed straight to the mud splattered across my clothing and caking my boots. With a great laugh, my interrogator threw one foot onto the seat of a dining chair, and leaned forward. 'I put the case that you were running away. But you changed your mind and returned.'

My days as a practised liar were still far in the future at this point, and even at this tender age I knew of Jaggers' reputation as a fine lawyer; he was used to dealing with adults far more cunning than I. There was little point withholding the truth, and so I told him all about my adventures.

His boots creaked as he shifted his weight. 'That was a foolish thing to do, child, and you had a lucky escape. Now – you have confessed that you were running away, but you have not told me why.'

I twisted the scratchy material of the boy's jacket in my fingers. 'To... to find my parents.'

Another creak as he seemed to roll back away from me, considering. His face softened as he nodded. 'I can see why you would feel like that, child. What made you suddenly decide to find them? You never will, you know.'

The material twisted again. 'Why? Why won't I? You know who they are, because you took me away from them, didn't you?'

'Are you asking, or do you know?' he said.

'I know.'

'This sounds like scurrilous conjecture to me. State the facts of the case.'

My head was muddy with fatigue, but I tried to formulate a response in a way the famous lawyer would approve of.

'I remember you taking me. At least, I remember some of it. That is a fact. You must know where I can find them.'

'They are gone, Estella, beyond where you or anybody else could find them. I am sure of that. Now you're trying to avoid my earlier question. Do not make me ask again why you wish to find your parents.'

I hesitated, but not for long. Mother trusted Mr Jaggers implicitly, and therefore so did I. Besides, I was so exhausted from my night's adventures, that with just one more tiny nudge it would all burst out of me.

'Come, come; out with it,' he badgered.

My dam burst. 'I wanted to find my parents because I was ashamed of my life here. Ashamed of Mother. I was, I was playing here in this room...'

Jaggers did not interrupt. His eyes merely flicked around the shadowed walls and the rotting banquet.

'I was playing with the mice who have their own city behind the wood panels, and caper across the floor without fear, and with the beetles who crawl across the tablecloth, and the fat-bodied spiders living in the cake. They are my friends! So I was talking and... and playing, and then' – I gave a great hiccup of emotion as tears almost overtook me – 'then Sarah and Camilla came in and... and they said I was adopted and I should seek out my real parents, because... Oh, I cannot say for they made me promise not to.'

Jaggers considered this, gnawing on his forefinger until he seemed to reach a conclusion. 'This is the conversation I interrupted this morning, is it not? When you all scattered like frightened mice. A promise made under duress is not enforceable in a court of law. Pray, continue.'

'Very well, sir, if you are sure. Well, Sarah told me that it was Mother's fault for changing me into this strange creature that plays with disgusting animals instead of people. That… that my adoptive mother's behaviour is the talk of the county, and I would be better off with my parents. They couldn't tell me anything about them but said I should seek them out as soon as possible, and London was the best place to start my search. They even gave me a guinea so that I would have money for the journey, and both were so happy to help me, sir.'

Jaggers lifted his foot from the seat and slumped heavily into it. The words continued to cascade from me.

'What they said made me look at everything in a different way. All that I had considered normal was not. Other people open their curtains and let in the light; others observe time — you yourself often consult your pocket watch; normal families do not have piles of rotten food sitting on a table for countless years, or wear the same clothes every single day. Oh, Mr Jaggers, I want to be like other people! But why is it strange for me to play with the creatures that are in this house?'

'It is not surprising that you do this, child, given the circumstances. Not surprising at all. Perhaps it might be best to stop, though, and play with your other friends.'

My blank expression was my only reply.

'Is there nobody in the village?' he probed.

'I never leave this house. Besides, why would anybody want to be friends with somebody strange like me?' Tears were threatening to overtake me again, so I dropped a curtsy to show that the conversation was over. 'I'm very tired, sir, and would very much like to go to bed. Thank you kindly for taking the time to speak with me. My adventures are over now and you need not fear any more about me doing anything so silly as trying to run away again. What's the point, when my parents are dead?'

As I walked towards the door, Mr Jaggers called out. 'Estella, today's Christmas Day. Did you know?'

'We don't celebrate Christmas.' I said it confidently, trying to disguise my ignorance from scant hours earlier. 'We don't recognise birthdays. You know that—'

'—every day of the year is the same in this house, every hour identical,' he finished.

He looked not at me but at the unmoving hands of the once-fine golden clock on the mantel.

'Good night, Estella,' Mr Jaggers said, his voice low, staring at the clock as if he had never seen it before.

With another curtsy, I left the room and finally stumbled to bed. Rather than sleep embracing me, I lay for many hours, exhausted but awake, running through the expression on Mr Jaggers' face when he'd heard about my conversation with the Pockets. Thinking about the dangerous convict who had threatened me in such a charming tone of voice, and the rough fellow who had saved me. Thinking about the terror of the world outside Satis House, and wondering why my heart was filled with foreboding that it would seep inside my home and poison me…

Chapter Twelve

NOW

PARIS, 1835

Since Bentley and I exchanged vows we have barely paused for breath. First, we rushed from our London wedding breakfast, abandoning our guests to travel to my family home of Satis House and share our evening with my thoroughly ungrateful mother. After that regrettable disagreement with her I did not fall asleep until the small hours. Then we newly-weds were up with the lark for our nine-hour coach journey to Dover, where we rested overnight, and finally crossed the Channel the following lunchtime, on a steamer – my first time on one, and the difference in speed was astonishing compared with sailing.

At last we arrived in Paris, and my husband immediately showed off the exquisite house he has in the city, in the Faubourg Saint-Germain. He has family here, and I spent four years here attending a finishing school to complete my transition to a lady, so we are both familiar with the city, and despite my own memories being... complicated... it feels good to see it again.

'It's perfect.' I smile as we finally come to rest. 'I shall ring for tea, and perhaps some light sandwiches to be served, for I am famished.'

As I look around for the bell pull, I untie the ribbon of my bonnet and remove it, then pluck the fingers of my gloves so that I might better smooth my hair with bare hands. Bentley glares accusingly at his pocket watch.

'No time,' he declares.

'Excuse me?' I pull a glove off.

'We must freshen up and change before leaving for my cousin's home.'

'Your cousin?'

'Lord, must you question everything? My cousin. My cousin!'

Travelling has made us both tired and short-tempered. As a show of tolerance and consideration I turn my back to hide the fact I'm rolling my eyes as I pull the cord to fetch a servant. Still, I can't resist a comment.

'Repeating it does not elucidate. I have no idea what you're talking about.'

'It has all been arranged. We are to attend the home of my cousin, Jean-François Dupont. He is a successful banker and an important person in Parisian politics, and we are keen to discuss our plans.'

'Our plans. Yours and mine. I see.'

'Damn it, woman, stop questioning everything and get ready. We have an hour before we need to leave for the Rue de la Chaussée-d'Antin – it's north of the Place Vendôme, don't you know, and we cannot be late because you are busy questioning and titivating.'

'I ask so that I may converse with him and support you. You say he works as a banker? This is surprising—'

'He's nobility, but prefers to work. Since they beheaded their king and queen the power has been shifting away from those born with power, and over to the bankers and industrialists who work for their money. Jean-François is no fool; he saw the way the wind was blowing and set himself up in business and now is not only successful but influential too. Enough of this! Get yourself ready.'

It is tiredness, that is all. It is making me equally prone to throw some barbs his way, but instead I remind myself that this is a fresh start for us both and our plans for the future are mighty. Working together will take some adjustment on both sides, but the benefits will make it worth the effort. So I push down my weariness, brighten my face, and retire to my room in order to change.

The rustle of my skirts makes Bentley turn. All ill temper has been forgotten as he smiles and holds out a hand to me, which I take.

'You look delightful,' he says. 'Though a little tired. Are you all right?'

'It is merely the journey. I shall be glad of rest, but I am looking forward to meeting your cousin, Dupont.'

'Of course, of course. And green is such a draining colour. Perhaps you should change into something else.'

'My, I did not realise you were such an expert on ladies' apparel. I am lucky indeed. Did you have anything in mind?'

'You sound annoyed. Don't you want to look your best for me?'

'I always strive to look my best for myself, certainly.'

He gives a long sigh. 'If you want to look drained and sad when meeting an important member of my family, by all means go ahead. I expected more of you, however. Don't you want to make me happy, and secure our future? Instead you cling to a silly, stubborn desire to wear a dress that doesn't suit you, just to win an argument.'

Other people have, so I am led to believe, an angel on one shoulder, whispering in their ear, and a devil on the other. I have Mother whispering in both ears, dripping poison.

Destroy men.

Break their hearts.

Never trust – they lie and manipulate.

I will not listen. I am tired of her and exhausted by the life she wished on me. This is a fresh start, the beginning of an exciting life. That means ignoring her intrusive thoughts.

'If it means that much to you, I'll change.'

Still, back in my new dressing room I find myself indecisive about which dress to pick. Aware of time ticking away, of Bentley waiting impatiently for me, I have to choose quickly because otherwise I will make us late – but I also must choose well. Finally, I remember that he has complimented me in pink before. The maid helps me into a beautiful gown that reminds me of sunrise through a soft mist over my marsh home, a thought that comforts me as the maid ties a pillow pad around each of my arms to keep the fashionably wide sleeves plumped up. That should impress this cousin, plus the gown suits the pearls already arranged about my person and hair.

The extra effort is worth it to see that Bentley is pleased with the overall effect.

'Jean-François will be green with envy when he sees my stunning bride,' he says.

I smile. 'What a draining colour.'

A pair of footmen open the doors and we sweep down the stone staircase to the coach. Taking Bentley's hand, I step up into it, settle into my seat and look around the area that will be my new home for the following months of our honeymoon. Suddenly my skin prickles, I search... and spot someone lurking in the shadows, staring. Who? Seemingly feeling my gaze, they flit away.

Chapter Thirteen

THEN

SATIS HOUSE, 1822

Jack Frost had visited in the night, painting his delicate leaf patterns across the windowpanes as he stole past the house. I was in one of the rooms not often used but which was a handy lookout for visitors arriving at the gate, huffing visible clouds of warmth on to the glass and rubbing my fingers back and forth to melt a viewing port. When it was done, I tucked my frozen fingers into my armpits, dancing around to keep the cold at bay. Hopefully, our expected visitors would arrive before my nose turned as blue as a blue tit's wing.

Camilla bustled into view, talking animatedly to Sarah. Though it wasn't possible to hear what was said through the window, both women were smiling and had a spring in their step such as I had never noticed before. Behind them trailed Raymond, and he too seemed filled with energy. My friends, my confidantes, had arrived.

It had been exactly one week since that awful Christmas Day, which meant that today was the start of a new year. I was determined that 1822 would be a fresh start and bring me answers, and already felt lighter at the prospect.

They rang the bell and a servant appeared, unlocking the gate with a great iron key and letting them in, before leading them in an unhurried manner across the courtyard while the Pockets hopped with impatience behind her like magpies in a flap over something shiny. I rapped on the window and beamed down at them, waving. Sarah looked up and stumbled into Camilla, who suddenly needed to be held up by Raymond. Perhaps the flagstones were icy, I surmised, racing from the room to greet them properly.

I knew exactly which room they would be shown to before seeing Mother – and that Mother would make them wait for some time, because she always did. The sprint through the house warmed me, so that by the time I burst into the reception room my cheeks were glowing. Sarah blinked rapidly at the sight of me.

'Estella, how, er, wonderful to see you,' she said.

'Happy new year,' chimed Camilla.

'And the best wishes to you all for health, wealth and happiness,' I replied, before diving straight in, unable to hold myself back. 'I want to ask you more about my parents—'

'Yes, you want to find them, don't you?' Sarah asked.

I proceeded to explain how I had attempted to do just that. Halfway through, Camilla started to fan herself, while Raymond moved silently to her side and held her up by one elbow.

'Oh, it sounds very upsetting,' said Sarah when I had reached the part where I had turned for home. 'But it was only a first attempt, and they so often end in failure.'

Camilla nodded. 'The key is to dust oneself off and-and-and—'

'Try again,' finished Sarah. 'If I know you—'

'—And we pride ourselves that we do—'

'—You have more mettle than that. Why, nothing will stop you from finding your parents.'

I tried to speak, but Sarah sallied on. My head turned back and forth between them, my eyebrows drawing together.

'They probably didn't want to give you up. I don't know, of course—'

'—We can't claim to know—'

'But family is very important, isn't it? Surely they wouldn't have wanted to give you up? Surely they'd be grateful to see you and gather you once again to their bosom.'

'Oh, what a picture you paint! I can just imagine it,' cried Camilla, producing a large handkerchief from a sleeve and dabbing at her eyes.

'Miss Havisham, bless her heart and bones, is not the gentlest of souls. She cares, of course, but is she really capable of love?'

'After everything she has suffered.'

'Indeed, after everything… Never let it be claimed that I would cast aspersions on anybody, but I think we can all agree that Miss Havisham is not capable, she won't allow herself to love any more. And who could blame her after the terrible way she was treated?'

'Since then she's never let anybody in, has she, not even us.'

'Not even you, you poor, dear soul. There may be some who might even claim that to take on a child when you are incapable of love is cruel. Not I, of course, never I. A child needs love, though.'

'So much love.' Camilla gave a great sigh, then continued to flap her fan.

My own head was spinning at this speech. Mother didn't ever talk of love, it was true – not unless it was to expound the futility of it. Yet having it spelled out to my young mind in this manner made something break inside me. From an early age I had learned the rules of the house, including never to climb on her lap asking for a hug, but she would embrace me sometimes and allow me to rest my head on her lap while she stroked my hair. She tucked me in bed at night and told me stories until sleep took me. Was that not love? I bit my lip to try to stop the tickling behind my nose that told of building tears.

Sarah was still speaking, piling my confusion higher.

'Somewhere out there is your real mother, crying herself to sleep every night over the loss of you.'

'That's how I'd be.' Raymond nodded eagerly.

'Be quiet,' hissed Camilla.

Sarah didn't break her flow once. 'Yes, poor, poor woman crying herself to sleep every night over the loss of you. It must be terrible. But if you would rather not end her sadness… If you would prefer to keep your long-suffering mother sobbing for the rest of her life, that is of course your decision.'

'It's not what I would do. But we respect your decision—'

'What do we know of such things?'

'We will take to task anyone who says you're a coward for that decision. The idea!'

'There might be those who would claim that to only try once and never dare to again *is* cowardly,' conceded Sarah. 'We will defend you against them all. What do they know? Why, anyone who has met you knows you are a brave girl. The way that you put up with living in this funny house, making the best of it by playing with… with the mice—'

'Anyone who called you a disgusting coward is out of their minds,' Camilla added cheerily.

Cowardly. I blinked to keep the tears at bay, clamping my teeth on my lip even harder.

'They are just plain wrong, for we *know* you will gather your courage again and this time be successful.'

Finally, the two of them paused for breath at the same time, allowing me to speak, despite my spinning head.

'Mr Jaggers says my parents are dead.'

'You told Jaggers?' Less a question from Camilla, more a shriek.

'He caught me returning so I'd no choice but to tell him everything.'

Sarah's eyes darted left and right. All three were frozen bundles of thrumming energy, reminding me of the mice when they sensed danger. Had I done the wrong thing by telling Mr Jaggers everything? But even if I had, surely it didn't warrant this reaction.

'You didn't mention us at all, did you?' Sarah asked after a long pause.

'I hope you assured him that the whole venture of running away in the night was your idea,' added Camilla.

The shame of that night flooded through me again. The hot tears. The confession. I didn't want to admit to it all. In the space of a week my life had gone from the uneventful monotony of every day being almost exactly the same, to non-stop worry. I wanted to find someone, anyone to confide in who would take all this burden from me and tell me what to do.

Perhaps I should speak to Mother. I hadn't until then because I didn't want to be yet another person hurting her. Instead, I had hoped the Pockets would provide answers and succour but the way all three of them were staring at me made me feel shivery and uncomfortable despite the fire. Could I trust them when they made me feel like a cornered rodent?

That thought gave me an idea of how to solve it once and for all. A solution that an adult would never use, I was sure, but which seemed obvious to my young self.

'I should check on whether Mother is ready to see you,' I said. And ran from the room before any of them could stop me.

Back in my bedroom, a little out of breath from running, I hurried straight to the corner where a chair covered in velvet of the deepest crushed raspberry sat. It was my favourite place to read, but that wasn't my intention for today; instead I pulled it away from the wall to reveal a hole in the plaster that was just big enough for me to wriggle into.

The best thing about living in an old house that was falling apart was the many opportunities for hidden holes and places to explore. I had discovered this particular treasure a long time ago when I was very little – probably about four – and since then had found the whole new world that it afforded me. For through this hole it was possible to crawl along the back of all the rooms on this floor. The crawl space was a wonder to me. I used to spend hours at a time in there, pretending it was a way into a magical world full of light and laughter and brilliant colours and all manner of fantastical creatures who were my friends. It was also a useful place to hide at night when sometimes I got a little bit silly, and felt scared by the sounds that had woken me as Mother roamed the house into the small hours, moaning and crying like a ghost doomed to replay the moment of its death until the end of time. I would curl up within the walls and feel protected enough to fall asleep, and only once the sun shining through a gap in the masonry had woken me did I return to my room and the darkness of my reality.

At that moment I had other plans though, and sidestepped along the between-world space as quickly as possible until I reached my destination: the back of the reception room where the Pockets waited. It was often said that eavesdroppers never hear good of themselves, and my plan was to test this theory and discover exactly what the Pockets thought of me, and whether they were trustworthy.

The fact was, the more I started thinking about them, the more confused my feelings became. I wanted to believe them but their words about Mother didn't marry up with the way they acted in front of her. She was often impatient with them, laughing at them for being fake and fawning and only interested in her money, yet all I saw was them being nice to her. Now it appeared they did not think as highly of her as I'd thought.

But perhaps they were right not to. Since discovering I was adopted I had felt betrayed. Unsure who to trust, Mother's own words kept rattling around my head like a loose ball bearing, tearing through all my thoughts: *never trust anyone.*

Through the rotting plaster I could hear low speech. Good, they were talking. A little further and I reached a place where the skirting board had been nibbled through by mice or creepy-crawlies or some such, and lay myself down beside it, first peering through the hole, which was just neatly eye-sized.

Chapter Fourteen

THEN

SATIS HOUSE, 1822

The hole through which I peered was just big enough to show the three cousins gathered in a knot beside the fire, talking busily. Camilla and Raymond had their backs to me, but Sarah's face was visible, her lips so drawn together that even her nose was wrinkled. Shifting position, I pressed my ear to the hole.

'—simple instructions. All you had to do was follow her to make sure she was gone, and you even messed that up,' Sarah fired through her screwed-up mouth.

'I told you, I did! All through the village. Once on the marsh, I saw no need, for she would have seen me. How was I to know she would change her mind and turn about?' Raymond replied in that plodding, mournful voice of his that made him sound permanently like a vicar delivering a particularly sorrowful sermon.

'You should have checked. To raise our hopes this way—'

'It was cruel of you, husband,' cried Camilla. Even from behind I could see her breathing was fast and her elbow moving up and down as if fanning herself. 'I hate to speak ill of people, you know I do, but wouldn't it have been easier for all if the scrawny little changeling had got lost permanently out on those marshes? You missed an opportunity there, Raymond dear, and I always say, you know it to be true, that there is nothing so tragic as a missed opportunity.'

'I don't think we need go that far,' said Sarah. 'We only need rid of her. If we can't get rid of a child without stooping to such tactics what does that say about us? I said as much when she fell through those rotten floorboards in the brewery.'

'That was beautiful; it looked exactly like an accident,' said Camilla. 'The hole was begging to be used, and what a merry dance it was as I led her toward it in the guise of a game. I shouldn't have had second thoughts and called for help when the deed was done.'

I pressed my hand over my mouth to stop from gasping out loud. My breathing mimicked Camilla's near-constant fake hysteria. I still bore the scar from that incident: a long cold-white rope across the inside of my thigh where the wood had sliced through soft skin. There had been so much blood that doctors had feared the end for me.

'You were always too generous of heart, dear,' said Raymond. 'It will get you into trouble one day.'

Camilla giggled. 'I might not be so generous another time, having learned the lesson. We must do something, though. I will not have that interloper inheriting the Havisham fortune. It should be ours. We are blood relatives, and we have put in the time and effort visiting Pandora despite her being deranged.'

'Perhaps the next step is to look at having Pandora committed,' said Sarah.

'Again? Jaggers will only step in, as he always does, and stop it. We can't afford to have him looking too closely at us. No, the key is to get rid of the child first, then move against Pandora once more – until the girl is gone the Havisham fortune will always be hers instead of ours.'

'No one can doubt your passion for the project, Camilla, but your plans are notoriously poor. Leave it to me—'

The sound of a door opening ended the discussion abruptly.

'Miss Havisham will see you now,' said one of the servants.

Their footsteps grew fainter, but I stayed where I was, curled up on my side, hugging my knees to my chest, too stunned to move.

Mother was right: there wasn't a single person in the world I could trust. What was I do to? Run away? My adventure on the marshes had shown me the dangers of that plan. That handsome man's face haunted my dreams, his Pied Piper voice calling me. No, there was nowhere safe out there for me, and with my parents gone there was no one for me to run to.

The only option was to stay at Satis House, which could prove even more dangerous – fatal even. At least there, though, I had a roof over my head, food, a place to think, and now that I was forewarned, hopefully I'd be able to see threats coming.

Perhaps I should tell Mother – but no, despite the fact she had lied to me I did not want to cause her upset when her everyday life was so filled with woe.

There was danger outside the house, and danger inside it, and no one I could turn to.

Then I realised. There was one person that could always be relied upon, one person who would always act in my best interests. Myself. From now on, I would fight for my place in the Havisham family. No one was going to part Mother and me. I pulled myself upright and wiped my face with my sleeves, sniffed and sat up straighter, my hands balled into tight, trembling fists.

I spent the rest of the day within the walls of Satis House, hidden and safe. There was a favourite spot of mine up in the attic, near one of the huge chimneys, which I sat with my back to, enjoying feeling the heat through my body. My chin was resting on my knees, which were drawn up with arms wrapped tight around them, tears making a wet patch on my skirt. But it was cosy, warm and safe where I was, and I even had some blankets and a couple of favourite books in this den. There was also a treasured window there, a small round decorative one that sat near the apex of the eaves, which no one had ever bothered to cover. Through it, winter sunlight shone pale yellow beams into the room, through which dust floated. Watching it, waiting for the occasional glints, stopped my chest from feeling so tight until at last I could breathe easier.

The Pockets want me gone. They want to hurt me. They wouldn't care if I was dead.

It was all I could think about. They had always been so nice to me. Smiling and asking questions and ruffling my hair in admittedly an annoying way but still… Many times they had given me little gifts of sweets, especially humbugs. How I loved that! The paper bag sometimes stuck to them so that I had to slowly peel it from one sweet at a time. Somehow the extra effort made them taste all the lovelier when I popped one at long last into my mouth and the sugar melted across my tongue.

Thinking about it, realisation hit: the Pockets always waited to give them to me in front of Mother. Everything they did was when around her. They would ask how I was but look away, towards her, rather than listen to my reply. They mostly ignored me when she wasn't there.

I was a fool never to have noticed, especially after all Mother had told me about people. That would be the last time I would be taken in, I vowed. From now on I would harden my heart to all comers.

Never trust. Never love.

The wind cut cold through the sunshine and sneaked through the chinks in the roof to raise a shrill howl. It was the sound my own soul made at that moment.

Chapter Fifteen

NOW

PARIS, 1835

Although I'd have preferred to rest after the long journey to Paris, I have to admit there are worse places to spend my first hours in the French capital than the Dupont family residence. The huge town house boasts impressive gardens outside, while inside it is the definition of 'opulent'. Huge mirrors are everywhere. Everywhere. Entire walls reflect and sparkle. It is a conspicuous show of wealth, along with the gold furniture, vast silk rugs, ostentatious decor and… yes, I espy a display of pineapples piled into a huge bowl.

The number of servants is so incredible I find myself wondering what on earth they all have to do. Surely, there aren't enough tasks to go around, and they spend most of their time idle. If that is the case, they really ought to look happier. I had thought places such as this ceased to exist after the revolution at the end of the last century.

Bentley and Jean-François share a grandparent. Despite spending a lot of time in France as a youth, Bentley's English accent is all too clear when he speaks the native tongue. Jean-François insists on speaking English for my sake, despite my replying in perfect French. His English, accent and all, is impeccable. When I remark on it Bentley guffaws, that abrupt explosion of amusement.

'Soon no one will speak anything but English all around the world.'

'Ah, see, my cousin, you are confusing your words again,' remarks Jean-François. 'Your bad grasp of my language made you make a mistake: you meant soon no one will speak anything but *French*.'

'Perhaps the two of you should create a new language for your world domination,' I quip.

'You have married a diplomat; she will make a good politician's wife. Certainly, she is easy enough on the eye – that is the saying, isn't it? – to satisfy any man.'

Why do men think they can comment on women's attractiveness as if she isn't there? They seem to evaluate us as though we are dogs to be bred, or horses to ride.

'Anything that can give me an edge,' Bentley replies. 'We have to stop the madness of the growing discontent within the working class – the fools think they should have the vote. When I am prime minister I will rescind the "Great" Reform Act.'

'The one extending the vote?' I ask. This is the first I've heard of this plan. The 1832 reformation gave the vote to men who occupy property with an annual value of £10. It is a big step forward, and one the government created to avoid the kind of revolution that has taken place in France. Still, it is hardly generous – from what I have read, the act still means six out of every seven adult men aren't eligible to vote. As for the chances of women getting the vote, I can't see it ever happening.

The men take no notice of my question, though. Bentley is busy ranting. 'They want voting by secret ballot. Have you ever heard of anything so ridiculous?'

'I can see merit in that,' I offer.

'Madam, it is better to leave the subtleties of power to men. Leave such ugliness to us – you are too beautiful to be sullied by it,' says Jean-François.

What a posturing peacock.

'It could possibly be turned to an advantage. If voting is done secretively there is the chance for forgeries,' I reply.

Jean-François's smile is as sharp as the tiny teeth it displays.

'You see, Jean-François. She is a clever one,' says Bentley.

'Indeed. Even a stopped clock is correct twice a day. You must be wise, though, Bentley. Hedge your bets. You've seen what happened here. My family survived the revolution and thrived in it because we worked for both sides. There was no way for us to lose. You must sound as though you are on the side of the common man, while doing everything to undermine these constitutional reforms. That is the key! As long as you tell them what they want to hear, you do not have to do any of it. Believe me, we have learned our lesson in France. Too much power has been given to filthy fools too ignorant to know what to do with it.'

Bentley hunches forward on his chair. 'If we don't stop the rot and take back control, they will push for more and more. Just like here. It used to be that cities such as Leeds and Birmingham, full of workers, didn't have a single MP. What did they need one for, when *we* know what's best for the country and for them? They're like animals, they need us to guide them and look after them—'

'—And work them until they drop,' laughs Jean-François. 'There are always more of them.'

'Yes, they complain about lack of food, but they always have enough vigour to be constantly breeding.'

'Like rats.' Both men say these two words at the same time. True brothers in ideation.

I knew Bentley was no egalitarian, but I've never heard him speak in such an extreme way before. We have talked of making money and building power for ourselves, but never about taking it away from people who already have virtually none. For a moment the thought occurs to me that perhaps we aren't as in tune as I thought... but no, he is simply showing off in front of his cousin.

I hold a finger aloft and clear my throat. 'So, you think we should go back to entire cities having no voters? Yet there is a constituency in Surrey, is there not, with a population of just fifty, which has two MPs.'

'Of course. I thought you grasped all of this, Estella, but clearly I've given you too much credit—'

'Ah, the blindness of amour, my cousin; it is understandable. And rectifiable. You see, Estella, the two MPs in such a small constituency can be controlled through patronage, which is to our advantage. In a large city, though... anything could happen and that cannot be allowed. It is too late to roll back the revolution here, but in England it is not yet.'

'Especially if some of your friends in my homeland back me,' says Bentley.

The two men shake hands.

'We already have a plan, do we not, Bentley?' I ask. 'Are you changing it now?'

My husband takes my hand and lifts it to his lips to kiss it. 'I have promised to make us one of the most powerful couples in the kingdom and I will deliver.' As his lips brush my skin gently, his fingers squeeze my middle finger so hard the bone might snap.

'You're hurting me,' I gasp, pulling free.

'Ah, such a delicate beauty.' Jean-François smiles. 'It is good to see my cousin has chosen a charming and intelligent bride. One who, no doubt, knows when to speak up and when to be quiet and supportive.'

Patronising, jolter-headed lobcock. Jean-François is outrageously rude, but that is the unsurprising usual reaction from men when women hint at having a thought in their heads. They really do think we have nothing between our ears except perhaps horsehair, like a stuffed cushion. Bentley though... I am disquieted. I rub my finger and keep quiet. Better to gather intelligence than argue – for the time being.

Chapter Sixteen

THEN

SATIS HOUSE, 1822

Mother had her hand on my shoulder, leaning on me and the stick she had recently begun to use, as we walked around the dining table, out of the room, across the hall and into the dressing room, then back again. It was a circuit she did daily, her form of taking the air. I always enjoyed our walks, a time when we talked freely and she would often tell me tales of the days when she was young and carefree, playing with friends, while the bustle of the workers around the brewery filled the buildings with talk and laughter and singing. It all disappeared when she closed the business down in her heartbreak. It was almost impossible for me to imagine this loud, vibrant world she had once inhabited.

Today, though, she seemed preoccupied with something, her fingers squeezing my shoulder.

'You're growing up, Estella,' she said.

I closed my eyes momentarily and tried not to show my dread at this turn of conversation. Mother did not approve of change, and that included my 'insistence' on getting taller. When I outgrew clothing I had to inform one of the servants to order new ones for me, as Mother got too upset about the visible proof of the passage of time. Nor was she interested in hearing about my educational progress. I had a tutor, a Mrs Sopper, who came to the house for several hours three times a week. Mother never to my knowledge met with her to hear reports of my progress. It was lucky that I recognised the potential benefits of an education and enjoyed the opportunity to learn new things in this never-changing house, and expand my horizons beyond the limits of its iron railings enclosing the grounds. If I had not it would have been easy for me to never do a lick of work. Mother was, however, impressed with my ever-improving needlework, which came in handy to repair the occasional tear in her outfit now that she couldn't see well enough to do the dainty stitching required for an invisible mend. We never talked of the future or what it might hold; she was happier to talk of the past, and I was content to listen. So her pointing out my growing up made me steel myself for the inevitable bad mood and melancholia it would trigger.

'Yes, you are growing,' she said again, her fingers digging into my shoulder like a claw then loosening. 'It gave me an idea that perhaps you may start to grow a little bored of life here. I know that for me life has stopped but it has been pointed out to me that some more responsibility would be good for you as you develop.'

'I don't mind staying as I am, Mother,' I said, dutifully, even as I felt a flutter of excitement at the opportunity for change.

'You alter daily.' There was that hollow sadness, echoing through her voice. I was letting her down, and must try harder. 'That is the way life is supposed to be. Though I resist, you cannot – nor can I expect you to, even though it pains me. From now on you will carry the key to the gate on your person at all times, and the comings and goings of the house are your responsibility. You can also take over collecting the rents from tenants. It is a simple enough task; all you have to do is note down in the ledger how much is given you and by whom. I assume Mrs Sopper has taught you how to tell the time, write neatly, and do arithmetic?'

I confirmed she had with no small beam of pride, although there seemed little use in reading a clock. However, to have a purpose would give my life some direction; something I had been too young to long for before, but which recently had started to make itself known to me. Mother nodded in approval. It was good news for her, too, for the servants were growing older – it was only the handful whom she had grown up with, who had spent a lifetime serving the Havisham family and therefore had a proven record of loyalty, who had been kept on when Mother had shut up the house – and of those, some had recently retired, and one died. She did not like to replace them with new ones (unless relatives of other servants) whom she feared would gossip about her.

'One more thing: I have arranged for someone your own age to come and play with you.'

It was so unexpected she might as well have told me Satis House was built from chocolate bricks or something equally ridiculous. A friend! Oh, this was wonderful news.

'The boy is called Herbert,' she added. 'Herbert Pocket.'

My stomach dropped. A Pocket? This could only be bad news for me...

Two days later Mother was still intent on her plan, and I kept thinking about ways I could get out of it. I wanted to make her happy, but perhaps I should tell her what had been happening between the Pockets and me. When I tried to raise the subject, however, she became full of forced jollity, which was such a strange sight that it disturbed me greatly. Why was she acting?

Finally, I decided she had been put up to this plan by someone. At first I suspected the Pockets for manipulating her, but despite spying on them during visits, I had overheard nothing to that effect, which seemed strange. They struck me as the type who couldn't resist congratulating themselves of any victory, no matter how small, because of its rarity in their sad lives.

The good thing about Mother's plan was that I was given the keys to the house. A great ring of them, which weighed heavy but felt comforting hanging from a belt about my waist at all times. Time was ticking down to the appointed day that Herbert was to visit, and still I hadn't thought of a way of stopping it. Even during my lessons I pondered, and even Mrs Sopper firing questions at me during an arithmetic lesson did not distract me from the problem of Herbert Pocket.

'Seven times nine?' she asked.

As I answered readily, she took a long sip from a flask she kept always on her person. Had it been the morning, I would have had to concentrate hard, but lessons tended to get easier as the hours wore by and her nose glowed redder.

'And five?' she asked.

If it wasn't the Pockets, who else had dreamed up this plan? Perhaps I was wrong and it was Mother's idea, after all. But why was she suddenly worrying about me having friends to play with when previously she had never given it a second's thought?

'And eight? And, I may, er, have a little sit down.' Mrs Sopper popped a peppermint into her mouth and sucked it until her cheeks hollowed, while I gave the answer. When not drinking from her flask, she was usually sucking a peppermint. Meanwhile, I mulled my problem further.

I was fine playing with the mice and spiders—

That's when it hit me. Of course! There was one other person who had spoken with me about making friends.

Mr Jaggers.

My teacher interrupted my thoughts. 'Now on to writing. Copy this passage from *The Pilgrim's Progress*.' She giggled for no apparent reason.

'Yes, miss.'

While I began the task, copying in immaculate copperplate, I kept one eye on Mrs Sopper. With each blink of her eyes, she became sleepier, until finally… a gentle snore rose from her lips. I didn't shirk my duties, though. Not only did I finish the passage, I also wrote to Mr Jaggers informing him of my disappointment that he had broken his word that he would not tell Mother about the night of my abortive attempt at running away. I added that any plan that involved one of the Pockets, even a young one, surely boded ill for me. Herbert would be their creature, spying on me, acting against me in whatever plan they had cooked up. I skimmed over the words, wondering if there was anything else to add to it, and decided I came across as worried, which would not do (even if it was the truth). And so I added a final line stating that I was not worried one bit by the Pockets, for they were stupid and would continue to underestimate me. Finally satisfied, I sent it.

The very next day I received a reply, the handwriting strong and bold, with thick, confident downstrokes that brooked no arguments, and sharp, spiky upstrokes that spoke of haste.

Estella,

Always be careful of what one commits to paper, particularly when expressing libellous thoughts.

I put it to you that if I were to speak to Miss Havisham and suggest you might like a companion now you are growing, is that breaking the contract?

No, it is nothing to do with the promise I made you.

As for young Master Herbert Pocket, you have nothing to fear. He is the son of Matthew, who was once close to your mother, and although they have long since stopped speaking to one another, he is as close to trustworthy as it is possible to get in this world.

Despite the people you referred to in your letter having nothing to do with this scheme of your mother's to find a playmate and companion for you, I will issue a warning to you: someone can be stupid and still be a threat. Sometimes they are more dangerous because they lack the wit to solve a problem in any way other than the most basic and physical. Bear that in mind in all dealings with people, but especially with those you mentioned in your letter.

Your servant

Mr Merryweather Jaggers

Although the letter soothed me, it did not completely dispel my fears. Perhaps Herbert would not be a danger to my position, but I could not risk anyone coming in and undermining me. As an orphan, I could easily be turned out of Satis House if Mother one day changed her mind about me – or rather, if someone turned her opinion against me. A rival for my place would not be countenanced; I would squash him like the flies that buzzed around the decaying wedding cake during the summers.

I would go through with my plan to make Herbert Pocket wish he had never set foot over the threshold of Satis House.

Chapter Seventeen

THEN

SATIS HOUSE, *1822*

Herbert Pocket's face stood out white as milk against his pewter-grey clothing, and the black of the gate's railings. Aged eleven, a year older than me (I had turned ten the previous week), he was already starting to shoot up, and was so very long and thin that he looked almost as if he had been stretched on a rack, which gave him a delicacy that hinted he might blow away in a strong breeze. He met me with a genuine smile that took over his entire face and made his enormous eyes disappear.

Weak in body and spirit, I decided.

I took on an almost regal manner, so stiff was my back, so set my face, in order to show not a hint of emotion or weakness that he might be able to pounce on and report back to his scheming relatives to use against me. One of the greatest weapons at my disposal, I decided, was the house itself. If the Pockets and my Christmas Day spent peering through windows at other households had taught me anything it was that Satis House was not like other homes. Where they were light and clean and inviting, it was dark and dirty and intimidating. Well, good; it would be the perfect location to rid myself of this interloper.

Leading him inside, I deliberately walked past the first candle and instead plunged on into the inky corridor which I knew by heart. Behind me there came a quiet gasp that made me smile.

'You're not afraid, are you?' I laughed.

'No, not truly,' he replied, though there was reluctance in his voice. 'Although… there are no ghosts here, are there?'

'If there were such things as ghosts then I would scare them away. They would never dare approach me. But I can see why you would fear them, for there's no fight in you at all, is there?'

'I'm learning to box.'

'Good luck knocking out spirits.'

We had reached the next candle, glowing at the bottom of the stairs, and began our ascent with no more words until we reached the top. Herbert seemed to have made a decision.

'I don't understand why Miss Havisham has invited me here. I think Father thought it might be an opportunity for bridges to be repaired between himself and your mother.'

'Yes, I've seen how keen your side of the family is to be close to the Havisham fortune.'

'Estella, I'm not interested in getting in Miss Havisham's good books or trying to get money. And I have plenty of friends and people to play with. What I'm trying to say is you need not fear me, Estella – though from what I hear I do fear *for* you. Don't you need a friend? Surely everyone needs people to laugh and commiserate with? Someone to be themselves with?'

'What a ridiculous thing to say. I am always exactly myself.'

'Are you? Aren't you rather what you have been told to be from the first moment you arrived here as an infant? My father has told me all about how you're being raised, but says it's still possible for you to change your fate. If you need someone to talk to, I'll be your friend.'

'You presume to tell me about my life, when your own fate is, what, to be one of a dozen children, with nothing to make you stand out from them. You are commonplace, dull, ordinary and always will be, Herbert, just like your father who was born as a gentleman, with so many opportunities open to him, yet has ended up working – a most ungentlemanly thing. Taking in students to study how to become a gentleman themselves! I can't think of anything more demeaning.'

His eyes grew wider as I spoke, his lips tightening together so that the rash of red and yellow pimples at one corner of his mouth stood out even more. I held my breath. But instead of an angry retort he gave a sigh and shook his head, and returned to his usual cheerful expression.

'Well, if that is how you feel about things then we shall probably never be friends, which is a shame,' he said, 'for I do feel a friend would be useful for you. We shall simply have to rub along until the end of the day, and that's that.'

It was as easy as that to be rid of Herbert. He didn't show any further interest in playing or conversing, and seemed quite happy to go off alone. Mother still insisted he come around, but even she noticed how little we had to do with one another.

My task completed, I told myself I could rest easy again in my home, but could never again find the ease I had previously taken for granted. Instead, I lived on a high alert, wondering if the Pockets might take my life or move against me some other way. And sometimes at night, I'd replay my dismissal of Herbert and worry at the words he had spoken.

'*Aren't you rather what you have been told to be from the first moment you arrived here as an infant? My father has told me all about how you're being raised, but says it's still possible for you to change your fate.*'

Yes, I did as I was told, but I was still my own person, wasn't I? Would I be different if I were being raised by my own parents? It was an impossible question to answer, for all I had ever known was this life. As for changing my fate, I didn't want to; in fact, I was going to do anything and everything to ensure no one was going to steal this life from me.

Chapter Eighteen

NOW

PARIS, 1835

The rest of the evening with Bentley's cousin goes along in the same vein. Jean-François and my husband talk about workers' wages and rights, about what a terrible decision abolishing slavery had been, while I listen and inwardly cringe. They have no interest in what I have to say, so I give up trying and instead collect information in silence. I had thought I knew everything about Bentley, but here he is showing me an unexpected side. I don't like being caught off guard.

'You're dead on your feet,' Bentley says at last, catching me trying to stop my eyes from closing. 'Apologies, I am used to being a bachelor having to take only myself into consideration. I should have realised how tired you were after so much travel.'

Ah, he has remembered me at last. Exhaustion is catching up with me, and probably him. Once we have rested fully we will both return to being the partnership we usually are and I can dissuade him from his more abhorrent views.

We say our farewells, and I am overwhelmed with relief. Bentley veers from my side as we cross the courtyard to our coach. Where is he going now? He's heading towards a beggar sitting on the pavement just outside the gated entrance. He pulls out a note and proffers it. The tattered man looks so grateful as he reaches for it – but Bentley snatches it back. Guffaws.

My food curdles in my stomach.

My husband is reaching into his pocket again. Produces a cigar and matches and…sets fire to the note and uses it to light his cigar.

'You really are a beast,' I snap when he reaches my side. 'That was unnecessarily cruel – I've never seen you do anything like that before. Don't do it again.'

He gives a wolfish laugh.

Furious, I try to climb into the coach, but my tiredness is so profound I stumble. Bentley reaches out a steadying hand. I settle back into my seat and can't wait for the comfort of bed. My eyes are gritty. I rub at them and—

There's someone watching us again. I'm sure of it. A cloak pulled tight around them, they stand in the shadow of the archway opposite. It was only the slightest movement that caught my eye, as they pulled up their hood to hide their face. They shrink further into shadow as the coach lurches forward and carries us away.

This is curious indeed. Is it something to do with Jean-François? Or something from my own murky Parisian past?

Back at our mansion I am heavy with fatigue. Bentley is solicitation itself, one arm around my waist as we go up the stairs. I don't actually want or need it, but it seems to make him feel better, as if he is making up for his earlier rudeness.

'You might trip and fall and break your neck, if you don't watch out,' he says. 'Rest yourself, Estella. Tomorrow is going to be a big day – the day when our honeymoon starts properly, and we can enjoy ourselves.'

'All the travelling and excitement since our wedding has left me wilting, I must admit. It has been a delightful time of celebration, though.'

'I greatly enjoyed showing you off to Jean-François. My beautiful bride, exquisitely dressed, your manners impeccable, your demeanour demure; in short, everything desirous in a good wife. That's what you should have been, anyway. Instead, you were argumentative. You humiliated me by speaking out so.'

His tone is light but his words are not.

I suppress a sigh. 'We're both tired. Perhaps it would be best to retire for the night, you to your bed, I to mine, and resume this discussion in the morning.'

'Do you like your view?' The change of subject surprises me.

'I haven't had a chance to look yet,' I admit.

'Come, then. Come! There is nothing like Paris at night.' He steps inside my bedroom and walks to the balcony. I hang back.

'All I want is sleep.'

'Grant me this one request, wife?'

I do sigh now. Would it seem ungrateful to remind him that far from being my first time in Paris, I lived here for four years? He knows this. A quick look won't kill me, though, and if Bentley is making the effort then I must, too. I am a married woman now, shackled to the whims of a husband. It was my choice and I must get used to it.

Paris positively glitters as we look out across the blaze of lights far brighter than the night sky, from the balcony of the mansion. Bentley points out various landmarks I already know.

'We must visit the Arc de Triomphe,' he says. 'They say it is almost completed now.'

'Another year, I believe; but it would certainly be interesting to see how it's coming on.'

'That is, if we are not too tired from our exertions.' He walks his fingers across the back of my neck, creating goosebumps. I jerk away.

'It's getting chilly, I must fetch my shawl.' As I move inside, Bentley comes with me, and I find myself chattering. It's unlike me. 'I am looking forward to tomorrow; perhaps we could have a quiet day, might I suggest a little promenade rather than sightseeing? At some point I would like to fit in some Parisian shopping, as it would be good to see what the latest fashions are here, but that can wait.'

'There's no need to waste money on more clothes, you have plenty. I'd rather see you out of them, anyway.'

I want to tell him not to be crude, but my instincts are whispering to me, low and soft and urgent, that this situation needs a gentle hand. My heart batters against my corset.

'It is my money to waste.' I add a smile to soften the comment.

'Estella, my dear wife.' He puts the shawl around my shoulders even though we are now inside. His fingers trail along my collarbone as he adjusts it. 'My dearest girl, you have nothing. What was yours is now mine, from your money to your body.'

His smile makes me go cold.

'Well!' I give a light laugh. 'This body needs to rest right now. Good night, husband.'

'I am definitely ready for bed.' He pulls me closer.

'What are—?'

He tries to kiss me. I turn my head, but he grips my face hard with one hand and covers my lips with his. Fear clutches me.

Chapter Nineteen

THEN

SATIS HOUSE, 1822

Nerves jolted through me when I saw the jealous triumvirate of Sarah, Camilla and Raymond Pocket waiting at the gates. It was the first time they had visited since I'd been given my new responsibilities, and the look Camilla gave me could have soured milk. Instead of running away I forced my shoulders back, put a little skip in my step and swung the ring, from which hung the keys, around and around my finger. When I was a few steps from the gate I stopped and put my head on one side as if considering them, the keys still swinging.

'Can I help you?' I asked.

'You can let us in,' said Camilla.

'Aye, come on, child. What are you doing with the key, anyway? Stole it from the servants, have you?'

'Not stolen, Raymond, I'm sure, just playing.' Sarah's voice was sharp, the look she gave him a warning. They still wanted to maintain the pretence of being my friend, while plotting against me.

'I would love to let you in,' I replied. 'Especially as Mother has now put me in charge of admitting visitors. But you see it isn't really down to me; I have to do as I'm told by Mother, and she has said no visitors today.'

'Well, I'm sure she didn't mean us.' Sarah's wooden face almost creaked as she tried to smile.

'Ah, but she did. She specifically said.'

'You've misunderstood. Run along and ask again.'

I lifted my chin and gazed at them down my nose as steady as you like. 'I understood perfectly. The instructions were clear. However, it is possible that Mother will change her mind. Come back in an hour and I'll let you know.'

With that I turned on my heel and skipped away, leaving them huffing and puffing in noisy indignation.

Inside the safety of the house and out of their sight, I leaned against the closed door and could scarcely believe my own cheek. They'd had no idea how fearful of them I'd been, and were totally fooled by my act. Even better, being treated that way had made them squirm. It seemed I could have some fun with this trio.

An hour later the Pockets were waiting patiently at the gate. This time I let them in and led them along the corridor, holding my candle aloft so they could see. Camilla tried to go straight into Mother's dressing room, but I neatly stepped in her way and opened the door to the reception room we used as a sort of waiting room.

'I'll let her know you're here, and will call for you when she is ready,' I said.

'You mean we have to wait again?' snapped Camilla. 'Well, really, my nerves can't take much more.'

'Yet we all know what a trooper you are. None of us would ever claim we suffer more than poor Miss Havisham herself, after all,' said Sarah.

Camilla flustered for a moment. 'Obviously, of course. As long as our dear Miss Havisham is feeling well enough to see us, that is the most important thing.'

I was playing a dangerous game, for Mother knew nothing of my delaying tactics. It felt good to take back some power from them, but if Mother were to somehow find out she would not be best pleased. The Pockets would never dare to seek her out themselves without her permission, however, and wouldn't dare reproach her for making them wait when they finally did see her, so it was theoretically safe for me to leave them to stew for a little longer before taking them to her.

At least I provided refreshments while they waited – in the form of a large silver pot of tea, laced with a hefty dose of dandelion for laxative purposes.

'Enjoy.' I smiled, backing away.

I ran to my room, threw a light cloak over my dress and hair to keep the dust and cobwebs at bay, and made my way along the crawl space until I reached the back of the waiting room.

'Time is running out. The child is growing up and we must act now if we're to stand a chance of ousting her – the longer we wait the harder it will become.' Camilla waved her hands around as she spoke, the backs of her arms and neck mottled red so high was her passion.

'Lower your voice or Miss Havisham will hear,' hissed Sarah.

'Perhaps we should encourage the child to run away again?' suggested Raymond.

'That ship has sailed, she won't be fooled into it again,' said Sarah. 'I had hoped Herbert would work out, but I hear it isn't looking hopeful.'

'Heard how?' asked Camilla.

'I sometimes pay one of the servants for information, not that I can afford it. Even though Matthew is hopeless and refuses to involve himself in family matters, I'd hoped we might get his son onside, get information that could be used to drive a wedge between Miss Havisham and the changeling.'

'It is no surprise to me that Herbert proved to be as useless as his father. Raymond, my fan.' Camilla snapped this last sentence. Her husband jumped and, after a quick search, produced her fan and began to wave it back and forth to cool his hot-headed wife. 'Did you see the swagger on that child today? Common little strumpet. "*Mother has put me in charge of admitting visitors*",' she mimicked, her voice a screeching falsetto.

'Miss Havisham must be quite mad putting so much trust in the hands of a stranger,' said Sarah. 'That child has bad blood – how else would she be up for adoption? Goodness knows what her parents were – thieves, murderers, peasants, most likely.'

'You only have to look at how she walks and talks to see she is coarse and common through and through,' Camilla agreed. 'It's in her face, the way she holds herself, even her hands – her horrid hands, so square, not delicate and tapered like a lady's should be. Breeding is everything.'

'She'll never be a Havisham, no matter how finely she dresses. Putting a crown on a pig doesn't make it a queen.'

'Oh! The idea!' giggled Camilla.

Once the laughter had settled, all three sighed.

'The question is: how are we going to rid ourselves of the little oinker?' said Camilla at last.

'Simple, we have to poison Miss Havisham against her once and for all.'

'In all the years we've been telling her that blood is thicker than adoption, and the fortune should stay in the family, has it made a jot of difference? No. So why will it work now?'

'Let me think on it. No, Camilla, before you say anything, we're not killing her. I won't go that far, no matter what you say. But we can destroy her.'

The talk drifted from me to what they were planning to eat that night, and the new bonnet Raymond had bought his wife, so I crawled away. One ugly, coarse, common hand in front of the other. Back in my room, I pulled the dusty cloak off and glared at myself in my full-length looking glass. Could people really tell by looking at me that I wasn't a true-born lady but a pretender?

Pondering that conundrum, I made my way slowly along the inky corridors and informed the Pockets that, unfortunately, Mother was too tired to see them. As I walked them back to the gate, Camilla's stomach gave a gurgle. They might make it home before the dandelion laxative took effect… then again, they might not. I was the one with the power now, and I was determined to enjoy it. Yet my triumphs were petty and hollow, and did nothing to make me happier or more secure.

The following months were busy. As winter thawed into spring, which warmed into summer, I successfully worked out which of the servants was spying for Sarah. By means of feeding each one a different piece of information, I devised from listening in to the Pockets' conversations that it was Martha. She was the granddaughter of the man who had apparently once been our head gardener until Mother let the grounds go to ruin, and she had been hired as scullery maid to set the fires, make the beds and do general work. It was tempting to tell Mother about it and have her dismissed on the spot, but instinct told me not to waste information that could prove useful. After all, I might be able to feed more false information to her, and thus the Pockets, at some point, and be able to make fools of them in front of Mother.

Besides, until it became clear what exactly they planned to do next to oust me from Mother's affections, it felt better to watch rather than act.

In addition to my sleuthing, there were my new duties to take care of. One was collecting the quarterly rent from various tenants. It had previously been carried out by Jaggers himself, despite him being always so busy – it was a testament to how much Mother paid him that he always found time in his schedule. There were occasions when Mother's signature was called for, but if she was in one of her moods it could be difficult getting her to put pen to paper, and so I started to sign on her behalf. Thus I discovered a skill for forgery, although I'm certain Jaggers wasn't fooled. Still, he pretended not to know, for he knew I never acted without her say-so.

Another duty was running errands to pick things up from the High Street. Sometimes the lists were so comprehensive that Mother gave me a gift to help me: a small ivory notebook, mounted in tarnished gold, with an accompanying pencil, all on a chain to hang around my neck. It was identical to a set Mother wore around her own neck, and it made me proud to think she so trusted me, and that in some ways I was becoming like her – for what little girl doesn't want to be like her mother, even if she does eventually outgrow the desire.

Although it was a mere fifteen-minute walk from the house I often dawdled through town, making the most of my time in the sunshine and among people. The world's many colours overloaded my brain so that afterwards I needed to lie down, and as for the noise, I covered my ears until acclimatised to it. I was not a part of this world, only an observer, an outsider, a creature different to everyone else. There seemed to be nowhere where I fitted in; not at Satis House any more, and not this outside place either. But I stayed out as long as possible, ignoring the urge to run, both enduring and enjoying the blissful torture of trying to learn its ways.

There was a butcher, saddler, coach maker, baker, grocer, chemist, watchmaker, dressmaker and corn chandler. The corn chandler – Mr Pumblechook – was one of Mother's tenants and I had never come across a man more desperate to ingratiate himself. A windy, wheezing man with a mouth always slightly agape like a fish, his sandy hair smeared across a thinning pate, and hands always fluttering as if holding himself back from doing something he knew he'd regret. And it was this man who created my next problem...

Chapter Twenty

THEN

SATIS HOUSE, 1822

It was rent day, and Pumblechook arrived with the other tenants to pay the monies owed.

'Miss Havisham wants a word with you,' I said, as instructed.

'It will be an honour. My word, an honour! To think that the great Miss Havisham should request a meeting with me...!'

He almost danced with joy as I led him along the corridor to the dressing room.

'Wait here,' I said, holding the door slightly ajar and calling: 'He's here.'

'Mr Pumblechook?' Mother's voice floated through the crack.

He started, and made to move. I barred the way. 'No, you stay here and speak through the open door.'

'I thought I was to see—?'

'Miss Havisham wishes to speak to you. I said nothing about seeing her.'

His disappointment was so great I suspected the downturned ends of his mouth might hit his boots.

'Mr Pumblechook,' came Mother's impatient voice. 'I have a fancy to have a child visit to play for Estella and me.'

Not again!

'Do you know of anyone in the village? I shall be asking all my tenants and—'

'No need, my good lady! I know just such a lad who shall fit the bill perfectly. If I might come in I can tell you all about him—'

'No.' The power of that single word.

Pumblechook's curiosity was so intense it made his hair stand on end as if he were underwater. He leaned closer, placing his mouth right next to the opening. 'He's an orphan being raised by hand by his sister, who herself is the wife of the local blacksmith, Joe Gargery,' he shouted.

How delightfully belittling of Mother to keep him standing so, speaking through the crack of the door; a grown man diminished with such a tiny gesture. It was inspired. When Pumblechook looked my way I did not hide my smirk, for why should I? I was swiftly learning that the best way to become superior to others was to act that way until they believed it.

I would treat this new playmate with equal disdain. The boy would retreat as swiftly as Herbert had.

But why was Mother so insistent? Jaggers must have done a fine job indeed in persuading her that I needed a companion more worthy than scuttling creatures; but it was only to be expected by one of the finest criminal barristers in the land. Even so, it had never bothered her before that I'd spent my entire childhood alone. Now she expected me to be able to interact with another child in a normal fashion. And if I didn't – or couldn't – might she be so disappointed in me that she would turn me out on to the streets?

A thought occurred that almost made me gasp. This boy was an orphan. What if Mother preferred him to me and took him on? What if he replaced me in her affections and my home?

That could not be allowed to happen.

'I shall bring the boy tomorrow!' Pumblechook promised.

There was no time for me to stop it, no time to make Mother realise she didn't need anyone but me to make her happy. Pumblechook puffed up like a dog that had performed a trick.

My stamping raised dust clouds as I took him back to daylight. When he went through the gate I slammed it shut so eagerly on him that it hit his vast behind and bounced off. I jumped back too slowly and it struck my shin painfully.

Let that be a lesson, I thought, rubbing my leg after turning the key: if you're going to be mean to people make sure it doesn't bounce back on you.

The following day I took my favourite seat at the window of the room overlooking the courtyard and gate, and waited for this supposed playmate to arrive with the wheezy Mr Pumblechook. Torn between eagerness for company and disdain for the people coming, I didn't know how to feel, so settled on a determination to do whatever was needed to secure my place and to make Mother happy.

First thing that morning she had come to my room and sat behind me to brush my hair.

'You grow prettier every day,' she had said. 'Use it, Estella, or it will be used against you. Men, that unfair sex, shape the world and make all the decisions; they can raise a person up or crush them. They pretend to fall in love until the whim passes. Do not be fooled by them. Make them love you, make them hate you, make them destroy themselves with their desire for you, because that is the only power a woman has.' She put the hairbrush down. 'There, your hair is shining beautifully. It will bewitch your new friend, I'm sure.'

Mother always said I was beautiful, but the words of the Pockets had burrowed deep inside me and taken root. I did not feel capable of bewitching anyone, with my strange ways, coarse, common hands and bad blood. As I looked anxiously down at the courtyard I tried to reconcile the two, but couldn't.

At last the bell beside the gate rang and I threw open the window. Pumblechook's double chins trembled with importance as he fussed over the boy beside him. He looked small for his age, smaller than I. Flaxen hair that stuck up despite him constantly forcing it down; a reflex from always being told he was a mess, I guessed. Ruddy cheeks dotted on pale skin. Wearing his best clothes, which were a little too small and becoming threadbare on the knees and elbows. He shuffled from one foot to the other and his eyes darted around, trying to take in all of Satis House at once. From the slackness of his mouth, it was clear he was overwhelmed.

'What name?' I demanded, flexing my minuscule power.

Pumblechook replied.

'Quite right,' said I, and slammed the window shut again.

When I appeared in the courtyard the corn chandler introduced the boy as Philip Pirrip, known as Pip. As he spoke, I swung the keys on my finger again, remembering how it had annoyed the Pockets. Pumblechook stared and huffed but gave an ingratiating smile as I finally unlocked the gate. The boy stepped in. Pumblechook tried, until I closed the gate slightly in front of him.

'Oh! Do you wish to see Miss Havisham?' I asked.

'If Miss Havisham wishes to see me,' he replied.

'Ah, but you see she don't.'

He looked at Pip as if it was his fault. 'Boy! Let your behaviour here be a credit unto them which brought you up by hand!' he ordered.

I had the immediate sense that 'by hand' meant slaps and beatings. The boy made no effort to stand up for himself as he was given his orders like a soldier going to war. Every emotion in him was clear to see – was I that easy to read? I determined to work harder at disguising my thoughts and feelings, because the last thing I wanted was to be like this frightened creature.

He seemed so much younger and more unworldly than I, an innocent abroad, with those wide eyes of his so full of questions.

It is a curious thing to observe the past through the lens of hindsight. What should have happened at that moment was that I bonded with Pip, for he was an orphan, like me, and completely at the mercy of the whims of bullying elders, too. Instead I only felt contempt, for he seemed to be everything that I was but did not want to be. The hatred that was growing within me for myself transferred to him, instantly, unreasonably.

Pip's curiosity made me see the house and grounds with fresh eyes. Ashamed at the state of it, I boasted about its history to try to impress him.

When I described how the storehouses had once heaved with malt, the vats filled always with beer, the fires in the furnace constantly glowing, he looked about him in wonder.

'Not that I ever saw it,' I admitted. 'No beer has been brewed at this manor in my lifetime, boy.'

A recent growing spurt made me a head taller than Pip, even though we were the same age. It made acting superior to him easier.

'The manor house, is that the name of the house, miss?' His voice was shy and soft. Filled with something I didn't recognise.

'It's called Satis House. It means "enough" in some language or other, for who could want more than all this?' Sarcasm iced my words. 'Don't loiter, boy.'

I wanted to move on quickly, for a chill had settled in my bones that had nothing to do with the biting wind. Mother had found no satisfaction or comfort within the walls of this house, nor her father. Its name seemed to be a warning that nothing here would ever be enough.

Once inside, Pip scurried behind me, our shadows looming over us as if to bar our way. I threw a glance at him cowering behind me, and pulled myself up further, my back ramrod straight, my manner icily regal. *Show no fear.*

At last we came to the door of the dressing room. I stopped and indicated he should enter.

'After you,' he said. There was the slightest tremor to his voice.

I smirked, realising he wanted me to go before him not out of politeness but fear. 'Don't be ridiculous, boy; I am not going in.'

Turning on my heel, I walked away, taking with me the only source of light in that long corridor and knowing how scared that would leave him. As I turned the corner, plunging him into total darkness, I heard him call after me.

'Thank you, miss.' What was that in his voice again? It irritated me.

A knock rang out that sounded far more confident than he had looked. What delicious tortures did Mother have in store for him, I wondered.

I stood in the corridor, tucked around the corner from Miss Havisham's dressing room, remembering the look on Pip's face, and laughing.

Tears rolled from my eyes. I doubled over, gasping. Still I laughed.

Something was wrong.

I held my sides, stomach aching, snatching breaths, and slid to the floor, wiping the tears from my cheeks, but they came faster and faster, and my breath, my chest was tighter than the ball I'd curled into, sobs bursting from me, from the depths of me, and what was happening to me, oh, dear, Lord, make it stop…

What was happening was that I'd finally identified what was in Pip's voice.

Kindness.

I hadn't recognised it.

Here was someone gentle and good.

I rejected it.

As quickly as the hysteria had come it swept away, leaving me feeling heavy with fatigue. Back in control, I dried my face, stood up and dusted myself down. Just as I finished, Pip's voice echoed along the corridor. He shouted like a common lout for me. Such a poor way of conducting oneself would not impress Miss Havisham. My mouth twisted into a smirk.

He called again, his voice filled not with kindness but fear. I waited in the darkness for as long as I could before my tardiness would begin to irk Mother, and then picked up my candle and walked towards the sound. I turned a corner and saw Pip's face white in a halo of warm candlelight. Eyes wide, eyebrows huddling together for comfort.

When I stepped into Mother's dressing room, she beckoned me to come close. Took a jewel from the table and tried its effect upon my fair young bosom, and pretty brown hair. She was showing me off for the blacksmith's boy.

'Play cards together,' she said.

She held my gaze and made the tiniest movement that looked to me like a nod. Confused, I turned to Pip. He was taking it all in, his eyes giving away nothing, but his mouth tightened to hold in tears. He was afraid of the darkness and cobwebs and the spectre of an ageing, wizened bride. He was judging us.

Two emotions swept over me simultaneously: shame and protectiveness. This stranger had no right to think badly of us – what did he know of our lives?

Mother's words from that morning returned to me. Men had all the power in the world. The fact Pip was weak at that moment did not alter his future. I must be a hawk striking while this boy was still tender enough to tear apart.

Chapter Twenty-One

THEN

SATIS HOUSE, 1822

'Play,' Mother said again. Time for me to show her what I was capable of.

'With this common labouring boy?' I sneered. He looked down.

'Well, you can break his heart.' Her answer was low. For me only. Yet I thought I saw a flush of fear across his face, gone in the flicker of a candle.

'What do you play, boy?' I asked, with the greatest disdain.

'Nothing but Beggar My Neighbour, miss.'

'Beggar him.' Mother's amusement was whip sharp. He flinched at her words, then huddled in on himself like a trapped mouse that knew whichever way it might run, it was doomed.

Poor Pip.

The thought flashed through me before I could control it. That made me angry at my weakness. And so I was all the harder on him that Mother might not glean my secret. I beggared him for fear of being turned into a beggar myself if I did not.

'He calls the knaves jacks, this boy,' I sneered halfway through our first game. His head lowered. What else could I say to hurt him? Inspiration hit, courtesy of the Pockets. 'What coarse hands he has. And what thick boots.'

Those boots, so like the ones I had stolen and worn when I ran away, were a terrible reminder of the way I had been duped by my own enemies. The memory made me dislike him all the more, as if it was his fault.

Look hard enough at anyone and it is easy to pick out something to criticise. I was relentlessly talented at victimising him. I thought I was fighting for my life, you see, and for that reason had to ensure he came away damaged. He looked at his hands, which before that day he had probably barely considered beyond how strong and capable they were. Now he was disgusted by his association with them. He shuffled his feet as far under his chair as he could to hide those thick boots. He started to make mistakes: silly, obvious ones that appeared to confirm my pronouncement of him as stupid and clumsy. By the time I was done, he couldn't hold his cards without dropping them.

Mother's hand played over her lips to disguise the cruel amusement that twisted them upwards in a rare smile.

'You say nothing of her,' she remarked. 'Estella says many hard things of you but you say nothing of her. What do you think of her?'

'I don't like to say,' he stammered.

Weakling.

'Tell me in my ear.' She bent down.

I could not hear the barbs, but Miss Havisham's eyes twinkled with delight as she listened, and that filled my heart with fear and hatred, those twin emotions that so often go hand in hand. He was sure to be saying all the things I had heard before from others: I was ugly, ungainly, unladylike, far more common than he.

Her smile dropped suddenly, and she waved her fingers again, silently telling us to return to our play.

Again and again I defeated him and insulted him, but the smile did not return to Mother's face. I threw down the cards I had won, hoping my triumph would mean the boy's banishment, at least. Finally, Mother spoke.

'When shall I have you here again?'

All my efforts had been in vain. Even when Pip tried to tell her what day of the week it was – a cardinal sin usually followed by swift punishment – she silenced him with an imperious movement of the fingers of her right hand, and merely gave that sonorous speech she was so fond of.

'I know nothing of days of the week. I know nothing of weeks of the year.'

Outside again, Pip blinked in the daylight, surprised that it was not night after enduring so much darkness. It could be discombobulating, time playing tricks on you when there was no change in the light to mark the passing of time, and no clocks to gauge by. It wasn't unknown for me to sleep through the day, then play under a sky as black as the house.

'Wait here while I fetch you something to eat,' I ordered.

I left him to wait in the courtyard, where he surveyed his hands and feet as if he wanted nothing to do with them ever again. Instinctively, I knew that I had landed a blow to his confidence that may never fully heal. I should have been pleased. But his helpless demeanour reminded me of something I did not wish to think of: me when dealing with the Pockets. I thought of the kindness in his voice when he had first spoken, and felt shame that I had not been able to do the same. That weakness must not be shown though, especially for a boy – for who were males to act hurt when the world was made for them?

I came back with some bread and meat and a little mug of beer. As he ate I gazed down my nose at him, and was rewarded with such a pleasing sight: his tears.

He saw my pleasure – and they disappeared.

That confirmed it for me: it had been an act on his part, and when he saw I would not pander in the usual feminine way expected, he knew there was no point continuing. It didn't occur to me that his small show of strength in stopping crying was the act.

After he had finished his repast, I came down with the keys to let him out, allowing my haughty sneer to slide over his strong hands, so used to helping out the blacksmith who raised him, and linger on those thick boots, before glaring into his face again. He met my gaze with unexpected strength.

'Why don't you cry?' I probed.

'Because I don't want to.'

'You do. You've been crying until you're half blind and you are near crying now.'

I laughed, pushed him out and locked the gate upon him.

Yet I ran to the top of Satis House and watched from that circular window as he traipsed down the High Street. There was a strange sensation of dislocation around my solar plexus, as if I was being pulled in opposite directions that threatened to tear me in two.

Mother clapped her hands together and smiled as I told her about Pip crying.

'I didn't think having this boy visit would be such fun,' I admitted. 'But I very much enjoyed it. Thank you.'

'I had intended you to become friends, but practice for the future was an even better idea that came to me. You were very good,' said Mother, picking up one of the jewelled hair combs from its dusty tomb. 'This is a beautiful diamond, see how it twinkles prettily in your hair? You will catch the eye of men this way one day. When you do, you will be prepared for their empty flattery and know exactly how to deal with them. You'll be strong as these diamonds, capable of cutting glass, where I was weak.'

I took the comb and put it in my hair, turning my head this way and that to make it catch the light.

'And then there is this...' Mother opened a jewellery box and brought out an elegant ring with a central stone of brilliant red, surrounded by smaller diamonds. I reached for it, but she held it up and studied it. The shadows on her face seemed to deepen. 'He gave me this. Compeyson. He told me he had spent all his savings on having it made, because I was worth more than all the money in the world. He said what I'd given him was the most precious thing under the heavens...' Her skeletal body sagged, concave, so that she looked scooped out. 'Then he sent me that letter. That he could be so cruel! I want to save you from that, Estella. Everything he said and did was as worthless and fake as these paste stones.'

She gripped the ring tight, knuckles white, and beat her chest.

'Mother, stop. Please!'

On and on she beat herself, each blow a hollow thump. She shook her head from side to side, her whole body swaying with the vehemence of her denial.

'Please,' I begged again, trying to take hold of her arms. 'Mother, you're bleeding.'

She stopped moving then and stared at the trickle of deep red that gathered into a drop from her fist, an identical colour to the ring clenched so tightly it had sliced into her flesh. The drop hung heavy, and for a moment there was horrified silence as we watched it drip onto her dress and seep into the ageing fabric.

'I'll clean it up,' I gasped. 'First, though, I need you to give me the ring. It's all right, I'll put it back exactly where it should be.' She resisted, pulling her fist away from me as I tried to prise it open. Fighting her would only make her more stubborn. I submerged my own fear and swallowed the threatening tears, forcing myself to be as blank as possible so that she would hopefully take that in herself and calm down. 'Come now, you need to give it to me or it will make more mess and we don't want that, do we?'

That caught her attention. She stared at me and slowly seemed to see me, a change coming over her expression. Docile as a lamb now, she allowed her clenched hand to unfurl, and I carefully caught the blood that dripped from it in my own cupped hands. Ordering her to hold her hand away from her, I tore a strip from the bottom of my dress for a makeshift bandage.

'Look at me,' I ordered. Although she was still confused and upset, her eyes snapped on to mine. 'I'm going to run to the kitchen to fetch salt and water. I'll be right back to clean all of this up. Soon it will be as if it never happened, I promise. Don't upset yourself.'

Slowly, the words seemed to sink in and she nodded. But I knew the moment I left the room she would become overwrought again. Any change sent her into hysteria.

I ran down the corridor, my heart breaking. Poor, shattered Mother. Her childhood of cosseting had left her vulnerable to emotional attacks from everyone; she was trying her best to prepare me for the world by teaching me the lessons she had learned.

Bursting into the kitchen, I shouted orders. Servants gathered everything, while my thoughts raced with realisation. Of course, Mother wanted to not only help me build armour against people such as Compeyson and the Pockets, she was also helping me to learn that sometimes attack was the best form of defence. She would do anything to stop me sharing her fate. She had told me this a thousand times before, but it only truly sank in at that moment.

A servant and I scurried back to the dressing room. Wailing drifted along the corridor as we approached. Mother was falling apart. She couldn't cope with change, the stain on the dress was more than she could take.

I sank down beside her and once again made her look into my eyes.

'Breathe with me, Mother. See how calm I am? There's nothing to worry about.'

When the servant approached her with the water, Mother struck out, sending her flying to the floor.

'I'll do it. Leave us,' I ordered, never taking my eyes off Mother's. Soaking a piece of cloth in the heavily salted water, I held it up for her to see. 'This will wash it all away. Everything will be fine.'

As I dabbed at the blood, my mother's moans grew quieter.

'See how it's disappearing. It's barely a pink spot now.'

Thanks to careful blotting and washing, soon there was no trace left. Next, with fresh water, I cleaned her hand. The cut was not deep and luckily did not need bandaging. When I told her, Mother sank against me, resting her head on my shoulder, listless with exhaustion.

We sat like that for several hours. My body became stiff from holding one position, but still I didn't move. Mother needed me. And I needed her. For I was growing up, and must start to learn how to become the revenge-wreaker and heartbreaker she wanted me to be. That meant listening to her lessons and practising all she taught. Herbert had been uninterested in me and walked away without harm, but Pip would be the perfect whetstone on which to sharpen my words until I learned how to wound more adeptly.

His coming to the house had nothing to do with finding a replacement for me: this was my apprenticeship.

Chapter Twenty-Two

NOW

PARIS, 1835

Cigar smoke, sour wine and whiskey, and the taste of Bentley, are breathed into my mouth, as my husband kisses me against my will and his slug tongue forces its way in. Fear starts to suffocate me.

I stamp my heel on his foot. He releases me and laughs, even as I wipe my lips. Pulling myself up to my full height, I stare him down despite him being a good head taller than I.

'We talked of this, Bentley, and reached an agreement when you proposed, did we not?'

He gives no reply, only smiles that fat-lipped smirk of his.

'This is a business arrangement for mutual benefit. There will be no children. No shared marriage bed. I will appear on your arm at engagements, I will do everything required and more to appear as the perfect couple, and to promote our ambitions with influential connections. But aside from that we will live separate lives.'

'Will we now? Oh, Lord!'

Sometimes when I knit, my yarn gets into an unpickable knot; my insides are starting to feel the same. Bentley has been uncharacteristically difficult with me since we married.

'Don't ever dare to touch me this way again. You said you were in agreement. You own all my worldly goods now that we are married, I don't argue with that, but is that not enough? You will not possess me.'

His smirk spreads to a full-blown smile, but he nods and walks across the room. The distance gives me space to breathe easier. He pours us each a glass of brandy. Although I refuse mine, he takes a large swig of his own, holding it in his mouth a moment before swallowing.

'I have been patient. More so than other men, for we have been busy. But it is time for this marriage to begin,' he says at last. 'I've lowered myself to have you, Estella. Show your gratitude.'

I tell him tartly that he has done rather well himself, considering that he has won the toast of the town; for all the gentlemen of standing had called for me, and my dance card had been overflowing at every ball.

'Didn't you hear everyone gossiping at our wedding? We're a laughing stock thanks to your guardian. You're clever enough – for a woman – and easy on the eye, but your "mother" is a liability,' he replies. 'Sitting in the dark, unwashed, unkempt, like something from a freak show.'

'You will not speak of her that way—'

A sudden movement, a shattering sound. Bentley has dashed his crystal glass against the wall, shards scattering everywhere. When his arm reaches the nadir of its arc, he throws it back up with even greater momentum and gives me a backhanded slap. My head snaps back, I fall to the floor.

The shock of it, the weight behind the blow, the way my brain seems almost to rattle against my skull, how hot pain continues to bloom across my skin, it all takes me by surprise – but not as much as Bentley's matter-of-factness about it, as though this is a normal occurrence, not something unusual. He stands over me, not even breathing heavily. In fact, he seems calmer and more comfortable within himself than I have ever seen him.

'Why on earth did you marry me if you feel that way?' I whisper.

He plucks at his lace cuffs until they sit in a way that pleases him, then returns his attention to me with such a cold contempt in his eyes that I shrink away like a flower caught by an early frost.

'It was Jean-François's idea, actually. Well, no, it was he who decided me once and for all. I wrote to him about you, about how you were the prize all of London was fighting to win and that therefore I must, of course, have you, but that my manservant Joseph had discovered the full truth about your mad mother. It turned my stomach. Even worse, though, you lack any good blood coursing through your veins.'

'Good blood?'

'You're adopted. Who knows what the devil your parents were: thieves, murderers, adulterers, you could be descended from anything. The lower classes are animals.' He appears to be studying me, as if I am an insect to be pinned to a board. 'You can't raise them up. No point trying to educate them. The only thing to do is use them.'

This is what I am to him: a creature to be owned. Our shared plans, though. All that talk, it surely wasn't... just to entrap me?

'So I ask again, why did you marry me? I know you don't love me, nor I you, but I thought we had a respectful understan—'

'Don't worry your pretty little head about it. Jean-François thinks you could be handy to soften my image, if it does get out about your background. In fact, he believes we should ensure the tale disseminates far and wide. It rankles, but I can see the wisdom of it, for he thinks the new voters, those so-called middle-class working men, could be persuaded to vote for me because you will make me more – what's the word he always uses? – relatable. They will think I understand them, that I'm soft and want to help them, when in reality they'll be geese voting for the butcher's axe.' He tilts his head. 'And you are rich enough and pretty enough that I can't deny the perks of our joining together.'

All our fine dreams have never been 'ours' at all. I thought I was being so clever choosing a husband who was awful; I thought it meant I knew all his flaws. It never occurred to me that he might be hiding even worse ones.

'We could still work together,' I say. Desperation has taken my voice up an octave. 'Everything we talked of—'

'You seem to think we are a team. But I am your lord and master. You will do exactly what I tell you, when I tell you – you do not get any say. Look at you, snivelling.' I am not, the bloody liar. 'We have a reputation to live up to, you and I. You must pull yourself up now you're married to someone who is almost a baronet.'

'*Almost*. Perhaps you should have taken another wife, let someone else win me, if you're so ashamed of me and my family.'

'Like the blacksmith?'

'What on earth do you mean?' My reply is sharper than I wished. Taking a breath to calm myself, I make my voice more placatory as I force myself to stand on shaking legs. Win him over for now and make him pay later, that's the plan. 'Bentley, is this because of my mother's little speech? I chose you. Can't you accept that? You know Pip declared his feelings for me, and I turned him down. There is nothing for you to fear.'

'Fear that creature? Oh, Lord! You are right, I have won the prize, for what it is worth – but you don't even know what I've gained. You know I loathe that man, that creature who thinks dressing like a gentleman makes him one. Now, I have stolen away the love of his life and struck a blow from which he will never recover. And I've done the same to you.'

'What—?'

'You're in love with him and you won't even admit it,' he laughs. 'I'll make you forget him, though.'

He pinches my tender face between his massive fingers and pulls it towards him until his nose is but whiskers away from mine. When he speaks, it is the low rumble of distant thunder on a stormy night.

'I will have you and you will be grateful for it. You will cry for me, my little star, and you will grovel in gratitude when I listen. You will forget all about Pip, and give everything to make me happy.'

Stupid with anger, I push my face forward until our noses press against each other. 'You seem far more interested in him than I. Perhaps you are wishing it was he you could have married?'

He stiffens with fury. Then smiles. 'You're going to regret that.'

I will not be cowed.

That is what I tell myself as Bentley shifts his weight.

I have survived murder plots. I have outwitted killers. I am clever and determined and—

And then Bentley attacks and I realise I had no idea what true brutality was until this moment.

Chapter Twenty-Three

THEN

SATIS HOUSE, 1822

For the rest of the week I worked on carefully building the blocks of hatred for Pip. The thought of that coarse boy hurrying home and discussing us made my flesh creep. The last thing I wanted was for common people to be talking about the strange Miss Havisham, who lived in squalor and darkness despite being the richest woman in the county. He was weak, and must be crushed. He was male and had all the opportunities of the world laid out before him; I was female and my only use in society was to be decorative.

By the time the appointed day arrived, I was filled with a delicious mix of anger and eagerness. It was Mother's birthday and even though she refused to mark it, the Pocket collective was already waiting to see her. Even Herbert was there, although he seemed to have disappeared off somewhere on his own to read or play.

Waiting for Pip's arrival, in addition to finding time at Mother's insistence to taunt the indifferent Herbert, meant I had no opportunity for spying on the adult Pockets. I could only pray they hadn't come up with a plan to attack me yet. The fact they might have done and were enacting it even at that moment without me realising stoked my mood.

When he arrived, I led Pip along the corridors, amazed by how good an actor he was. He seemed sweet and scared, but I needed to discover what was hiding beneath the façade. I stopped so suddenly he almost bumped into the back of me as I turned to face him.

'Well?'

'Well, miss?' He looked back at me, blinking rapidly those eyes that seemed to take in everything and always be full of questions.

'Am I pretty?'

'Yes, I think you are very pretty.'

I cursed myself for asking such a silly question first, and showing my weakness to him. Cursed even more the little flip my stomach gave at his reply.

'Am I insulting?'

'Not so much as you were last time,' he said.

'Not so much so?' I fired.

'No.'

I slapped his face with all my strength. He tottered a step back, stunned mentally if not physically. The thrill of the impact! I'd never hit anyone before, but suddenly my insecurities seemed to disappear into power.

Power through cruelty.

I leaned closer. 'Now, you little coarse monster, what do you think of me?'

'I shall not tell you.'

'Because you're going to tell upstairs, is that it?'

He denied it. Worse, I believed him. My feeling of superiority hadn't lasted long, I needed to be more ruthless to him to bring it back.

'Why don't you cry again, you little wretch?'

His lips tightened, brows drawing together with some internal struggle until he burst: 'Because I'll never cry for you again.'

The confusion in Pip's eyes and the sinking of his head almost to his chest told me he was lying. I'd won this round.

Yet I didn't feel victorious.

Pip and Mother had been together for some quarter of the hour when I heard him bellow my name, voice bouncing down the corridor to me where I sat reading a book Mother had recommended to me from the library: *The Prince*, by Niccolò Machiavelli.

His call was the signal for me to bring the loathsome cousins along, which I duly did – although Herbert was still nowhere to be found. Pip and Mother were no longer in the dressing room but across the way in the dining room, which made me unaccountably uncomfortable.

Around and around the festering feast they walked, Mother slightly behind Pip, hand laid on his shoulder as well as leaning on her stick. Fingers twitching, mouth working, her thoughts racing even if her body moved slowly.

Exercising with her was my job, why was she making him take on this responsibility? Why was she trusting him with her safety this way, for she was given to unsteadiness and falls if she was not careful.

As we watched, it became increasingly obvious she had told him about the feast, about her pain and suffering. It was embarrassing. These were private family matters, but she was so proud of her hurt, even in front of a stranger. So unaware of the gossip – or perhaps she revelled in it. Either way it made me uncomfortable that Pip should know so much about us that I wished to keep hidden.

Mother was enjoying herself, though, that much was clear. She was showing off in front of this new visitor. Pip so obviously wanted to stop because the Pockets were trying to converse with her, but she wouldn't have it. She insisted on continuing past them, going around the dining table until we all felt quite dizzy watching her.

'How well you look,' said Sarah.

'I do not. I am yellow skin and bone,' snapped Mother.

Camilla brightened at this, I noticed. That was interesting – perhaps the allies were not so close as I had imagined. I wondered if there were a way to divide and conquer. Perhaps Machiavelli would have some interesting ideas on the subject.

Mother noted Camilla's perky mood, too. She turned her hawk eyes on the cousin, asking how she was – an unexpected enquiry, as she didn't normally care how others felt.

'As well as can be expected,' Camilla replied.

'Why, what is wrong with you?'

Camilla fluttered, realising she had walked into a trap.

'Nothing worth mentioning,' she replied. 'I don't wish to make a display of my feelings, but I have habitually thought of you in the night.'

'Then don't.'

Camilla then brought on the tears, which she seemed to be able to do on demand – she should have been on the stage! – and proceeded to go into great detail of how her digestion and health had suffered.

'If I could be less affectionate and sensitive I should have a better digestion and an iron set of nerves,' she cried. 'But as to not thinking of you in the night – the idea!'

Raymond patted her on the back. 'Camilla, my dear, it is well known that your family feelings are gradually undermining you, to the extent of making one of your legs shorter than the other.'

I bit my lip at the absurdity, and as I looked up I caught Pip's eye. He was fighting the upturning of his mouth, too, and barely winning.

Balancing a plate of doorstop sandwiches and a drink in one hand while carrying a candle in the other was no easy feat. My tongue stuck out in concentration, until I imagined Camilla coming across me and then telling Sarah all about the common and coarse sight she had seen. Tongue returned to mouth, I almost dropped the sandwich and had to stop to reorganise. This was all for Pip, who was waiting to be fed after his day of playing in front of Mother and the toadies and humbugs. I'd left him waiting in the courtyard, wringing his cap between his hands and scuffing with his thick-soled boots the light dusting of snow that had fallen that morning.

I placed everything on a handy windowsill for a moment. At that second Herbert hurried past me, carrying a bowl of water, which sloshed over the sides in his haste.

'What on earth are you doing?' I shouted.

He didn't slow, but called over his shoulder: 'Water and vinegar for the sponge. For the fight!'

What fight? Food abandoned, I followed after him.

Chapter Twenty-Four

THEN

SATIS HOUSE, 1822

I abandoned Pip's victuals and stomped after Herbert, who moved swiftly despite his gangly limbs surely risking getting tangled. Outside, he disappeared around a corner that led to a dead end where two walls and some rubbish left over from the brewery days created a nook. He was trapped. But someone was with him, I could hear voices, so slowed and listened.

'Is this to your satisfaction?' Herbert asked, in that light voice of his.

'Erm, yes, I suppose?' Pip. Always questioning, even when making a statement.

What were those two doing together? Cautiously, I edged over and peered around the wall. Herbert was pulling off his jacket, waistcoat, and even his shirt, an expression of determined delight in his red-lidded eyes. His ribs shadowed his white skin, goosebumps blooming, as he started to jump backwards and forwards and side to side and spin and fling one leg out behind him. It must be some kind of strange jig – why on earth were he and Pip dancing together? Pip looked equally as bemused as I.

'Ah-ha!' Herbert slapped his hands together, formed fists again, dodged towards Pip and threw a punch.

I gasped.

The blacksmith's boy swung wildly, clearly taken by surprise. Although a good head shorter than Herbert, he was far stronger. My cousin flew onto his back, his nose squashed and bloodied.

Herbert jumped up, sponged himself down, then skipped from leg to leg. Threw a punch which smacked Pip squarely on the jaw. He didn't flinch. Quick as a flash, Herbert was on his back again, this time with a rapidly swelling eye.

They were fighting, but why? It had to be over me. A thrill ran through me.

Watching those two boys sparring made something stir in me that I'd never felt before. Again and again, Pip hit Herbert in reply to a poor punch, each time harder than the last. Herbert's nose streamed with blood. I watched it course down his pale skin, standing out so bright from the alabaster white. Already his eye was puffing up, and the skin around it changing colour; a lump on the back of his head where he had hit a wall was visible even from my viewpoint, yet he never stopped jumping up, sponging himself down and then jabbing Pip's way.

My blood pumped ever faster at the sight of Pip's reluctant brutality. I had never witnessed violence before... I enjoyed it.

Finally, panting like a bellows, Herbert reached for the sponge and threw it down. 'That means you have won.'

Pip acted the perfect gentleman by complying.

It was a shame it was over but, my word, that had been brilliant; like nothing I'd ever experienced before.

Two boys fighting. *Over me.*

Herbert was getting dressed again, Pip making his goodbyes and saying it was time to go home. After all that, they were so polite, sharing their 'good afternoons'.

Reluctant to be seen, I hurried away, almost skipping with glee, to wait beside the gate. When Pip appeared, my heart thumped against my ribcage and I couldn't stop the smile spreading. He had a small cut on his right cheek, that was all. But his hands – those big, strong, capable hands – had grazes running across the knuckles, and he was bleeding from where Herbert's teeth had broken the skin during one punch.

Euphoria rushed through me. My champion should be rewarded for his victory on my behalf. I beckoned him into the passageway so no one might see us.

'Come here. You may kiss me if you like.'

I generously offered my cheek and Pip kissed it. For all his strength, he was gentle as a butterfly's wings against my flushed skin.

He looked so sad, though. His fists hung loose by his sides and seemed to weigh him down as he slid through the gate and trudged away. I stood for a long time with my cheek pressed against the wrought-iron curls, waiting for the heat from where his lips had touched my skin to disperse, for my heart to slow, so that I could sift through all the strange feelings inside me. The strongest thought of all was that my first kiss had been received from the right person, but for all the wrong reasons.

I sat on a low stool by my mother's feet and knitted while she played dress-up with my hair, brushing it into different styles and experimenting with the placement of jewels, combs and other decorations, while talking in a low voice almost to herself about the balls she had attended once upon a time. Myriad men had admired her and vied for her hand, her father measuring each of them and finding none rich enough, or of a high enough social class, or with good enough prospects or... The marriage game was a serious one and wise choices were made with the head rather than the heart, she had been warned, and so Mother had trusted her father to make the right choice for her. She had been content to do as she was told.

All the time she spoke of her would-be suitors, she arranged my hair and the glittering decorations. She was happy to be lost in the past when she had been a different person. Her cheeks seemed less sunken, her eyes brighter, movements stronger, as if the past were reinvigorating her.

The names marched past me, forgotten as soon as heard, as the stitches marched along my knitting needles. I had been taught by my governess, Mrs Sopper, a few months earlier, as she seemed to think it might help calm my nerves. She had patted her pocket in a strange way, her wedding ring clinking on the hip flask she always carried, and told me there were other ways to deal with anxiety but they weren't recommended.

'No one captured my attention until that Derby Day at Epsom races,' said Mother. 'I had not long come out of mourning for my father and this was the first event I attended. As soon as I saw *him* – ah, that man, that cursed, beautiful man – all was lost. Matthew tried to warn me.'

'Speaking of Matthew reminds me: Herbert and Pip were sparring today.' I said it to head off the inevitable downward spiral whenever Mother's former fiancé was mentioned. Her eyes brightened again, so I told her all about it in lurid detail.

'This is wonderful, Estella.'

'I don't think Herbert gives a jot what I think of him, so I don't understand why they were fighting over me, but I can't think of any other reason for them to box.'

'Some people, particularly men, like to fight simply for the pleasure of it. Whatever the reason, it's good to know Herbert has his uses. As for him not caring about you, that may change with time.'

I expressed my doubt.

Mother conceded I may have a point. 'Herbert has parents who, though eccentric, do love him, as do his countless siblings, and he loves them all in return. In short, his life has given him certain assurances about his worthiness as a person. Though Herbert's family are poor, they are rich in affection. Although eager to please, Herbert is secure enough to stand up for himself. There are no betrayals to blow a hole in his armour.

'Pip is a far more suitable target for you to practise on, for he is an orphan being raised by a sister who (according to the gossip of my tenants) is a hard woman not averse to disciplining him with a good thrashing – and does the same to her husband the blacksmith. Think how vulnerable Pip is as a result, and how desperate that makes him to win approval and love. You did well practising on the blacksmith boy.'

The compliment made me preen. The more superior I acted, the more people responded to it and gave me power, from servants, to Pockets, to Pip. It was all an act, though. Appearing powerful while terrified of losing my place in the family; attacking to defend myself from others; spreading hate while all the time longing for kindness.

These were the vital lessons I must learn, though, if I was to survive the world and not be broken like my mother. I put away my knitting and the rest of the evening was spent in pleasant conversation, tearing down each of that day's visitors in turn.

It was only in bed, huddling beneath the sheets to hide from the grasping shadow man, that I thought again about what we had said: *Pip was a better person for me to practise on because he was sensitive and vulnerable...*

That didn't make sense. Why was I picking on him if he was nice? Surely, I should only be attacking terrible people?

But then, all males were untrustworthy, weren't they?

Yet in Pip I recognised a kindred damaged soul.

Chapter Twenty-Five

NOW

PARIS, 1835

I pull my voluminous sleeve up over my shoulder. It flops back down again.

I try to gather the dress' skirts around me, to huddle inside the heavy brocade material. Seeing its colour, that distinctive soft pink of a sunrise, makes me long for the marshes and big skies of my distant home. The material springs free from my shaking hands. After several attempts to cover my bare thigh, I give up. Bentley shredded the material to pieces last night, and my spirit with it.

If I could just stop the shaking, that would be something. I can't seem to control my own body, though, only look at it helplessly as it judders as if I had spent an entire winter's night exposed to the elements. Perhaps I am cold. I don't seem to feel anything, instead I am a bystander watching myself.

Everything hurts.

The fire in the grate must have gone out some time ago. I've no idea how long I've been sitting in the same spot, my mind as blank as a wiped chalkboard, staring at the marble mantel that is pristine white apart from a constellation of spattered blood. Noticing it brings a flare of memories, pain and terror.

Too soon, too soon, I cannot think about that yet.

What my husband subjected me to the previous night is beyond my imaginings. I descended into hell and, just as he promised, indeed begged, pleaded, bargained, played dead even, in order to make it stop. I'd have done anything.

Bentley is so much bigger than me, so very strong, that it takes my breath away. Literally. Fight as I might, he took my maidenhead.

This morning when he woke he covered me with kisses as though everything was normal and loving.

'You asked for that.' He smiled as he stretched. 'I'm meeting Jean-François at his club; it was all arranged when we saw him yesterday. You will stay here and rest. After all, you said last night you were tired, and what kind of husband would I be if I didn't indulge you?'

For a wonderful moment I hoped to escape, though without my passport or travel papers, and with no money of my own or even untorn clothes on my back – for Bentley had taken up some scissors last night and threatened to use them on me, but instead had cut my entire wardrobe to shreds. But Bentley first shut and locked the shutters across the windows, pitching me into Satis House-like twilight, then he pulled at a chain that I had not noticed around his neck and showed me the key that hung from it.

'I shall lock you in, my little star, for a wife is a husband's greatest treasure; I must look after you.'

The click of the lock is the last thing I remember until just now, and must have been many hours ago, as it is once again getting dark.

Something warm is trickling down my legs. Perhaps it is that which has brought me out of my stupor. There is blood between my legs and soaking into the back of my gown.

It will be ruined unless I do something.

It is already destroyed beyond redemption, yet that doesn't stop me stirring into action at last, against all logic, and removing the remnants of the heavy gown even though every movement makes me whimper.

Finally, I turn my attention to myself. Though unable to bring myself to look in a mirror, I do at least find a still-upright pitcher of water, and by soaking pieces of material torn from my petticoats, I wash away some of the blood from my skin.

More keeps coming, though.

Is this the way it is with all marriages? Surely, not every man and woman experience this? But there is no one for me to ask, and so I must endure or refuse.

Or die.

Bentley sees nothing wrong with what he has done to me, for I am his property now and it is his right to treat me as he pleases. Society expects the demands of the husband to be accepted meekly by the wife. He couldn't resist the challenge of beating his competitors (beating Pip was particularly sweet for him, and he mentions it often) and now he has the challenge of breaking me in like a horse. His cruelty to horses is, while quite notorious, nothing in comparison to his treatment of me.

On the ground is a jagged piece of the crystal tumbler my husband smashed last night. I pick it up and test its weight in my hand. Not too bad. There's enough left of the base for me to wield it without cutting myself. It will do the job, if I'm fast enough.

Many hours pass with me making experimental thrusts. It helps me to get to know how much damage Bentley has wrought on me. It's bad. There's no food to give me strength, either, and all the water was used on washing myself down. All I can do is stand behind the door, which opens inwards, and wait... Every moment that passes weakens me further, so that I'm torn between dreading his return and hoping he'll come home soon.

Come on, Bentley, where are you?

My eyelids are heavy. They won't stay open, even though I'm standing. They won't...

A slight rattle from the door handle pushing down. The shush of the door opening across the soft, thick Chinese rug. My eyes fly open.

He steps in, I lunge forward and slash towards his neck. It slices his shoulder. I try again. He is suddenly behind me, choking me and laughing. I can't breathe, try to get my hands up but Bentley has them both pinned against me with one arm, while the other is about my neck, squeezing on my windpipe with the crook of his elbow as strong as a nutcracker taking on a walnut.

Vision reddening, darkening...

When I come around, Bentley holds something out to me. A handkerchief? No, a piece of paper.

'Take it,' he urges. 'It's from Jaggers.'

I stretch for it. He snatches it from my reach. Holds it tantalisingly close. 'Come on, don't you want to read it?'

I pull myself up, coughing. Try again. Almost topple flat on my face I strain so far. Bentley holds it that little too far away.

'Don't want it? Well, let me tell you, then. Your mother has had some kind of accident.'

'Is she all right? What happened? I must go to her.'

He says nothing.

'Let me see.' I try to reach for the letter again. Bentley holds it too high.

'I'll let you see it, if you're good.'

If I'm...? I want to double over and cry but won't give him the satisfaction. This is why he's doing this, I realise, to torture me emotionally as well as physically. Another thought occurs. Is Mother even ill? He could easily be lying, to hurt me.

'Jaggers wants you to go back,' Bentley says. 'Are you two having an affair?'

'I— no! Of course not.' Talking hurts like swallowing glass.

'That's it, isn't it? It's all a plot to get you away from me. Do you think I'm stupid?'

Amongst other things. 'If Mother is ill I must go to her. Please let me go.'

'Please let me go,' he mimics in a mewling voice. 'Go to your fancy man? Cuckold me? I think not.'

He tucks the letter into his jacket's inside pocket. 'Your face looks terrible. And it's your only redeeming feature. I won't mess with it again – I have to look at the bally thing.'

Is this... good news? Does he feel sorry for what he's done?

But no. He has other plans. He is on me again and though I try to fight him, he wins easily. The pain, the cruelty, it seems endless. My body is so broken there is nothing left of me.

Perhaps he'll kill me soon. If I'm lucky it will be today.

Chapter Twenty-Six

THEN

SATIS HOUSE, 1823

For months life was steady. Pip and I developed a strange relationship where he arrived weekly and I made his life a misery, yet somehow he hung on my every word all the more. The worse I was, the more he appeared to yearn for my approval. He never did cry in front of me again, though. He became a favourite pet of Mother's, too, always well behaved, well meaning, kind and thoughtful.

I continued to wait for the Pockets to move against me, but even that lost its edge of urgency. My eleventh birthday had passed, and it seemed perhaps they had decided my place was too embedded and strong to risk tackling. After all, what had they done in the past? Tried to persuade Mother to return me to an orphanage, which now I was older I realised would never happen; tried to lure me into danger, which would not work again now their technique was known to me; and persuaded me to run away to search for my parents, which was another gambit I was too old and wise to fall for a second time.

Still, I kept an eye on the servant girl Martha, who I sometimes fed silly stories to and listened with delight as the Pockets discussed them in consternation. My favourite had been when they thought I was going to get Mother to buy a freak show to stage in the grounds of Satis House. That kept them talking and plotting for weeks. Hearing them drop hints to Mother about the local people only having so much tolerance for eccentricity meant I had to leave the room so I could laugh out in the corridor alone.

One February day in 1823, I sat inside the increasingly tight crawl space, wondering how long it would be before I was too big to fit inside it to spy on the Pockets. The voices of Sarah and Raymond droned fitfully, while Camilla's voice followed her usual fluctuating pattern of either worked up or so bored she could barely suppress a yawn – depending on whether she was talking about herself or having to listen to someone else. As usual she was wearing a new dress; she wore something different every time she visited, whereas Sarah lived in the same brown drab, although it was possible she had an array of almost identical brown drabs.

'It can't be much longer,' Camilla said on the other side of the wall. I yawned in sympathetic boredom. Mother did so enjoy making them wait, almost as much as I did.

'Patience is a virtue, dearest,' replied Raymond.

'In that case—'

A low moan filled the air, coming from somewhere else in the house. It gained velocity, building to a shriek. *Mother!*

'Ah, she's found it,' said Camilla. It sounded as if she clapped her hands together. 'Time for the fun to begin. The brat will never wriggle out of this one.'

'She'll be on the streets where she belongs before the end of the day.'

'On the streets? My dear Sarah, she will become close friends with the hangman's noose for this – although not for long.' Camilla's laugh tinkled again.

'And what will you do once we have all the money?' asked Sarah. Not so long ago she had said she did not want me killed. Clearly in her mind having someone official kill me was more acceptable.

'Eat pineapples all day long.'

On one side of the wall they all stood and hurried to the door towards the screaming, on the other side I moved crabwise as quickly as possible, desperate to escape the claustrophobic, cobwebbed tunnel.

What had they done to Mother? And why was I going to get the blame?

I pelted down the corridor, dark as a mining shaft, towards Mother's room, no need for a candle when I knew the way with my eyes shut.

As I grew closer to the dressing room the echoing shouts from inside changed to distinct words.

'Call a constable, Miss Havisham,' cried Sarah.

The dressing room was chaos. Mother had sunk to the floor and was crying and beating herself in a frenzy, while around her the Pockets ran about like chickens with a fox in the coop. Instead of calming Mother they seemed intent on stirring up pandemonium.

'Yes, yes, the lawmen will soon find the culprit,' shouted Camilla, trying to fan herself and Mother at the same time. 'You should not have to deal with such wanton dishonesty. The person responsible should never be allowed to set foot over the threshold of this honourable house again. To think that—'

She was cut off mid-flow by another moaning cry from Mother.

'What's happened?' They scattered as I moved to her side, but their non-stop chatter continued.

'I've rung for the servants, we'll search the whole house,' said Sarah.

'There won't be a nook or cranny left unchecked. We'll find it,' added Camilla.

'Find what?'

Mother's eyes lifted to mine. There was such devastation there. I'd never seen her look so vulnerable. Clinging on to me with one claw-like hand, she pointed with the other to her dressing table. Then she uttered one word: 'Gone!'

The heavy diamond necklace that she so loved to put on me had disappeared from the dressing table where it was usually draped half in, half out of an inlaid jewellery box. All that was left to show of its existence was its outline in the dust and cobwebbed debris.

I glanced at the Pockets. Camilla gave me the wide smile of an imp doing the devil's work. 'Shall we start the search now?' she asked.

The servants were arriving, breathless and scared. Once again, the Pockets demanded someone fetch the local constabulary.

'Having strangers in the house will only upset Mother more,' I said. 'Lydia, send an urgent note to the doctor, and also Mr Jaggers; tell them to come immediately. Jaggers has long arms that can reach into all worlds and find not only the necklace but the culprit.'

'There's no need for the lawyer,' fluttered Camilla.

'We shouldn't delay. Let us search now, before the nasty little thief has a chance to escape.'

Sarah's words tugged at me. There was something about the way she said 'nasty little thief' and threw a look my way.

I went cold all over. My first instinct had been correct. This theft was about me, and causing upset to Mother was merely collateral damage. But why? *Think, think, think…*

If they had stolen the necklace it must be in order to blame me, I decided. Mother would never accept such a betrayal. The Pockets were right, I'd be out on the streets before the end of the day, homeless and ruined, without a single friend or family member to fall back on.

That was if I was lucky.

If I was unlucky, I could hang.

Sarah's efficiency at organising the servants' search of the house from top to bottom was admirable – almost as if she'd had hours or even days to plan it. At her suggestion everyone was split into pairs and given a floor and wing to search. She stayed with me – presumably, to keep an eye on me – and, surprisingly, the usually inseparable Raymond and Camilla split up and each went with a servant. I could think of only one reason why. They wanted to make sure they were the ones to find the necklace and point the finger at me, while ensuring there was an independent witness, in the form of a servant, to corroborate their find. It would ensure everyone believed they were innocent even if I were to accuse them of setting me up.

Sarah allocated the servants' quarters for she and I to search. It was the place furthest away from my own bedroom, and surely the necklace had been planted in my quarters, for the Pockets weren't ones for subtlety. I squirmed with the effort of trying to think of how to get away from her.

'Someone should stay with Mother,' I said. She truly wasn't in a fit state to stay alone.

'Martha,' Sarah snapped.

Damnation. Of course she'd choose her lackey.

Everyone bustled from the room, with me trailing behind.

'Come on, child, don't dawdle,' called Sarah, clicking her fingers at me. I wanted to snap them in half.

For all her words of hurry, Sarah moved slowly, as if wading through marsh mud. I tried to race ahead, keen to lose her. Perhaps I should just make a run for it?

'With me, please, Estella,' she ordered. 'The whole point is that we all work together.'

Finally, we reached the servants' quarters, which were in a separate building from the main house. Only a handful of servants remained with us, and of those, only half stayed on-site. The others lived in the village, in cottages where they paid no rent in exchange for a lower wage from Mother. Here at the manor they were also charged board and keep, but got to keep more of their wages to make up for being at our beck and call. Each room was for one person, and was generous enough to house a single bed, bedside cabinet, armchair, chest of drawers and either a wardrobe or built-in closet, depending on which room you were in. Their windows were not blacked out, either, although the lower ones were barred. The building itself was not as derelict as the rest of the property, including the manor house, because the tenants sneakily did repairs when they thought Mother and I wouldn't notice.

We searched the first room we came to. Sarah placed herself near the door, so there was no way to escape if I gave in to the growing urge to run. She felt so comfortable that I was trapped that she turned her back to me as she searched through the chest of drawers.

My mind galloped, precious time disappearing, and all the while a pressure grew in my throat as if my neck was already in the hangman's noose.

Sarah looked at me like I was an imbecile. 'Don't just stand there in the middle of the room.'

There was no point to this search, but I opened the bedside cabinet drawer and pretended to move a few things around. This invasion of privacy made me uncomfortable when we both knew the servants were loyal and honest.

Everyone except Martha.

Finally, Sarah indicated we move to the next room. Again, she took the chest of drawers, taking advantage of the excuse to nose around.

We were in one of the rooms with a cupboard. In fact... I looked around – yes, I remembered playing inside the one in that very room, for the cupboard had a badly fitted panel at the back, to cover a hole.

Holding my breath and staring at Sarah's back, I took a step backwards, towards the wardrobe. She didn't notice as she moved away from the door and over to the bed and checked under the pillows.

I took another step. Turned and disappeared inside the wardrobe, quietly pushed aside the clothes hanging. There was the panel, in the bottom right of the back wall. It looked nailed on, but if I remembered rightly... Yes! It came away easily.

I glanced over my shoulder. Sarah's back was still to me as she lifted the mattress while monologuing about cleanliness and tidiness.

I dipped down and backed into the hole, cursing my growing height. Somehow I managed to quickly pack myself in, knees up to my ears, then pulled the panel back in place, knowing the nails would slide into the overlarge holes in the rotten surrounding wood panels, and look as if they had been hammered into place – that is, as long as it was given no more than a cursory glance.

Within a few uncomfortable, painfully shallow breaths I heard Sarah call me. Footsteps grew closer. The sound of the clothes sliding along the rail one way then another. Any second now I'd be discovered and told off. The desire to take a deep breath was growing. My legs were cramping, my neck aching from my head being pushed to one side to fit into this hellhole.

Sarah stamped around the room, her calls growing louder and more impatient.

I can't take much more. I need to stretch. To breathe deep.

Muttering and cursing, Sarah flounced from the room. Still I didn't dare move.

Must breathe!

No. Stay still.

My hands quivered with the twin forces making them reach out and pull back. Sarah might be searching the other rooms, or waiting in the corridor for me to emerge.

Have to...

No.

Can't—

I pushed my way free, wanting to scream like a newborn as I took in lungfuls of air. Finally, I tiptoed to the bedroom door and spied through the crack at the hinge. No sign of Sarah. Cautiously, I made my way towards the main entrance and peered through a nearby side window.

There she was, glaring at the door. Waiting.

I couldn't get out that way. But she wouldn't be aware of my alternative route, climbing through an upstairs window onto the branch of an overgrown tree, and shimmying down it.

Then all I had to do was run to my bedroom and find the necklace.

It's not here! It's not here!

I sank to the floor of my bedroom in despair. I was a child, what chance did I stand against adults? Despite tearing my bedroom apart I could find no sign of the missing diamond necklace. The Pockets had outwitted me.

The books! I'd moved them from the shelves, but hadn't checked inside them.

Leaping forward, I picked one up and shook it. Nothing. I shook them all, each time hoping this would be the one, until... The last one flapped upside down in my hands like an injured bird, and absolutely nothing fell from its pages.

If I didn't find the necklace my place within the Havisham family, and the safety of Satis House, would be torn from me. Where would they put it that would illustrate my guilt and mine alone? They didn't know about my hidey-holes, did they? The only way to find out was to check.

I raced along the corridors, darting around to avoid the searchers who were moving noisily about the house. One hiding place after another I searched, but there was nothing out of place in any of them. Had I got it wrong? Perhaps the Pockets were as innocent as I? Or perhaps they had simply stolen the necklace in order to get some money, as they always seemed to be complaining about lack of funds, especially Camilla and Raymond. Whatever my doubts, I continued running – because what else could I do? I raced past the dressing room, slowing only so that Martha wouldn't hear me. She was talking to Mother in soothing tones. Poor Mother. She was quiet now but looked catatonic, curled up on the floor, nothing more than a pile of rags.

Martha... she was working alongside the Pockets. Perhaps she was privy to their plan.

Chapter Twenty-Seven

THEN

SATIS HOUSE, 1823

 walked into the room, greeted Martha confidently, then bobbed down so that I was beside Mother, stroking her cheek and murmuring a few comforting noises.

'I can't believe someone could do this to her,' I said. 'We both know the people that are involved – don't we, Martha?'

Her eyes widened and her cherry cheeks drained of colour. 'Oh, do you know who? And why? I'm clueless, miss.' Her voice was unnaturally high.

'Come now, we both know the people that are behind most of the nasty things that happen in this house. *You* know, because you're working for them.'

She shook her head. It shook free tears from her eyes, sending them cascading down her cheeks. 'I-I don't know anything.'

'I would have sacked you long ago had it not been useful and entertaining not to. But now the game is up. Tell me where the necklace is.'

The shake of her head was more like a tremble. I pushed on.

'Maybe the Pockets aren't involved. Perhaps you stole the necklace and hid it somewhere—'

'No!' The word burst from her lips before she could stop it.

I stood up, put my hands on my hips, and stared her straight in the eye. 'Tell me the truth, right now, and I'll give you severance pay. Make me wait any longer and I'll have the authorities hang you from the highest gibbet.'

Whether this was possible I knew not, but I was already learning that sounding confident was the key to being confident. Although Martha was aged around fourteen, and therefore probably three years older than I, she was used to being ordered around, having worked in Satis House since the age of twelve, just as her mother and grandmother had. And just like them, she would probably die in childbirth.

'Please, miss, I can't—'

'No one in this county will employ any member of your family, either, when they hear what I have to say.'

'That's evil! You and your family are all the same.'

'But you doing this is fine?' I gestured to Mother, still unmoving, unhearing, unseeing. 'As for my "family", don't think I don't know how much they hate me.'

'They do. They want to get rid of you because they feel that you're taking their inheritance.'

'I know all of this. Tell me about the necklace.'

'But I don't know nothing else. I swear on my life. I swear on my family's lives (and all they have is that, for they've lost everything else). You say I'm working with Raymond, but I'm not; I had no choice.'

Raymond? I had thought she was working for Sarah Pocket – after all, that was what Sarah had told Camilla. I said nothing, though.

'He saw me one day taking some of the food. I was only taking it because my dad had just lost his job, and my wage was the only one coming in. We're starving. Raymond said he'd tell Miss Havisham and get me sacked if I didn't spy on you. I'll pay you back for the food, miss, just please don't—'

'Don't worry about the food. I can help you – but only if we find the necklace.' Every word spoken wasted more time. 'Tell me.'

'I don't know nothing, miss. But I'll help you look for it.'

Martha and I pattered along the corridor together, not knowing where to head next but determined to get there quickly.

We had reluctantly left Mother lying on the floor after she resisted all attempts to move her. Her silence was even more worrying than her usual hysteria, and I wondered what on earth was taking the doctor so long.

'Where are we going?' Martha asked.

'My bedroom. Perhaps you can think of somewhere I have missed.'

She grabbed my arm, pulling me to a stop. 'I just remembered something Raymond kept saying to me. It could be nothing, but... he's been making odd jokes and comments, and he's not the type to try to be funny.' She shook her head. 'No, it can't be anything.'

'Tell me, anyway. We've nothing to lose.'

'It doesn't make sense.' Martha frowned as she remembered. 'Raymond was on about someone getting stitched up. That's it, he said: "They'll find themselves in a real tangle and get stitched up. And everything that's been woolly in my life will be so much clearer." He was really chuckling. Now, it makes me wonder if—'

'My knitting bag! It's in the dressing room.'

'Surely, he wouldn't be so obvious, though? Why say all that to me?'

'Raymond isn't the brightest. It's typical of him to make such bad puns, chuckling to himself, thinking he's being terribly clever. He'll have arrogantly assumed a servant would be too stupid to pick up on it.'

'He thinks he's a cut above, that's for sure.'

We turned back, and I hurried to my knitting bag. It was always hidden beneath the stool beside Mother, where I sat. Turning it upside down, I sent the contents tumbling across the rug. The necklace fell with a gentle thud. Thank goodness.

'Oh, what's that?' Martha darted forward and picked at something small tangled in the wool.

'We've got more important things to worry about than – what? – a button.'

She held it out. It was a soft pink mother-of-pearl button worked to look like a flower. With a sigh, I took it and popped it into my pocket, and went over to the dressing table to put the necklace back in its usual place.

But I paused.

'What are you waiting for?' asked Martha.

'It occurs to me that what's good for the goose is good for the gander...'

Before she could ask more, I ran across the corridor to the reception room where the Pockets had left their coats and reticules. Sliding my hand into Camilla's bag, I deposited the necklace inside.

All three deserved punishment for what they had done, but while Sarah had thwarted me, and Raymond had been the one blackmailing Martha, Camilla deserved my revenge the most for she wanted me dead. She had earned everything she wished on to me.

'Miss? What's happening now?' asked Martha, when I returned to the dressing room.

'Well, you can...' I tipped my head, hearing footsteps coming closer. 'Ah, you can stay here and watch the fun, if you like.'

Sarah walked into the room, her mouth a line of disapproval. 'Oh, Estella, so this is where you've been hiding. How kind of you to look after your mother, while the rest of us labour around the house.' Her eyes darted to the dressing table where the necklace should have been, and seemed to relax when she saw the dusty void.

Others were joining us, murmuring between one another. Camilla walked in and found Raymond, whom she sagged against.

'Oh, such a shocking turn of events! What a terrible sin for someone to have *thieved* from so generous a benefactor. Who would do such a thing?'

'Now, my dear, do not work yourself up. You do so worry on the behalf of others,' intoned Raymond.

'It's true!' She clutched her chest and began to hiccup. 'See how my digestion is already playing up! But what are we to do? We have searched everywhere. Everywhere!'

She waved her hands around for emphasis, one sleeve flapping at her wrist, and looked pointedly at Sarah.

'We've searched everywhere but this room,' said Sarah.

Her partner in crime gave a gasp of mock shock. 'Oh, how clever you are, cousin. I can't believe we've all forgotten to search this room.

The *idea*! There are so many of us here that we will make quick work of it.'

Raymond made a beeline for the knitting bag, but I headed for Camilla.

'Why, cousin, you have a button missing – and on a brand new day dress, how awful.'

She looked at her sleeve hanging loose at her wrist. 'Perhaps we can all search for that after we find the diamonds, eh, Estella?'

Across the room came an 'ah-ha' noise from Raymond, who was such a bad actor that he hadn't even opened my carpet bag yet. Everyone stopped to watch as he finally rooted through it, triumph on his face.

Triumph turned to confusion to consternation. His search became more frantic.

Camilla marched over. 'Have you found something, Raymond?'

She snatched the bag from him and dug deep into the contents. Sarah, the cleverer of the three, glanced at me and frowned.

'Are you looking for this?' I asked, holding the button up. 'I found it in my knitting bag earlier.'

Sarah started sidling over to her cronies.

'Oh, you and that button,' said Camilla, head still buried in bag. 'It's lovely of you to care so much, Estella, but priorities! Priorities! Besides, it's nothing like my buttons.'

'Looks identical.' I shrugged. 'I saw it sparkling in amongst my knitting. *Like a diamond.*'

Her searching slowed.

It stopped.

She looked at me, at the button, then back to the empty bag, and finally the penny dropped.

As all three conspirators turned their eyes to the space where the necklace should have been, I realised how much I was enjoying myself.

'I've just remembered, this isn't the only room we haven't searched,' I said. 'There's—'

'The reception room.' Raymond's voice was a pained groan. Sarah elbowed him.

'That's right!' My grin widened.

'Well, this is, this is ridiculous,' Sarah said.

'Who-whoever has stolen the necklace has clearly got away with it,' agreed Camilla.

'There are only a couple of chairs and our things in there so there is nothing to search.' Sarah's sallow face looked pasty, but her voice was firm.

'Nothing. Unless someone is trying to imply something,' Camilla agreed.

'And what could this child imply? We are Pockets, we have Havisham blood running through us. To accuse one who has such noble lineage would be ridiculous.'

'Indeed. Blood and breeding always win.'

As the two women batted words back and forth, their confidence grew. Together they had strength.

At that moment the gate's bell chimed.

'You had better answer that,' said Sarah.

'I'll get one of the servants to—' I began.

'But after all, it was entrusted to you and only you by Miss Havisham. Would you let her down in her hour of need?' Camilla asked.

Mother was still curled on the floor, no sound, no movement from her. She needed me to protect her. She needed the doctor, for surely it was he who was at the gate.

The ringing was becoming insistent. Filling my brain. Mother was starting to twitch.

I was going to have to go and answer it.

But this was my chance to triumph over the Pockets.

'You answer it and I will stay here with Mother. She needs me to keep her calm.' It was my final throw of the dice.

'Estella,' said Sarah sternly, 'I am the adult here, and I'm telling you now: *we* will stay and *you* will go to the gate.'

I turned to the servants. 'Start the search of the reception room—'

'*Now*, Estella. Stop dawdling.'

The servants looked like sheep who did not know which wolf was in charge. This was supposed to be the moment I bested the Pockets; instead, tears of frustration gathered at their dismissal of me, and I could not ever, ever, let myself cry in front of them.

I ran from the room, the bell jingling so hard it sounded as if it might fall off.

When I returned, with Dr Hawkins in tow, the necklace was back in place.

'You'll never guess where it was,' said Sarah.

Camilla's laugh tinkled out. 'While I stayed to help the servants search the other room, Raymond and Sarah lifted Miss Havisham into a chair, as she was starting to move.'

'We thought only to make her more comfortable, but – lo! – there was the necklace. Beneath her all the time.'

The doctor was feeling Mother's forehead. She was discombobulated, but the ringing bell seemed to have woken her from her catatonic state. She blinked slowly, still not seeming to see what was before her. In that moment I knew the Pockets had got away with their sleight of hand, for Camilla must have found the necklace first, distracted the servants somehow, and got it to her counterparts. Mother was still not herself, and would have little to no memory of her episode and so would never realise she was taking the blame for something she had not done.

Mother was in bed resting, after being checked over by Dr Hawkins. He had prescribed a small vial of that great cure-all, laudanum tincture, to aid her recovery.

'To be taken, ah-hum, with rhubarb water. Ah-hum, it's the rhubarb that'll make her better, all right, but the opium won't hurt,' he said.

Meanwhile, I had ordered all guests from the house. Now it was evening on what felt like the longest day, and Mr Jaggers had finally arrived. We sat in the firelight as I apologised to him for his wasted journey.

'I would have wanted to check with my own eyes that all was well here, anyway,' he said, waving his forefinger before returning to gnawing it. The fire cast shadows on his face, emphasising his strong black stubble, and the bumps on his nose from where it had once been broken, by the looks of things.

'So you say the necklace was beneath Miss Havisham the entire time?' he asked.

'Mr Jaggers, you surprise me. I say, rather, that the Pockets told me that.'

'Your version of events differs?'

I told him everything, for there was no point in holding back from this bloodhound for lies.

'What would the penalty have been had I been charged with the theft?' I checked when my story was complete.

'Death. The theft of anything worth more than twelve pence is punishable by hanging.'

'They wanted me to die. I knew it, I knew it. I'm a child, barely turned eleven; how could society be so cruel as to endorse their plotting?'

'What is a child? Plenty your age and far younger hold down jobs and earn their livings, else face starvation. To quote George Savile, the First Marquess of Halifax: "men are not hanged for stealing horses, but that horses may not be stolen."'

'So you believe that such harsh penalty is just? Even in those so young? And you mentioned children working or else facing starvation – what of them, should they be put to death if they steal food for their bellies?'

'The world is not just. I apply the law, Estella, and work night and day to ensure that the hangman is kept as idle as possible. That is all I can do. The law and justice are two separate things. Only once have I tried to rescue a soul I felt deserved to tread a finer path than the one they had been placed on.'

The usually beetling brows were softened, his stern mouth almost unrecognisable as he stopped chewing his finger, and let his hands fall to his lap and his lips form a melancholy smile.

'Me. You rescued me. But why?'

'I don't know. My life is, and always has been, about evidence. For once I wanted to do something that was about the evidence of my heart, which spoke out upon seeing you, grubby and tattered but with such sharp eyes. There is something about you that speaks to my soul and tells me you are marked for great things. You see the world the way I do, I suspect.' He took a deep sigh, then gave a rumbling laugh. 'Anyway, the Pockets would not have been successful in their ploy, because I would have defended you, and my track record is impressive. Although I suspect what made them take this gamble now is that a new law is being discussed in Parliament, the Judgement of Death Act, which will give powers to judges to commute an automatic death sentence.'

'In which case, they can't try something like this again.'

'Not like this, no; but stay on your toes. Evidence supports the theory that this will not be their final attempt to be rid of you.'

Indeed. My place at Satis House seemed to grow ever more unstable.

Chapter Twenty-Eight

NOW

PARIS, 1835

I am alone again, locked into the ruins of the bedroom suite. Curled up into a ball on the floor, the butcher's shop smell of blood in the air. Breathing hurts.

Bentley has been gone for some time. He comes and goes as he pleases, sometimes bringing food and drink for me, sometimes not. I never know what to expect, but that is part of his purpose, I suspect. Has it been two days, three, a week perhaps, that I have been languishing here beyond time, past fear, wandering in a wilderness of pain? I've no idea. I need to get away.

I need to get to Mother. How ill is she?

I watch a spider scuttle across the colourful silk rug and it reminds me of home, of darkness. It pauses to watch me, its body crouching low. Darts towards me. Veers away.

'Don't go,' I croak. 'Don't leave me.'

It continues its journey across the rug, finally disappearing behind a chair leg.

No matter how clean and tidy you are, no matter the war you wage against them, the spiders are always there, hidden in plain sight, and far stronger than they first appear.

There is a sound from below. I freeze, listening.

Footsteps. Coming up the stairs.

The doors. Bentley will unlock them and then...

I can't survive another attack. I don't think he plans to kill me, but if it were to happen he will, I believe, welcome being a tragic widower; it will gain much sympathy with voters.

There must be something I can use to barricade myself in. But what? *There!*

Throwing all my weight behind my travelling trunk, I cry out in pain at the exertion. I don't stop. It is huge and heavy and if I can only get it across the doors...

It won't budge. I'm too weakened.

I push and push as if my life depends on it.

Because it does.

He's coming. The footsteps are closer. He's almost here.

I was a fool to have married Bentley Drummle, and to think that anyone other than myself would be punished by my decision.

What had I expected when I turned down offers of marriage from far superior men in favour of a man who has nothing going for him? Pip poured his heart out to me and I deliberately pushed him away so that I could be with Bentley. That this almost-baronet has been confirmed as the worst type of husband possible should not have surprised me. The evidence was plain to see. Yet despite all my best-laid plans and machinations, I've been naïve.

I have paid for my stupidity in blood and sweat. Last night's pain, my screams, his busy silences that were so much worse than his threats, revisit me...

I throw myself against the mahogany trunk. *Thud, thud, thud.* It must weigh three times as much as I do, filled as it is with countless gowns and my trousseau. While picking my new outfits for my wedding tour I'd felt a thrill of excitement – for the clothing, not the man.

Fool! What am I going to do? Time is running out.

I haul the heavy lid open and pull out armfuls of shredded garments. Lightened of its load, I force it across the door, then fill it up again.

The footsteps stop. The sound of a door being unlocked. The doorknob turns. I imagine Bentley's hulking body trying to push it open, and hold my breath, hoping, ridiculously, that he might just give up.

A knock, gentle, barely more than a tap. The doorknob turns again. My time is up. Last night, when he had thrown me on the bed, I had known the truth: that despite being raised to break the hearts of all men, it was I who would be broken. Mother had always warned me that: 'Men shape the world. Women must shape themselves around it.' How I wish I could be with her now, giving her comfort, instead of facing more terror. Yet in her own way, she has broken and shaped me as surely as Bentley intends to.

The knock on the bedroom door comes again, harder and more insistent this time.

Memories of last night make me cringe like a beaten dog, but what choice do I have but to open the door to him? The thought of defying him and making him angry again, of *that* happening once more... I'd rather end my life. That is what he has reduced me to.

I pull myself over to the golden frame that has until last night housed a stunning mirror. Now all that is left are splinters on the floor and a few clinging to their original housing. Bentley has broken every single thing in this room, every stick of furniture except the bed. A long piece of the mirror catches my attention. It's perfect for my purpose, and when I pick it up parts of my face reflect back at me. Two swollen eyes, a split lip, dried blood beneath my nose, storm-cloud bruises ringing my neck...

I want to fight. I long to feel this shard sink into his flesh and skewer him. If I can lure him close enough, perhaps I can stab him as he draws me to him once again.

But no, I've already tried and failed. My movements are slow and painful, my reactions leaden. He'll overpower me again.

Only one choice left, I hold the shard against my wrist and close my eyes. Giving up is against my nature, but at least this way my death is on my terms and not his.

Another knock.

'Estella, open up.'

That voice.

My hand jerks, flesh slicing open. Blood blooms, but the mirrored weapon falls to the floor. My ears must be playing tricks on me...

The familiar voice calls again, reaching out to me from the past. 'Quickly, open the door!'

Droplets of blood leave a trail from my self-inflicted flesh wound as I rush to the trunk and empty it of its contents once again. Last time fear had given me strength, but now it has ebbed away, replaced by exhaustion. Even the hope fluttering inside me can't stop my gasps at every movement. My ribs are on fire, I can barely breathe with the exertion, and the pain between my legs makes it hard to walk. Worse, something inside me aches as if it has been profoundly injured.

Again that voice calls my name. Perhaps in my pain I am imagining it. Surely, it can't be…?

Finally, I open the door.

Chapter Twenty-Nine

THEN

SATIS HOUSE, 1823

Mother recovered fully from her trauma over the diamond necklace. In fact, she seemed to not recall it at all. Her mind skipped over such glitches in the continuity of her life; she was only interested in dwelling on the minutiae of years long past. A few days later, however, I sat at her feet and, as I knitted, I told her everything that had passed between her cousins and myself in recent months.

She listened, her hand stroking my hair the whole time, and at the end of it she chuckled.

'You seem surprisingly sanguine,' I said.

'Of course they hate you. What do you expect? You have my ear and my affection, not them, and you will inherit my fortune. Torturing them was one of the amusing appeals of adopting you, silly girl. You aren't only useful against men, you know.'

She continued to stroke my hair, and if she feared for me she gave no indication. Her hand landed heavy on my head, resonating through my skull in gentle rhythmic torture, and pulled me down, down, down with her fingers as they scraped through my hair. Dragging me to a fate I didn't understand and burying me.

Revenge. It was my only reason for existence in that house. I didn't want to become a monster, but my survival depended on it.

Somehow life continued and time, whether we marked it or not, continued its march ever onward. The Pockets knew that I was no longer the ignorant dupe of the past, and that made them more cautious. Instead of trying anything direct against me, they constantly undermined me to Mother. She amused herself by passing these vicious lies on to me when we were alone together, me sitting beside her and knitting or embroidering, longing to stab those conniving cousins with whatever was to hand. I refused to let it show, though, for it would only make Mother chuckle and call me silly for letting them get to me.

My pettifogging revenge was amusing but dissatisfying. My skill at forgery had grown from faking Mother's signature to mimicking all kinds of handwriting. It began as a hobby to pass the days in a house with little to distract one. The best and most accurate way to practise, I had discovered, was to hold a letter up against a window on a sunny day, and place another piece of paper over the top of it, then trace various letters and words to form the wording that I wanted. I particularly practised the Pockets' writings, and often created amusing missives confessing they had soiled themselves while walking down the High Street or that Sarah had once stolen a large hake from the fishmonger because she had fallen in love with it and wished to marry. Silly things for my own amusement. I'd never thought of a way of using the skill to truly strike against the Pockets, though.

And so my frustrations were taken out on Pip, who continued to visit weekly, faithful hound that he was.

The seasons came and went, but his visits invariably ran the same way. He would first walk with Mother, either with her hand on his shoulder to steady her as she moved beside him or, on her unsteady days, he pushed her in the wheeled bath chair. Around the dressing room, along and across the hall, and into the dining room they went for hours on end. It was the same perambulation as Mother and I made daily, and in some ways it was a relief for me to get time off from it. Not that I could admit that even to myself at the time. Sometimes we all walked together, and on such an occasion Pip taught us a smithy song called 'Old Clem', with a strong beat. After that, it became a regular for us to sing together, for Mother adored the hammer-blow tempo of the tune.

After the walk, Pip and I would play cards while Mother watched. These were my favourite moments, for I could take out all of my anger at the Pockets on him. Being cruel to him also bought me favour with Mother, and it was a currency I'm ashamed to admit I banked greedily.

Once Mother was tired, I would be called upon to take Pip away for food. At first I always flounced away, but eventually began to linger. Occasionally, we played hopscotch on the barrels, a game I always won because I made him too nervous to ever beat me. Slowly, we fell into the habit of talking. Against all odds, and thanks only to Pip's remarkable patience and kindness, the impossible happened. We became, not friends, but something so adjacent as to be in friendship's shadow.

One day while giving Pip his customary victuals at the end of a day spent marching Mother, he told me about his parents being dead.

'They lie in the churchyard over yonder, on the marsh,' he said, picking at a thread on his worn jacket sleeve.

Yonder. I almost laughed. But the goading words were swallowed down, for once. 'I'm sorry to hear that, boy,' I said instead. Certainly, there was an odd, tight sensation around my chest.

'I wish there was a likeness of them; it would be nice to see them, to know what they looked like. I've decided Father was a square, stout man with black curly hair, and Mother had freckles.'

'Neither sound like you. What is this based on?'

He gave a shy laugh. 'The lettering on their tombstones, for there is nothing else to go on. I am not much like my sister, you see, and it makes me wonder...'

'How much you are like them,' I finished quietly. Then roused myself. 'Perhaps it is better not to know. Deal with what is rather than what might be.'

'Wise words, miss. I struggle with that, though. I'm always losing myself in fancies of what was and how differently things might be if only other decisions had been made. Even small ones can forge new links in the chains we make during life.'

'Decisions such as?'

'Perhaps if I had not been born, my parents might still be alive. For once Mother died, Father was not far behind, according to my sister.'

'If they were alive now and you weren't would it make a difference to the world? No, I don't mean to insult your parents, but... well, you are here, so make the most of it.' I thought of Mother, sitting in the dark, reliving one moment. 'Doesn't this house teach you anything about moving on from the past?'

He picked some daisies within reach and began plaiting them. 'I wish I was as strong as you,' he said quietly, presenting me with the daisy chain.

There was no room any longer for curiosity about my own parentage. My place in the Havisham family was too precarious for me to waste energy thinking about parents who had not wanted me enough to keep me – and were probably common oafs, to boot. Still, hearing him talk about being an orphan, and voice thoughts I'd sometimes had myself, built a sort of kinship between myself and Pip.

When he wasn't there, I drew strength from him. Imagining the stoic way he would have dealt with the Pockets gave me the strength to fight back when I felt like giving up. When they made me want to cry, I would think of a compliment Pip had given me, or something he had said that made me laugh at its kindness and innocence, and I'd smile a wide, taunting grin at my cousins. Thinking of the admiration he always held me in lent me the courage to get up every day when I felt like staying abed and weeping, because I knew to do so would be to shatter the image he held of me. Pip thought I was strong, and felt nothing, and was beautiful – to be anything else would be a betrayal. He was always in my thoughts, though it never entered my head to intimate as much.

I was being torn in two, and it took all I had to hold myself together. The pull of Pip's kindness and friendship, the push of Mother's constant orders.

'*Break his heart.*'

'*Torment him.*'

'*All men are evil.*'

Every time I hurt him, Mother praised me – and I lived for that, because she was the one who gave me food and shelter. Had I not seen how dreadful the world outside could be when I had tried to run away across the marsh? No, there was only one person to whom my heart belonged, and that was Mother. There was nothing I would not do for her, either at her bidding or to protect her.

So I hurled the cruel barbs whether she was there to witness or not, and Pip absorbed them. Sometimes he was so gentle it boiled my blood until there was no release but to slap him, desperate to make him snap so that I could know once and for all he was as awful as all men. And as awful as me. Never once did he cry, or reprimand me. The only evidence of hurt was that sometimes he would turn his head away, bowed momentarily, before continuing as if nothing had happened. Those soft brown eyes of his were as gentle as those of an ox given a heavy burden to pull.

He was growing as strong as an ox, too. When he had started coming to us, he was smaller than I and scrawny as if undernourished, though always clean and tidy. After a year of visiting, he had grown level with me so that he could have looked me in the eye, if only he had dared. Another year, and he had to bend his neck to look down on me.

All the time our strange relationship grew, as twisted as the weeds in Satis House's gardens.

I could have confided to him why I was so mean: that it was a form of self-preservation. He would never have betrayed my confidence, for he had always been kindness itself to me, and there was no one else I could say that about in my life. Not one single person. Instead, though, I kept him always off balance, never sure whether I would be nice or nasty from one moment to the next. I think somewhere, somehow, I forgot that he was hurting as much as I. That I was being as terrible to him and inflicting permanent damage on him in the same way my nemeses the Pockets were to me.

One time, around the time I turned thirteen, Mother had been telling us a story about the balls she used to attend. Only recently I had begun dance lessons, and so the steps were fresh in my mind and I longed to show off my new knowledge once he and I were alone.

'Come,' I ordered. Taking him by the hand, I led him from the courtyard and back inside the house.

'Where are we going?' he whispered.

'You'll see.' Excitement trilled through me. 'This room hasn't been used in many a long year. Just wait and see… the ballroom.'

At that, I pushed open one of the ornate double doors. From the ceiling hung a huge crystal chandelier, which despite being heavy with dust and webs still managed to sparkle in the dim light of my candle. Pip stopped in amazement.

'Over here there is room for an orchestra. Over there, on that trestle table, would be punch bowls and refreshments, and the floor used to tremble with all the dancing, apparently.' I swept into the middle of the room and twirled, my skirts flaring away, my arms open wide. 'Shall we dance?'

I knew he wouldn't know how, and that I would teach him.

First we ran a slow and stately minuet, then a French quadrille. Pip's face grew flushed with exertion. He had to take his jacket and waistcoat off. His cheeks glowed red and his brows drew together in concentration, a smile spreading across his lips.

Seeing that smile made me so happy!

'A waltz next. A scandalous German waltz,' I declared.

'Scandalous?' His cow eyes widened with worry.

'Don't worry, boy, you're in safe hands. Now hold me close – not like that, like this.'

One hand, large and strong and warm, splayed across my back while the other encased my own. Our hearts were pressed against each other, beating in time as we began to move.

At first I hummed the tune low, and then he picked it up, and soon we were singing together and laughing, and there was such a look in his eye that my heart beat faster than the tempo of the music.

Breathless, we stopped finally and grinned at each other.

'I'll have to teach Biddy this dance,' Pip said. 'She'll love it.'

Biddy was some girl he went to school with. He'd mentioned her a few times, innocently enough, but it always made me furious.

I dropped my hands as if burned, and stepped away from him, arranging my face into a sneer.

'That's enough, boy. Why, you stamped on my toes so many times with those thick boots of yours that I'm surprised I can stand.'

It was a lie, and the confusion blooming on his face made me guilty – which only fed my anger.

'I hate you! Get away from me,' I screamed. My fingers blazed five scarlet lines across his cheek.

Chapter Thirty

THEN

SATIS HOUSE, 1825

That night I sat at Mother's feet while she arranged jewels in my hair.

'Careful who does the breaking, Estella. You are meant to skewer Pip's heart, not the other way around.'

I scoffed. 'The best way to hurt someone is to pull them close first, surely?'

'True. That is what *he* did to me. He always wore dark colours, you know, which made him stand out amongst the peacock outfits of the other men. But when he danced with me he was filled with gaiety that only seemed to be expressed in my company. Ah, how light I felt in his arms, how dazzling the world was as we spun in the ballrooms; how supported I felt − as if he were my rock, my Atlas holding up my entire world, and I could swoon against him safely, knowing he would always be there to hold me up.

'But he dropped me and let me shatter on the ground like that crystal chandelier you danced beneath today, Estella. Love is for fools. It is a tool with which to inflict the deepest and most deadly of wounds. Trust is for those who wish to gamble with their hearts and lose everything.'

'Exactly that − I will take the blacksmith boy's heart and crush it in my embrace until it hurts him to breathe.'

Pip was always 'the boy', 'the blacksmith', I never called him by his name anywhere but the privacy of my mind, for that was another way of diminishing him.

'That is the game you trained me to play, is it not?' I added. I moved to pick up the pack of cards rather than look at her. I could feel her eyes on me. Moments passed before she spoke.

'All men do is take. Suck you dry of your energy, your looks, your wealth, your joie de vivre, your very sanity. They take it all. From their first breath they are told that whatever they want is theirs for the taking. It comes naturally to them – but we women must be schooled in it.'

'Fear not, Mother, your lessons are taught well.'

Hers and everyone's. For I thought I knew by then that to survive in this world I could only rely on my own wits, and must always ensure I struck quickest and hardest. My armoury was growing daily, I believed.

Hubris rarely goes unpunished. For all my confidence, it took just five words to make my world fall apart, and they came the following week as Pip walked Mother around the rotting feast, her hand resting on his shoulder.

Suddenly, her fingers twitched impatiently and she declared with distaste: 'How tall you are growing.'

Pip's transformation from short and scrawny to tall and broadening had not happened overnight, but Mother reacted as if it had. It was a change she refused to countenance, she said, and so it was time for his visits to stop.

The look of bewildered betrayal on his face matched my own, better-masked, feelings. When he left that afternoon my back was ramrod straight, and if my nose had been any higher in the air it would have taken flight.

'Farewell, Estella. I… I shall miss you.'

'Don't be ridiculous; you're coming back tomorrow to get your indentures signed by Mother,' I said.

As soon as the gate was locked behind him, I crept to my attic space and cried into the darkness, my arms wrapped around myself.

Only when I knew my puffy lips and red eyes had returned to normal did I venture out again, and flounce carelessly into the dressing room where Mother sat hunched over her cane, staring into the fire. I sat beside her, trying to think of how best to tackle the subject without giving my true feeling away. She knew me better, though, and broached it herself.

'You are grown too fond of him,' she said, speaking as if to the fire.

'I am very fond of tormenting him, exactly as you wanted. Have I let you down?'

'You have been perfectly vicious. It has done me such good to see you gain in skill and confidence.'

'Yet more practice can never be a bad thing. I can't help but wonder that you decided to send the boy away.'

'You'll miss him.'

I dug my nails into my hand. 'In the same way the cats in the barn miss the sparrows they trap beneath their paws and pet for a while, only to let them go so that they can have the pleasure of trapping them again. Perhaps now we have let the boy go... we can have the entertainment of enticing him back.'

'I will not have change here. No time, no turn of the seasons, no ageing.' Her walking stick thumped the floor.

A fizzle of annoyance ran across my skin. 'What of me? I change and grow and age. Will you throw me out for doing something I am powerless to stop?'

'Where has this come from? Have I ever shown you anything but love?'

My head sank to my chest. 'I'm sorry, Mother; you're right. I don't know why I said that.'

She slipped her hand beneath my chin and forced it up until I looked at her. For long moments she studied me, then with a grunt let me go.

The fire crackled and cast dancing shadows, and for the first time I felt a shadow between myself and Mother. Despite the heat, goosebumps bloomed across my flesh, and it was not long before I said my goodnights.

The next day Pip returned with his guardian, the blacksmith Joe Gargery, so that his indentures could be signed and his new life as apprentice blacksmith started. Part of me wanted to tell Pip that he would be missed, but I lacked the ability to identify such emotion, or the language to convey it. Instead, I ignored them both.

'This draws an end to our relationship, Pip. We will not meet again, or have any further dealings,' said Mother firmly.

The back of his neck flushed, his lips trembled momentarily, but he gave no reply except a bow.

He and Gargery left. Their next stop would be the justices who were sitting in the nearby town hall. It would be the official seal that he would no longer be part of my life.

What a good thing, I told myself.

So I slipped after them and watched him being bound over and apprenticed, in the magisterial presence. I even followed as Pip was dragged along to celebrations in the Blue Boar.

'Hurrah!' his sister cried.

'Hurrah!' everyone echoed.

All except Pip and me.

Chapter Thirty-One

NOW

PARIS, 1835

I open the door to the voice from my past, still terrified it will be a trick and Bentley will be waiting to pounce, a sly smile on his face.

Standing there is not my husband but Yvette Reno.

Yvette! I sway not from pain or exhaustion but shock at this sight. The past six years melt away and I am back at the Parisian finishing school for ladies again, back on the pavement after receiving the most shattering news of my life up to that point... I was a different person then, but Yvette...

I run my eyes over her, grateful and wary all at once. She is exactly the same. Stillness surrounds her, filled with a sense of so much going on behind her eyes that will never be spoken.

'Is it really you?' I gasp, but already she is stepping through the door and putting her arm around my waist to support me.

'Can you walk?' she asks.

'What are you doing here?'

'Later. Don't worry, I'm here to help.'

'Help like you did last time? I can do without that, thanks.'

'There's no time; we've got to act fast. I know the kind of man you've married, Estella, and I'm here to get you away. Don't fear – I've taken care of him.'

Her arm tightens around me as I sag in both relief and fear. 'What do you mean, you've taken care of him? You haven't done anything stupid, have you?'

'Fewer questions, more hurry. *Vite, vite!*'

Yvette is certainly the lesser of two evils, and so I do as I'm told. I only pray history isn't going to repeat itself – I'm not sure I'm strong enough to deal with her again.

At the bottom of the stairs, I cling to the banister for a moment to catch my breath, my ribs seeming to stab me with each inhalation.

'Yvette, what do you mean, you've taken care of him?' I ask for what feels like the hundredth time. 'Have you killed him? They'll hang you.'

'So melodramatic! I distracted him, that is all. You worry too much. He was already so drunk that he won't be in a hurry to return. And men like him never notice servants—'

An exchanged look brings her sentence up short.

'Servants,' I gasp. 'What about—'

'His butler is dealing with a delivery mix-up, also arranged courtesy of *moi.*'

'Where will I go? We need a plan. I've no passport, no clothes except for what I stand up in.' Yvette had quickly got me into a cotton day dress that has only one tear in the shoulder, before we'd hurried from the bedroom, but now I am cursing myself for not taking a moment to think instead of being rushed along.

'Think while you're running,' she urges. 'We can't take forever planning.'

She patters across the black and white tiles of the hallway and opens the front door ahead of me, beckoning me to follow while asking if I need her support to walk. It isn't pain that brings me to a halt, though, it is a letter with my name on it resting on the highly polished mahogany side table. I recognise the writing: it is from Jaggers. It must be the letter Bentley tormented me with. Snatching it up, I limp towards the door.

One of the footmen appears and cries out in shock at the sight of me. I bark at him to stand aside, and years of ingrained obedience to that tone of voice keep him in place despite whatever his brain may be telling him. Fatigue is already catching up with me, but I drive myself to keep up with Yvette.

Whether I trust her completely or not, she has risked a lot – everything, perhaps – to rescue me, and this is probably my one chance. I can't survive another night like the last at my husband's hands.

The edges of my vision are darkening. A stumble has me hissing through gritted teeth as pain fires through every part of my body. I force myself forward by focusing on Yvette, who is running ahead towards the corner of the street.

Please don't let safety be far away, I pray. My strength is fading fast.

We are safely at Yvette's house, which sits in a compact cobbled court-yard surrounded by tall, run-down buildings. It is a small place, little more than a tiny room. Although nothing like Pip's forge on the marshes, I'm reminded of it nonetheless because it has that same feel to it: homely. Inside the one room is the range for cooking, a stool beside it, a table where Yvette eats and two chairs, one of which is a rocker that I already know is Yvette's favourite place to sit. A small looking glass hangs on the wall, a prized possession of hers. Its familiarity is bittersweet, but right now I embrace the comfort of being somewhere safe rather than dwelling on the awful memories these items stir.

One of Yvette's friends is a coachman and he'd been waiting for us at the corner of the street, and brought us here. The favours she must have called in to pull this off amaze me, but I'm grateful. I'm not sure how much further I could have run.

She tends to my wounds as best she can, shushing me whenever I try to talk.

'Rest your mind for a while,' she soothes.

'You just want me to shut up because you don't want to hear what I have to say.'

The upturn of her lips as she wraps a bandage tightly around my ribcage tells me I am right. She has a point, though. I feel utterly broken. I can barely walk, hardly think. Breathing hurts, every inhalation returning the memory of Bentley's weight pressing down on me, pushing on my lungs tighter than any corset. After days of torture, I'm hanging on to sanity by a single, unravelling thread.

Even so, I can't rest until I know I am truly safe – and how can I be without knowing what is happening? Then there are practical considerations such as lack of money, clothes, status. When I try to question Yvette again about her plans for me she pours some brandy into a thick-bottomed shot glass and pushes it towards me.

'Drink. Then bed. Tomorrow is the time for talk.'

Too traumatised to be my usual argumentative self, I drain it, and then the milk she fills the glass with twice. As I wipe my hand across my mouth, I gasp as pain fires.

'Rest now,' orders Yvette, her voice firm. She helps me stand and leads me to a curtained section of the room, behind which is her narrow bed. On it is a counterpane that I remember her stitching when I thought we were friends; the patchwork design is so familiar that my heart constricts at the sight of it. We stare at each other a moment before she hands me a nightdress.

'Thank you,' I mumble, feeling suddenly awkward.

'I will sleep on the floor.'

'You shouldn't have to give up your bed for me,' I say.

'The bed is too small to share; I wouldn't want to accidentally hurt you.' She makes a gesture with her hands to illustrate us turning in bed and clashing.

I grimace. Perhaps it's for the best.

The exertions of the preceding days and nights are overwhelming me. Yvette tries to help me out of my clothes, but still I stubbornly protest.

'You're not my maid any more. I can manage.'

She leaves at my insistence. My legs feel insubstantial, my head as if it is floating somewhere far above the ceiling, looking down on me as I pull on the nightdress.

Thank God Yvette was at the mansion. Why had she been there, though? The obvious question only occurs to me now. Despite crushing fatigue I open my mouth to call out and ask her – but the sound of crinkling paper as I fold my one and only dress makes me stop. There's something in my pocket.

Of course! I'd forgotten the letter from Jaggers.

As I pull it out I almost drop it, my fingers trembling with so much hope that Bentley was lying about its contents, and fear that he wasn't.

The words are short and to the point.

> *Dear Estella,*
> *Miss Havisham has met with a terrible accident. Her doctor recommends you return immediately. He says her wounds are fatal.*
> *Merryweather Jaggers*

Mother is dying. Bentley must have been saving that piece of information as a final piece of emotional torture.

I scan the words again, as if this time they will say something different, less shocking.

If anything it is worse the second time. Those sparse words leave no room for misinterpretation. I launch myself across the space and throw back the curtain. Yvette, who was in the process of sitting on her single chair beside the table, jumps at the noise. The heat that had been roaring across me disappears as quickly as it came. I feel cold and strange and my heart is thudding but so slowly it brings to mind the ponderous beat of a drum foretelling impending black deeds. Something is squeezing my body far harder than even my husband managed; I can barely breathe against the vice. My face is wet.

'I've got to get home,' I gasp. 'I've got to get home and see Mother. Now, Yvette!'

She doesn't ask questions. She knows me too well to waste time asking what has happened and why, when she can see the letter I still clutch has devastated me. Her hands are on my shoulders, her eyes looking into mine to make sure I'm listening. Her mouth moves. Silence. I cannot hear a word over the beat of my heart.

Thump.

Thump.

Thump.

The world tips sideways and I slide into unconsciousness.

Chapter Thirty-Two

THEN

SATIS HOUSE, 1825

Nothing changed in that midnight-black mansion except me. My body, my mind, my emotions all altered, despite everything else continuing as usual after Pip stopped visiting. The Pockets still plotted against me, and I them. Mother still cackled at our machinations when I informed her of them. And she still dripped daily resentment into the open wounds in my soul. Instead of trying to understand or win or please, I felt only frustration. A longing to escape grew.

Pip had only visited once a week but that had been enough to lighten me. Without him all felt heavier.

'I miss having the boy to practise on,' I said. Despite my pouting, Mother refused to discuss it further.

Months passed. Pip did not return.

Perhaps I could find a new friend, I decided. I walked the streets of the village, searching for someone to approach. All the children seemed huddled in groups, heads bent close to each other, or playing raucous games, the rules of which baffled me.

How did one become friends with someone? After days of watching I was none the wiser. It was perplexing. I was an observer of a language I did not speak.

Two girls were sitting on a wall, deep in conversation. I pushed my shoulders back and walked over.

'Good day to you.' Nerves put ice into my tone.

They stopped speaking.

I tried again. 'What are you talking about?'

'You live in the ghost house.'

'No, I li—'

'Ghost girl! Ghost girl!'

'Come on, Katy, run!'

They grabbed each other's hands, jumped from the wall and sprinted away. I wrinkled my nose.

That was the other thing friends seemed to do a lot: touch. Plaiting hair or tapping shoulders or hugging. It was strange. Apart from when she wanted to arrange my hair or put jewels on me, Mother barely touched me, although sometimes she allowed me to put my head in her lap.

I bit my lip until blood trickled into my mouth. There was something about me that people didn't like. My parents had taken one look and rejected me. The Pockets had hated me from the moment I arrived at Satis House. Mother loved me, but only because I was useful to her future plans.

There's Pip, I reminded myself. *He likes me.*

And look what I'd done to him.

My feet led me inevitably away from the village. The two girls from earlier were sitting on a low bridge over the shallow stream, heads bent together once more. They didn't even look up as I walked past, not until I was right beside them, reaching out with both hands… One quick shove and they both tumbled backwards into the stream with a splash. Without even slowing, I continued on my way as they shrieked their rage.

Despite feeling lighter, I still wasn't ready to go home. On I walked, heading across the marsh to the one place where I could find true comfort. Light faded, and in the twilight an orange glow appeared before me, welcoming me.

It was the blacksmith's forge, where Pip lived.

As silent as a shadow, I approached, then stood on tiptoes at the forge window. There he was. His face so serious and hard as he shaped the metal, first heating it until it glowed white-hot, then taking a hammer and, with expertly judged blows, flattening and curving it.

I entered the world as malleable as if I were that iron glowing white in the smithy's fire. Each of Mother's life lessons was a hammer blow that bent and broke me. She would only be satisfied when she had forged me into a weapon.

Suddenly, Pip glanced up as if he heard someone call his name, and seemed to look straight at me. His eyes had the unfocused appearance of one in a dream, though, and he didn't follow my face as I withdrew quickly.

My heart pounded and shame hotter than a furnace blazed across my cheeks as I scuttled away, praying I hadn't been seen.

Yet, for all my mortification, spying on Pip became a habit over the following months. Seeing him at the forge at his grimiest and most common, working away, covered in soot, and with black face and black hands lit up by the fire, which threw such huge, harsh shadows, calmed me. When he and Joe Gargery, and the journeyman who worked alongside them, would sing out 'Old Clem', how I wanted to join in, as in old times.

At the time I could not tell you why I felt compelled to commit these frequent night-time visits, though it is patently obvious in hindsight. I fought the urge often, trying to limit myself to once a month, and usually failing. I couldn't understand why I wanted to see someone whom I told myself I despised so much and my confusion made me all the angrier with Pip, with Mother, with the world.

The sense of alienation from my home grew as I did. My clothes no longer fit the way they used to. It wasn't just that they were getting shorter, it was something else. I bound my swelling chest down until it pained me. But what to do about my hips?

Thankfully, fashion was moving away from the slim silhouette that had changed little from when Mother had dressed on her wedding day, and towards a fuller skirt. I hoped my new dresses, with flounced petticoats, would stop her noticing my altering figure – for if she did, I feared she might cast me out on to the street. The shadow between us was thickening, fed on a diet of resentment and anger on my part.

One night I went to bed with an ache in my stomach so deep I thought it might kill me. Upon waking the next day, I sat up and… blood soaked my sheets. A scream ripped from me.

A maid ran in.

''Ere, miss, it's all right. Has no one talked to you...? No, I supposed not. You go find Lydia, tell her your courses have started, she'll know what to do. I'll sort this out.'

I did as instructed, hiccupping the news to the housekeeper. Lydia dried my face and explained the lot of a woman, along with how to tie rags to absorb the flow.

It was yet another thing in my life that was out of my control.

A Christmas passed, then a new year began. Time continued to fly, until Pip had been gone for almost twelve months. Through all that period the Pockets stayed remarkably quiet, apart from the occasional goading comment to Mother or me. At the time I gave it little thought, but hindsight clearly shows they were, to use that well-worn phrase, giving me enough rope to hang myself with; and I was courteous enough to tie the knot for them.

During one visit Sarah plucked at me continually as we walked up the stairs.

'You are so lucky to live here, Estella,' she said, turning me around so that she could speak.

'No one could be luckier than to be raised so high from their place in the gutter,' agreed Camilla.

My temper, always smouldering, flared. 'You take my place and live in the filth and darkness, then. You'd happily crawl in the mire to impress a woman incapable of being impressed, wouldn't you? Her soft sentiments were hollowed out from her years ago, and into the space left has been poured all the bitterness of the world, yet still you try to ingratiate yourself. She's straining at the seams with it, and the fuller she becomes—'

'Oh, Miss Havisham, how it must pain you to hear someone you treat as a daughter talk of you in this way.' Sarah's hand went to the straight line of her mouth in mock shock.

Mother was behind me, and I had not realised. So that was why they had turned me around and engaged me in conversation, while I had stepped into their noose willingly. I closed my eyes and waited for the tirade. The sound came of Mother's walking stick hitting the ground, as it always did when she was in high emotion.

'Do you prefer honeyed lies over sour truth? People who don't wish to hear honest words about themselves should not eavesdrop. You perhaps would not like to hear what is said about you,' she said.

She sounded amused. I opened my eyes and looked at her in shock.

'I am pleased to hear Estella give such an honest review, for it is how I would describe myself. Anyone who refuses to see the evidence before them is a fool.'

She put her hand on my shoulder and gave it the tiniest squeeze. We felt united – a rare occurrence at that time.

For the rest of their visit Mother gleefully punished her relatives by telling them in great detail the plans she had for her funeral, and exactly where she wanted each relative to stand around the table she would be laid on.

'I will lay where the rotting wedding feast now lies. And they will stand ready to feed on me in death as they have in life,' she pronounced.

They fluttered and quivered and claimed such a day could never possibly happen, but there was a clear glint in their eyes at the prospect. Their silent question screamed loud from their minds: *If she wants death so badly, why doesn't she just get on with it?*

Mother's equally eloquent silence spoke: *Why would I give up on life when tormenting you is far more satisfying?*

I wanted more to life than constant one-upmanship. It was time to tackle Mother with my plan – but what would her reaction be?

Chapter Thirty-Three

THEN

SATIS HOUSE, 1826

ater, after the Pockets' visit had ended, I sat at Mother's feet, as of old.

'I do know I'm fortunate to be here, Mother,' I said.

'You earn your keep, and more,' she replied.

That I did. Thus my gratitude and my anger became yet another set of emotions to pull at me, opening up the hole inside me further. But an idea had germinated in my mind, as a result of spying on my cousins of late. They were convinced I was being groomed to reopen the brewery business that had been left to Mother, who had closed it after her heart was broken. The idea appealed to me.

Broaching the subject with Mother would mean having to be brave, though, and tackle the issue of my growing up.

'Talking of earning my keep...' I began. 'May I talk with you about a daring plan growing in my heart? A while ago you made me your mouthpiece, speaking for you to tenants, collecting their rents and so on.'

Her fingers adjusted over her walking stick. 'Go on, go on.'

'With your blessing, I feel ready to start taking over the Havisham legacy, although it will take many years to get me fully acquainted, of course. The brewery was once the biggest employer in the area, and made the family the richest in the county. That could happen again.

'I will be a rare thing indeed – a woman of business. But why not? I can do it, Mother, I promise I will not let you down.'

She started to shake her head and gave a moan. I hurried on.

'You have a good head for numbers and knew the industry inside out once, thanks to your father's teachings. You could pass that acumen on to me. I am a good student, capable of being more than a mouthpiece.'

'Do you wish to pluck at my carcass, too? To pick at my brains like a carrion crow until there is nothing left? I will not have it.'

'But once it is done I can take care of everything. There will be no need to disturb you. It means I will have a purpose in life—'

'You have the purpose I gave you, and there is none higher.' Her voice cracked, so loud was her shout. Her body shook. 'You dare to want more when I give you all? Your education has been specific to your goal, Estella Havisham. You have been taught how to play piano, how to dance, paint, read, write, and know all that's required to hold an intelligent conversation with men to attract them, trap them and break them.'

'I am simply a tool for your revenge.'

'That is correct. Who are we, either of us, to ask for more? It is a noble thing you do, to avenge your entire sex. It's a higher calling than *businesswoman*.'

She could not have put more distaste behind the word if she had said prostitute. Yet she was asking me to one day soon draw the attention of men I did not like or love, to conduct her enterprise – that of revenge – like a common courtesan.

I tried once more.

'But wouldn't it be the sweetest retaliation of all to show men that we can achieve a full life without any input from them? We do not need them to run our business, or tell us how to dress, or when to speak or that we should smile—'

'You will captivate them, and then you will crush them. That is what is required of you—'

I clenched my fists. 'Why can't I be more than that, though? You were chosen over your half-brother to inherit the business – that's so rare! Most women must marry because society won't allow them to work, and so wedlock is their sole means of keeping a roof over their heads. Their well-being rests on the goodwill of another; but you were given this almost unique gift of independence.'

'How dare—'

'Let me have the opportunity to defy societal expectations and prove that women can be brilliant in business. I can blaze a trail that other women will be inspired to follow. When men see my success, they'll know every cliché about women being silly, emotional creatures who can't be trusted in matters of business is nonsense.'

I swelled in elation at my view of the future laid out before us. The bang of the cane shook me from my reverie.

'Enough! I will not hear of this! Go to your room or I shall do something I regret.'

I opened my mouth, then closed it. There was simply too much to lose. So I swallowed my furious enthusiasm, feeling it stick in my craw, and sloped from the room, hating her for making me cower because one false move on my part could leave me homeless.

The darkness, the constant smell of decay, the filth of the cobwebs and dust, it all seemed to press on me. I ran from the house, and out on to the expanse of the marshes. My lungs burned, yet I could breathe more freely there than in that oppressive house. Throwing my arms open, I screamed with rage into the sky.

As the weeks went by, my emotions grew more fiery rather than less. Mother seemed to sense it and tried to reach out. She really did. It was what I longed for and for brief seconds I was soothed, but the blaze inside me refused to be extinguished.

Even now it is hard to understand what was going on. Thinking on it, I can only say that I often felt pulled in all directions by what I wanted. My desire for love and my by-then automatic rejection of it. A longing for freedom, against a genuine desire to please Mother, which meant following her plan. Growing up, stacked against desperation to remain stuck in time. Spying on Pip while feeling ashamed of my weakness.

Each diametrically opposed craving pulled something inside me further apart. I had heard tell of places in other countries where the very ground cracked open, and the insides of the earth spilled out as a hot and fiery blood that ignited all in its path. That was how I felt inside.

And so, when Mother put her jewels against my hair as though I were her plaything, in a way that used to make me feel comforted and closer to her, it made my flesh crawl. When she advised me, I tutted, rolled my eyes and dismissed her. Her monologues about the great love of her life turning out to be a liar made my well of sympathy drought-dry.

One day I walked into her dressing room while she was studying something. It appeared to be a miniature portrait, an item I had never previously seen, but before I could look properly she tucked it swiftly away into a purse she carried always on a chain around her neck. Her jaw was defiant, her eyes embarrassed.

I had an idea of who it was – and was filled with disdain.

'Why did you allow one measly man to ruin your life?' I asked.

'What did you say to me?' Her hand clasped and unclasped the handle of her walking stick, those fingers working overtime as if she wished it were my neck.

'I don't know how else to say it.' I made to pick up my knitting and shrugged at her. 'You've allowed one man to destroy your entire existence. You've given him so much more power than he deserves. Over my life, as well as yours. I know he jilted you, and it was scandalous and embarrassing, and damaged your reputation... but honestly, Mother, it isn't unheard of, and would have been possible to recover from—'

'Do not talk of things you don't know.'

'But I do know. Because it's the only thing you talk about.'

She reared her head back as if slapped. I was appalled by what I'd done – and exhilarated.

'You're rich and were beautiful; you could have got another match, eventually, and the gossips would have moved on to another scandal. Instead you did all this. It's madness.'

'*Madness* she says. Others have tried to make that claim and failed. They've tried to get me locked away so they could lay claim to my riches; is that what you want, Estella? Oh, to think that—'

'Not this again. I'm trying to tell you, for your own good. Look at the damage you let him do – yes, let him. I understand it hurt at the time but why, even now, can you not move on and accept the passage of time?'

Her mouth worked. 'At your age everything is so easy. There are things I cannot tell, will never tell,' she said, finally.

'Why? It might be interesting to hear something different.'

'Oh, you serpent, to strike at my heart this way.'

'I thought you didn't have a heart any more – that's what you always say, isn't it? You've committed your whole life to cursing this man.' Each sentence lightened me. I stood taller. 'Let's say that one day Compeyson discovers what you've done to yourself: what do you imagine his reaction will be? That he'll finally realise the terrible impact of his actions, and is hurt by that? That he'll be moved to beg your forgiveness? No, wait, don't tell me.' I put my hand over my own callous heart and laughed. 'Do you imagine that he'll see the destruction he wrought in you and… realise he still loves you and ask for a second chance?'

Mother's jaundiced skin paled so much I thought she might faint. My laughter became a crow.

'Yes, that's it! Your actions are those of a woman hurting – and if you're continuing to hurt, why, then you must still love him… in your own selfish, destructive way.'

She picked up her cane and swiped through the air in my direction. Strands of my hair lifted in the breeze from it, it came so close. I grabbed it, wrenched it from her hands and flung it across the room.

'Be careful, old woman. If you beat me I will strike back harder.'

We stared at each other for a long time, our breath coming heavy and fast, both realising we had reached a precipice.

Both backing away from it. For now.

'Please, Estella,' she said at last. 'I would never, could never, sully your innocence by telling you the contents of the letter that man sent me on our would-be wedding day. I can never explain to you how he shattered not only my heart but every piece of me, and why I must punish him and myself by never moving on from it. At the end of days he will know what he did, and he will pay the price.'

I shook my head, unable to understand. 'I will never give my heart to someone,' I vowed.

Mother broke into a smile and nodded as if I had made her proud at last.

Chapter Thirty-Four

NOW

PARIS, 1835

There is fire in my veins. My whole body is burning. There is a voice calling to me.

Mother is standing over me. She is at the end of my bed, shrieking my name. I try to speak, to tell her about the awful dream I had where Mr Jaggers wrote and told me she was dying, but when I open my mouth there is no sound. Her begging stare burns into me, an unfelt wind lifting her hair and veil from her face to create an unholy halo. My hands tangle in the sheets as I fight to sit up. She points at me and begins to speak but I can't hear. Why can't I hear...?

Yvette is placing a cool, damp cloth across my forehead. When I whisper her name my throat feels like I've swallowed broken glass.

'You're awake at last. You gave me a scare.'

'How...' I try again. 'How long have I been asleep?'

'The fever has gripped you for three days. I thought we might lose you. Here, drink this.'

She takes another cloth and soaks it in water, then squeezes drops into my eager mouth.

'More,' I beg. She acquiesces, doing it several times.

'That's enough for now,' she says. 'Too much at once will make you ill. Slowly, slowly. I will make you some broth now, to build strength.'

A nod is enough to exhaust me back to sleep.

When I next wake I feel more alert. Yvette helps me drink a glass of water then spoon-feeds me salty chicken broth that is easily the most delicious thing I have ever eaten. All too soon it is finished and Yvette brings a second helping.

'So Bentley almost killed me?' I ask. Speaking makes the room waver. I close my eyes, take a breath, before opening them again. Yvette is looking at me intently.

'He came very close. You hovered between worlds and we could not guess which you would choose.' She lifts another spoonful. 'Now open wide. Tasty, yes? I shall make more.'

I swallow. 'Did... did I dream a letter about Mother?'

'Alas, *non.*'

I push the blankets back with as much force as I can muster. 'I have to get to her!'

'How? You can stand, can you? No, I thought not. Patience, Estella; for even as you lie in bed recovering, plans are being laid. Now, just let me wipe your chin.'

'There's no time. I have to go now.'

'Let us disregard your terrible injuries for a moment, huh? Let us pretend you are strong enough to run all the way to the coast and then swim La Manche. Still I would advise caution. *Pourquoi?*' She pauses to ladle more broth into my mouth. 'Your husband is searching for you. His cousin is very powerful – I will explain another time, when you are stronger, all about him, but it is enough to say that he is searching around every corner and beneath every cobblestone to find you. He has the authorities searching houses everywhere for you. He fails to get information only because he is so hated. But a big enough reward can soon turn hate to love in some people.' She gives a shrug of apology for the nature of humankind.

'All the more need for me to leave now.'

'Leave then. But first, feed yourself.'

Challenge accepted, I take the spoon and bowl. The bowl plummets, feeling lead-filled, and only Yvette's cupped hand beneath it stops it slopping into my lap.

Weakness. How I despise it. 'I have to get back to Mother. You don't understand, we argued before I left for France. I need to see her and apologise. She can't die alone. Can't leave this earth thinking I'm angry with her.'

Mother had been correct about everything, from the evils of men, to Bentley. I must make things right between us.

Yvette's brow puckers. 'Look how well we distracted your husband. We had seen how he went out every night after beating you, so knew he would do the same again. Visiting his cousin and planning and boasting and drinking. Pig. Ha, the wheel coming off his barouche on his homeward journey was perfectly timed – apparently, his face was a picture! So, you see what we can do. We are planning. I promise you that soon you will be home.'

Her skin is cool against my still-feverish flesh as she squeezes my hand. She looks so genuine. But she's fooled me before into believing her, and the consequences were profound.

I pull my hand away. 'You keep saying we.'

'My brother, Gérard, of course. He has been here, worrying about you, running around getting medicine.'

Weak as I am, I have strength to blush at the thought of Gérard and the memory of the last time we saw each other. I'd been such a different girl then. Full of enthusiasm for the future, for the first time in my life. I'd been so head over heels in love that the thought of turning my world upside down had felt natural.

Then Yvette had brought it all crashing down.

'What were you thinking, marrying such a man?' asks Yvette, a few days later.

'What sort of man would you prefer me to have wed?' I snap back.

I should be more grateful to my rescuer, for there can be no doubt she's saved my life. But the more time we spend in each other's company the more we bicker. The truth is, I can't stand the sight of her for fear of letting my guard down. Her secrets and lies – and her brother's manipulations – will not ruin my life again. At least Gérard hasn't shown his face yet, but I worry what we will say when he finally does.

'Just tell me the plan,' I demand.

She is peeling potatoes and brandishes the knife in the air. 'Ah, you haven't changed one bit. Ungrateful, stubborn—'

'Neither have you – slippery, untrustworthy, won't give a straight answer to a ruler.'

She viciously stabs her knife into a potato eye and twists the blade to pop it out. She's glaring at me while she does it.

'Don't even think about it,' I say.

'In your condition? Where is the challenge?'

'I need to get home. Quickly.' Mother is alone on her deathbed. Even now I may be too late. How I wish I had listened to her.

There had been something she wanted to tell me, too: a secret to share. What could it be? What possible enigma could a woman possess who never leaves the house?

'Why can't I go now?'

'Do you hear any words I speak? You aren't strong enough; your husband's cousin scours the city and beyond for you; the ship isn't ready yet… Which of these do you want to pick?' She gives a dramatic sigh involving her whole body. 'You know me, yes? I have lots of friends, and one I'm waiting to hear from that I contacted earlier. A ship's captain. Yes? Clothes you can take from me, you only need a spare dress.'

I open my mouth, but Yvette holds up a finger dripping with water. Wipes it dry on a tea towel that she has flung over her shoulder.

'Voila, here is your passport.' She produces it from her pocket. 'I searched your husband's paperwork before knocking on your bedroom door. Hopefully, you can be on a ship the day after tomorrow or the day after that, at the latest. *C'est ça.* You know that he will be watching your home, yes? What will you do then, in England, with no friends to hide you?'

'I'll be safe at home,' I insist, licking my dry lips.

'Huh. And this Jaggers, he will do what he's promised?'

I nod. I've written to him asking for transport from Portsmouth, where I will be disembarking. It will be a hellishly long journey, and hard on my already shaken bones, but Bentley is more likely to be scouring Calais and Dover for me than Le Havre and Portsmouth.

Between us we have thought of everything, but Yvette has been the one to make it all happen. Perhaps she is trying to make amends for past hurts. With everything else that is going on, I haven't the strength to unpick that knot, but if not now… when?

'Yvette, it's about time—' I begin.

A heavy bang on the door interrupts me.

'Open up! In the name of the law, open up!'

Chapter Thirty-Five

THEN

SATIS HOUSE, 1826

My fourteenth birthday had been and gone. It was coming up to a year since Pip had left us, and still I was lost in a dark solitude, with no chance of ever stumbling across daylight. The loneliness was desperate, whether because I needed Pip or simply someone my own age who understood my pain – to this day I am unable to decipher. Most likely it was both.

One particularly grumpy day I was knitting in the dressing room, tutting and harrumphing loudly at the complex lacework pattern.

'Perhaps you would be better to take a break for a time. Come back to it fresh,' suggested Mother.

'And do what instead?' I demanded.

'What is the name of that servant girl you sometimes talk to? Why don't you find her?'

'Martha? She left a couple of years ago.'

I had stayed true to my word, aiding Martha after she had helped me find that necklace the Pockets had stolen. She had been an unwilling player in their game, and helped me to beat them that time. I had considered keeping her at Satis House as an ally, but ultimately did not think her completely trustworthy. She'd had her reasons – strong ones – for betraying Mother and me, but there was no coming back from that. At my request Mr Jaggers had found her a new employer who was thoroughly respectable, and who offered Martha a higher station and better salary.

That she'd been gone for so long and Mother hadn't even noticed was ridiculous. Seeming to sense this discourse might trigger one of my little tirades, Mother changed tack.

'Perhaps you could go down to the kitchens and see what Cook is up to. Get something to eat while you're there.'

I frowned. 'Why don't you ever eat with me?'

She did not reply, just threw me a gaze that would have outstared an eagle. I wouldn't be put off.

'Why do you pretend not to eat or drink and instead do it in hiding at night, so no one can ever see?'

'Off you go, Estella. Your knitting will still be here when you return.'

'Of course it will be, nothing here ever moves. Why must everything go back in the exact same place? Why must we pretend time does not move on in this place when it so clearly does – look at how I have grown over the years; see how you shrink and fade as you age. What do you think will happen if you let in the light?'

I expected anger. Instead Mother bit her lip, as if considering. 'I will not have change,' she said, finally. 'I–I cannot. The world outside is cruel and full of pain. If anything changes in here, if something is not put back in place in the exact right way, then my world here ends, do you not see? It is the only way I have of keeping us all safe from an ever-changing tumult outside. It would destroy us.'

Something inside me melted at this attempt at honesty. My poor mother; she was trying to protect us in her own futile manner. But that was why it was all the more important to show her the error of her thinking. I would confront her with the truth.

'Change isn't bad, it's natural,' I said.

I reached out and snatched up the small looking glass that always sat on the dressing table.

'Change won't hurt you,' I said, swinging it, 'it will set you free!'

'Estella! No!' Mother's shriek chimed pitch-perfectly with the shattering sound of the mirror as it hit the ground.

It was a stupid and cruel thing to do. I see that clearly now, as a grown woman looking back. Any alteration was a threat to the mirage she had woven around herself that time stood still in Satis House. A smashed mirror, an item moved an inch out of place, a change of any sort would have had a profound impact on her state of mind. Her hold on life was fragile, and her mind veered between razor-sharp and meandering. Even her hair was deserting her, falling out in handfuls despite her being less than forty. Although aware of all that, I could not in my youth understand it; all that mattered in that moment was my conviction that I was right.

'You see!' I crowed. 'The world hasn't ended just because the mirror is in pieces. We're safe and healthy—'

Mother fell onto the floor, picking up the shards and trying to push them back together. 'What have you done? Why? Why?'

Ribbons of blood snaked down her hands. I knelt on the floor with her, trying to pull her away.

'Mother, please, you're the one making something bad happen. Let me clear it up, and you'll see that everything is fine.'

She wouldn't have it. Of course she wouldn't. I had seen her break down too many times over the tiniest of changes, why on earth had I thought that smashing one of her treasured items would force her to see the error of the way she lived? It was the arrogance of youth, I suppose.

I prepared for her to go into hysteria, to have to call the doctor. Instead she grew calm and stared at me, her hands dripping blood onto the shattered mirror.

'I'm-I'm sorry, Mother,' I whispered.

'No, it is I who am sorry. You are turning wild with frustration, fear and anger; you need more in your life than you can find within the boundaries of Satis House. I cannot hold back the passage of time as far as you are concerned, you are right, although I have tried to deny it for many seasons; and so I must enact something I have been considering for a while. It is for your own good...'

She could see the icy fury that was growing inside me. I went cold all over. 'What are you talking about?'

'I'm sending you away, Estella.'

I wanted to cry, to beg, but nothing would come except the slightest prickle at the back of my nose. I had denied myself emotion so often that now the only thing I seemed capable of feeling was anger – and at that moment even that had been robbed from me. The Pockets had finally got their way, and they hadn't even had to lift a finger to make it happen. I had been the master of my own downfall.

'You're throwing me out?' My voice was so small, so different from the strident shouts of moments ago.

'Child, this will always be your home, as long as you want it.' Mother's voice was gentle, too. 'For a long time now you have been frustrated, though, and asked for more than your present lot. There is a school for young ladies that I should like you to attend. There you will learn all you need to about how to become a gentlewoman, what is expected of you when out in society, the best way to dress and act. It is in Paris, the perfect place to learn about the world. This is the true start of your apprenticeship, Estella, for Pip was mere practice. You will work hard and become a beautiful young woman who any gentleman will desire to marry and call his own. And you will break all your suitors' hearts.'

So this was to be the next step on my journey toward fulfilling Mother's dreams. I didn't dare argue, not when I saw how close I had pushed her to delirium. Her whole being trembled as she spoke, and the effort to hold herself together was considerable. She did that for my sake, I knew. Sending me away would cost her dearly, but she was doing it for my good as much as hers, that much was clear. I set my shoulders back and nodded, then got on with cleaning up the mess I had created, the broken mask of my face reflected back at me in myriad shards.

Chapter Thirty-Six

THEN

SATIS HOUSE, 1826

Arrangements for my departure from Satis House were made swiftly. How did I feel at such a huge change? Once again, I was feeling lots of things at once and all seemed to radiate in differing directions from my chest. I had never been anywhere else but the village, had barely left the walls of Satis House, and was now moving to another country. It was impossible to comprehend how much my life would change. It was terrifying. However, there was no denying it was also exciting. Luckily, my haphazard tutor Mrs Sopper had been proficient in French and by a small miracle had managed to impart her knowledge to me over the years, so at least communication was not a worry. I decided to look upon the move as a dream come true, rather than banishment.

My enthusiasm, feigned or real, helped to soothe Mother's wrecked nerves at the thought of me going. The delicate détente between us was holding because I knew how close I had come to smashing *her* when I broke that mirror. Only her strength and love for me had made her hold herself together, but the effort took everything she had and she seemed to be shrinking before my very eyes.

One evening, not long before my departure for France, I walked briskly to the marshes as soon as dusk fell, needing to feel free, to have the space to breathe. Across the wide expanse I strode, looking at the endless line of perfectly flat land squeezed into a few horizontal inches. Above it rose the vast dome of the bruised sky. I told myself I was walking aimlessly but found myself at the forge. Pip's sister was outside, unpegging washing that flapped and snapped in the wind.

Step forward, I urged my feet.

I asked for Pip. He came outside, blinking rapidly in disbelief, the smile on his face growing innocently wide as I said hello – and growing tragically earnest as I bade my final farewell to him. It made my own shrivelled heart swell…

That's what happened in my mind's eye, anyway.

Instead, coward that I was, I hunkered down behind a woodpile for long minutes before Mrs Gargery bustled inside, muttering angrily to herself about dunderheads and work-shy fools. When I was certain the coast was clear, I crept forward to the forge's window and peered over the sill.

There was Pip, shaping some white-hot metal. Ash smudged across his cheek, sweat dripping down his neck and the muscles of his bare back.

Goodbye, dearest friend. I shall miss you.

He looked up. I swear he stared straight at me and saw my hair fluttering in the wind. He shook his head, and returned to his work. Sorrow seemed to give weight to the mighty blows he landed on the metal he hammered, although perhaps that was only my fancy.

I wanted to call out but his name caught in my mouth. I was going to Paris to be educated and turned into a lady, and this time I was keen to be forged into something fresh. If I did not learn to control my temper, one day I risked losing it so profoundly that the damage to myself or others would be irrevocable.

The following day I was nervously putting the final touches to my packing. It was here: my last day before I moved to Paris. I planned to spend my final evening with Mother playing cards. It was hard to comprehend I would not see her again for some considerable time. I walked through the trails I'd trodden in the dust-filled corridors, and tried to imagine sleeping elsewhere, in a place that was clean and tidy, and was not haunted by the sound of Mother's shuffling and wailing through the night.

It was impossible to envision.

'Ah, Estella, there you are. Are you all set for your adventure?' asked Mother. She held a hand out to me and when I held out my own, she pulled me to her and kissed the back of it. Her gaze seemed to devour me.

Before I could answer, Sarah entered, plumped up with self-importance now that the huge key to the gate swung from a chain at her waist, not mine.

'Will there be anything else, Miss Havisham?' she asked.

'You have shown Pip out? Then that will be all.'

'The boy was here?' I asked, trying to keep my voice disinterested. I dropped my hand and seemingly idly picked up the emerald drop earrings that were Mother's favourites. I twisted them in the light as she replied, and hoped she did not see them trembling.

His visit could not be coincidence. He must have spotted me at the forge. What if he had come to complain about my spying? No, that was unlikely. Still, even if he was pleased, if he mentioned it to Mother I was sure to get into trouble...

'He came because it is a year today since he was last here, and said he wanted to thank me as he was doing well in his apprenticeship. Strange boy. He did not fool me, though – you should have seen how he looked around for you. And the disappointment on his face when I told him you had left for Paris.'

'Why did you lie? I mean, this would have been an opportunity to tease him one last time. Give him hope then tear it away because I am leaving.' Still I stared at the reflected candlelight captured by the deep green stone.

'I must admit I couldn't resist the opportunity to break his heart myself. When I asked if he felt he had lost you, he knew not what to say.'

'He looked like he didn't want to leave when I closed the gate on him,' Sarah added.

So I had only missed him by moments? Hope rose in my chest. I could catch him up and we could say our farewells to one another, away from the gaze of either of our families. It seemed as if fate had handed me this chance.

'Hmm, well, I am to bed, for tomorrow will be a long and tiring day,' I said, finally placing the jewellery back where it belonged. A light kiss on both of Mother's cheeks and I slid from the room.

I sneaked out the way I had when I was a child, over the wall, praying no one would notice this undignified exit, but left with little choice now Sarah held the keys to the gate. Just as yesterday, the light was fading. There was plenty enough to see as I walked into town proper, and scurried along the High Street, always on the lookout for Pip but never seeing him. He could probably walk far faster than I, and so I pushed on even after hitting the marsh and beyond, expecting at every moment to espy him. Finally, I arrived at the forge once again.

There were voices coming from within. The sound of arguing. A man and a woman. There was no sign of Pip.

I stepped closer to the window. Trod on a twig which gave way with a snap. I held my breath, praying no one would come out to investigate. Through the window Pip's sister was clearly visible, standing with her hands on her hips and her head thrown back in scorn as she sneered at the man in front of her. He was tall and broad, though not so much as her husband, and from the curious way he seemed to hunch and rumble, I recognised him even though his back was to me. It was Dolge Orlick, the blacksmith's journeyman. I had seen him at work when spying on Pip, and noticed this Orlick disliked my dear friend. He always beat his sparks towards Pip, and when Pip sang 'Old Clem', Orlick deliberately came in late.

I didn't like him – and it appeared Mrs Gargery didn't either.

'You great idle hulker, you come here expecting me to apologise! You've done no work all afternoon and been paid for the privilege. It's I who deserves the apology!'

'I know what I'll give you, you evil shrew, and ain't no one would calls it apology.' He stepped towards her, towering over her. Using his huge size to leer down at her. She did not shrink. She laughed.

I liked this feisty woman. She reminded me of myself.

'Shrew, am I? Aren't you the bold one when my husband isn't here to teach you a lesson. How weak, to pick on a woman alone. I don't need him to deal with you, though he'll hear soon what you've done. Away with you, you knuckle-headed ninny, and don't bother coming back, for you've lost your employment here.'

'You fink you've got any say over me, you shrew, you crone.' His fists closed, forming two great hammers. He leaned in further.

Mrs Gargery, hands still on hips, worked her way up to her full height, a triumphant grin on her face. She leaned in closer, too, glaring right into Orlick's face. The fire threw orange and black relief over her face, her features seeming to dance with delight at her power.

'My husband is a fool, but he won't argue when he hears you come back here all high and mighty with me. Even he won't put up with that. Now get out of my sight.'

The mighty muscles of the journeyman's back bulked together beneath his shirt. In the light of the fire he seemed almost to be shapeshifting into a demon.

He's going to attack her.

The thought flashed through my mind – along with a delicious shiver as fast as a bolt of lightning and gone just as quick. I needed to help her. I cast around for something to hit him with – perhaps a log?

The muscles flexed further. Those hammer fists tightening so hard his knuckles cracked in the quiet.

He's going to kill her. She doesn't stand a chance.

'Why you—' he rumbled. Glowered. Breathed. Straightened, turned and walked out of the building. Nothing more to say.

How swiftly that scene had changed – I'd been certain something terrible was about to happen. Releasing a long, slow exhalation, I put down the measly branch I'd pulled from the top of the pile of kindling I was hiding behind, then peered through the window again.

'Ha! Go on, you coward, run away. And don't come back!' Another laugh, and then Mrs Gargery faced the fire, seemingly satisfied with the outcome.

She did not see Orlick striding back in.

She did not see the iron shackles in his hands raised up and swung towards her with such speed the candle on the kitchen table was snuffed out.

The mighty blow connected with the back of her head with a heavy thud. She grunted. Toppled forward. Sprawled on the floor, face down. Her fingers twitched and scrabbled at the floorboards. All that came from her mouth was soft nonsense.

My hand flew over my mouth, clamping in the sounds of shock and fear. All I could do was stare.

Orlick stepped towards the prone woman. Watching. Waiting. She didn't get up. She'd never get up again.

'You ast for that. Don't ever accuse old Dolge Orlick of being weak.'

He cast the chains down with such violence it silenced her feeble noises. I bit my lip. When he walked away, unhurried, I threw myself against the wall, hoping the shadows would make me invisible. He did not glance my way.

When he was gone, I sneaked into the forge. Mrs Gargery was insensible, probably dead. Her skull had a dent in it, and blood oozed steady and strong, soaking through her hair, running down her face, collecting in a pool that spread out in a scarlet halo. I prodded her.

'Mrs Gargery? Can you hear me? Move your fingers if you can understand me.'

No movement nor sound. I tilted my head to one side to consider the gore. The fight between Herbert and Pip those years before had exhilarated me, for they had been evenly matched. This was something different. I felt pity for Pip's sister. She had stood up to Orlick, but she hadn't stood a chance – for even if he had not come upon her as a coward, while her back was turned, he still would have beaten her easily. The raw power of him was incredible and terrifying.

In a fight, women did not stand a chance against a man.

Most women, against most men, I silently qualified.

Bubbles were forming in the blood closest to Mrs Gargery's mouth. Perhaps she was alive, after all, I reasoned.

I didn't know what to do. I should get help but... that would mean admitting my presence at the crime, which was not desirable. Pip, Mother, constables of the law, the whole village would have questions. No, it was better to do nothing, for no one could help the blacksmith's wife now. That meant Orlick getting away with his crime unpunished, and that didn't sit well with me, but...

I felt guilty about it as I walked home, but did not change my mind. Not even when I heard a commotion in the village that meant Mrs Gargery had been found and word of her attack was spreading.

The next day, I moved from the cobwebs and darkness of Satis House into the bright world of Paris.

Chapter Thirty-Seven

NOW

PARIS, 1835

The blows to Yvette's door are so hard it shakes on the hinges. Dupont's men must have found me somehow.

'Open up in the name of the law!' a gruff voice shouts.

Yvette pulls at me, urgent, silent. Sickness shivers through me as I shuffle as fast as I can to the corner of the room, and watch as she moves a barrel and sacks to reveal a hole in the ground.

'In there,' she mouths.

Doing as I'm told, I curl up, ignoring the pain. Darkness swiftly falls as I'm covered over. For a few moments all I can hear is blood thudding in my ears. I'm so close to passing out.

Muffled voices slowly drift into my hiding place.

'—have you seen her?'

'Ha, what kind of lady would spend time in this neighbourhood?' jokes Yvette.

'The kind that's been kidnapped. There's a handsome reward for information. You don't mind if we take a look around—'

'You've no right—'

'We are the *garde municipale de Paris*, we can do what we want.'

There's the sound of cupboards being opened, the bed moved. They're searching the place. I hunker down further, as if the tighter I pull myself the less likely they are to discover my hiding place. The pain! I clamp my teeth down on a wad of my sleeve to keep from screaming.

'Looks like thirsty work. Want a drink?' asks Yvette. What on earth is she doing?

More sounds come that I can't make out. Lowered voices.

My knees hurt, my ribs are on fire. This reminds me of being young, when I spent all my time hiding in the dark, listening to other people making plans about me. Is Yvette telling them where I am, is that why everyone is talking indistinctly now? Perhaps Bentley has been sent for by them and is getting closer…

I feel around for something I can use as a weapon, but there is nothing but dusty earth surrounding me. I gather together a handful.

Finally, there is the sound of scraping. Light chinks before me. It widens. I throw the handful of soil and shove forward, pushing my assailant to the ground.

'Estella! What are you doing?'

It's Yvette. Only Yvette.

The weight of relief has me sinking to the floor.

It's been a fortnight since Yvette pulled off my daring rescue. Although still dangerously weak, I'm glad to be on my way home at last. Yvette and her brother Gérard had wanted to wait until I was stronger before moving me, but their hand is being forced by the net closing in on us. Jean-François, we have discovered, is a good friend of the prefect of police in Paris, and the authorities continue to scour the capital for me, often doing door-to-door searches of houses on a whim.

And so Gérard and I are travelling from Paris in style – lying in the back of a wagon, covered over with hay.

With nothing to do but close my eyes and drift through the pain haze, I think about the past. About the last time Gérard and I were alone together and the conversation we had.

Does he still remember it as vividly as I? Seeing him again has made me awkward and angry but also grateful.

Then there is Bentley… How furious is he at my flight, I wonder. It's impossible to tell what he will do next, for I have been proved a fool many times over in my assumptions about him.

How could I have been so stupid? Pride, that's how. It is always my greatest failing.

A bump in the road shakes through my bones, making me gasp.

'Are you all right?' Gérard's voice is nearby but I can't see him beneath the straw.

The absurdity of the question makes me snort.

'Sorry, of course you're not. I just—'

'Why has Yvette done all of this?' I blurt out.

Being hidden makes it easier to say what has been almost bursting from me ever since I saw her framed in my pale blue bedroom doorway.

There's a rustle. Gérard must be shifting position.

'Because she is a kind-hearted person beneath the hardness. You know that; you were good friends once, before you left Paris. Though the way you said goodbye to each other this morning was as if to strangers.'

My silence does the talking.

'Why did you fall out? I've never been able to get a straight answer from Yvette.'

'I'm not surprised; she is someone to whom truth and honesty are fluid concepts.'

'Steady! My sister is incredibly loyal and brave. She's put her life and all she owns on the line to save me before.'

'Well, family is different, perhaps. I can only speak of my own experience.'

'So how do you explain her doing all this for you?'

I can't. That's the simple answer. Unless... 'Payback. It is to make amends for the past. And you – is this why you're involved? After everything you said last time we spoke? You're not exactly an innocent party in all this.'

'The last time...? Oh, you don't approve of my actions. I see.'

'No, Gérard, it is I who see.' I'm blushing and hate it. 'What you did and said – I was shocked. Let's not rake over the past, though, let's just... I'm grateful for what you're both doing for me. I truly am. The past is the past.'

How rarely that is true, though. The past never stays where it should, but leaks into the present. It informs everything we do, every decision we make, shapes the people we are. The past has been the cast into which I've been poured by Mother.

'It is safe. You can come out now,' calls the man driving the wagon.

We push out from our itchy, scratchy covering and any sense of secrets shared dissolves in the watery sunlight.

The rest of the journey is spent in silence. It is only when we transfer to a coach, once we are several miles away, that Gérard speaks again.

'You have been told the plan?' he checks.

'I'm sailing from Le Havre, correct? I've never been there.'

'It is a busy port on the coast, but slightly isolated from the rest of France – certainly more than Calais. Yvette and I have connections there.'

'Revolutionaries?'

He says nothing, but runs a finger around the neckline of his shirt, tugging at the cravat.

'You're a very bad liar,' I add.

'It is a shame that honest people must sometimes make themselves better bad people, in order to survive this world.' He smiles at the dichotomy of his words. A shy smile which I remember so well from all the evenings we spent together, talking about how to put the world right, all those years ago.

But that's all gone now. The only thing that matters is getting to Mother's side once more.

If I'm not already too late.

Chapter Thirty-Eight

THEN

PARIS, 1826

Every movement conveys meaning, each glance must be considered. These lessons in the art of secret communication must be learned well, for no woman must ever commit the sin of saying what she means.' Madame Flaubert's heels clicked with the precision of a metronome as she walked across the front of the classroom and back again, holding the gaze of each pupil. She was twice as colourful, big and bright as the rest of the world, and was at all times accompanied by her tiny dog, who would peek from beneath her skirts, or even a sleeve. In her hand almost permanently was a willow switch, which served as both a pointer and a form of punishment.

'Why ever not?' Everyone turned to me, eyes wide, when I spoke.

'Pardon?' asked Madame Flaubert.

'Why can we not simply say what we want to say? Men do.'

'We women are creatures of subtlety. There is delicacy and beauty in secrecy, it comes naturally to us, and enthrals the men who must rise to the challenge of breaking the code. Men love a challenge, and the harder we make them work for us the more we will capture their hearts.'

'It's not much of a code if everyone knows it,' I grumbled. 'And why should we pander to men's ideals? Surely, our goals should be more than wanting to be chased and captured?'

'Estella, to the front of the class, please. *Bon.* Hold out your hand. *Et la!*' The switch flicked heat across my palm, making me gasp.

The gasp as Mrs Gargery crumpled to the floor. The angel halo of blood spreading around her head. Orlick standing over her, breathing hard, triumph on his face.

Paris was a fresh start, yet there was no leaving the past behind. The violence I had witnessed bled into my thoughts often in those first weeks of arrival, casting a blood-red hue over my new world.

The switch cracked against my skin again. Quick as a flash, I closed both hands over it and yanked it free from my tutor's grasp and bent it in half, expecting it to snap. It simply sprang back.

'Are you quite finished? Then hand it back, please?' Madame Flaubert's cheeks were as red as her hair, but that was the only indication that she was flustered by my actions.

As I made my way back to my seat the other girls laughed cruelly, flapping their fans in my direction. So loud! I wanted to clap my hands over my ears and run to somewhere quieter. There were too many people here, too much noise. It overwhelmed me, and I longed for the peace of Satis House. There were a dozen of us in total, young ladies from good families which were paying handsomely for us to attend one of the finest finishing schools in Europe. Madame Flaubert continued speaking as if there had been no interruption and everyone quickly settled down.

'Every movement of a fan is choreographed, every glance has hidden meaning, even the flowers given, received, displayed, have a secret language of their own. Estella, show me how to convey "go away".'

I bit the tip of my glove.

'Excellent! Well done, Estella.'

I blushed. Madame Flaubert was hard on us when we got something wrong, but dished out praise with equal generosity.

'Now, everyone, let me show you the opposite – this is how you can tell a suitor: "I love you."' Excitement rippled through the classroom as our teacher drew a handkerchief across her face in such an artful manner. 'Your turn.'

We repeated the movement.

'Careful, Bernadette; I do not think you mean what you just said with your kerchief!'

We continued in this vein for some time before moving on to the language of flowers, and the art of flower arranging (tuberose, for dangerous pleasures; red carnations, for pure love; and yellow roses for friendship and joy – a mixed message if ever there was one). Suddenly, there was a squeal. One of the girls held her hand forth in dramatic fashion, a drop of blood on her finger. The other young ladies began a loud panic at the sight, with several starting to swoon. Madame Flaubert took charge with swift efficiency, tending to the girl so the class could begin again.

By the end of the lesson my head was thumping, as it had been every single day since my arrival. There was too much of everything here, and my senses were overloaded. Although the sun was falling behind the buildings – and there were so many buildings in Paris – the light barely dimmed thanks to gaslights in the streets and even inside. There was never true darkness. Squinting to try to block out some of the brightness, I stumbled to my room, assaulted constantly by the aromas of beeswax furniture polish, fresh flowers in vases, the different perfumes each person in the house wore... Safely in my haven at last, I pulled a pillow over my head to try to block out the noise of a dozen girls and at least twice as many servants rushing about the house, talking, laughing, stamping their feet. The noise of other people was overwhelming, along with the onslaught of colours. The finishing school was officially a private house, but contained so many people that I was aware of every whisper in the day and every gentle night-time snore. Nowhere offered the peace of the marshes or the comforting, smothering quietude of Satis House.

Beneath the pillow everything was, at least, muffled and subdued...

There was Mrs Gargery again. Fingers twitching against the floorboards. Always she flashed into my mind. The violence had shocked me but not, I was starting to realise, the way it would have other people. The way the girls had reacted in class to the sight of a few drops of blood from their friend's finger had been ridiculous. I hadn't flinched at all. Even when Mrs Gargery had been struck down I hadn't screamed or cried or fainted. My feelings were closer to... fascination.

Her back turned, with no clue that her death was rushing towards her. No idea that in moments her looking glass would be a pool of her own blood.

With a sigh, I threw the pillow across the room. There was no point in thinking about it, I needed to write my daily letter to Mother, as instructed. When I had finished telling her how happy I was, I hugged my pillow once again and cried myself to sleep with longing for home.

Chapter Thirty-Nine

THEN

PARIS, 1828

It was my sixteenth birthday and Paris seemed to be celebrating with me as the sun shone through the delicate pink blossoms on tree-lined avenues along the Seine. After almost two years there I knew the capital city well, from the reflective sheen of rain on the pavements, to the best place to promenade with my schoolfellows. It was my home, and the young woman it had turned me into was barely recognisable from the argumentative, almost feral, creature I had been on arrival. At last I was fluent not only in French but the 'secret communication' of flirtation.

I sometimes thought of the brutal attack against Mrs Gargery, although less frequently. That moment, seeing how easily a man could take a woman's life, solidified all my anger against men as well as my frustration with the way society viewed women, stymying our intellect and ambitions at every turn and seeing us only as decorative breeding machines. Just as a piece of grit irritates an oyster to produce a pearl, my emotions wrapped intricate layers around the event until it became something else, although I was still many years away from identifying what...

As it was my birthday I was rebelliously walking out alone – for among the many changes, some traits remained the same, and I still loved my freedom. I hung back in some places and strode purposefully in others, chin up, with such confidence that few gave me a second glance to question why I was alone.

The air was full of the sounds of people and horses, the shouts of street vendors selling everything from pies to posies. I walked through the food market at Les Halles. A stall had a brilliant display of fresh lemons. I held one to my nose and breathed in its sharp citrus smell, and bought two on a whim. In another brown paper bag I held a croissant, still warm from baking; I made a discreet hole in the bag and popped buttery-sweet crumbs into my mouth when no one was looking. They melted on my tongue like snowflakes.

If Madame Flaubert could see me now she'd be scandalised, I thought.

Madame Flaubert and I had an unspoken understanding that she did not ask and I did not tell. Despite our shaky start, we had bonded. She was a wonderful woman; her manners were impeccable, of course, as was her dress, but despite her no-nonsense demeanour, there was something pleasingly eccentric about her. She was not afraid of punishing me when I did something wrong; something I was not used to. But she rewarded with equal vigour. Her husband had died several years ago, possibly from the flu, although some of the girls at school liked to gossip without foundation that he had taken a lover who killed him, which was why, they claimed, Madame Flaubert had refused all offers of marriage since for fear of having her heart broken again.

It was Madame Flaubert who had taught me how to control the fire inside me. She understood, I think, that sometimes I had to get away from conformity in order to maintain that discipline, but it was unspoken between us, and she had not seen me slip from the school grounds that day. Only a new servant I had not seen before had glanced at me, her curious eyes lingering before they slid away.

It had taken me a long time to feel even a little settled in the French capital. I never admitted it to Mother in my daily letters to her, for fear of causing upset, but my sleepless nights had been many.

Now I slid through the multi-coloured scenes and felt total ease.

Suddenly, a shout of a different pitch sliced through the calls of the stallholders.

'No! I have nothing – nothing. You're hurting me!'

It was a young woman, about my age, clasping her hands together imploringly at a man just a few years older than us, but far taller and dressed as a merchant or some such. She herself looked to be a servant, judging from her attire. He struck her. People turned their backs. They did not want to step in to help a lowly servant.

'I will have what is mine,' he said. 'This isn't the end.'

His eyes blazed as he strode away, towards me. The girl had tears in her eyes, her lower lip trembling, but it wasn't her helplessness that caught my eye, it was the flash of anger that burned. She wasn't crying out of fear but frustration, for like me she realised that if she acted to defend herself it wouldn't be him that got into trouble with the law but her.

Onwards this man strode. As he got closer time seemed to elongate. This bullying, condescending buffoon needed taking down a peg or two. It was none of my business and yet I found myself waiting, anticipating, and...

At the last second I pushed the tip of my parasol along the pavement and neatly tripped him up.

He dipped forward so hard his glasses flew from the end of his nose. After he had picked them up, he adjusted them and glared at me.

'What on earth do you think you're doing, getting in the way.'

'Excuse me, sir, but you walked into me not the other way around. I thought Parisians were gentlemen.'

People were stopping, taking notice now that he was arguing with a young woman of breeding. I looked around in helpless appeal at the onlookers.

'As you can hear, I am not from this part of the world; I am a stranger.'

'Yes, well.' He dusted himself off, pulled himself up, and seemed to gather himself before giving a cursory bow. 'I apologise, mademoiselle.'

Off he stalked, weaving through the crowd.

The girl and I looked at each other and smiled.

'Thank you for helping me,' she said.

'It was no help at all, but at least it gave him a taste of his own medicine. I can't stand bullies,' I said.

Even as the words left my mouth I blushed, thinking of how I had made Pip suffer without mercy. There is none so evangelical as the reformed, though, and it was true that I found any bullying abhorrent.

'Well, you rescued me. I shall not forget.'

I dipped my head in acknowledgement, then looked at her properly. That steady gaze looked familiar.

'You work at the finishing school?'

'Today is my first day. I am only supposed to be running a quick errand and shall be for it for being so late. So if you'll excuse me.'

She turned and scurried away before it even entered my head to ask her name. Another chance at friendship lost – not that it could flourish when we were in such different social strata.

There were no friends at my new home, though at first I had tried to make some. Somehow I always alienated people with a comment or a look or simply by being me; whatever, it was always something that I couldn't identify. The other girls kept themselves from me at best; at worst, they picked on me.

I missed Pip.

Men were easier creatures, I was discovering as I grew up. Although, unlike my blacksmith friend, most were not interested in conversation, had no desire to get to know me, and only cared about how I appeared. For that reason, I proved popular with men of all ages, even at that tender age – or rather, *particularly* at that age.

No one had noticed my sojourn outside, and my little adventure had left me so tired that I took an afternoon nap when I reached the gentlewomen's school, and did not wake until the gentle tap of my lady's maid on the door. I was rubbing my eyes as she entered and drew back the curtains. Late afternoon sun flooded in – how I had grown to love the light! I adored how clean and fresh everything looked in it. A smile spread over my face, fighting with a yawn as I stretched.

'Good afternoon, mademoiselle.' As she spoke she continued bustling around, opening the wardrobe to pull out a gown. 'I am Yvette, your new maid. I thought perhaps this evening you might wear th—'

As she turned around, I gasped.

'I know you,' I said, pulling myself upright. 'You're the girl from earlier!'

'It is you! Oh, mademoiselle, how wonderful that we should be reunited. I hope you do not find it awkward, however; I can excuse myself and ask for you to be given someone else.' Her eyes were lowered respectfully the whole time she spoke, her hands clasped in front of her.

'Not at all.' In fact, I was pleased – not least because she was smiling, too.

Now I could look at her properly, I saw she had an air of stillness about her. She seemed to be someone completely in control of herself at all times, though it was hard to put my finger on what gave this impression, especially now that I look back and wonder if hindsight colours my memories. Did I notice that day how, despite her respectful and serious expression, something of mischief played at the corners of her mouth? Surely not, for her face was lowered, yet when this memory is viewed in my mind, I see that hint of devilment vividly.

'So, what was that trouble all about with that gentleman on the street?'

'A silly misunderstanding, mademoiselle, nothing more. I have chosen this outfit for you today, if it meets your approval?'

She showed me my favourite dress of cornflower-blue velvet, which had the flower embroidered around the neckline and cascading down the bodice in a way that accentuated my waist. The bloom's meaning was delicacy, refinement and good fortune and was a favourite of mine – even if it was a lie.

'If it meets your approval, I suggest the Ceylon sapphires. And this.' She picked up a huge ostrich feather. 'It adds a touch of exotic glamour, *non*? Something a little daring would suit you, I think?'

I nodded in approval as she held it against me, but—

'Yvette,' I said, voice sharp. 'There's a smudge on the mirror. I will not have dirt and dust in this room. Everything must be pristine at all times, do you understand?'

She bowed her head and curtsied an apology.

'I thought a simple hairstyle for you?' she said quietly, after wiping the mirror.

'Definitely. I hate looking too fussy, especially with such a beautiful dress.'

'There is no need to gild the lily, when the flower is such a beauty already.'

The flattery was to keep me from pursuing the previous subject, I was sure. Well, it was no business of mine, I told myself, as we dressed me for dinner and a night at the theatre. But I found myself studying this servant with silvery-blonde hair and curious grey eyes that seemed to take in so much but give away so little.

After she had left the room I gave myself one last check in the looking glass. She had done a fine job, right down to the belt of pierced silver metal she'd chosen to adorn my waist.

I lay my hand on my dressing table, palm up, and tapped lightly on the wood. A house spider with long legs ran from a crack in the skirting board, up the leg of the furniture, and onto my hand. Her touch tickled as she played over my fingers.

'What do you make of Yvette?' I asked. 'Yes, she's hiding something, isn't she? There are few things more irresistible to me than solving a puzzle, though.'

The spider seemed to agree as I fed her a titbit of juicy steak I'd been saving.

Chapter Forty

THEN

PARIS, 1828

Months had passed uneventfully, yet I was the happiest I had ever been. I looked forward to being woken by Yvette and talking about the humdrum of the day to come, and to the evenings when I changed for dinner or an evening out, and particularly to telling her all about what had happened that day. She in turn shared gossip from the servants' quarters, doing impressions of other members of staff, though never of the other ladies or Madame Flaubert.

I laughed freely. For the first time I had a friend, someone who didn't have to be viewed as a potential rival, and whom I didn't have to protect myself from. I trusted her.

She didn't seem swayed at all by the way the other ladies laughed at me.

'*Estella doesn't know how to tell the time.*' Not true, I had learned.

'*Estella is so backward she doesn't even know what gaslights are.*' I'd never heard of such a thing before arriving in Paris. At Satis House we had candles. When the girls had found out they had been merciless.

But their favourite was: '*Estella is so unlovable even her family don't send her Christmas or birthday gifts.*'

Even the other servants fought to hide their smiles at these taunts, and treated me with a slight air of disdain, as if they had just smelled some milk that was on the turn but were too polite to say anything about it. Not Yvette. In fact, the more she heard the barbs, the more she told me stories and tried to befriend me.

Madame Flaubert was aware to a certain extent of how the others shunned me. She had taken me aside on one occasion and advised me that a lady should 'never respond; simply rise above comments. Imagine, if you will, there is a plate of glass between you and those who say such things. The glass protects you from those words truly reaching you – they cannot hurt you. But if you respond, you will shatter that glass and be left vulnerable to hurt.'

It was a sound theory, but the practice was a struggle. Those little bitches all needed to be taught a lesson, and if Madame Flaubert wasn't willing to, then I was.

One day we were sitting embroidering together. It had been a long and dull afternoon, where the most exciting thing to happen had been Collette pricking her finger with a squeal from her piggy face. The way she sucked on her sausage-like digit, setting her tight dark curls quivering, was as though she had severed it, and everyone fussed over her. Despite her lack of looks or intellect, her family was so rich that everyone fawned over her and treated her as if each word from her mouth was a diamond to be prized. She liked to show off how rich she was by doing silly things such as declaring that her brand new cream shoes – with a lace overlay and forget-me-nots embroidered across the toe – were ugly. That anyone who wore such things must be mad (which had all the girls looking at their footwear and finding it wanting, for they always liked to wear what Collette was wearing. All apart from I, who wore plain ones of midnight blue). She then took them off and forced them so they were almost bent in half, then forced them back the other way, intent on destroying them.

'You could simply wear some other shoes,' said I.

'They are so grotesque that I feel it my duty to rid the world of them. You would understand if you had any taste or breeding.' She looked me up and down in a pointed manner and declared: 'I simply can't stand ugly things.'

Remembering the plate of glass, I decided not to retort that it must be difficult for her never being able to look in the mirror.

The rest of the afternoon passed without incident until Collette glanced over and called to me.

'What time is it? I cannot see the clock from here, for the sun is on the glass.'

A quick look and I was able to tell her what the time was. This seemed to cause stifled amusement, with much elbowing and bitten lips and barely concealed sniggers.

Oh, how hilarious to ask me the time when the running joke was that I could not read a clock. Because I'd been unused to the concept when I first moved to Paris, there had been a number of incidents where I was late or had been slow to tell the time when asked. I'd quickly learned.

Despite there being another hour until we had to change for dinner, the girls all started to drift from the room, making various excuses. It seemed a little odd to me, but the relief of having time alone overcame the oddness.

Half an hour later Yvette came scurrying into the room.

'I hope you don't think me impertinent, mademoiselle, but... well, if you do not come now it will be too late for you to change.'

I looked at the clock. 'I always come up an hour before dinner – and there's half an hour before I need to move.'

'Mademoiselle, that clock is wrong.'

Suddenly, I realised what had happened. Collette or someone in her herd at her bidding, no doubt, had changed the mantel clock so that it was a full hour behind where it should have been. No wonder everyone had thought it so funny when I told them the time. No wonder all had left the room, ensuring they would arrive as expected and I would be late – knowing that Madame Flaubert would punish tardiness by sending me to bed with no food.

'I'll kill them.' I stood, embroidery falling to the floor, hands clenched into fists. 'I'll—'

'Do nothing for now. We will make sure they get their comeuppance. Eventually.'

But I was already striding across the room, calling Collette's name. The plate of glass would be smashed over her stupid head when I caught up with her.

'Mademoiselle, Miss Estella, please. Think before you act.' Yvette caught my arm, holding me back.

From down the corridor I could hear group laughter. Those—

'Act now and they will see you coming. They will get you into trouble and win. You think they haven't already considered this? Wait and—'

She chased after me down the hallway and up the stairs to Collette's room. All the other girls poked their heads from their rooms, eager to see the fireworks. Yvette was right, I knew, but anger had control over my body. I marched into Collette's room.

'Estella! You're a little earlier than anticipated.' She grinned. *Thud!* I punched her straight in her smug face, felt her nose crunch beneath my fist, saw the blood that poured down her face, and heard her shriek of agony.

For that, I wasn't allowed to have dinner for a whole week, nor was I permitted to leave the house for two months.

It was worth it.

Through all of my punishment, Yvette sat with me in my room every evening. Her talk of the servants' goings-on kept me sustained, and I no longer felt so lonely. It made my 'punishment' a pleasure.

Finally, one night I raised the subject of the circumstances of how we had first met. She looked at me almost as if she had forgotten the drama.

'It is a sad fact that even in these modern times there are some men who though they have the money and the clothes, are no gentlemen. That man – for I will not call him a gentleman – he, well, he—' She cut herself off for a beat, blushing. 'He propositioned me, and when I refused, he insulted me further by offering money. I may be poor, mademoiselle, but never will I be that poor.'

I remembered his arrogant glare, the way he ordered rather than spoke. He seemed exactly the kind of man Mother had warned me about.

Mystery solved, friendship grew between us, despite the disparity in position. She was exactly as she appeared: a sweet, funny young woman with a mischievous sense of humour and a sharp eye for observing characters. This breath of fresh air was precisely what I needed in my life, I decided.

One evening, several months after I had punched Colette and been allowed once more to join the school's social engagements, Yvette dressed me for the opera and we were all about to leave for our outing together, we ladies of the school. I was showing off my latest purchase, a pair of cream satin slipper shoes, chosen deliberately since Collette declared anyone who wore such a thing persona non grata. She looked down and sneered while I tapped my toes in her direction, making the warm white pearls that adorned the slipper catch the light.

Suddenly, I realised I had stupidly left my fan on my bed. I could ring for a servant to fetch it, but that would take longer than if going myself, as I wasn't certain where it was, so I glided upstairs – glided, not hurried, for a lady never hurries.

In the privacy of my bedroom I could at last make haste and threw things around until I uncovered it under the dressing table, where it must have fallen.

Relieved, I turned – and heard a tearing sound. In my haste I'd caught my dress so hard that I feared it had torn. Luckily it had not, but it had pulled loose my fastenings. I couldn't go out like that, I needed Yvette.

Again, I thought about ringing down for her, but I was already running late. Knowing that Madame Flaubert would only wait for me so long before leaving without me, I instead decided to go down to the servants' quarters, get her to fix me quickly there, and then I could go straight to our hallway and meet everyone there.

I hurried, unashamed now, down the servants' stairs that ran down the back of the house. One of the footmen came across me, stepping back out of my way and looking at me in shock before he managed to rearrange his face into a more respectful expression.

'Where might I find Yvette?' I asked.

'She'll be in the servants' parlour, at the right of the stairs when you reach the bottom.' I raced off, as he called: 'She has a visitor, mademoiselle.'

Outside the door of the servants' parlour I paused for a moment to catch my breath. Yvette surely wouldn't mind me interrupting her, for we were more like friends than servant and mistress, and I would only be there a moment. Still, I decided to press my ear against the door, prompted by my desire not to interrupt something important, but also, I cannot lie, curiosity.

Yvette indeed was not alone – she was with a man.

From his accent he sounded as if he was Parisian, like her. They were familiar with each other, judging from the tone they used.

'What is the point of fighting the system?' asked Yvette. She sounded annoyed. 'It is better to accept, and not waste energy on fighting things that will never change.'

'They will not change unless we fight.' It was not a rumbling bass that sounded, more of a light baritone. Was he her lover? Could he even be the man who had been on the street with her all those weeks ago?

'That's been tried, remember? The people of this country did rise up and fight.' Her voice dripped with sarcasm. I frowned. I'd never heard her like this before. 'Lives were lost to the cause, blood ran in the streets and fields, and to what end? Still the poor are poor and the rich are rich. We even have a king again. Nothing has changed, there is no point in fighting.'

'We have to close that gap. Never has there been such disparity between the way we are told the world is, and the way things actually are. If we accept, then all that went before was for nothing.'

'You're an idealistic fool. I am a realist. Society will not change and accept us. Instead we must take what we want, all while putting on an acceptable face so that no one will ever suspect.'

'There is power in hidden things, I'll admit. But sometimes there is no choice but to come out and fight – for the greater good.'

'Don't make me laugh. You—'

I knocked on the door, interrupting her. As fascinating as the conversation was, I still had to get my state of dress sorted and meet the other ladies.

Without waiting for permission to enter, and thus give time for the mystery man to hide, I pushed open the door. Yvette appeared the picture of composure, apart from being caught in the act of sitting up straighter, and tugging at her dress skirts to tidy herself. A light-haired man sat on a chair opposite, hunched forward with his elbows on his knees and looking up with his mouth agape at my intrusion. He leapt up. I ignored him and sallied forward, explaining my problem.

While Yvette swiftly took care of it, I seized my chance to study the two of them. The atmosphere from him was charged.

He greeted me with a smile, yet did not introduce himself properly. He was handsome, this man, with intelligent eyes, high cheekbones and generous mouth beneath a neat moustache. There was an attractive delicacy about him.

'And you are?' I pressed, holding out my hand.

'Oh, pardon. I am Gérard—'

'Voila, all done. The time, mademoiselle! You will be late.'

'I have a few minutes. Time enough for introductions.'

'Of course. I apologise,' said Yvette. 'I only hope Madame Flaubert will not be angry with me when she discovers it is my fault you are late.'

She would not be, for she was not an unfair woman. She would, however, be extremely disappointed in me, which would result in my being banned from the next few outings.

There was no time for interrogation. I had an appointment to meet. Defeated for now, I made swift farewells. Who was Yvette's visitor? And whom did he want to fight? That was vaguely interesting. But what piqued my curiosity far more was Yvette. Now here was a woman with interesting secrets. What's more, she had fooled me into thinking she was straightforward. Someone who could take me in was someone I definitely needed to study.

Chapter Forty-One

NOW

SATIS HOUSE, 1835

ome at last after my epic escape from France and my husband, I sag in my seat with relief as the coach makes its way along the familiar street towards Satis House. How welcomed I feel by the ivy overtaking the exterior of the dull old house so that barely a red brick shows; the squeal of the rusting gate as it opens; the hummocks of grasses growing through the paving stones on the paths, and the overgrown briars tugging at my skirts. Inside, the cobweb-filled darkness smells of decay, and welcomes me. I stumble and almost collapse in relief. Bentley will no doubt come here, and when he does I dread to think of the outcome, yet still being home makes me feel safe for now.

It has surely been a hundred years since last I walked these corridors, for I am wholly changed. Broken, beaten, utterly defeated as I am, my suffering has given me empathy for Mother at least: it's now possible to understand why she chose to hide from the world here, where she could control everything, and nothing could hurt her. For myself, my ribs still make breathing painful, but thankfully the bleeding from inside me stopped before I left France, my split lip is no longer so swollen, nor my eyes (though they are still black as storm clouds). I will be wearing long sleeves and high necks for some time to come…

Without pausing to pick up a candle, I hurry to find Mother, as fast as my injuries allow. Along the corridors I go, running my fingers across the almost invisible walls to help me find my way; feeling familiar bumps in the cold, damp plaster, or the rise and fall of warped wood panelling beneath my touch. I marvel at the things I used to take for granted; nothing has changed here. Nothing.

It fills me with a conviction that Mother will be fine – for she never alters either. Jaggers, for the first time in his life, has run away with himself and exaggerated the situation. Yes, that's right. It's not so unlikely – he is a man, after all, not an automaton, and so is prone to weakness, mistakes, overblowing facts, even if it is only once in his entire life.

Still, my limping feet hurry. There is no sign of Mother in the dressing room, where I half expected to find her sitting as usual, perhaps holding some jewels against herself in a bored fashion. I run into the great hall next, where the wedding feast always sits. Throw open the door – and stop short, blinking in disbelief.

Daylight floods the room.

The curtains have been ripped down, one still hanging from a couple of curtain rings while the rest of the material droops and pools onto the floor, mid-pour. Sunlight piles onto the dining table, lighting it like a cheap actress in a music hall act. It is bare.

I step forward, a low groan escaping my lips. This can't be real. There is no sign of the feast at all. The table is barren, even the tablecloth has gone. My astonished hands move back and forth through empty air where the monstrous, blackened cake should be. The home of countless, nameless friends has gone.

'Mother!' I shout. 'Mother, where are you?'

There is no reply.

Then…

Footsteps. Pattering towards me.

I run to the door. 'Mother—!'

It is one of the servants, Lydia. One of the original staff who were there that terrible day over twenty years ago, when the clocks were stopped. Only a handful have remained loyal to Mother, but their loyalty is fierce and they are well rewarded for their refusal to gossip in the village. I almost run headlong into her.

'Miss Estella – I mean, Mrs Drummle, of course…' The name jars. 'Thank goodness you're here. Permit me to take you to Miss Havisham. She's in her bedroom.'

'What has happened here? I know only the bare bones.'

'I know little myself, miss. Only that Mr Pip visited your mother, and that while he was taking some air, a coal fell from the fire and,' she dabbed at her eyes with the corner of her apron, 'her dress caught. Mr

Pip heard the screams and raced in. He saved her, Mrs Drummle. Tore the curtains down and the tablecloth to smother the flames.'

Dear Pip, always there for us when we most need him.

'She lives?' It is a struggle to form the words, but I steel myself.

'That she does. The doctor says 'tis a miracle. Rubbish. "She's holding on for her daughter," I told him. She lives and breathes for you.'

'What are her chances of recovery? Has he said?'

She stops, turns. 'Sometimes she seems to be improving. Others… But the longer she holds on, the greater the chance.'

I sway but keep my head high, and start walking again, forcing Lydia to hurry to keep up with me. She has taken in my injuries but knows her place enough not to comment. 'And what of Mr Pip?'

'I heard tell he was injured himself. His hands required dressing, and were quite the state, but that's according to Jane, who helped the doctor when he arrived – I didn't see it myself. I've no stomach for such things so kept busy with the tea.' She prattles on and I let her, though I am barely listening. It seems a relief to her to finally be able to talk to someone about what happened.

Finally, we reach Mother's bedroom. Lydia pauses to check I'm all right but I bat her hand away from the doorknob and turn it myself. Let us face this head-on. Whatever state Mother is in, I can nurse her. I can put things right. I shall never leave her side again, content to remain here at Satis House and decay slowly with her.

At my touch, the bedroom door swings open. Lying on the bed is a pile of rags. Where is Mother?

A moan comes from the bed. From the rags. Is it—?

'Mother!' Five steps and I'm at her side, my own pains forgotten.

Her legs are swathed in bandages, like the Egyptian mummies I have heard tell about in penny dreadfuls and tall tales. Patches of skin on her face are pink and shiny, swollen so that her normally sunken cheeks are a cruel parody of the plumpness of youth, like the painting of her as a thirteen-year-old, which hangs downstairs. There is a strong smell of iodine and alcohol. Her eyes are the same, though: sharp, even while clouded with pain.

This is the first time I've ever seen her in something other than her wedding gown. Gosh, how strange to think she will never wear it again. I wonder where the pale pink nightgown has come from, then recognise it as an old one of mine. Her hair is neat, and there is no veil half-attached.

'Mother, can you hear me?'

'The doctor has told her to rest her voice. I've put pencil and paper nearby, though.' It is kind of Lydia, but Mother's right hand is bandaged. Briefly, I wonder what has happened to the notebook identical to the one I wear about my neck. It must have been destroyed in the fire, like the bridal gown, and so much more.

Mother moans again. She is awake but her eyes are closed and I'm not sure how aware she is. Still, I call her name again.

Her eyes flutter open. 'Estella.' Her voice is a painful rasp. 'Is that really you?'

It's exactly what she said last time I returned from Paris, all those years ago. I search for a part of her I can touch without causing her pain, and gently stroke an un-blistered patch of skin.

'Feel that? It's real, Mother; I'm here.'

Tears gather in her eyes. Then overspill, running into her hair. Her bandage-mittened hand reaches towards me, but she cries in pain and drops it again. 'It's been a long time since I was grateful for anything,' she says. 'But my heart is full at the sight of you. I feared I'd never get the chance to say I was sorry.'

'Hush, now. There's nothing to apologise for—'

'There is so much! Too much for me to ever hope for forgiveness.'

I hush her in ways learned through a lifetime of soothing her. Finally, I resort to a threat.

'If you do not rest now, then I will not listen to one word of your apology later.'

She closes her eyes, at last. Her breath is uneven and shallow, as if it pains her to fill her lungs. There is the slightest rattle to her chest. First checking that she is asleep, I ease a chair over to her bed, drop my head to the mattress and let my own tears come. Allow myself to take in the enormity of what has happened to her.

For Mother to apologise, to admit to having a heart left to feel gratitude and fullness, hammers home what my own eyes tell me.

She is dying.

My body has been broken by Bentley. But seeing Mother like this has demolished my heart.

Chapter Forty-Two

THEN

PARIS, 1828

It became my business to watch Yvette. She was a brilliant dissembler, never giving away in speech or demeanour that she was anything other than a meek and mild servant. There was no hint of the 'take what you want' attitude she had shared so freely with her male visitor. Only because I now knew her true nature did I study her so minutely and realise she always quietly got her own way in all things. I spied on her around the school, using the skills acquired as a child. Yvette was breathtakingly good at what she did, her hands so speedy it was easy to miss it even though I was watching closely, but on occasion she slipped into her pockets change left lying about by my rich fellow students – only small amounts, and never with enough regularity for it to be noticed by any one besides me. Sometimes she would be bolder, working loose a stone from a necklace or brooch, for example, but not taking the whole piece, instead making it appear as though the missing stone had fallen out and been lost. Other times she might swipe a single earring, never the pair and always from someone who had been out and returned. At first I could not puzzle out the reasoning behind it, then it dawned: of course, a missing pair of earrings would seem suspicious, but a single one could be assumed to be lost outside, gone forever. I remembered how, when Yvette had first started as my ladies' maid, a single earring of my own had disappeared and I'd been vexed with myself for not noticing it dropping while I had perambulated around the park. Now I knew Yvette had taken it. Yet it was only that one time that she had done it to me.

What was she doing with these random items? I followed her through the streets to try to find out. She led me to the rougher parts of the city. I sank further into the dark cloak I wore, pleased it disguised my expensive clothing. Perhaps we would go to a pawnbroker? She hurried to a door, glanced over her shoulder, then slid inside.

Strange. It wasn't a pawnbroker but a tavern.

I followed her inside, cautious. Everyone seemed to give me sidelong looks. I stayed long enough to see Yvette disappear into the back.

I would have to return another time in a better disguise, I decided, walking nonchalantly away.

A few days later, I had the opportunity, and just like I had as a child trying to escape across the marsh, I dressed as a man, hiding my hair beneath a cap and making my strides longer and swaggering. This time, knowing – or hoping I knew – where Yvette was heading, I hurried there and arrived first, taking position at a table near the door to the back room. She didn't give me a second glance as she passed by. Her transaction was swift; she was selling the jewellery to a fence who broke the pieces up into their individual gems and then sold them on, presumably.

What was she doing with her profits from the theft? Keeping it all for herself? Giving them to the revolutionaries, in support of her lover? That I doubted, as from everything she had said to him, she did not share his zeal for direct action.

A few more hours of investigation revealed that she was giving some to paupers she came across on the street.

She's like a French, female Robin Hood, I thought, even more intrigued.

Her slim figure was always in front of me, slipping through crowds easily. The neighbourhood we were in changed slowly, until we were on a street of respectable, residential town houses. Yvette went up to a black front door and swung the brass lion's-head knocker. She was allowed in, without being sent around to the servants' entrance. Curious...

I looked around. It was bright daylight but no one was taking any notice of me. Taking my chance, I walked confidently down the side of the house, and then sank into the shadow it cast and peered into a side window. There was Yvette, handing over the remainder of the money she'd received from the fence.

A man took it from her. Her lover? No; too tall, too slim. Judging from Yvette's face, although I could not hear what was being said, she did not like him. Fear was smeared across her features. As she swiftly left the room again, he turned, and I gasped in shock.

It was the man I'd tripped up all those months ago on the day she and I had first met.

She was giving money to her enemy.

That Yvette had kept a secret from me shocked me to my core. Growing up surrounded by liars, plotters, toadies and humbugs, I had assumed I would be good at identifying those who were dishonest. Mother had made me considerably more suspicious of men than women, but my experiences with Sarah and Camilla meant I was all too aware that women could be untrustworthy to the point of being dangerous, too.

After hurrying back to the finishing school to ensure I arrived well before she did, I pondered over what to do about her. Should I continue to follow her to find out more? It was tempting. I had a feeling, however, that though I may discover more lies I would not find the reason behind them without a more direct approach.

There was no more evidence to gather. I was going to confront her, angry as I was for being taken in. The more I thought about it, the more the fire within me was stoked – she had probably only befriended me because she knew I was the most likely to catch on to her thievery. Was anything she had shared with me true? I paced the room fairly crackling with anticipation of how I would destroy this liar.

She came into my room all smiles. There was nothing at all to show she had only two hours earlier been in the company of someone she despised, handing over money made from thefts in this house.

'What have you been doing today? Any tales to share, impressions to entertain me with?' I asked.

'Today was very dull, mademoiselle. I spent a little time with my brother, then—'

'I did not know you had a brother.' Another lie? Was her enemy actually family? That might explain why she was giving him money. That house belonged to someone far more well-to-do than a servant, though.

'Ah, well, I… You met him; he was the gentleman you saw me with when you came down to the servants' quarters. I did not introduce you formally then as I was a little… caught off-guard by seeing you there. Anyway, I was thinking you could wear these earrings today, with this necklace, to go with…' As she spoke, she turned her back to me, reaching out towards my jewellery box. Her fingers were trembling, and her voice sounded thicker.

All my anger disappeared, replaced with worry for her. It was a new sensation. If she was lying to me, there had to be a reason, I decided; if she was handing over money to someone she so clearly hated and feared, it wasn't of her own free will. In my anger, I had made the situation all about me.

What I tried next was something of a novelty to me: I put myself in someone else's shoes, and this change of perspective gave me compassion. Truly, Paris was changing me.

I put my hand over hers and spoke, gentle and low. 'I know, Yvette. I know you have been stealing and I know what you've been doing with the proceeds. Tell me what is going on.'

Chapter Forty-Three

THEN

PARIS, 1828

Under my touch, I could feel Yvette tremor. Her hand turned palm upwards, to hold mine.

Then she pulled away, as if burned.

'Oh, you know everything, do you?' she spat. 'Well, I have no need to tell, do I?'

'Yvette—'

'No, run to Madame Flaubert and have me sacked. Tell all those horrible girls all about me, so they can have me locked up for my crimes. They will love you then, Estella, as surely as they now hate you.' She did not shout, but her words had power behind them and her eyes sparkled with tears. She pulled herself up and looked at me like she was a queen and I was the servant. 'You know nothing about me or the world. You are a child and always will be, sheltered from harm by your money.'

'Sheltered!' I couldn't hold in a small laugh. 'Now it's you who knows nothing. But I don't want to argue with you, Yvette; I want to help you. Tell me what is happening, and perhaps together—'

'Oh, you rich, you are so arrogant! You have no idea what it is like to be born with nothing; to scrape and scrimp and work until the bones ache and skin bleeds; to spend carefully and save hard, and still have nothing to show from a lifetime of it. You all think you are in your rarefied place because of talent and intelligence, but it's just luck at being born into riches. If one of your class tries an enterprise, of course it will be a success – because you have money behind you to help if something goes wrong. You have no fear that if the venture fails you will lose everything. You have the freedom to try and fail and try again. The poor do not have that.

'Nor can we educate ourselves out of the mire when schooling is barely available to us. And those who are given the chance have to work such long hours that all we can do at the end of the day is eat – and not good food that will make us strong and feed our minds, but whatever is going cheap, and then is barely enough to stop the belly growling; and so we fall into our beds, before the day starts all over again. That is how we are kept stupid and obedient.

'So I steal. Yes, I steal. If you think that is unfair, there are far bigger injustices in the world. I take nothing that will make any difference to anyone here; no lives are ruined. And who notices me? A poor servant; a woman; a good girl who curtseys and minds her manners and does exactly as she is told – that makes me invisible. So run to the authorities and do your worst, for I have nothing to be ashamed of.'

'Peace, Yvette,' I begged. I held my hands out to her and when she ignored me I sat on the bed and patted the eiderdown. 'Please, come and sit with me. I don't disagree with anything you've said—'

'How easy it is to be egalitarian when you have everything and risk nothing. You're a strange one, Estella, you don't fit in here. You're such a fool you'd probably join in the revolution.'

'And get my head chopped off by Madame la Guillotine, while you sit and watch? You can't think me that foolish?'

My joke did not make her smile. She threw her hands up and made a noise of anger. She was like nothing I'd ever seen before. All her meekness, even her mischief, had been burned away. She was haughty and proud and fiery and magnificent and would not be quieted. 'If I thought it would work I'd be the first on to the streets screaming: *Vive la révolution!* But it is a waste of time. We tried it and the world didn't start afresh just because we got rid of the aristocrats, because those who replaced them were equally as greedy and determined to keep everything they acquired to themselves.

'The poor are still down-beaten, the gap between the haves and the have-nots grows ever wider. And no one with the power to make real change wants to, because it is not in their interests. They do not think of the greater good, only their own. So fuck it. Why shouldn't I be as selfish? I'm going to take what I want – *everything* I want. And while all the time looking as if it is the last thing in the world I would do. No apologies. No denial.

'My brother thinks we need another revolution and that will change everything. He is even more stubborn than I. It will be the death of him.' Her laugh was hollow.

'So you're robbing the rich to feed the poor?' I waited a beat. 'Liar.'

The anger that had powered her through this speech flowed from her so suddenly that she swayed, exhausted. I jumped up, and guided her to the bed, where she sank down as if in a trance.

After a few moments of quiet, I spoke. 'You say you will take everything you want, but you don't. You're too clever for that – and too kind. No, no, do not try to deny it, for I know you would never take anything that might get someone into trouble. Yet for all that, I know you're lying to me. As impressive as that speech was, you said it all to hide the truth.'

She said nothing. I took her hand, and tried a change of subject, working on instinct. 'Tell me about your brother.'

Yvette shook her head, quiet still. Finally, she spoke. 'He is a fool. A beautiful, idealistic fool who should have been born into a rich family so that big brain of his and that absolute kindness could have been put to good use. You should see his inventions! Ah, he longs to make the world a better place. Instead, he works as a groom for Jean-François Dupont.'

'Is he the reason why you are in trouble? There's something going on, so do not lie to me. Let me help you. You said yourself, I'm different, and I don't deny it. One day I'll tell you all, but for now let's concentrate on you. Come, share your troubles.'

'Gérard is... a worry,' she admitted slowly. 'It is dangerous, the things he plans, and that is a big enough fear. Someone is following him, I think. But there is something else happening. I-I don't know if I can... You'll never look at me the same way again if I tell all.'

'I will never look at you as if you are anything other than Yvette, my friend.' I squeezed her hand. She squeezed back and gave a suspicion of a sniff that sounded full of tears. 'But if you don't want to tell me all, don't. Reveal only what is needed so that I may help. There are things about me that, if you knew them, would change your perceptions. One day... well, perhaps one day we will trust that we won't judge each other.'

'Even a pinch of the truth may change you.' Even so, she sniffed again and sat straighter. 'What do I have to lose after that little explosion?'

'Little?' I laughed gently.

Her pale eyes were downcast. 'Shh. Listen. And try to be kind when you have heard all...'

Chapter Forty-Four

THEN

PARIS, 1828

We must go back to before I was born for this story to make sense, for this began with my mother and her sister, Marian. They were inseparable growing up, with just ten months between them. Despite their family being of modest means the girls were beautiful enough that they were expected to marry well and advance their stations – for that is all a woman can do, is it not, to advance her lot, when she is not allowed to make or keep her own wealth and must instead rely on another to provide it.

'Marian exceeded expectation. The youngest son of an aristocrat, who was joining the clergy and had a beautiful parish within Paris, proposed to her. My mother was equally happy in her love, but alas he was as poor as a church mouse. Her parents, my grandparents, disowned her and I have never met them.

'She and Marian remained close, though, despite the social gulf between them. Spending time together was not easy, for Maman would not allow her sister to come to our lowly home for fear her reputation would be sullied, nor would she visit Marian in case her presence caused gossip. Still, they managed between them. My aunt was a great comfort when my dear Papa died when I was eight.

'When their parents died they left nothing to Maman. It all went to Marian. Maman wouldn't really have benefitted, anyway, for she died of consumption half a year later. Ah, thank you for your condolences but it was long ago, though the pain never lessens.

'Four months ago, Marian joined her beloved sister. Of course, everything she owned went automatically to her son, but she left me a personal gift: a ring. Oh, it is beautiful, Estella; a diamond, no less, with two smaller diamonds on each side. It had apparently been owned by her husband's mother, a great lady; it was said she had worn it in the company of Marie Antoinette! That I should receive such a gift. The note Marian left was explicit – that the ring must be sold to fund a better life for Gérard and I, and that this might atone for everything her parents had given her and not my mother.

'Her kindness! I cried such tears of relief. My brother could afford to be schooled in the workings of engines or chemicals or whatever was needed for him to thrive as an inventor. And I... I could get an education, too, and become a governess.

'But Marian's only child – a son named Jacques – is furious that such a valuable piece of jewellery has fallen into the hands of someone who, in his eyes, is not his family at all – for he thinks we are far below him. He is demanding it back.

'When he first came to my home ranting at me I reasoned with him, trying to appeal to his heart because this was what his mother had wanted. I showed him the note she had written. He tore it up in a frenzy.

'The ring was apparently not mentioned directly in the will. The letter was the only proof that it was given to me and now it is gone. Still I kept the jewellery. I'd readily go to jail to give Gérard the life he deserves. When Jacques realised the threat of arrest wasn't going to work on me, he... he said he would reveal my brother's revolutionary activities if I didn't hand over the ring.

'Of course, I did as he asked, but he is not satisfied. He still threatens to go to the authorities about Gérard unless I pay him what he calls reparations. Every week I must find money to pay this vile creature. If I don't, my brother will be thrown in jail, maybe even killed, Estella.'

After Yvette finished speaking we sat in silence and I tried to take it in: she stole to find the money to pay her blackmailer. At last I broke the quiet.

'He'll never be satisfied, no matter how much you pay.'

Yvette nodded. 'Already he wants more. He wants to bed me. He has no wish to marry me, you understand, only use me. If I don't give him what he wants he says not only will Gérard be thrown in prison but he will have me put into an asylum.'

'On what evidence?' I demanded.

She shrugged. 'Something and nothing. Men do not need any real reason, do they; it only takes the whim and we women are helpless against them.'

'Is it really so easy?' Although I knew nothing about such things, the suggestion left me cold because it had the ring of truth to it.

'Rank was and still is everything in this world and, if one has it, it is incredible what one can get away with. Justice is for sale to those who can afford it.'

Yet still I felt Yvette was holding something back. For the time being I knew enough, though. I shrugged. 'Let me speak with him. I am above him socially. He wants money, so I'll offer him money. Your predicament may be caused by men – how typical – but this woman will solve it.'

Yvette made sounds of protests (not least because she believed her brother to be a victim of Jacques as much as she), but in the end it was agreed I would aid her. It was rather nice to be someone's solution for once, rather than the cause of the dilemma.

Jacques reclined on his sofa as though it was a chaise, and stared at me through the perfect circles of his glasses. It was most ungentlemanly and ill-mannered. I expected nothing less, however, and so his attempt to ruffle me did not work – the condescending ass.

I'd 'accidentally' bumped into him after waiting for hours outside his house, walking backwards and forwards until my feet ached.

Finally, his distinctive figure had appeared in the distance; a real Duke of Limbs, he was long, thin, and all arms and legs. He had not recognised me, but when he heard that I had information on Yvette that could be of use to him, he had been intrigued enough to let me into his house.

Not intrigued enough to treat me with any politeness, though; not only was he positively lounging in front of me, he hadn't even called a servant to offer me refreshment.

'Out with it, then, dear woman. What do you wish to say?' he said in his nasal voice.

'Straight to business, I see. I admire that,' I said. 'Very well, I shall do the same. How much will it cost to get my friend, Yvette, out of trouble with you? She has told me everything, and I am happy to pay you what you deem to be a realistic reparation for any trauma or financial loss you believe she has caused you.'

He shifted so that the light fell across his glasses; he appeared to have white coins instead of eyes. It was intentional, I was sure. I sidestepped a little to the right and my shadow cast across him – all made possible because he had not offered me a seat.

He gave a sigh and shook his head in sadness. 'Women should not try to involve themselves in matters of business.'

'It is a matter of friendship. The transaction is simple: I give you money and in return you leave Yvette alone.'

'I won't be told what to do by two women,' he said, as if suggesting that a couple of donkeys had tried to order him over a cliff, rather than me offering cash and compromise. 'Tell the serving girl that unless she does as I say I will be going to the authorities at the end of the month.' He plucked an imaginary piece of fluff from his waistcoat and flicked it to the floor.

'You're turning down a lot of money. Name your price.'

'I see you are cut from the same cloth as she. What you need is a man to show you the real ways of the world. Really, I can't take you seriously.'

I will not kick him between the legs. Why? Because I'm a lady.

I nodded. 'In that case I shall show myself out. Thank you for your time. Oh, you've, er, got a little something between your teeth, by the way.'

His lips closed over his smile. My victory was pyrrhic, however. I hadn't solved Yvette's problem – I'd made it worse, and created a deadline.

Yvette was annoyed. It was easy to tell because she'd gone very still –
she was not someone who threw her hands about when angry, unlike
me. Instead she spoke more quietly, went more still, as she thought.

I stared at the sunrays falling on Yvette's hands, so neatly clasped
in front of her, and tried to think of what words of comfort could be
offered. This was not my forte, but there was no doubt my interference
had made things worse. There was an unfamiliar feeling nagging at me.
It took a while to identify: guilt. Discombobulated, I turned to the
mirror on my dressing table and patted at my hair.

'Let me have a look at any correspondence you have from him, oh,
and also his mother,' I asked.

'There's nothing in them to either exonerate me or incriminate him,'
she replied. 'And time is running out now – thanks to you.'

'Well, a fresh perspective never hurts, you know. If we don't find
something there, we'll get it elsewhere, never fear.'

The only movement she made was the slightest squint around her
eyes to glare at my reflection.

I continued, anyway, while picking up a decorative hair comb with
butterflies twinkling across it, and holding it against my hair. 'The
solution is obvious: if he's blackmailing you, then do the same to him.'
It was like talking to a brick wall. I spelled it out. 'Someone like him is
bound to have secrets. We'll blackmail him back.'

'How are we supposed to discover his secrets, pray tell?'

'Oh, I'm good at this sort of thing. And if they're so well buried that
we can't find them, we'll make some up. He will pay for making you
suffer – and for foolishly thinking he could dismiss me.'

The long, sharp teeth of the comb sank into my hair and glittered
as I turned this way and that. 'It's amazing how even the tiniest thing
hidden away can inflict dreadful injury,' I added, sotto voce.

Chapter Forty-Five

NOW

SATIS HOUSE, 1835

I barely leave Mother's side for the next few days. A mattress has been set up beside her so that if she needs me in the night, I'm there. The servants, particularly Lydia, offer to take shifts, too, encouraging me to rest, but Mother draws strength from knowing her daughter is with her.

The skin on her legs is swollen so tight it sometimes bursts anew, oozing a clear substance more watery than pus, and mixed with blood. She is brave and never complains, but the pain is constant and terrible for her, I can tell from the way she clutches at her sheets, and the pinch of her lips, the tightness around her eyes.

She barely eats or drinks at the best of times, and never in front of anyone, but now it is terrifying how little sustenance she takes. Dr Hawkins attends daily. He's as kindly as ever, and has prescribed what he always does for any illness or injury: laudanum and rhubarb water. He has impressed upon me the importance of keeping her constantly topped up with water particularly.

What magical properties he imagines rhubarb to contain can only be guessed at – however, I do as I am told. The laudanum is always given before the twice-daily changing of the bandages.

'The pain!' she whimpers, trying to pull free from me.

'The quicker we do it, the faster it's over,' I say firmly. 'Some of this lotion will soothe you, it's lovely and cooling, isn't it? Ooh, but it smells odd! Now for the bandages.'

I bind them the way I've been told, not so tight as to cause pain, not so loose that they come undone.

'All done. Better?'

Her eyes are watery but she nods at me, then passes out into an opium-induced sleep.

When she wakes, I feed her chicken broth, thinking of how much good it did me. She takes it as best she can. Sometimes she seems traumatised that she's eating in front of me, other times the pain of swallowing appears to be almost unbearable for her.

'Five more mouthfuls and I'll stop,' I order.

'Enough! Enough!' She moves her head to one side, sending the liquid spilling into the napkin I hold beneath her chin.

'Three more, then. Come on, one.'

She swallows. Gasps.

'Two.'

A tear spills down her cheek but she takes it.

'Last one. There, all done.'

It is pitiful to see my proud mother reduced to weeping over eating and drinking, but still I threaten, cajole, mock – if it makes her well it will be worth it, even if she hates me by the end.

There is an unexpected benefit for me in caring for her: it stops me from thinking about my own woes, for which I can only be grateful. Every day I fear Bentley's arrival yet can think of no plan for what I'll do when he finally comes.

My physical pains are many, every movement hurts. It's all I can do to keep body and soul together – quite literally, as I feel I've been pulled apart and thrown to the four winds by what has happened. It has utterly destroyed all thoughts of my ever being superior to my husband. I am defeated. Every creaking floorboard makes me jump in case it is him creeping up on me. A flickering shadow in the candlelight makes me turn, heart hammering. I can't control my imagination, but at least I can nurse my mother.

Sometimes she tries to tell me what happened when she was injured, but I tell her not to tax herself because I know enough. I catch her eyeing the bruises daubed over my features, or glancing at me when I audibly wince, but she says not a word. I don't know whether to be grateful or annoyed at her lack of curiosity, but then remind myself that if she asks, I won't answer. How can I possibly share with Mother the shame and trauma of what I have endured at the hands of my husband, when she has never known the intimate touch of a man? Despite all her talk of shattered hearts, she is an innocent about the physical side of relationships, and I am not going to risk setting her back further by sharing my reality of a marriage bed.

Right now she is staring at a yellowing handprint around my right wrist, as I plump her pillows and pull them into a more comfortable position for her. Her expression pains me.

'Which would you prefer me to read,' I ask as way of distraction, 'Jane Austen or the Brothers Grimm?'

A wavering finger points towards the fairy tales. It's a relief – all Austen's stories seem to have happy endings. I begin to read and her eyes slowly close.

Being back at Satis House has made me notice again the weird disconnect it creates between it and the real world. With no light I lose all sense of where I am in the day, and find myself falling asleep when I am tired rather than at bedtime, and waking with no clue of how long I have slumbered. Stepping outside makes me blink in surprise at finding the stars are out when I assume it is daytime, or walking into bright sunshine when I fancy a moonlight stroll. I lose track not only of hours but days. I have no concept of how long I have been here, apart from my storm of bruises fading gradually. All I do is sleep and talk with Mother; talk with Mother and sleep. This is the home of Morpheus, and we are both under his spell, though not even he can stop Bentley terrorising my dreams.

Dr Hawkins' arrival is the only marker of time. After a week, he seems cautiously pleased. Mother is managing to take her food with a little more enthusiasm and her sleep seems more restful.

'Ah-ha-a-hem, she seems to be turning a corner under your ministrations, Mrs Drummle. Ah-hem, yes indeed. Quite encouraging,' he pronounces. 'Keep up the regular dressing changes and lotion application. And do not forget to administer the rhubarb water.'

'And the laudanum? That seems to help her exponentially.'

'Yes, yes, that, too.' He nods as if to say, 'these newfangled inventions cannot possibly be as effective as rhubarb water', but gives an old-fashioned courtly bow and leaves.

I palm Mother's hand gently. 'How are you feeling?'

'Better than I have in many years.'

'The medication must be working well,' I reply with a gentle smile.

'It is a lightening of the soul that makes me feel better. Though I know there is much, much to atone for.'

'I don't—'

'Listen to me, child. I had no idea that I had inflicted the same fate on to Pip – that of a forever broken heart – as I had suffered all those years ago. Not until I saw his face and heard him speak of his love for you. There was no falsehood to his devastation; I know, for I have seen one of the greatest deceivers.' She halts, gasping a little. I hold a glass of water to her lips and help her take small sips.

'Save your strength,' I beg. She shakes her head, a flash of her old stubbornness. I can't help smiling at it – it's surely another sign of her returning strength.

'Tell me, am I right about Drummle – he is not a good husband, is he?'

I stiffen. Give the barest of nods.

'You might have been happy had I not interfered in your life. Had I not been so set on my own pain, I might have seen what I inflicted on others. You have paid the greatest price of anyone. Pip the second highest.'

'I never understood why you wanted Pip to come here in the first place and play for you. It was bizarre.' The words are out before I can stop them. Hopefully, there is not too much recrimination in my tone.

She nods as well as she can in her prone position. 'Mr Jaggers confided in me his belief that you would do well to have a friend. Only a fool disregards that man's advice. You were growing up, Estella, and needed more stimulation than it was possible for me to give, and so the search for a companion began. Having a day to yourself lightened the burden of caring for me always. I had hoped Herbert would serve, but you dispatched him with admirable efficiency.'

We share a smile at the memory.

'Then along came Pip,' she continues. 'Dear, kind, gentle Pip, so out of his depth here. Yet when I looked at him I saw only a creature to be used by you. Even a child could not get past my bitter barriers.'

I catch my lip between my teeth and my head sinks at how cruelly I sharpened myself on him as if he were a whetstone. There is no pride in that memory. 'There's no need to worry about that now. It's in the past,' I say hurriedly.

She looks at me for so long that eventually her eyes flutter closed. How long she sleeps for can only be guessed at as the clocks still do not function. When she opens her eyes again, she starts speaking as if no time has lapsed.

'Yes, I sent Pip a note, via Jaggers, asking him to visit me here, and he was good enough to do so. Of course he was. Even when given a fatal blow, he can be relied upon – after all, that is what *I* relied on for all these years.'

Her eyes wander about the room for a moment, then refocus.

'What have I done? What have I done?' she cries suddenly. 'When I shut out the world, the pain was trapped inside with me. The doors and windows were barred instead to anything good that could eventually have healed me. Do not make that mistake, Estella. There was such vanity in my agony. I was determined to make it the biggest, the worst; to make it mean more than anyone else's pain ever had. Oh, what have I done?'

'It's in the past, do not exhaust yourself over such things—'

'He forgives me, you know. Despite everything inflicted on him: teased and cruelly used as a child; misled into love, and into believing he was fated for a life that could never be his; and now he faces ruin, though at least that is not at my hand. But instead of hating me, Pip begs only for me to try to right the wrong I have forged in you.'

'I am who I am. Nothing more, nothing less.'

'You don't despise me?'

'How can I when you saved me from a life of probable poverty and early death?'

'Because I kept you in the darkness and told you to fear the light. Is it too late, Estella, for you to find a way to kindness and love after a lifetime of my poison forcing those emotions to wither within you?'

There's no answer to that, for it is a question I've asked myself to no avail. Mother turns her head from me to wipe at her eyes. When she is finished, I take the opportunity to give her rhubarb water. It isn't long before she speaks again.

'Estella, my dear girl, I was desperate for a little girl to call my own. I thought only of pouring all my love into you and raising you up to have a good life – one better than mine. You were so trusting, though. It scared me; I feared what would happen once you reached adulthood, and so started to tell you things in order to protect you – only to protect you... at first. My lessons lost their point somewhere, though. When it altered I cannot pinpoint, but change it did, and so it was no longer about shielding you but making you into a sword of justice. No, even that is a lie I told myself to justify it, for it was not about fairness but punishment, and not about *him*' – I did not need to ask who 'him' was, for the momentary venom on her face spoke of one person only: her ex-fiancé Compeyson – 'but every male, old or young, deserving or innocent. They were all I saw. I lost sight of you, darling girl.'

That Mother should talk like this seems incomprehensible. Never have I seen her this way. Her expression soft and pleading for forgiveness.

'There is ice in my heart and hardness,' I admit. 'There is no point denying what the world knows. It is unlikely to melt.'

'Try. Only for your sake, try!' She clutches my hand to her cheek.

'I will, but I cannot promise, for who can say what of me is down to you or my nature—'

'Or Bentley. Tell me, what has happened.'

'He is in Paris; I left as soon as I could when I read your letter. Now, rest.'

She struggles to raise herself from her pillows, her white hair a swirling mist about her face. 'You're keeping things from me. I recognise pain, I am an expert on it.'

I shake my head, and try a diversionary tactic. 'Mother, I must ask about Pip. You've mentioned several times that his great expectations have crumbled to nothing. What happened?'

'I don't know the details, only that his benefactor is no more. All his dreams are ended.'

Poor Pip. How cruelly life has dealt with him. With us all. I will never tell Mother what happened in Paris.

A sound makes me turn, clutching at my necklace of yellowing bruises. It is only a candle spitting and sputtering. It is not Bentley, come for me.

He is out there somewhere, though. Biding his time and plotting.

Chapter Forty-Six

THEN

PARIS, 1828

For several days I tried to work out a full plan of how best to free Yvette from the problem that was Jacques. Finally, the solution came to me one morning as I was reading a book, the sun shining so strongly through the library window that the pages were turned almost translucent. The Pockets were my inspiration, and what they had done to me as a child when setting me up for theft. Jacques had real secrets worth discovering, I had no doubt of that, but trying to discover them would be a time-consuming affair. There was a risk he might act against Yvette before we had time to find anything useful. Far better to manufacture something, I decided.

When Yvette heard the plan, her silvery eyes widened, and she paled until her skin was the same colour as her white cotton apron. For two weeks she continued to pay her blackmailer. Time was running out.

'He forced a kiss on me and tried to make me touch him.' She shuddered. 'He says I have just a fortnight left to give myself to him, or he will tell the authorities about Gérard.'

'Once he has had his way with you, he'll probably do that, anyway. We need to act – now.'

The next time Yvette went to Jacques' house to pay him off, she took with her some of my jewellery. Her hands were usually swift at stealing, but this time she hid my gems in his front room.

She walked out, past where I waited, but did not look my way. She nodded to herself, which let me know the deed had been done.

We had timed the visit carefully with the moment that a local gendarme passed by on his daily patrol. As he rounded the corner, whistling to himself, I put my hand to my forehead in dramatic fashion and stumbled as I weakly cried: 'Help! Oh, Lord, someone please help me!'

The gendarme came running over.

'Oh, thank goodness. Sir, I have been robbed of my jewels. A scoundrel pretending to be a gentleman approached me and demanded I hand over anything precious on my person. He ran into that house.'

I proceeded to explain that a ruby ring, along with matching earrings and necklace, had been taken from me, as well as another, particularly precious, diamond ring.

'It was foolish of me to carry them, but I was going to send them to my mother at her request – see?'

I sobbed while producing a letter in Mother's hand, which asked for the jewellery to be sent to her, complete with a description of exactly which pieces she wanted.

'He threatened me with violence unless I handed them over. I can't understand how such a well-turned-out gentleman could be driven to such desperate actions.'

'Ah, mademoiselle, people are not always what they seem. But never fear, I shall take care of this so-called gentleman.'

Quite the crowd gathered, thanks to my histrionics and the gendarme blowing on his whistle to bring his colleagues running. They marched up to the door and hammered on it, demanding to be let in. I caught a glimpse of Jacques' stunned face through the window. Within minutes the jewellery that fitted my detailed description had been located and handed over to me. The disgraced owner of the house was dragged outside between two gendarmes, protesting his innocence.

'You! I recognise you!' He twisted towards his captors. 'She is in league with relatives of mine. An insane woman who is little more than a harlot and thief, and a brother who is—'

'Never have I been so insulted. This man is clearly demented,' I said, dabbing at my eyes with a handkerchief. 'I apologise for this emotional display, it is far from ladylike, but this experience has terrified me.'

My gaze fluttered over the handkerchief to the officers. Head down, I peered up at them with eyes wide and innocent, just as I had been taught to do over the top of a fan to lure a man in.

'You should never have to experience such rough treatment,' replied one officer. 'You are of the gentle sex, not able to deal with the harsh realities of the world. You have nothing to apologise for – it is this pig who should apologise.'

I laid a gentling hand on his arm. 'Call me foolish and too soft, but I hate to see someone in such torment. If he apologises to me and promises he has seen the error of his ways then I would rather he be released than punished. Might he and I speak in private?'

The men looked from him to me in confusion, then gave a shrug as if to say: *Women, eh? They're fools but who are we to argue with their nonsensical ways?*

Jacques shrugged off their hands as if he had broken free rather than been let go. Glaring at me, he stalked back inside, barking: 'Come.' As if I was a dog.

Meek and mild, I glided behind him, then paused in the doorway.

'Forgive me for asking, but could you please come, too, if it's not too much trouble,' I called to the gendarmes, 'and stand outside the door – for although I'm willing to help him, I'm also scared he might try to hurt me.'

They almost fell over themselves in their hurry to do so.

As soon as Jacques closed the door to his study, he glared at me.

'You are making a very big mistake. You and Yvette are in league.'

I smiled sweetly. 'Prove it.'

'You bitc—'

A heavy knock on the door came at his raised voice. 'Mademoiselle, are you all right?' a gendarme called.

'Just about.' My voice lowered again. 'Oh, please, if you're going to insult me, show some imagination. Better yet, be quiet and listen. That diamond ring of Yvette's that you've stolen from her – yes, stolen – that's mine now. The police have given it to me, for I described it to them along with the jewellery that is mine, which Yvette planted.'

He was going puce and looked like he might explode again. 'When I've finished with you, you'll all be in jail.'

'Hush, now.' My finger on his lips was as gentle as my tone. 'It will only take one shout from me to bring those lovely officers in to drag you to jail. But I won't do that unless you give me no other choice.'

'Once they hear what Gérard has done he will be thrown into prison and the key thrown away. As for you and that depraved bitch, Yvette—'

'Read this letter,' I interrupted.

'I'm not—'

'I think you'll find it interesting. You see, it's a letter from you, detailing your plot to kill the king.'

He spluttered. 'That's ridiculous. I would never—'

'And yet here it is, in what is irrefutably your handwriting, no?'

He snatched the proffered paper from me, mouth opening as he scanned the incriminating words. They were enough to have him hanged for treason.

'That is just a sample of your criminal plotting,' I explained. 'There are some others that Yvette has secreted about the house during each of her last few visits here, and I've a whole stack more of them should those ones disappear. Some of the things you admit to... well, it's shocking. You would be the talk of France if they were found.'

'But I didn't – I'd never – how did—?' He blinked rapidly and shook his head. 'I didn't write this.'

'No one will believe you, though. It's your handwriting.'

'I-it's my handwriting.' He nodded. 'But I didn't... You did this.'

'Of course I did. But as I said earlier: prove it.' The thrill of besting him sent tingles all over my body. Always a lover of hidden things, I felt the knife I kept in a pocket of my skirt. It was a curiosity picked up from a shop in Paris and at first glance looked like a fan, but the intricate filigree in the bone guard hid a marvellously sharp blade that could slide out at the press of a little button. Pulling blade from sheath, I sat beside Jacques and eyed him flirtatiously, bit my lip... and ran the knife slowly and gently up the front of his waistcoat.

'I am a woman of position, why on earth would I frame you? Now, leave Yvette and Gérard alone and these incriminating letters from you will never see the light of day.' My blade paused just under the top button. 'Misbehave and I'll have no choice but to have you hanged for treason.'

With the tiniest flick of my wrist, his button came free and fell to the floor. We both watched it tumble.

Jacques' mouth opened and closed but no sound came out. He reminded me of the fish in the marsh creeks.

Finally, he nodded, utterly defeated.

Chapter Forty-Seven

THEN

PARIS, 1828

The skill at forgery that I had discovered as a child had finally paid off. I'd never thought of a way of using it against the Pockets, but it had come in handy for creating something with which to blackmail Jacques.

All this I explained to Yvette when she had finally got over her relief that her problems were solved and she and Gérard were free to make their dreams come true. For her relief had soon turned to curiosity about my skills. As she had been so honest with me about her past, I told her a little about mine. Over the following days and weeks, we shared more.

Yvette loved hearing about my life, and it was a novelty to be able to speak freely with someone who was not going to use anything against me. For if she did confess to anyone what I had done, she would be incriminating herself, too. It was more than that, though: I trusted her.

'Hearing about how easily I forge letters probably doesn't make it easy to trust me,' I said, suddenly realising. We were walking together through a park, enjoying the summer sunshine as we talked. The thought made me feel cold despite the warmth of the sun through my parasol.

'I know you don't like yourself – don't look like that, it's obvious – but you've shown your true self to me,' replied Yvette. 'You were there for me when I needed someone, even though there was no reason for you to put yourself out for me.'

I waved my hand, trying to act dismissive even though I flushed with pleasure at the unexpected compliment.

'Your mettle was tested. I have seen what you are made of, Estella Havisham.'

'If I were a metal I'd be fool's gold,' I joked, deliberately misunderstanding.

'You are nobody's fool.' She stopped and took my hand in hers, interlacing her fingers through mine and holding them up. 'Some metals are stronger when they are combined than when they are alone. That's us. We are an alloy.'

My heart inflated so that the ends of my mouth refused to do anything but lift into a smile, no matter how much I tried to hide it. 'We do make a good team,' I conceded.

At last, I was no longer alone; instead, I had someone who made me stronger, better, kinder.

Yvette was a normal person, teaching me the normal world. From Mother I had learned how she wanted things to be, and all the terrible things to look out for; from Madame Flaubert I had been taught the way things 'should be' and the expectation to be meek, mild, malleable. Yvette's world was the real world. We went for walks together or even to a tea shop – now that I had given her some of my old clothes to wear we did not get a second glance. When the other girls at the finishing school laughed at me I no longer noticed or minded.

She calmed me, too, showing me the power and joy of hidden emotions. How to manipulate gently instead of with cruelty. How to target only those who deserved it, and to protect and help those who didn't.

Yvette taught me so much – all while making me more open. More vulnerable.

I never saw what was coming.

I had been away from home for well over two years, and not returned in all that time, despite Mother often asking me. There was always an excuse, be it a social event or feigned illness, for I loved my place in the bright, colourful world and had no desire to return to my old life even for a week.

To assuage Mother's neediness, I wrote to her daily. She loved to hear about my world and all the skills I was honing, knowing that each one brought her plan closer to completion. Her own letters to me were filled with questions, along with the occasional amusing story about what the Pockets had been up to. One day she wrote with some interesting news, however.

Pip had been to visit her, and it seemed he had come into a fortune.

> *He has great expectations for a future as a gentleman, and is to receive training for such from none other than Matthew Pocket. It was, I believe, Mr Jaggers who suggested my cousin to Pip, for it is he who is acting on behalf of the boy's benefactor. Now here is what is particularly interesting, for the person paying for Pip to live as a gentleman (and so no longer have to earn a living) wishes to remain anonymous for unknown reasons. How very mysterious!*
>
> *I have to say, when he came to see me, he did look splendid in his new clothes, but no amount of riches can make a gentleman from a commoner.*

The comment gave me goosebumps. That was exactly the kind of sentiment Sarah and Camilla would express about me never being a true gentlewoman. I shivered then read on.

> *Jaggers had already told me of the boy's luck, and so I was able to have a little fun at the expense of Sarah — she does lurk so, listening in on conversations with my visitors. Usually it is vexing, but on this occasion I was pleased. Her face was positively verdant with envy. A game sprang to my mind, and so I used the information Jaggers had given me to make it appear I was Pip's benefactor. It was perfectly played. Sarah looked like she might faint away by the end of it.*

It was interesting news. Pip was no longer an apprentice blacksmith, instead he was a gentleman on my level. Humming to myself, I folded the letter up and put it in the drawer of my writing desk, for safe keeping, and for some reason throughout the remainder of the day people commented on what an agreeable mood I was in.

There was a sour note, though. Sarah's jealousy did sound amusing, but I couldn't help wondering what impact this charade had on Pip, given that he didn't know who his real benefactor was. I only hoped he hadn't also been fooled by Mother's game into believing her. I had a bad feeling…

Chapter Forty-Eight

THEN

PARIS, 1829

It was a little over a year since Yvette and I had got rid of Jacques. Since then, things had remained quiet and uneventful.

'You've never heard from him?' I checked as we took our usual stroll around the park to chat freely.

'Never, thank goodness.' Her reply was listless. It was early morning and already the midsummer heat was building. By lunchtime it would be too much for outdoor activities.

'And Gérard is doing well now? How is his education coming on? Last time I saw him he mentioned exams coming up soon.'

Yvette had sold the ring and given almost all the money to her brother, forgoing her own plans to become a governess because the price fetched had not been as much as anticipated. It wasn't a decision I had agreed with, but when I offered money to her myself it was made clear it was none of my business, so I had limited myself to one lecture and a couple of barbed comments when I couldn't resist. That and a dose of dandelion added to his tea one day when he visited Yvette – not much, but enough to make him uncomfortable.

Under my current questioning, she quickened her pace.

'Yvette? Is Gérard all right?'

'He's fine, absolutely fine.'

I stopped walking. She went on a few more steps then turned to look at me. 'Very well, you're clearly not going to give up until I tell you.' She sighed. 'I've discovered he has been skipping his lectures.'

'But... I thought all he wanted was to become an inventor or engineer or some such. Has he any idea how much you've given up for him?'

'It was my decision, no one made me, least of all him.'

'Of all the stupid, lazy—!'

Her glare silenced my tongue. We continued walking in silence, both of us stewing. Gérard wasn't lazy, so what was driving his malaise? I had only met him a handful of times over the year, true, but he came across as honest, hard-working and clearly had a brilliantly quick mind. He was a bit of an idealist, just as Yvette had said all those months ago when I had first spied on them in the servants' parlour, assuming he was her lover. How they had laughed when I told them that! I smiled to myself at the memory, then frowned, wondering what type of man she would one day marry. She was such an independent spirit it was hard to imagine her ever falling for a man and agreeing to obey him in all things. Perhaps she would choose someone as feckless as her brother...

How typical of a man to have opportunities spread before his feet and choose to turn his back on them, while women had to fight tooth and nail for everything. To work for our fortune was frowned on; to be independent was to be a freak; even inheritance was often barred to us. Our only option was marriage, every road we went down always turned us back to that dead end. Yet there was Gérard, wasting his chance to improve his lot. He'd be getting a lot more than dandelion in his tea the next time I saw him.

As I pondered, Yvette veered off the path towards a young woman selling matches. With her was a scrawny scrap of a child, who looked around three but was probably older and stunted by malnutrition. He sat on the ground beside her and played with her skirt, tugging it so that he almost hid completely beneath it, shivering occasionally.

'That is Clare,' Yvette whispered as we approached. 'She is a soldier's widow. When her husband died she took in laundry to make ends meet, but fell behind on her rent and was thrown out. It meant she lost not only the single room she called home, but also her means of earning a living. Now she earns just enough to buy food by selling matches, but not enough to afford a roof over her head.'

'That's terrible!' I gasped.

'It is – but it's not unusual. We often chat and sometimes I give her a little money, if I can spare any.'

'Wouldn't they be better off in the workhouse? Do you not have them here?'

'We have something similar. If they went there she would be separated from her son. She would rather have him with her – even if they are on the streets.'

What a ridiculous decision, I thought. Then again, a child being separated from its mother was something I knew a little about, having been given up or taken from my birth parents. If I were still with my birth mother would I be a different person: happy, light-hearted, content? Or would I be ground down by poverty myself, and reduced to begging for scraps? What would I do as a mother in the same position as this woman? Was there a right and a wrong decision?

The fact I was even thinking that hard about it showed how far I had come since Yvette and I had become friends. Before, I probably wouldn't even have noticed this match girl – or at least, I may have, but not given her a thought.

Yvette introduced Clare and me to one another, and when we said farewell I shook the young mother's hand while surreptitiously slipping money into her palm and hurrying away as she looked at it, stunned. There but for the grace of luck, it could have been me relying on the generous whims of richer people. What I had gifted was enough to pay rent on a room for a month or two and perhaps change her fortune, yet giving it away made no difference to my way of life. Yvette, though… What she gave really was the equivalent of the widow's mite. Her generosity, given how little she had, was incredible.

Back at the school, in my room, I told her as much as she helped me dress for dinner.

'You've changed me, you've changed my life. You are such a force for good,' I said.

'No better than the next person.' Still her cheeks flushed and she looked pleased at the compliment.

'Well, the next person is me, and you're definitely better than that!' I laughed.

She stopped lacing up my dress and turned me to face her. 'Estella, I keep trying to make you believe you are a kind and beautiful person. Why do you refuse?'

Thoughts of Pip had me shaking my head. The memory of watching the blacksmith's wife be murdered, and deciding not to name the killer because I was embarrassed about what people might think, made me squirm. 'You'll never convince me.' I smiled, trying to make light of it.

She took my face in her hands. 'Ridiculous girl. I wish you could see what I see.'

Her eyes burned so brightly into mine. They looked so full of love. For me.

An invisible force as strong as gravity pulled us closer. My lips planted on hers. So warm, so soft. My stomach fluttered, my skin felt the way the air did in a storm just before lightning struck. Yvette's hands were on my shoulders.

She shoved me back so hard I stumbled and almost fell as my unfastened dress slid to my feet.

'Why did you do that?' she hissed. 'How...? How dare you!'

She hurried from the room and closed the door behind her – didn't even slam it, she closed it with a careful click. I wrapped my arms around my naked shoulders and sank to the floor. Cold, vulnerable, rejected, unlovable.

Chapter Forty-Nine

NOW

SATIS HOUSE, 1835

Mother and I are connecting in a way we never have before, since she had her painful epiphany and apologised for how much damage her sorrow and bitterness had wrought on me and others. She tells me tales of the past, but instead of choosing them to illustrate her pain or hurt, or to show that no one can ever be trusted, she shares memories of when I was a child.

'You were such a strong, independent little thing.' Mother smiles. 'You could just about toddle when you first came to me. You loved running! Your little legs so chubby I could have eaten them up, going nineteen to the dozen. No regard for obstacles, you wanted to run through them instead of around. The number of times I had to chase after you, and scoop you up, for you were about to go headlong into a table or sharp corner.' Her eyes light up with joy, and we laugh, bringing our heads together.

It is as if her mind is healing for the first time, along with her body. Her physical pains are lessening slightly, which is a blessing. The skin on her legs seems more pink and less red now, and fewer blisters are coming up.

It is good to hear these moments and laugh, but I have no memory of them. By the time my memories begin properly, Mother had already shut down completely. I can only think that in her attempts to protect me, her constant warning lessons to me forced her to relive her hurts and they cut her deep again. It's so sad for us both and what might have been. When asleep, I dream of being a child again, and instead of feeling Mother stiffen when I reach to climb onto her lap, she lifts me up and cuddles me close, telling how much she loves me.

It is to a certain extent an echo of what is happening in real life. Sometimes when I'm reading, Mother gazes at me and announces: 'I love you.'

It's hard to know what to reply. I smile, nod back. Sometimes say: 'And I, you.' I wish there were more I could give her but the words feel like cotton wool in my mouth, choking me and grating on my teeth, unable to be spat out or swallowed down.

In rare moments when I'm alone, Bentley slips into my mind like a snake into a bird's nest, to wreak havoc. His memory is a constant reminder of how fragile our peace is here at Satis House; our haven is an illusion, for there will be no stopping him once he decides to come for me. Mother may try to take the blame for this disaster of a marriage, but there is only one person at fault: me. She begged me not to wed him and I stubbornly held to my plan. It's all too late for me to be able to do anything. I am married to him and our union consummated. His granting me a divorce is highly unlikely. The bed I have made I must lie upon, and most likely die in, eventually – for whether by design or not, his brutality can only have one ending for me. I wrap my arms around myself to keep my fearful shivers from shattering me.

I do wonder, though, about what Mother said, about how different my life could have been if she had stuck to her plan to raise me with love instead of force-feeding me hatred. Would Pip and I have married? Lived happily ever after like the fairy tales I read to Mother?

There is little point thinking that way.

Est quod est.

But what on earth am I going to do about Bentley? His silence scares me. What is he up to?

Mother's strength is returning. It is a slow process, but her skin is no longer covered in pustules, although even as it begins to heal it is painfully tender to the touch. Her temperature no longer rages. She has a long way to go, but everything is going in the right direction.

When awake, she tries her best to talk, though her throat still troubles her and she has to drink constantly as she is so dehydrated all the time. It is around four weeks since her accident when she asks to be pulled upright in bed so she may talk to me. Her head lolls against my shoulder as I do just that, and it takes her a moment even now to recover from almost passing out with pain. Finally, she blinks into focus again and takes a grateful draught of barley water (she is growing heartily tired of rhubarb).

'Despite all this,' she says, waving a dismissive hand towards her legs, 'these last days have been some of the happiest of my life because you are here with me. It's strange to think that we're so much closer now than ever before. I wonder if it is because I have let my guard down and at last let love into my heart... So, Estella, my love, will you finally tell me what happened to you on your honeymoon?'

I stand and move from the bed, turn my back and make a great pretence of tidying. Answer with my back still turned. 'Why, I had barely arrived in Paris before rushing back here.'

'Please. You can trust me, tell me anything. I might understand more than you suspect.'

Finally, I turn. 'Mother, I think your medication is playing with your imagination.'

She nods her head. There is such sadness in the droop of her shoulders, but her eyes seem more accepting. 'Very well. Perhaps it might be easier if I went first. You know – by heart and backwards, by now, I'm sure – many stories about Everard Compeyson and me.'

Everard? This is the first time I have ever heard his given name.

'There are certain things that have always been omitted, though. Things no one knows. Indulge me by listening to my tale one last time?'

What else could possibly be revealed when I know every detail down to the colour of their clothes and the turn of the weather? Still, I am intrigued and settle on the winged leather armchair beside her and lay a hand on the mattress, in case she needs my touch for comfort.

'You remember, of course, how I was at Epsom Downs Racecourse, watching the Derby, when first I met Compeyson. He was with a group of friends when we saw each other. It was my first outing after ending my mourning period following Father's death, and so perhaps I was more vulnerable than usual, for he swept me off my feet. First he started talking to one of my companions, Matthew Pocket, but soon his attention turned to me, advising on which horses to back, what to look for. What a handsome man he was, with exquisite manners, quick-witted, and with such charm that he could have called forth the bees from their hives had he so desired, and bade them give him all their stores of honey. Such care was taken over his dress, too, yet he never appeared as a vain peacock. I went from never having experienced love to being so deeply under its spell there was nothing I would not have done for that man – not one thing. All sense and reason flew from me; I, who had always prided myself on being more astute and level-headed than others of my sex.'

I shift slightly in my seat.

'All this you already know. When he proposed to me it was the easiest decision to accept. This was a clever man who, although not quite at my level in society, had all the attributes to be able to step up to my side, and take over the family business and continue its success.' She leans forward, conspiratorial. 'I was a proud little thing. I thought I had shown more wisdom than most by holding out for the right man, and it seemed my patience had paid off. My fortune in life thus far had been down to my superior judgement, I believed, and not dumb luck.'

She sags back into her pillows and gives a hollow chuckle. Her eyes seem to have sunk into shadow.

'Mother, perhaps it is best not to upset yourself—'

'Hear me, I beg you.'

Arguing will take more of her strength, so I let her continue but vow that if she becomes too upset I will slip some laudanum into her rhubarb water in order to give her peace.

'My head was filled with the wedding. Everything needed to be perfect, for it would be the society wedding of the county and further. Everyone who was anyone was invited. Preparations helped to distract from my grief, too, for my father had only died the year before. As an orphan estranged from her half-brother, it fell to me to arrange everything for the wedding.

'Arthur had already been banished from my life after proving to be as much of a wastrel as I'd feared. Before his death, Father had also seen how weak and foolish his son was, and unbeknown to us all had changed his will. Instead of leaving the entirety of the business to Arthur, as anticipated, Father had bequeathed his son a few personal items and a minor share of the brewery only. All else was mine. Even though

I disliked my half-brother I had given him some money, and tried to include him in the running of the business, but he was a wastrel. He burned through cash the way a forge furnace burns through coals. He begged for more, more, more, but always wasted it until finally I refused. Even then he railed against me and cursed. Only when Everard spoke stern words to him did Arthur stop visiting me. How grateful I had been, little realising it was all part of the ruse to gain my trust, and he and Arthur were working together.

'Still, innocent child that I was, I ordered my trousseau and even bought Compeyson a fine wardrobe of new clothes fit for the leading man of the county that he would become when we joined together. For his wedding suit I chose dove grey, for I did not want him to marry in his customary black. Although I paid for everything, I did not mind, for what was mine would soon be his.

'And so I come to the part you have not heard before...'

Chapter Fifty

THEN

PARIS, *1829*

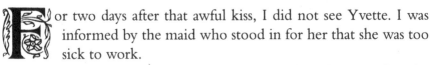or two days after that awful kiss, I did not see Yvette. I was informed by the maid who stood in for her that she was too sick to work.

The truth seemed obvious: she found me so abhorrent that she couldn't stand to have anything to do with me. I didn't blame her, for I hated myself.

Yet for all my disgust at myself, my feelings were honest and true. I loved her. There was no doubt in my heart at all.

It made the expression on her face when she rejected me all the more painful. The more I saw it in my mind's eye, the more it hurt. Her lips so red against her paling skin, and twin roses of anger blooming on her cheeks. She'd pushed me away with all her strength, utterly shocked.

What could I do to make it up to her? How could I rescue our friendship? The thought of losing her forever was more than I could stand.

I would make a joke of it, I decided. Next time I saw her I would apologise profusely and say it was a miscalculated jape, and the last thing I'd wanted was to offend.

That would work, I told myself.

Yet my nights were sleepless.

The following morning a familiar knock on the door made my stomach lurch. I sat up, tidied my hair and tried to quell my nerves before calling, 'Enter.'

Yvette bustled in, avoiding my eye as she gave me a cheery 'good morning' and went to my wardrobe to pick out a dress. 'Perhaps the pinstripe and flowers today? It's a nice weight for the weather – it looks very grey and autumnal out there,' she burbled. 'Did you have any thoughts?'

'Only that you must accept my apology. Could you stop for a minute, please, and look at me?'

She stilled, but remained with her back to me.

'Yvette, I'm so, so sorry for what happened. It was a prank, a silly joke. That's all...'

'What made you think of doing it, though?'

Still she didn't turn. It was both hurtful and made it easier for me to talk. To lie. 'It was just an idea that popped into my head and felt right at the time. Funny, you know. Like it would shock you and make you laugh.'

'So you don't feel... romantic towards me?'

'We're friends. I cherish our relationship, and would never risk losing you.'

The silence seemed to fill the room, drowning out all the sounds from outside. Finally, she spoke. 'I never told you why Jacques was threatening to put me into an asylum, did I?'

'Because he's an evil, addle-pated numbskull, presumably.'

'Because he discovered that I love women the way most women love men.'

I found myself climbing out of bed. 'You mean...?'

Even if she was attracted to women, there was no reason why she would want me. Still, hope inflated inside me. If I did not seize this moment to tell my truth I would regret it forever, I just knew it. 'Yvette, I love you. We could be together.'

She turned and looked at me. 'We can't, Estella. No. Never.'

'Why?'

'Just know we can't. I-I don't feel that way about you.'

The emotional punch hit hard. 'Of course you don't. Why on earth would you or anyone?'

She stared at me, thinking, then walked across the room. I braced myself for the home truths she had clearly decided to give me. I closed my eyes in readiness…

…and felt her lips on mine. The heat of her arms around me, her body pressing against mine and burning through the thin cotton of my nightgown.

'You fool, Estella. Don't you know how much I love you?'

'But you just said—'

'Being together is impossible; the world will never allow it. But I love you, Estella. With all my heart, I love you.'

I couldn't stop smiling. Love made everything right. And best of all, I didn't need to fear for my heart, or try to break Yvette's as Mother had always told me to, because this was no man I'd fallen for.

Our affair was easy to conduct, despite Yvette's fears. She was in my bedroom first thing in the morning, last thing at night, and throughout the day as much as possible without anyone becoming suspicious – why should they have been when it was our usual routine? Instead of waking me with a gentle knock on the door, I awoke to kisses and caresses. Our friendship continued as ever, only it was even better.

Happiness became my constant companion. When Yvette mentioned anyone who needed money, I offered mine. It was so easy – and worth every franc to see others become as happy as I.

'I don't have enough to change the world, but I can change one person's world easily,' I told her. Yvette's smile was my payment.

Away from the critical gaze of Mother, I felt totally carefree. I didn't care what people thought, but Yvette was more cautious, counselling that even my money could not buffer us from the condemnation of the world if they discovered how we felt. We were careful.

But we both knew that secrets can only be hidden for so long. Like a splinter, they work their way to the surface eventually, but often not before starting to fester…

As the months passed, a niggle of fear of discovery began to grow alongside a desire for more. We would hold hands and dream of living together, perhaps claiming to be sisters. And so we made plans to run away. I began gathering my money so that we could finance a new life. It didn't matter where, as long as we were together. Finally, we plumped for the warmth of Italy, that 'paradise of exiles' which had been so welcoming to the romantics: Byron, Shelley and Keats.

It would be hard abandoning Mother, but the pull of freedom and happiness was far greater than guilt. She had made it clear she had adopted me to give me a mission, but now love made it impossible for me to fulfil. She was once again being let down by someone she trusted, but even that thought could not make me turn from my bright new future.

Gérard and Yvette were close. He spent time with us, sometimes, when he wasn't busy with his revolutionary friends. He seemed kind-hearted, but lacked the lightness of his sister. He would monologue earnestly about the haves and the have-nots, and his determination to strive for equality.

'The city government does not trust Parisians since the Reign of Terror, yet if they do not, how can we trust them?' he would say.

Not knowing what to reply, I simply continued sipping my tea.

Often I wondered what he thought of my friendship with Yvette. Did he think me too rich, and therefore part of society's problems? It was all too easy to imagine him whispering criticisms to his sister…

One day Yvette was finishing up her work in another room, while he and I waited.

'If the workers all banded together and refused to work, it would not be long before the country ground to a halt. The rich would have to cave to our demands for better pay and work conditions,' he said.

'Why on earth would they? It's giving in to blackmail,' I replied. 'No one likes having a knife held to their throats.'

'And how else are we to get equality? What makes them – you – better than someone born poor, apart from opportunity to better your lot?'

I opened my mouth to argue – and closed it, thinking. 'My own life could have been very different had I not been adopted by a rich woman,' I admitted.

'Yvette mentioned that.' He extracted a pipe from his pocket and began packing it with tobacco in meditative fashion. 'You are close, the two of you.'

Was that slight pause before the word 'close' in my imagination, or did he know about us?

'Sometimes we want to do things. Sometimes it seems like the only way forward. But does that mean we should give in to our desires?' He lit his pipe as if he were asking the most profound of questions. I wanted to slap it out of his mouth.

'If you're talking about what I think you're talking about, you should mind your own business.'

He clamped down on his pipe with an audible click. Furious smoke puffed into the air. 'I had hoped you might be open to discussion. Yvette respects your opinion, so I thought to see if I… But, no, I can see I was wrong to even try. I won't trouble you again.'

Heat crept over my cheeks. If he knew and objected – which must be the case – that would surely impact on Yvette's feelings. I had to try to rescue the situation, win him over, make him realise that our love was true and unshakeable, and that I was not some rich person taking advantage of his sister only to drop her when I grew bored. Emotions were not my area of expertise, though; the thought of spilling my innermost feelings to anyone, even the person I loved, was difficult, let alone her brother. I tried to find words, to force them up, but already he was standing, giving a wooden bow. Closing the door behind him.

Red with anger, I held my teacup so hard the delicate bone china cracked at the handle. When Yvette came bustling in minutes later, I told her only that her brother had said he was busy and had to leave. Luckily for me, she accepted this without question, for he was always doing such things.

For days after our disagreement I worried what Gérard might say to his sister, but if he did mention anything she gave no indication. Instead, she talked of nothing but our plans. A room in a Rome *pensione* had been booked, and from there we would search for a villa to rent, somewhere more remote in the countryside.

'Ideally overlooking a lake,' Yvette dreamed.

'Of the brightest blue.'

'The colour of your eyes.'

Finally, the escape day dawned. Yvette dressed me as usual, her hands deft as she pinned my hair.

I kissed her palm. 'Just think, we'll be together soon, in our own home.'

She gave a laugh. 'Are you packed?' she checked.

'My portmanteau is under the bed. We can buy everything new when we arrive in Rome, for everything we own is probably too heavy for that climate. I can't wait!' I almost squealed this last. I grabbed Yvette and twirled, then dipped, kissing her. She laughed and slapped me playfully on the shoulder.

'Come, you'll be late – and you don't want to be punished by Madame Flaubert and miss our coach.'

That made me sensible. With a last kiss, and a final 'I love you' we bid farewell and promised to meet at the arranged spot for the coach.

'Here's the money to buy the tickets,' I added.

The morning dragged, but I felt giddy rather than impatient. Even Collette didn't dent my joy when she made a spiteful comment about my smile being wide enough 'to mar what little looks you have'.

At lunchtime I pleaded that I was feeling unwell and excused myself from afternoon lessons. No one suspected a thing, and I caught a cab to the station. Yvette wasn't there, so I bought our tickets. And waited.

The coach arrived.

Yvette did not.

Where was she? What on earth could have held her up? I kept checking my watch against the clock in the square: both agreed the time. Something must have happened to her. I was flagging down a cab when a child ran up to me, breathless, and waving a note.

I went cold. Thoughts of Mother came to mind, of the note her fiancé had sent her on her wedding day, the unknown contents of which shattered her heart so completely that it could never be put together again. I pushed it away as hard as Yvette had pushed me when we first kissed.

I'm going to be sick, I thought as I unfolded the note. The words were brief.

Don't wait. I'm not coming.

No signature, no kiss, no explanation.

My fist closed over the notepaper, and with it my heart crumpled.

After all my criticism of Mother and her actions after her wedding, I finally understood why she had been left so broken by what Compeyson had done to her. There was no feeling in the world like falling in love for the first time – and then having your heart broken. No joy soars higher, no pain cuts deeper, and both change you forever.

Chapter Fifty-One

NOW

SATIS HOUSE, 1835

Mother smooths the bed sheets to delay the inevitable. 'You will look at me differently after this, but I hope you can add it to the list of things you will try to forgive me for—'

'You are already forgiven for anything you have done to me, Mother. There is nothing to forgive you for no matter what you tell me in relation to Compeyson.'

She pats my hand and looks past me into the years gone by.

'As I say, what was mine would soon be his, in my mind, so why not buy him expensive things? With no parents or loved ones about me to enforce the correct behaviour...' Her voice trails off. She catches the flash of surprise on my face before I can hide it, guessing where this tale might lead. 'In private, we used one another's first names, and I already thought of him as my husband. We would kiss – I'm sorry that you should hear these things and worse from me, but I need you to understand everything. We spent time alone that should have been stopped. Matthew – Matthew Pocket – did once catch us alone. He was scandalised. But my embarrassment made me angry and I refused to listen to his warnings of the rumours he was starting to hear about my fiancé. He claimed that Everard Compeyson was a man whose manners were only a veneer, beneath which hid a trickster and rake. I thought Matthew was jealous. Not romantically jealous, for I knew he didn't love me in any way other than a cousin – no, I convinced myself he wanted the Havisham fortune. I should have known that was not the case, for Matthew has always been independent and hard-working, and not afflicted by the desire to acquire money that haunts the rest of the family.

'The wedding grew closer. It was just months away. My happiness grew daily, for Compeyson showered adoration onto me. "My heart is yours and only yours; my life is in your hands," he would say. The most fulsome words are always the emptiest, I realise now, but at the time? How I warmed to them and melted against him.

'Still I refused to give him the thing he wanted most. Not until after our marriage. "Am I not already your husband in your heart?" he pressed. And of course, I assured him he was... and not only with words... The thought that I was hurting him by not giving him what he longed for cut me deeply, and so at last I gave him all that was in my power to gift – and we lay together as man and wife. Why not? I wanted to. It was safe, for the wedding was almost here, the banns read, the outfits bought, everyone had been invited. He loved me and I loved him and he acted every inch like a man who thought of me as his beloved. Besides, I was not some common strumpet, I was the catch of the county, and for all my fierce love for him, I knew that Everard would benefit from our match. He would be a fool to walk away from me. There was no earthly reason that could stop us becoming man and wife and so... and so we joined together.

'Those months were a bliss of discovery. We found any excuse to be alone. It seemed such a marvel, an incredible gift that men were so very different from women. It seemed to me that we were created as two halves of one creature, meant to be drawn together again, in order to find true happiness.'

I thought of the joy of being with Yvette and blushed, remembering my own awakening.

'The day before the wedding my good friend and matron of honour came to visit me. You know her, Estella, for she is Mrs Brandley. She had been married for nine months or thereabouts, and was just showing the bloom of her first child. As I had no mother, she felt it her duty to sit down with me and, hesitant as a fawn, tried to warn me what would be in store for my wedding night. I remember her saying: "With the right person it can be wonderful, but it may take time to accommodate one another. Patience may be needed by you both until you get used to each other." I did not have the heart to tell her how my body constantly ached deep inside me for my husband-to-be and that the wedding night would be only a continuation of our beautiful relationship. How smug

I felt, guessing that her marriage bed had not been as natural as the one I shared with Everard.

'He came to me that night and we felt closer than ever. The day of the wedding, he did not take his leave until the sun had risen. He quoted *Romeo and Juliet* – the nonsense where Romeo denies he can see dawn. Then he added: "Today is the last time I shall have to leave you like this." Neither of us could stop laughing as we kissed our farewell. I, of course, thought he meant he would never have to leave my side again because we would be man and wife; he must have thought himself so amusing, knowing how I misconstrued a meaning only he knew.'

My heart breaks for her. She had loved him completely, and he had comprehensively used her. It makes a sad sort of sense.

'Now I have reached the sorry part of my story.'

There is more?

'I was dressing for my wedding when my world began to fall apart. I remember standing in front of my full-length cheval mirror, admiring how my gown suited me: the way it clung to my shoulders and bust, then flowed loosely over my figure as was the latest mode. We were running late – but that is a bride's prerogative, after all – and one maid was just starting to fix my veil to my hair, while another slipped my foot into a shoe. That's when the letter was pushed into my hand by a red-faced pageboy. As you know, the coward Compeyson's note informed me he wasn't coming to the wedding. That he and my brother had been working together to grift me out of money, jewels, my very fortune. He had been hired by Arthur to humiliate and break me, for what I had done. My crime? Being a "mere woman" who had "presumed to steal" a man's rightful place by inheriting the business and fortune over Arthur.

'I've never shown anyone that letter. Its details were horrifying. There were family secrets Arthur had shared with him... Everard took great pleasure in telling me that of all the things he had stolen, including my heart, the best had been my body. He wrote that he had spoiled me for all other men, and they would be horrified by the unnatural things he had taught me to do – things I now wanted to do, things I enjoyed. He had never loved me, never cared a jot for me, had only wanted to see how far he could take me, and even if he were not already married (yes, he'd been married well before he ever started to romance me) he would not have tied himself to me, because I was too ugly and proud and did not know my place.'

Mother's voice is faint with fatigue, and she is trembling. I tend to her, wiping the sweat that has gathered on her brow and upper lip.

'I dismissed all but my most trusted staff, so ashamed was I at being the talk of the county. They wanted to clear away the wedding feast and all signs of what would have happened that day, but I ordered them to leave and not return until sent for. Then I took to my bed to cry and rage, and—'

'It's time to rest,' I say firmly.

She sinks her fingers into her hair and grips the roots, as if trying to lift herself up. 'Not yet. Soon, but not yet. There is more I need to share.'

I do not argue. Instead I suggest a drink to soothe her throat from all the talking, then help her take the rhubarb water, and its sly laudanum addition.

Chapter Fifty-Two

NOW

SATIS HOUSE, 1835

Somewhere outside, a crescent moon casts a faint silvery glow over the world, but inside Mother's bedroom there is no indication of time as she once again takes up the story of Everard Compeyson. She is rested and composed as she speaks, though there is the slightest hint of a tremor as she raises one hand to fiddle with the Honiton lace trim at the neck of her nightgown.

'I was the richest woman in the county and also the proudest. To have to inform everyone the wedding was cancelled, that I had been jilted, virtually at the altar, almost broke me. Almost. Of course, I was furious and embarrassed. I threw things and raged. But every storm passes eventually. A rich woman such as I could survive a setback of this nature. Oh, there would be talk and my prospects with other suitors would be damaged, but eventually my money would overcome any squeamishness a prospective husband might feel about me.

'Everard's talk of my unnaturalness in bed was hurtful and worrisome, but I could act the winsome innocent if required, at least long enough to fool anyone new who came along. It would be a long time before I would trust again, and certainly would never love, but I was lucky to have social standing to shield me.'

So if Compeyson using her and casting her aside on her wedding day had not destroyed her, what on earth had?

'Logic does not heal a broken heart, however. The future I had thought was assured had been stolen from me in the cruellest manner. I took to my bed, my pillow soaked with tears as day turned to night while I lay unmoving, clutching Everard's letter to my heart. Every happy memory between us was tainted and destroyed. As I mulled over our last night together the cruel double meaning of his goodbye occurred to me – how amused he must have been.'

She shakes her head. But the movement is heavy with sadness rather than her usual quick anger.

'My heartache was so strong it manifested as a deep, painful ache in my back and across my stomach, as though some giant were wringing me out. It grew in strength, making me cry anew. I surmised my courses were coming, and cursed it for its timing and the horrifying strength of the pain it brought. Reluctantly, I rolled across the bed, leaving the note crumpled in the middle of the mattress, in order to light a candle and put on my monthly rags. As my feet hit the floor a wave of heat then of absolute cold went through me, before pain doubled me over the edge of the bed. I gathered my skirts up in one hand and with the other felt between my legs as blood gushed down them. A shiver of sickness and the oddest sensation… and suddenly there was a strange protuberance between my legs, a bulge that should not be there. I screamed with shock. But there was no one to hear me, no servant to come to my aid for they had all been sent away. I was alone in the darkness.

'I was dying, I was convinced of it. The pain, the strange growth, it seemed the only explanation. I kept my gripped skirts tight around me, gathered high into a ball in one hand, and bit down on the material as wave after wave of agony tightened around me. There was an urge to push through the pain, and as I gave in my only companion was the moon shining through the window. I had never been so scared, or felt so utterly alone.'

She can't look at me. Her hands claw at her chest in her familiar way. I want to stop her from causing herself pain but something makes me pause, knowing she needs to say this. She has kept her story hidden for so many years. Some secrets can be turned into pearls and used for good, others become a canker that never heals and slowly poisons the blood. Sharing her secret will lance it.

'Lydia found me in this vulnerable position, my feet on the floor, my nether regions naked, and my top half prostrate across the mattress as I bore down with bent knees. She had come to check on me despite my orders, and thank the Lord she had. She reached my side as something came free from my body and fell to the ground.

'"Oh my days! A babe!" Lydia gasped.

'She cleaned me and the child down as best she could with water from my washbowl and pitcher. I did not speak, did not move, so in shock was I at the news. A babe. It could not be. Yet I could see her, defying all reason.

'A child. Begat between Everard and myself. Our daughter. *My* daughter.'

Might she announce me as her natural child? It isn't unheard of for rich families to 'adopt' a child in order to disguise a true relative born in scandalous circumstances. It saves not only embarrassment for the family, but also society the effort of having to condemn and shun. I want to ask, but hold my tongue so that this tale can play out.

'I sat on the edge of the bed as if stunned by a great blow, while Lydia bustled endlessly. Quite suddenly I remembered something that my dear friend Mrs Brandley had told me: that the point of lying with one's husband was so he could quicken the womb with his seed. That the earliest sign of success was the halting of courses. At that moment I sat up straighter and thought hard. My bed sheets had been pristine for all the months since lying with Everard – I'd had no courses.

'He'd assured me it wasn't possible to become pregnant because as a man of experience he knew a way to stop it. I had trusted him. And besides, I had reasoned, even if it did happen, it would not matter, for the baby would be born well after wedlock. I hadn't given the consequences much thought at all, I admit.'

'Were there no other signs?' I curse myself for asking but cannot help myself.

'I had noticed some changes in my body, a certain Rubenesque quality; my stomach more rounded, my breasts plumper, but I had thought it was simply because love was making me eat more than usual.'

Oh, Mother. You poor, naïve fool! But we women are not fore-warned about what to expect, all is shrouded in mystery. I remember well the shock of my own courses starting – how much worse must it have been for Mother as she realised she had given birth? And was I that child? I bit the question back, waiting…

'Of course, there was panic and fear. I was a fallen woman, unmar-ried with a child out of wedlock, who would be shunned by society. It took only moments to decide what to do, though: Lydia could find a wet nurse to look after the babe for a few months and eventually I could adopt her.

'Oh, Estella, how good it felt in that moment to be back in control of my life. It was only then that I realised how quiet the room was. Lydia and I were making no sound – and neither was my daughter.

'"See how good she is already, not crying," I said, despite an instinctive fear in my heart. "Do you not think?"

'Lydia was tying the rags to me to mop up the blood still leaving my body, and she said nothing. When she was done, she took the material of my gown from my still-clenched fist and tried to pull it over my head. I pushed her away with arms as weak as water and repeated my question. She did not look at me as she answered. "She's gone, miss. She was too early, too small."'

Mother's hands rest on her stomach as if trying to reconnect with the life she once held inside her. Her words paint such a vivid picture that I feel as if I have stepped back in time to see it all. Good, loyal, level-headed Lydia, how it must have hurt her to break that news to her beloved mistress.

'"You're lying. Show her to me," I demanded.' Mother's voice as she speaks echoes the imperious tone from all those years ago. 'She refused, told me it was too late, that it was better this way. I gathered all my strength and channelled it into a cold fury that brooked no argument as I ordered her to give me my child. At last Lydia did so.'

Her voice catches, strength gone. I lean forward to ensure I miss nothing.

'Curled up, she was about the size of my hand from tip to wrist. Miniature but perfect, she was, with pale eyelashes and rosebud mouth. Lydia had swaddled her in one of my finest scarves of soft lambswool, but my baby's skin was softer still. I gently stroked her face – and my heart leapt at the warmth of her cheek. "She lives! Open your eyes for Mother," I crooned. "Come little one, show the world your strength. I shall name you Aurora, for you are the light of my life."

'I found her tiny hands among the folds of material and put my finger to them to feel her strong grip curl around it. Nothing. No matter how I held Aurora to me or blew gently on her little hands, she grew colder. I held her against my flesh and rocked, trying to protect her, trying to fill her with enough love that she might breathe. I ordered the Lord to help me, offering myself in exchange of her. I called for Everard to be by my side, promising that all would be forgiven if he would only return and protect me and his child for evermore. I kissed each of Aurora's toes, begging her to stay. Her rose-red lips paled. Her petal-soft skin grew icy. Her eyelashes did not flutter.'

'Oh, Mother! Speak no more; you do not have to relive your heart-break.'

But her eyes are fixed on the past and she neither sees nor hears me.

'The sun was peeping through the window before Lydia persuaded me to let Aurora go. My child had not lived to see her first sunrise. I never heard her voice nor her laugh. She did not take a single step; she could not grow tall and strong. A lifetime was lost.

'"What will become of her?" I asked aloud.

'"Don't fear, miss, I'll bury her in the grounds, so no one will know she ever existed except for us. It's better this way," she replied. "And you can visit whenever you wish, so she'll be ever with you."

'She thought she was doing me a kindness – she was, for there was no alternative. The church would not allow a bastard child in consecrated ground. Lydia emptied a large jewellery box and placed Aurora inside. When she asked if I thought it was fitting I said yes even though I barely knew what to think or feel. Yet the thought of people walking over her unmarked grave, unknowing, disrespectful... No, I could not allow that.

'I uttered not a word of protest, however. Too weak. How I despised myself.'

Her head rolls back into the pillow, her white hair a wave of foam. Tears course down her cheeks, and her voice is thick. Yet somehow she keeps talking.

'How long Lydia took to bury Aurora I couldn't tell you. I did not go with her. I seemed rooted to the spot. I stared at three drops of blood on my pristine wedding gown. How had I suffered so much, lost so much, since dressing less than four and twenty hours earlier, and yet it looked unchanged but for three small spots in livid red? They were the only sign that the desolation of my world had not been imagined.

'When Lydia returned to my side she once again tried to take off my veil and gown. "We need to get you out of this and into some clean clothes," she said.

'I hit out then. Finally striking out against the numbness. "No. Once my wedding dress is gone it will be as if the whole day has been a dream. I don't want to forget Aurora," I told her.

'"Come, we need to tidy you up," Lydia urged. "Cleanliness is next to godliness."

'My dress was virgin white, pure – as I should have been. It taunted me for not being a good girl, a virtuous woman. If I had not sinned, I would not have been punished and Aurora would have survived. Her birth changed me irrevocably. I had gained and lost everything, *everything* in that moment. Because of Everard Compeyson. Because I chose him to give my heart to.

'"I'll never wear anything else," I told Lydia. "I shall close the brewery and house so that no one can ever walk over my daughter's grave. I will never again see the world. Close all the shutters, for the sun, the moon and all people are not welcome here. Stop all the clocks, for the house will never move on from this day."

'But why, Mother?' I can't help myself. 'Why would you want to relive that time for the rest of your life? Shut yourself away; I suppose that's understandable to a certain point. But to replicate that awful moment and live with the constant reminder of—'

'It was the punishment I deserved. I had been the fool that let liars into my life and believed them. That was the thought that circled me, like a lone wolf whose snapping jaws took chunks of my mind until there was nothing left but that awful certainty: that I was to blame for my little one's death.

'So I stopped the clocks at the time I received the news of Everard's betrayal, because that was the moment everything fell to pieces. I couldn't move on if I had wanted to – and didn't deserve to when my follies had cost a life. I hoped that vile man might hear of it and realise how much pain he had inflicted. That he might be hurt by that realisation and suffer, too. But of course he didn't care. The punishment was always mine to bear.

'The spots of blood on my dress dried, flaked away to dust, the tiny marks left behind faded to nothing over the years. Everything changes whether we want it to or not. I look at the space where my jewellery box was every single day and think of Aurora, but I have never visited the spot where she was buried. I don't need to. She is buried deep in my heart; she is a part of me always and forever.'

The room feels heavy with her words.

'Do you think differently of your old mother now?' A soft, sidelong look begs me for forgiveness.

'I do,' I admit.

Her nod is eloquent in its pain.

'Now I see how strong you were, where in the past I thought you weak,' I say. 'You have endured so much. As for the rake that did this to you, he should be strung up. None of this is your fault, you don't deserve punishment.'

I understand as only a woman who has experienced terrible pain inflicted by a man can. Now is not the time to reveal it, for this moment is about Mother sharing her sufferings with me. Instead I ask a question.

'Is this why you adopted me? Did it... help you at all?'

'The loss of my child was a gaping hole in me that wouldn't heal. I hoped adopting would knit it together. Mr Jaggers was working for me by then. I don't know how long I had been shut up in this house, for by then time had lost its meaning for me, but I asked him to find me an orphan child and one night he brought you to me.

'How innocent you were, lying in his arms, fast asleep. You were a little rosebud, only three years old. Such long eyelashes! You snuffled into my neck when I held you for the first time. At that moment I lost myself to you, Estella. I named you so that you might be my shining star in the darkness. There was nothing in my heart at that moment but a desire to raise you well; I did not mean to lead you into the night with me.'

For so many years I had judged Mother and found her lacking for allowing being jilted by a mere man to taint her life and those of others. Now I understand how terribly she's been used, and how much she has lost. I have been afraid of that woman; I have loved her, hated her, and even felt indifferent to her when I, too, isolated myself from all emotions. Now I feel pity for her. She held her hurt to her bosom, not because she wanted to make the world pay, but because she felt it was a sentence she deserved. She indoctrinated me so that I might never suffer the way she had. Her zealous passion for the project carried her away from her original plan, however, and instead she weaponised me. We have both paid dearly for that.

But who can blame her for her actions? Not I. Her suffering hurts my soul.

Chapter Fifty-Three

THEN

SATIS HOUSE, 1829

After the turmoil of my speedy retreat from Paris, my heart shattered by Yvette's cruel note which broke our affair, all I wanted was to reach Satis House. As the coach approached with deadened hooves, it appeared out of the heavy marsh mist whispering promises of the comfort of stepping out of time. It was as if I had never been away, and Paris had been only a dream – which was perfect as it was my most fervent desire to banish Yvette from my thoughts and act as if I were as frozen as Satis House itself.

There was one significant change I noticed upon my arrival, however. When the coach pulled up outside Satis House, a large man dressed head to toe in grey lumbered from the gatekeeper's cottage, the familiar set of keys swinging from the chain around his waist.

Dolge Orlick. That murderous villain. What was he doing in my home?

He lowered his head and breathed heavy and bullish, peering with malevolent curiosity at the coachman who pulled down my luggage.

The last time I had seen this man had been the night before I left for France. How curious he should be the first to greet me on my return.

That last time he'd been standing over Pip's sister after smashing her over the head from behind with a manacle. He'd had no idea someone had been spying on him and seen it all.

The coachman opened my door and proffered a hand for me to steady myself as I stepped down. Once out of the carriage I gave Orlick a look dripping with bored superiority and ordered him to open the gate instantly. The fool hesitated, but luckily Sarah Pocket – yes, what a welcoming committee: a killer and a calculating bitch – appeared at that moment and clicked her fingers in a show of power aimed more at me than him.

Sarah walked deliberately slowly in front of me, as if I needed escorting through my own home. She wore a dress so dark her head seemed to float before me in the corridor. I swept past, leaving her, her candle and my goosebumps in my wake. The darkness enveloped me. Though more than three years had passed, there was no hesitation in my step. Lack of light does not blind when there is such familiarity. From the smell of decay in the damp air to the scritch-scratch of scuttling mice behind the walls, everything was the same. I knew exactly where the door to the dressing room was, and turned the unseen handle without first knocking.

The welcome sight of a faded spectre in her ragged wedding finery, sitting in the soft yellow candle glow, greeted me. Ever-present, never-changing, that was my mother. Still in her tattered lace gown and half-attached veil; still staring into the fire as if the answers to all questions lay in its dance. I called to her. She started and turned, her stare sliding into a frown.

'Is this a phantom come to plague my lonely heart?'

'Only if it is possible to touch a phantom.' I surged forward and wrapped my arms around her skeletal frame.

It was good to see her again. 'Never-changing' I had thought her, but when I held her she felt more frail than ever. She had lost more weight, her gown looser. Her bird's-nest hair was thinner, her skin more papery. For all she tried to keep time stopped at that moment in 1813 when her wedding had been abandoned, she was ageing faster than her contemporaries.

There were other alterations, too. I expected her to pull away from my embrace after a count of three, as she always had. Instead she clung to me, her hands like hooks tangling in my hair and clothes to keep me in place as she pulled me so tight I thought her bones might crack. Would she recognise my heartbreak, I worried. When she finally let go, she kept hold of my hands as if to reassure herself I truly was there. A smile stretched over her skull.

'Is it really you? What a wonderful surprise! Are you home again now? Had I forgotten this was happening?'

'I didn't have time to send word of my return. I missed home and was desperate to return, and when I explained to Madame Flaubert she told me that my learning was completed, anyway. So – it was perfect timing.'

The best lies are built around truth, and it was true that Madame Flaubert had told me this. After receiving Yvette's note I had not returned to the finishing school. Instead, I had sent a letter to my teacher telling her to have my trunks packed and sent to Calais as I would be sailing for home as soon as possible. What I hadn't expected was for her to accompany my luggage so that she could check on me. She was a good woman, and had wanted to ascertain for herself how I was, but when she saw my desperation to return home, she accepted my decision.

Mother gripped my hands and looked at me as if she were starving and I were a feast. I broke the reverie.

'The person at the gate, what on earth made you hire him?'

'Orlick? He's a big, strong man, and sometimes circumstances call for brute strength. There was a time when the Havisham name demanded instant respect in the community, but how quickly the people forget. There has been some trouble with youngsters recently, throwing stones to smash the windows, climbing over the wall to explore. Mischief, nothing more, but... but disconcerting.' She wrapped her thin arms about herself and shivered. 'Jaggers suggested getting someone in as a sort of guard, and found this Orlick fellow. Said he was the perfect man for the job.'

The unspoken 'why?' stayed on my lips.

'It was a surprise seeing him, that is all – Sarah, too,' I explained. To tell her the truth about Orlick would scare her further. 'He is such an oaf, a true gollumpus—'

'He is not allowed any further into the house than the main passage. He rings a bell to alert Sarah of his presence and that of visitors. *We* have nothing to do with him.' Subject closed, she leaned further over her walking stick, kestrel-like as she gazed at me. 'How you have grown. How beautiful and regal you've become. And your clothes! So elegant. I must show you off.' She gave a cadaverous chuckle. 'Let us send word to Pip. We shall surprise him.'

'Or we could leave him alone.'

'Nonsense. Think of how awestruck he'll be by you. This will give me the chance to see for myself all that you have learned about entrapment.'

Her grip on my hands grew tighter still. I nodded and smiled, simply so that I could pull away from her. How typical that her obsession with her own broken heart stopped her from seeing mine.

'You have his London address?' I asked.

'I'll send it to the forge, they can forward it. I'll tell him to come immediately.'

Would Pip be the same, I wondered. He had come into great expectations himself, from what Mother had told me, but it was impossible to imagine him as anything but the young innocent I had brutally taunted and haunted.

I told myself that I would never revisit those dark insecurities that had made me hurt Pip, nor the tempers that had led to me having to leave Satis House. In those last years before Paris I had felt there was a fire inside me about to rage out of control and set ablaze everything I touched. No longer. Instead, I was ice, I decided: an untouchable ice queen.

What a fool I was, thinking that I was worldly-wise and could see with such clarity how things were. But youth is often blessed with certainty that life experience clouds rather than clarifies further. There were so many more mistakes ahead of me. Deadly ones.

'It is time for the next move in the plan, Estella, my dear,' Mother announced.

'Do I have a say in it?' I asked, my voice crisp.

The look she shot through the gloom was hooded. She tapped her cane on the floor. 'You do not wish to do as I ask after I have given you love, a home, education; lavished you with all you could need.'

It was true; compared to what my life could have been had the Pockets had their way – returned to an orphanage, left destitute and friendless, with no money, no shelter, no prospects – what would have become of me? In Paris I'd seen the reality of poverty. I owed Mother everything and as much as I desired to break free from her grasp, I also longed to win her approval, too.

'Of course I do, Mother; I was being facetious. I apologise.'

'Plans are in place for you to go to stay with an acquaintance of mine, Mrs Brandley, and her daughter.'

'Brandley? I've heard you speak of her.'

'We were once close. Very close. Before...' She completed the sentence with a regal wave that took in the destruction of her world. 'She will oil the wheels to ensure your introduction to the most powerful and eligible bachelors in society.' Mother leaned forward and grasped my hand in her claw. The candlelight slashed shadows of madness into her face. 'You will destroy them all, Estella. Just think of it!'

I closed my eyes and nodded, tired of fighting, exhausted from years of raging against the bars stronger than iron that caged me. I would accept my fate and become a knife wielded by my adoptive mother's hand, and have no more feelings about my victims than a blade would.

'Oh, I quite forgot to say,' said Mother, as I kissed her good night, 'a letter arrived for you, but as I did not know you were coming I can't remember where I put it.'

My heart gave a painful jump that took my stomach with it. Who would be writing to me? Could it be Yvette?

Chapter Fifty-Four

THEN

SATIS HOUSE, 1829

The paper was cheap and thin, the sort a servant might buy and think they had spent much on a luxury. The writing spidery and poorly educated, and so familiar to me. I held the letter opener in my right hand like a knife about to stab someone through the heart, but its only movement was a slight tremble from the war within me. Half of me wanted to tear the missive open and discover what the liar who had broken my heart had to say, the other never wanted to have anything to do with her again and was repelled by the parchment gripped in my left hand.

What to do?

The letter had been hidden away in my old knitting bag, which itself had been pushed beneath a table so that the tablecloth cascaded over the edges to the floor, thus concealing it and retaining the fiction that the room was ever unchanged. Once I'd located the missive, I said good night and left the room so Mother couldn't see my reaction.

Yvette's last note had shattered me so completely that I wasn't sure I could ever be whole again. The person who had laughed and loved and felt complete for a few short months was gone. It was impossible to imagine me ever being her again. No, all that Yvette could do now was hurt me more, and why should I give her the pleasure? She had already plunged her knife into my heart up to the hilt with that note, why curl my own hand over hers and help her give it a final twist by reading this new letter?

I threw it onto the fire and watched it curl at the edges and blacken, as my lips curled in grim satisfaction. I would not let anyone turn me into Mother. I would recover and move on and never think of love again.

Only, of course, I did, the moment my head hit the pillow.

That Yvette could end things with a one-line note was cruelty I had never expected from her. I should have, though, I reminded myself ruefully. Had Mother not spent her every moment with me trying to warn and protect me from the ravages of so-called love, its fakery and the bear pits in which it trapped us? It wasn't only Yvette I was angry with; it was myself. I had been taken in with soft words and lingering looks and gentle touches like some naïve idiot instead of a hardened soul. The same mistake would not be made again.

It didn't help that Mother had spent the remainder of the day inter-rogating me about all the men who had wanted me and could not have me.

'Make them love you,' she had said. Her eyes wide, her crypt-breath poisoning me as she leaned close. 'When they smile and flatter, make them love you; when they cry and wail, make them love you; when they are sick with it, make them love you, love you, love you all the more until they die from it.'

Thinking of it made me shudder.

I took my razor-sharp letter opener and lifted my nightgown to expose the scar on my leg. I had been an innocent, trusting child when Camilla had lured me across the rotten beams in the brewery, where I had broken through and slashed my skin and vein open. I had almost bled to death, and a thick white scar twisted over the pale skin of my inner thigh to remind me of my brush with mortality.

Yet what Yvette had done to me hurt more, cut more deeply, and the wound would, I feared, never heal. Pressing the letter opener against the scar, the flesh resisted before parting and blood blossoming. It felt good to be in control of my pain.

I will never love again, I vowed into the night. The spiders and mice witnessed my blood oath.

The thin scarlet line trickled down my leg and onto the sheet before drying as I lay back and pondered the more urgent problem. Orlick. In him was a clear physical danger to the entire household. He was a violent offender, and could not be allowed to stay at the manor when Mother was so vulnerable. Like Mrs Gargery, she was not known for holding her tongue – and one wrong word could have her paying with her life.

He could kill us both in our beds.

After all the emotional drama of Paris I'd been looking forward to the monotony of life at home to heal me. Instead, I found myself once again thrown into intrigue and violence. Like a fly in a spider's web, the more I ran from the situation the closer to it I seemed to come; the more I struggled the more I was trapped.

This time I was determined not to place myself at the front of the action, though. I was not the fiery, headstrong girl who had left Satis House all those years ago, who acted first and thought a month later. Nor was I blinded by love, as I'd been in Paris. Instead, I was a lady of breeding and it was time to act as such, with decorum.

In other words, this problem was of Jaggers' making, and he could damn well get rid of it.

The very next morning I ascertained from Mother that Jaggers was due to visit the following day. In the meantime, I bided my time by watching Orlick. He seemed happy to stay in the gatehouse, sleeping in a sort of feral nest he'd created from blankets and a patchwork counterpane.

When he went to patrol the grounds, he took with him a large hammer. It was easy to imagine the damage he could do with such a weapon. All too well I remembered the blacksmith's wife prone on the floor, her vitality snuffed by Orlick's heavy blows. His cowardly attack as her back was turned. That would not happen here.

I slipped into his room and had a look around. In the creases of his blanket was hidden a massive knife. No elegance to it, an ugly two-sided blade with notches in it, but no less deadly for all that. On the chimney breast hung a gun with a brass-bound stock. It was loaded. I carefully emptied it out and retreated, having done more than I'd promised myself, but feeling better all the same for snuffing out a threat to the house.

Still, I watched him. I found my lip curling every time I looked at him as he growled to himself. I felt like growling, too; he seemed to echo the frustration I felt inside. Waiting was not something I was good at.

The moment Sarah Pocket, who had unfortunately become a permanent helper around the house, walked into the dressing room I could guess what she was going say. Her stiff, disapproving face silently shouted that Pip had arrived. He must have dropped everything to come at once, for it had only been two days since the note had been sent to the forge.

Mother was positively gleeful as she told me to sit quietly. 'Do not speak, let him notice you, gaze upon you and realise he cannot resist your beauty.'

We were both just pieces on her chessboard, to be arranged for her entertainment.

She sat in her usual chair beside the fire, two hands crossed on her stick in that familiar pose. Meanwhile I sat on the footstool, as I had as a child, my wide skirt pooling around me, my head slightly bowed as I gazed at the fire and prepared to play my part.

There came a rap on the door.

'Pip's knock,' said Mother, looking up like an eager hound.

Why did I suddenly feel nervous? I looked down, ashamed, remembering all the times I had spied on him, and how I'd witnessed his sister's attack...

Mother was almost capering as she greeted him, and he kissed her hand.

'Well?' she smiled, grimly playful.

Pip stuttered some reply or other – ah, how little he had changed, for all the wrapping was more luxurious. He cut a fine figure in his tall hat, neckcloth, waistcoat, trousers and fine boots made from the softest calfskin. Yet he wore the clothes uncomfortably, looking rather more as though the clothes wore him, for he had no confidence in himself. From the way he stood, to the constant little tweak of his neck to one side because he was unused to the stiffness of the collar, right down to the way he still fell over his words when faced with Mother, he remained the same old Pip on the inside.

My own nerves melted at the realisation and I raised my head just as Pip noticed me. He seemed unable to speak as he took me in. When I gave him my hand he glanced at his own and gave the slightest twitch as if he were about to hide them, as if once again my taunts about his thick, coarse hands might ring out. My own coarse, common hands shaped themselves into an approximation of elegance, as they had been drilled to by Madame Flaubert.

Mother invited Pip to sit and started to verbally nip at him immediately.

'Has she changed?'

'Not so very much.'

'Really? And yet you thought her proud and haughty and you wanted to leave here to be away from her. Do you still feel that way?'

Poor Pip, no matter what he said he was not going to win. Mother herded him into mistake after mistake.

I could not stay quiet. 'Mother, really, he was quite right, I was most disagreeable back then.'

'Is he changed?' she asked. Her stare tried to penetrate my practised mask. I picked up the bridal shoe from the dressing table and pretended to study it as if I had never seen it before.

'Very much,' I told the shoe.

Mother ran her fingers through my hair. 'Less coarse and common?' she asked.

I laughed, and suggested Pip and I take a turn around the garden. Anything to escape Mother's haranguing.

Once outside, I explained that after returning from Paris, Mother had decided my next move should be to London to join society there.

'I believe Mother plans to ask you to aid me in my move. I'm giving you warning so that you may find an excuse, if you wish, for it is unfair of her to expect you to do this.'

'You know I would do anything for you,' said Pip.

The years had not diluted his adoration of me. Rather than pleasing me, it made me uncomfortable – and the more I became discomforted, the stiffer I held myself and the more precisely I spoke. For love was tainted as far as I was concerned; and as much as Mother clearly wanted Pip and I to slip back into our former roles of unfortunate sailor and siren, it was the last thing I wanted now that I knew what it was like to have a broken heart. Mother had always warned me that love hurts, and now I had learned first-hand. It would be easy to do it to others, but to Pip, my childhood friend, it was impossible. In all else I would be Mother's creature but not this.

Perhaps there was a way to use my cruelty as a kindness...

Chapter Fifty-Five

THEN

SATIS HOUSE, 1829

decided the best way to warn Pip away from me was to remind him of our past. We were drawing close to the place where he and Herbert had fought.

'What a nasty little creature I must have been to hide and see that fight that day. But I did and enjoyed it very much.'

'Do you remember the reward you gave for being your champion?'

Of course I did. For many hours after I had put my hand to the spot, to warm my cheek again as when his lips had touched there; but instead of telling him that, I pretended to think then gave a light shake of my head. He looked suitably hurt by my feigned forgetfulness. Why did his injury cause a clench in my own stomach?

'How I disliked Herbert for daring to come here and trying to be my companion – as if he had any more choice in the matter than I,' I said.

'Herbert and I share lodgings now and are good friends.'

The talk moved to Pip's change in fortune. He retained the deference of someone talking to a great princess. He had put me on a pedestal so high it was a surprise we could speak without having to raise our voices to be heard across the distance.

As we spoke an impression grew that Pip felt Mother had chosen him for me. There was nothing I could put my finger on, only a general aspect in the words he spoke and the way he acted. Where had he got this impression from? Nothing in Mother's demeanour lent itself to the role of fairy godmother.

By this time we had gone round the evergreen garden three times, and were passing the brewery, when Pip began reminiscing about the first time he had come to Satis House, when he had seen me walk on the casks, and I'd given him food and drink and cause to cry.

If my surmises were correct, this was my opportunity to hurt him just enough to save him from further injury.

'Do you know, I don't remember that at all. Are you sure you didn't make it up?'

Pip's face had always been open, as easy to read as a book of fairy tales. Now the tips of his ears flushed and his eyes sparkled with gathering tears that he blinked away.

'You must know that there is no heart here.' I touched my chest.

'You are too beautiful for that to be true.'

If anyone else but Pip had said that I would have rolled my eyes at the bare-faced flattery. But the thing about Pip was this: he meant it. I may have been the one named Estella, but Pip was always the light to my darkness.

'Believe me,' I said bluntly. 'There is nothing of softness there, no empathy for other people's feelings, only a muscle that would cease to beat if it were stabbed or shot. We are to spend much time together, so please take heed – this honesty is the one act of kindness I will undertake.'

He gave me such a curious look, as if trying to work out a difficult sum. He did not believe me.

'I have never loved and never will,' I lied.

Still he argued, saying he didn't believe me. My patience was all used up.

'It is said, and I have tried. The rest is up to you,' I finished. Picking up the hem of my dress in one hand, I rested the other lightly on his shoulder and we continued back to the house.

Once inside, Mother reminded me that Jaggers would soon be arriving, and suggested I change for dinner while Pip pushed her around the dining room as he had in days past.

When I agreed, she seized my hand and pulled it against her cheek, kissing it as if she wanted to feast upon me. Her eyes were greedy on mine even as she urged me to go. She had never been like this before; absence seemed to have made her fonder and more demonstrative but instead of it feeling like the comfort I'd longed for as a child, it was disagreeable. Her love wanted to devour me.

'Use him, Estella. Use them all,' she whispered into my ear.

The vehemence made me hurry from the room. Outside, I paused, though, curiosity winning over. Old habits die hard and my former habit of listening illicitly to conversations in Satis House was calling to me. The door was still open a crack so I pressed my ear to it.

Mother was pushing Pip on how beautiful I was and urging him to love me at all costs and against all reason. He said nothing as she hissed her poisonous words.

Through the thin crack I peered. She had her arm around his neck, pulling him ever closer, her veins standing out in her passion.

'Hear me, Pip, she was adopted to be loved; educated to be loved; developed and formed in every way that she would be loved. Love her.'

That four-letter word was her curse.

Sickened, I withdrew and gladly let the darkness enfold me.

As I turned, I jumped – Sarah Pocket was standing behind me. So intent had I been on the play before me I had not noticed her approach.

'Mr Jaggers has arrived,' she said. Her face said more. Her superior smirk was carved in light and shadow, for she had seen exactly what I was doing. Once again I was a naughty guttersnipe child and she the lady.

I found Mr Jaggers in the waiting room, where a large bowl of water, an unused bar of soap and several towels had been laid out for him, for his custom of extreme cleanliness was well known.

He was greatly struck by my new look, which is to say he glanced at me from the side of his eye for a full three seconds, and spent even longer than usual scrubbing his nails with an air of distraction most unlike him.

'*Make them love you and lose all reason,*' Mother seemed to whisper in my ear. I shuddered. I could not do it; could not flirt and flutter around a man I had known all my life.

'I would like your help in a matter of security,' I said simply. With Mr Jaggers, preamble and sweet words were a waste of precious time, flattery was something he saw through instantly and used against one.

I told him of my concerns that Orlick was a danger. He threw one leg over the back of a chair and rested his foot on the seat as he listened, leather boots creaking occasionally.

'Do not allow your imagination to put fear into your heart or head,' he said when I had finished.

'I don't have that active an imagination. These are facts I present.' My reply was sharp.

'You have nothing to worry about concerning this man. He is of interest, that is for sure, but I keep my eye on him and he knows it. Do you imagine he would defy me? I put the case that only a fool would cross me.'

'That is for sure, and yet, Mr Jaggers, if he were to do something violent in this house it would be too late for Mother or I to be able to tell you that you were wrong.'

A creak as he assessed the argument.

'I say again there is no hard evidence that he would ever consider such a thing. You're being emotional.' He gave me a long look, producing a huge silk handkerchief and proceeding to elaborately dab at his face with it, like a magician using a prop as distraction. He was giving me time to think, I realised, as if he knew there was more to my story than I'd thus far revealed.

Telling him I had witnessed a murder and said nothing at the time would only lead to trouble for me, I surmised. An idea sprang suddenly into my mind, though, and I presented Mr Jaggers with a penny as a token for his services, thus buying his silence, for a lawyer's client is protected by confidentiality.

'I can provide evidence. This is an eyewitness account.'

And so, I told him everything.

'He is living up to my expectations,' mused Jaggers. 'It isn't in his best interests to hurt you, though – in fact, it is detrimental to him and he knows it. Still, if you fear for yourself, I could protect you, Estella.' Creak, creak. 'I have to confess I am most struck by the way you have grown and would, most earnestly, like to offer you protection at my side for life.'

'Mr Jaggers—'

'You will not call me by my first name of—?'

'I will not, for you wish to turn my trust in you into something different and I will not give you the slightest hint of encouragement. You have let me down, Mr Jaggers. Further, you have let yourself down. You are the closest I've had to a father figure, and you would use that to manipulate me into a fake romance for which I am meant to feel grateful? You would pose as my protector while leveraging a position of power? Does that sound like love? It doesn't to me. Marriage should be a meeting of equals, should it not?'

'I put the case to you—'

'The case? I am not something to be won. Let me put a case before you instead. A man has chosen a child, plucked her when she was little more than a babe in arms, watched her grow in her innocence, and now that she has turned into a woman he wants to possess her. He has acted alongside her adoptive mother to groom her and shape her into the person they wish her to be. And then he proposes to "protect" her for the remainder of her life now she is grown to womanhood.

'I put the case, Mr Jaggers, that this way of acting is abnormal. It hints at dark deeds and perverse thoughts. But what would I know of such things, for I am a mere woman, so I shall leave it to you – you, man of not only the world but the underworld, who walks through grime unsullied and smelling of carbolic – to put me right and correct the fictional case I put forward.'

Mr Jaggers' stance was as sure as ever, one leg over the back of a chair as he stood. Yet his finger was in his mouth, and he gnawed at it before flinging it toward me with a laugh.

'What fun it is to intellectually joust against a worthy opponent. I have missed our little talks,' he said.

Fun? Mr Jaggers? Seeing me truly had thrown him.

He made his excuses and began to wash his hands again.

Chapter Fifty-Six

THEN

SATIS HOUSE, 1829

hat a weird quartet we made around the fireplace. The cadaverous bride, the lovelorn cynic, the out-of-depth innocent, and the bitter siren.

Mother, as ever, had not eaten with us, preferring instead to keep up the pretence that she was a ghost who needed no sustenance. Instead Jaggers, Pip and I had the dubious pleasure of dining with Sarah Pocket. Mr Jaggers had been seated opposite me, yet managed not to speak or look at me once during the entire meal. Instead he'd thrown his conversation at Sarah, making her grow greener than a lush jungle with his deliberate talk of Pip's newfound wealth. The object of the jealousy had squirmed in his new clothes, uncomfortably torn between pleasure and the knowledge that taking such pleasure was a sign of ill breeding.

Now we had returned to Mother's company in the dressing room, while Sarah slid away after Mother had pointedly asked her if she were not required elsewhere. I am certain Sarah tortured herself, imagining all the fascinating things we spoke of, all the secrets shared and alliances made. The reality was far duller: a game of cards where Mr Jaggers took everyone's winning hands into custody; and Mother's far crueller game of playing him and Pip against each other by bedecking me with jewels as she had of old and begging for compliments they were all too willing to give. Pip stammered and dropped his cards and was as naïve as if he were still wearing his blacksmithing clothes rather than the expensive finery that adorned him right down to the lace cascading over his hands. Jaggers pulled out his large silk handkerchief and appeared and disappeared behind it with such calculation as to remind me of the tales of Spanish bullfighters waving their red cloaks to control the raging bull, his thick eyebrows undulating like the roar of a crowd whenever he felt he had dealt a successful blow to Pip.

I, the bait, sat like a cut of succulent meat, showing no favour either way, while the dogs fought over me with cutting looks to each other, and careful words of empty flattery to me. Let them fight over me if they wished. Let them dash themselves on the rocks for want of being with me. I no longer wanted to think or feel, I would simply do whatever was required of me without argument. I was too tired of the world and everyone in it. The cards would fall as they may.

We played until nine o'clock, when Pip took his leave; but not before it was arranged for him to meet me at the coach when I arrived in London.

As I took my own leave to bed, Jaggers appeared at my side.

'I have dismissed the gatekeeper,' he said without preamble.

'Thank you for listening to my fears.'

'Pip shared concerns with me. Action became inevitable.'

We stared at each other for several moments, neither speaking. He knew I was furious but there was no point in my wasting energy saying so. For although I had got what I wanted the victory had not been mine. My words had been dismissed as the fears of a weak woman with an overactive imagination, but those of a man had been deemed worthy of acting on instantly. I wrapped my hand around the metal comb I kept hidden in my pocket and clenched tighter and tighter until the sharp teeth bit into me, the pain keeping me clear-headed and dry-eyed. After several more moments, Jaggers inclined his head, and took his leave with a creak of leather.

After that day Jaggers was always more careful with me, as if he saw me differently and realised the changed creature I was – and as if he felt guilt and did not know how to make up for it.

The following two days flew by, as I busied myself in preparation for my move to London, and Mother grew more and more possessive of me at the looming prospect of losing me again after we had only so recently been reunited. When I wasn't packing, she wanted me by her side, both day and night – or as much of the night as I could stand, for I had not the drive of the damned that she possessed to float along the long-abandoned corridors and rooms for eternal hours.

'We have received a letter,' she said.

Was it Yvette again? As she spoke she waved the paper at me, and I saw words written in an unfamiliar, childlike scrawl.

'It is anonymous, but there are some particularly serious accusations in here. I shall read it aloud:

> *'Dear Miss Havisham,*
>
> *'Please forgive me for writing to you. You do not know me, but I have heard of you and the terrible pain you suffered so many years ago. May I take this opportunity to extend my deepest and most heartfelt emotions on this subject, as there is no one less deserving of such pain as you. You will notice that I do not sign my name to this missive, and it is for the simple reason that I am in fear of terrible reprisals should the subject of this letter discover I have contacted you. When you read what I have to say you will understand why.*
>
> *'I must tell you that Mr Philip Pirrip, known as Pip, is not to be trusted. He is a gold digger, intent on inveigling himself into your trust and into your will. He will do whatever it takes. A master of manipulation, he deliberately appears mild-mannered when in reality he is evil, two-faced, and dangerous.*
>
> *'Oh, if you could hear the way he speaks of you in London! He talks of his grand plans to spend all of your money and dance on your grave once you have passed away, in front of the deeply grieving relatives that adore you and have stayed ever true to you.*
>
> *'I do not wish to cause upset but feel it my duty to share with you the terrible tales I have not only heard tell but seen with mine own eyes.'*

She lifted her gaze from the letter and stared at me sternly. I went cold.

'Do you believe these accusations?' I asked.

Instead of answering, Mother read on. '*He is trying to take you for a fool and use your name for his ill-gotten gains. The idea!*' she read.

'The idea,' I repeated, thoughtfully.

Our eyes met. Mother's mouth twitched.

We started to laugh at the exact same moment.

'The *idea!*' we repeated with an intonation so familiar to us.

'She is not at all subtle, is she?' I chuckled, wiping at my eyes.

Even in written form, Camilla could not help using her well-worn phrase. Presumably, she had used her left hand to disguise her usual lettering. The Pockets were up to their old tricks. Clearly, they feared that now Pip had been raised up, Mother might be tempted to raise him further.

I remembered his misguided belief that Mother had somehow earmarked him to be my husband. Had the same thought occurred to them? That, combined with their conviction that Mother was the rich benefactor behind his own great expectations, was surely more than enough for them to act against him now.

I mentioned it to Mother, who laughed all the longer and harder for it – so hard that she began to cough.

In the days that followed more letters arrived. Some anonymous; others that were more subtle and begging, written in their own hand, and signed by Sarah, Raymond and Camilla. How they hated Pip! How they tried to poison Mother against him with their constant insinuations and false reporting. Yet for all Mother spoke of never trusting anyone, her faith in Pip remained curiously unshaken.

Even more curiously, I did not think to question it – which just went to show how much I trusted him, too. Instead, I was grateful to Pip, for while the Pockets were busying themselves hating him they were leaving me alone.

No longer fighting, simply accepting my fate, was working well. Having no feelings was far preferable to the pain of opening up to people. I barely thought of Yvette, and when I did I imagined pushing her into a lead-lined coffin and slamming it shut. Instead of brooding, I would do as Mother asked. She knew best.

Go to London, entrap men, coolly break their hearts, and keep moving on, like a never-ending dance. Easy.

Chapter Fifty-Seven

NOW

SATIS HOUSE, 1835

There is a new understanding between Mother and me, now that I know fully everything she suffered because of that cad, Everard Compeyson. She has never recovered from the loss of her baby, and never will, but unburdening herself to me seems to have made a difference because she seems stronger. There is a brightness in her cheeks and eyes the like of which I have never seen before.

Encouraged by this, a few days later I tell her my own truth.

No details – it's not necessary; the bare bones are enough. I am cold and strong as I speak about the attack by Bentley, being locked in, how close I came to death. I am describing something that happened to someone else.

So why am I trembling?

When I finish she says nothing. She eases across to the far side of the mattress, then pats the space created. I don't understand. She pats again, hard enough to make an audible sound.

She can't mean…?

I hesitate, thinking of my dreams, of how much I longed for a hug as a child, and frown, trying to work out what Mother means.

She opens her arms and moves her fingers, every inch of her body saying: *Come here.*

I climb up. Pause. Then lie down beside her. Put my head on her chest. She doesn't stiffen. Doesn't silently count to three then ease me away. She curls her arms around me and sways gently, as if rocking me.

'It is not your fault,' she says softly and kisses the top of my head. 'None of this is.' She hums a lullaby under her breath.

Great, wracking sobs heave up from somewhere so deep inside me it must echo. Through it all, Mother holds me tight, and croons until I fall asleep in her arms.

When I wake, I'm still in her arms. A boulder of emotion I hadn't known was weighing me down has lifted. I look up at her. Smile.

'I love you,' I say.

'Dr Hawkins has suggested something that might speed up your recovery.' My gaze is firmly on my knitting as I speak, because Mother is going to be angry when she hears the idea.

'Pray tell.'

'He says you need to be trying to walk a little, and that... and...' There's no point dilly-dallying. I put the knitting down. 'Some light – sunlight – would be efficacious.'

She shakes her head. A tear escapes from one eye. Her fingers twist in the counterpane.

'He was quite firm. Aside from the umming and ah-ing. "It, ah-hem, ah-hem, speeds healing – almost as well as, ah-hem, rhubarb water",' I mimic.

It fails to stop her fingers twisting.

'It will be a shock for you to see daylight, but if it can help, isn't it worth trying?'

'I can't. I-I can't.'

'You can.' My reply is firm. 'You simply won't try.'

She bites her lip and looks down like a child trying to avoid a scolding.

'Everard Compeyson.' Her head shoots up when I speak his name. 'He has taken enough from you. Don't let him have one more moment of control over you. You've been so much better since you told me everything. Just think how far you've progressed in these few short days: you're eating better, you're talking more, and I can see for myself the strength returning.'

She ponders. Looks as if she will argue. Relents.

This is a huge step for her. I'm stunned she's agreeing – but I'm not going to say so, as to draw attention to it might make her change her mind. I walk over to the window and open one side of the wooden shutter. Daylight steals through the gap, slicing the darkness and playing over Mother's bed.

The sound she makes is somewhere between a gasp and a whimper. She puts her hand into the sun patch as if she expects to be incinerated on touch. When the warmth hits her skin she pulls back... then eases forward again, turning her palm up as if to catch it.

'How does it feel?' I ask.

'Good,' she says, as if she can't believe it.

Now that the sun is finally shining on her it is all too obvious how frail she is. Her skin is as white as the bed sheets – whiter, as they are grubby from age – and is like tissue paper that has been crumpled up then smoothed flat again, crazed with lines fine and deep. I think again of Mrs Brandley, with her bustling energy, pink cheeks and plump skin, and find it impossible that she and Mother are both forty-seven.

'Come, then,' she says, suddenly. 'Let us do what must be done.'

My mouth gapes, but I recover. 'You mean...?'

'The bath chair, the bath chair. The longer we wait, the worse it will be.'

'Are you sure? You haven't seen daylight in almost twenty-five years.' The words slip from my mouth before I can stop them.

'You make a persuasive argument, Estella. Everard Compeyson will have no more of my life. My gown is gone forever, the feast was cast to the floor when Pip used the tablecloth to put out the flames engulfing me, and more importantly, I have shared my shame at last—'

'Not shame,' I reply.

She raises her arms up and makes that familiar movement of impatience with her fingers. She is light as a sparrow as she wraps her skeletal arms around my neck, and I lift her into the bath chair with ease.

I wheel her towards the window, but she turns away at the last moment. Concern clutches me. 'Is it too bright? Does it hurt your eyes?'

'It does, child, but that is not why I recoil. No, it is shame that has me showing my back. This is something I should have done long, long ago, and now I wonder if it is too late.'

'Never—'

'If it is, that is all the more reason to go forth. It is time to be brave and face the world at last.'

The wooden shutters creak in protest as I push them back fully. At one point they stick so badly I have to use all my strength to move them on, but with a clank and squeak they give in.

The early spring day is overcast, but I only have eyes for Mother's face as she looks through the window. Her fear melts away, replaced by wonder. Deep lines on her face became shallower as her eyes flit from place to place as if following something.

'Birds,' she says. I've never heard her voice sound like this before – high and full of childlike awe. 'How could I have forgotten birds?'

Chapter Fifty-Eight

THEN

LONDON, 1829

As long as I didn't feel anything, all would be well, I reminded myself on the journey to London. The streets were even more crowded, filthy and narrow than Paris, the buildings more crooked, and there were people thronging everywhere. Even in my carriage I could smell them, packed together like animals. I held my kerchief to my nose and breathed in the comforting smell of lavender.

It was midday by the time I arrived at the coach office in Wood Street, Cheapside. As I alighted, I pulled the furred collar of my dolman a little closer around me, and found solace in the hidden things: the lavender pomade secreted in my bonnet; the small bag of humbugs in my travel bag; the pocket-knife up my sleeve. No sooner had I adjusted my dress than Pip appeared, hurrying towards me, his tall hat and stiff clothes looking taller and stiffer than ever before. My heart sank: clearly, he had dressed for the occasion and gone to great pains to impress me.

'Mother has requested you take me to my new lodgings in Richmond,' I said. 'It irks me that I require a chaperone to do even this simple thing when I am perfectly capable of doing so alone.'

He looked shocked, then rearranged his features. 'It's no trouble, I assure you.'

'You don't even know where we're going. It's ridiculous that I have to give you the address to pass to the driver – why could I not do that myself? Because it is frowned on by society. Because I am a helpless female.'

I rolled my eyes and felt annoyance heating me, until I took a deep breath, pushed it down. Pushed it into that handy coffin of my mind, which was getting more crowded with occupants by the day.

'Here,' I added, giving him the fare for the cab. It would be expensive, as it was a further ten miles to my final destination in Surrey. He tried to refuse it. 'Do not fight our fate,' I told him. 'It is easier this way. No thought is required of us, we need only do as we are told.'

'Let me take care of you,' he began.

'Neither of us is expected to follow our free will,' I reminded him. 'We are creatures in a story of someone else's devising and can only act as instructed. Life will be easier when you give in and accept the inevitable.'

His eyes widened, but he agreed eventually. Though the lingering look he gave me seemed to search for more meaning behind my words than there was, for what could there possibly be behind them but welcoming, blissful emptiness?

Once in the cab, we began rattling along. The cobbles seemed determined to shake my skeleton to pieces, but I kept my back ramrod straight, showed the fortitude of spirit a lady must always present, and gazed out of the window to take my mind off the journey.

'What is this place?' I asked. The high walls and stench of misery, the drooping shoulders and wringing hands, the fear twisting faces, all shouted at me.

'Newgate,' Pip replied reluctantly. 'A place of law courts and prisons and...'

And executions.

So much suffering. How many had started out as orphans or been born into abject poverty and never given a true start at life? Never educated or given a decent job with which they could work their way out of the mire? How many had been prejudged simply for their station, and treated more harshly as a result? Their end was almost inevitable from birth unless someone helped them.

'Poor wretches,' I whispered.

Not long after we had jounced through that place of penury, Pip's curiosity got the better of him.

'What will you do in Richmond?' he asked.

'I shall live with an old friend of Mother's – yes, she had friends once, although no longer. Now they are acquaintances, but nevertheless Mrs Brandley shall be taking me in, thanks to an incredibly generous payment from my mother. She has the power to introduce me to society.

I am to be dressed finely and shown about, and will make intelligent conversation when required.'

'That sounds like grand fun.' He smiled, settling into his seat and spreading his arms out so they rested along the back.

'Does it? Yes, it must be, I suppose.'

'You speak as if you're talking about someone other than yourself.'

Ah, Pip, he knew me too well. Somehow he had guessed that I had removed myself from all that happened, and viewed myself only from a distance. Could he tell that it was a way to protect myself? His slight frown told of confusion rather than insight.

'You don't know how I speak of others – or to others.' I smiled with levity. 'I don't talk to you the way I speak with other people, you know.'

'How do you speak to others?'

'I school them, just as I did you when we were children; but you and I are past all that now.' I said the words gently, for Pip had received enough hurt at the hands of my family and me. Besides, we still had miles to pass in our carriage journey to my new place of residence in Surrey, and I did not wish them to be awkward. 'You now live with Mr Pocket, Herbert's father, I believe?'

'I do. It is very pleasant there – as pleasant as anywhere can be where you are not.' He spoke with a sweet yearning that reminded me of Paris.

He realised we were going through Hammersmith, and pointed out the place where Matthew lived. In return, I shared how Mr Matthew Pocket was far above the rest of the Pockets, who all did their best to tear Pip down with poison-pen letters. He shot forward with such a look of concern.

'Fear not,' I comforted. 'Mother and I would never believe such rot.'

His relief was palpable, the grip on the gloves he clutched in his hands relaxing.

How good it felt, to have someone with whom honest opinions could be shared without fear. But opening oneself up to good things comes with the danger of the bad pushing themselves to the fore. In my head my emotional coffin seemed to shake as if its contents were hammering to escape.

Pip took hold of my hand. Pulling it away would be the right thing to do, but I was so very tired of fighting. I would let fate make its decision. He put it to his lips.

'Silly boy.' There was sadness in my voice.

An awkward silence rose like mist on the marsh. Pip broke it. 'I hope we might see each other sometimes, now you are here in London.'

'Oh, yes, Mother has already decided you are to see me, and may act as my chaperone at dances, for you are almost like a brother.'

He blinked rapidly at that word.

I continued: 'Mrs Brandley has been told about you already, and that you may come as and when you think proper. She is of some station and will be able to elevate my introduction into society so that I may meet all the right people, and they may meet me, and Mother's hopes and dreams will all come true.'

'Again you talk as if you have no choice.'

'No one has choice. Choice is an illusion. People cannot help what life they are born into, who they fall in love with, the luck they receive. There is no point in struggling to swim upstream all the time when life has determined you should be swept downstream.'

'But look at me; I have improved my position in life, have I not?'

'Thanks to a chance circumstance. You have done nothing to elevate yourself.'

He had been leaning forward, eager to engage, but sank back at this comment.

'I did not mean to insult you,' I added, more gently. 'You have clearly worked hard to improve your manners, bearing and speech. You endeavour to better yourself and you succeed, Pip.'

Had he, though? True, his exterior had been given a buff, but what was inside him had always shone. It was why I had tried hard in childhood to tarnish his spirit. I feared his obsession with appearance would lead to a degrading of his very Pip-ness.

'Ah, here we are,' I said, for the carriage had stopped.

The house was so unremarkable as to be identical to the others on the street. All large, grand, symmetrical, with vast windows and small panels, and columns either side of the door, and in all everything that the previous era had been so overly fond of. A square of garden was at the front, which overlooked a communal green. My heart sank. If I was going to be in London I had hoped for something more modern and exciting. A fresh start.

Pip offered his hand and walked me through the parade of trees lined up to greet us, towards the front door, before ringing a bell that sounded as dull as the house looked.

Two maids with cherry cheeks hurried out to receive me and organise my baggage to be brought in. Pip lingered awkwardly, apparently waiting to be dismissed. Words of thanks ran through my head but stuck in my throat as Mother's reproaches replaced them.

Do not trust men. Never let your guard down. They will all hurt you given the chance – so you must strike first.

I gave him my hand as a master would throw a titbit to their dog. There was something reverential in the way he planted a farewell kiss to the knuckles.

Oh, Pip, will you never learn? I silently sighed.

But I did not pause; instead I sallied on through the door without a backward glance, and heard it click closed behind me.

Chapter Fifty-Nine

THEN

LONDON, 1829

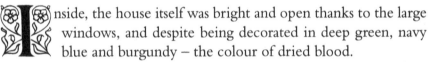nside, the house itself was bright and open thanks to the large windows, and despite being decorated in deep green, navy blue and burgundy – the colour of dried blood.

Later I discovered the decor had been chosen not by Mrs Brandley but her late husband – 'may he rest in peace'. She always prefaced any comment about him with that phrase, to such an extent that I began to wonder, after months of hearing the repeated hope, whether she suspected that might not be the case.

When I entered the room into which I was led by a maid, two ladies rose from their seats to greet me. Mrs Brandley was a woman of smiles. She opened her arms to me for a welcoming embrace. I flinched back before steeling myself to accept it.

'How wonderful to meet you, Miss Estella. My, but you're elegant – I can see the hand of Pandora guiding you. She was always so very particular about her appearance, you know; always had to have the latest fashions.'

My smile clenched with shock. Mother had told me about her previous life, of course, but it had always felt like listening to an impossible fairy tale. To hear it spoken about out in the real world, by a stranger…

Mrs Brandley rescued me from my confusion with a: 'Come! Sit! You must be quite exhausted from your journey.'

She twittered on, asking me about how long it had taken to get from Kent to London, and then across the city. She was so full of energy, and looked so much younger than Mother, yet they were the same age. Was this the life my mother could have had, had she not been deliberately left heartbroken and then chosen to shut out the world? Would she still be at the cutting edge of fashions, embracing the change from neoclassical, slim-fitting, high-busted gowns in pale shades, to romanticism, with its bright colours, patterns and curvaceous shapes? The thought of Mother with coiffured hair, wearing something other than her ghostly garb, was jarring; for her to show her natural waist, and wear petticoats to give volume in her skirts, and show off the same leg-of-mutton style sleeves as I wore, in every shade conceivable... why, it seemed ridiculous. If I could not comprehend even such a shallow change, how much more impossible was the thought of my mother, the famously bitter recluse, as a bon viveur?

Through all Mrs Brandley's flutterings, her daughter remained quiet, apart from a brief greeting when her mother had introduced us. Lucy Brandley was so different from her mother that I wondered moment-arily if she was adopted, like me. Closer inspection showed a similarity about the eyes, though the mother's danced with curiosity and her daughter's were so disinterested they almost appeared hooded behind the unfortunate half-moon glasses that perched on the end of her nose no matter how many times she pushed them up.

From their demeanour I would have thought Miss Lucy to be the elder of the two. My guess at the time was that she was already despairing about her marriage prospects and this was what made her so quiet. Bitterness was already drying her up like an apple left to wrinkle in a fruit bowl, I decided. At twenty-eight, she was several years older than I, and considered an old maid.

How sad, I thought, that a woman's lot so depended on a few brief years when she bloomed into womanhood. If she were not plucked, she was destined to fade and, at best, live with her family, a drain on their income, solely dependent upon their charity. At worst, a woman could be cast out and live in poverty. All because she had not found a husband.

What was to become of me, I suddenly wondered. If I did as Mother asked and broke all the hearts I could, what then? Did she expect me to return to Satis House and see out my days with her?

'Oh, my dear, you're shivering,' gasped Mrs Brandley. Despite my protestations she insisted on calling a maid to build the fire up, even though it was a warm spring day. 'We can't have you falling ill on your first day here,' she said. 'You have been entrusted to me and after everything your mother... well, it is an honour that she should put her most precious daughter into my care. Tell me...' She hesitated. 'Tell me, how is she? I have heard rumours, of course, and have tried numerous times myself to engage her in letter writing, but...'

'She corresponded with you in order to arrange this,' I replied.

'Well, yes, but it was all business. She would not answer any questions of a personal nature.' Mrs Brandley picked up her teacup then set it down again without taking a sip. Her quiet voice was filled with concern. 'I don't ask in order to pry, you understand. We were, once, great friends. As close as sisters. I was her maid of honour that... that day. I was there when she read the letter. I saw what it did to her. She went so pale it was as if her heart had stopped. Together we went to the church, her veil still only half-arranged, and only one shoe on her foot, she was in such a state – she wouldn't listen to me, you see, when I begged her to stay at home and send servants, instead. The congregation was kind, when they realised what must have happened, and at first she—'

'Do you know, Mrs Brandley, you are quite right: I am feeling a little under the weather. I wonder if I might withdraw to my room.'

'Of course! How silly of me! The maids should have finished unpacking your things by now, so you can rest undisturbed until dinner time.'

She knew what I had done, but seemed unhurt by it. Mrs Brandley wanted to be friends, a confidante even. I see that now, years down the line. She, perhaps, suspected that Mother had not provided the warmest of upbringings and wanted to be a substitute for me. It's possible that if I had met her years earlier she might have succeeded, and then how different my tale would be. Instead, I was too formed in my nature. Too shaped by others to allow myself to be moulded yet again. And so, I rejected her advances. Her enquiries brought out the urge to protect Mother from the gaze of outsiders and gawpers, so I refused to engage in conversation with her.

As long as I lived with her all was civil politeness only, and the more she bent towards me the more I buttressed myself against that cheerful, well-meaning woman and her daughter whose head was always in a book. Whatever it took to protect Mother from scrutiny and criticism, I would do, even if it was to my detriment.

I went upstairs and flopped onto the bed, already exhausted from pretence and all that lay before me. With a sigh I sat up again and found paper, pen and ink, and began my promised daily letter to Mother.

Chapter Sixty

THEN

LONDON, 1833

Making men fall in love was ridiculously easy. I ticked all the boxes that were required of a good wife: beauty, breeding, accomplishments in every feminine field, from embroidery to singing. My manners were impeccable, my deportment that of a dancer's; even my clothes and jewels were immaculate, and I was always at pains to be at the cutting edge of fashion without ever looking as if I was trying too hard. It's all easy to do when there is enough money to draw on.

Over the years, I successfully broke many a man's heart and, as requested, faithfully wrote to Mother every day of my successes. She absorbed each detail, and so I spared none, reliving every breath in conversations, a speck of lint on someone's clothing, no detail was too small, so that she could live the moments as if she were by my side. Indeed, I often perceived that she was there, peering over my shoulder, whispering advice into my ear of how best to entrap the hapless suitors.

The first society heart I shattered was Samuel Jonson, the son of someone or other high up who owned a bank. I think. He had a habit of saying 'what, what' as if he were the old King George III, and insisted on bringing his small dog with him everywhere. The more casually cruel I was to him, the more he wanted to dance with me. A fortnight after we first met, he proposed. He can't have been too broken by my refusal, as two months later he was engaged to the daughter of a lawyer, a woman of generous proportions and sympathetic demeanour.

Thinking about it, I seem to remember her sister snagged another of my cast-offs. Number four or five, I can't remember which. I think his name was Peter someone, or perhaps someone Peters. Either way, I do know he was obsessed with boating. He talked constantly about rowing on the Thames, and liked to pose with his jacket off, to better show off the physique the pursuit had given him. He had plenty of time to row and do other sporting pursuits because he was the eldest son of a family that owned a large estate in Derbyshire, which he would one day inherit.

The suitors became blurred in my memory, there were so many. They all used the same sort of lines: that I was beautiful, a wonder to behold, that they desired to spend time with me... and then proceeded to attempt to dazzle me with their achievements and prospects. None asked about me. Who I really was. What I desired. The life I longed to live. What my ideal marriage partner would be like.

If they had I could not have answered. I didn't know the answers myself.

It's a curious thing that, rather than putting men off, seeing so many of their rivals propose and fail seemed to spur them on. It became a competition between them, and I was the prize they all coveted, shot for and missed. Madame Flaubert had been correct.

I was perfection – provided no one looked beneath the surface. Inside I was devoid of anything but a restlessly roiling, ice-cold anger. All my efforts went into keeping it in check and trying to convince myself I felt nothing.

Every year that passed brought a new batch of fresh-faced and eager young men to the marriage market to replace those who had settled down. Some were naïve and hopeful as I drew them near and removed their hearts; others had heard about the danger of falling for me but saw me as a challenge that must be conquered, as if my heart were the impenetrable jungles of deepest, undiscovered Africa.

By the time I turned twenty-one, four years of living an empty life were beginning to take their toll. In public I appeared to be the same dispassionate siren, but in the privacy of my room at Mrs Brandley's I became obsessed with cleaning, and insomnia stalked me. There was no one in whom I could confide. Most women on the marriage circuit grew to despise me because they knew they were doomed to marry men who had chosen them second.

Pip was by my side through it all, though. In that great swirling marriage market of society balls, dainty teas and elegant promenades around London parks, only he knew me. He became my friend and confidant, as of old. Like me, he would neither confirm nor deny any rumours swirling about Mother, and most people heard them and dismissed them because the truth was too bizarre for acceptance. It is a strange thing that the more weird and twisted the reality, the more blind people become to it.

When Pip turned twenty-one he came into his full annuity and his life as a gentleman was set, which made me look at my own life. What would become of me at the end of Mother's game, once I was too old for any man to wish for my hand? Still, I urged myself only to do as I was told.

Don't react to the lying letters from the Pockets about you and Pip that Mother loves to read aloud, I told myself.

Don't think.

Don't feel.

Don't try to work out why you enjoy Pip's company so much.

Ah, my poor, hapless blacksmith boy.

He often cradled his chin in his hand as he leaned on a table and simply watched me, as if awestruck. He never spoke plainly, but it was clear he loved me and wanted more. I wondered if he held back from saying the words he danced around because he knew I would refuse him, as I did all others.

Indeed, I would have turned him down without hesitation.

I told myself he did not love the real me any more than the others did. He had fallen for a perfect princess in a fairy tale, up in an ivory tower. If he knew the scarred soul inside me, if he knew I'd watched his sister die, if he knew of my relationship with Yvette, if... he would hate me.

The truth was, while everyone else's love was something to be discarded as carelessly as a rose whose petals had browned, the thought of losing Pip's love was more than I could stand.

The truth was, I could not trust anyone after Yvette. Especially myself.

The truth was that Pip was the only person in the whole world with the power to hurt me again. To destroy me, in fact. I would not hand that over for anything. Not even the chance of happiness.

How insanely stupid of me. Still, I like to think there was something more noble at play, too: a desire to protect Pip from any further harm by me, Mother or anyone else. That urge was the only decent thing in my life and as long as it remained there was some hope for me, surely. I couldn't be all bad, could I; not as long as that silent promise was honoured.

I was growing so tired of my life, though. One can only live empty for so long before one must be filled up with something.

That was when I met Bentley Drummle.

Chapter Sixty-One

NOW

SATIS HOUSE, 1835

How about ten pounds for Camilla, to pay for a lifetime's supply of buttons?' I suggest.

Mother laughs. 'No, five pounds for rushlights, to put her in spirits when she wakes up in the night.'

'Perfect! Although not the return she expected for a lifetime of scheming and creeping.' I clap my hands together.

She writes it down, adding the codicil to her will. Her hands have healed sufficiently that she no longer needs bandages, and can hold a pen without pain. Every day her vitality strengthens, and she's putting me to shame as I still slowly recover. Still, her brush with mortality has made her decide to make a few changes to her will – and to have a little fun at the expense of her odious relatives.

'Sarah next. This one is easy.' She begins to write, reading as she does so: 'To receive twenty-five per annum to buy pills, on account of her being bilious.'

Oh, how green that will turn her! Particularly when she discovers that Matthew Pocket will receive £4,000 'because of Pip's account of him'.

It's now April, and in the two months since Mother's accident Sarah, Camilla and Raymond have not visited. I had braced myself for their sycophantic faces buzzing around her, dripping fake concern and drowning her in honeyed words. But they have stayed away. I can only assume they think there's no point making an effort if she's dying, as it's too late to get a better deal in the will. How disappointed they'll be when they hear of her recovery.

The two of us enjoy looking through the open window and watching spring developing, mirroring Mother's own journey from heart's winter to thaw. The snowdrops have been and gone, the daffodils are wilting, delicate blossom has bloomed in the orchard, while the bare branches of other trees tease with the buds of leaves. There is birdsong when we open the windows, and the deep drone of bumblebees. When Mother heard that for the first time she asked what it was and was amazed when I reminded her. It has been over a score of years since she shut the door on the world, and there is much she must become acquainted with again. There's such comfort in watching her grow stronger; it makes me feel that way, too.

The sun may finally be welcomed back in Satis House, but Bentley still casts his long shadow over everything. I can never fully relax, always watching, waiting, for him. I am a woman reduced to pandering to the whims of a man, even though he isn't here. I still feel his breath on me when I close my eyes; feel his weight crack my ribs, and his hands encircle my neck; hear him whisper: 'I'll make you beg, little star...'

Mr Jaggers is due to arrive momentarily, summoned to see the new will. The prospect of a visitor has been a timely reminder that the world outside these walls is real, and that Bentley lurks there. He has been uncharacteristically quiet, and much as I hope he has decided that pursuing me is more trouble than it's worth, I know him better. He is planning something. Waiting, toad-like as ever, to crawl out when he has decided how best to act with maximum impact and minimum effort. And so it is time to dip my hesitant toes back into reality, and who better to do that with than Jaggers?

'There has been much happening of late,' Jaggers says. The smell of soap fills the air of the morning room, which we have now opened up to receive the sun all day. 'The first thing I must inform you of is a matter that resides close to your heart. This is not a matter of speculation but fact.'

Mother looks at him keenly from her bath chair. Her oil-painted younger self mirrors the expression from above the mantelpiece. 'Go on, go on.' She gives a rapid nod of her head, as if urging him forward.

'I must tell you, Miss Havisham, that your former fiancé Mr Everard Compeyson is no more.'

She says nothing. Her hand twitches up to her chest and pulls closer around her the lapels of a dressing gown that I've lent her. It swamps her spare frame.

'He died in an unfortunate incident during an altercation. Drowned, in fact.'

'Can it be?' she seems to whisper more to herself than to Jaggers. 'It can't be true. I thought I would feel something, that I would know, without having to be told, when he left this realm.'

'You know this for certain?' I check with Jaggers.

'I have not laid eyes on the body myself, but have been reliably informed by officers of the law that his body was found following a fight that was witnessed in part by Mr Pip.'

We look at each other and then Mr Jaggers in astonishment. He takes out his huge silk handkerchief and makes a show of wiping his face with it, enjoying holding us in his thrall for a little longer, before continuing.

Mother seems to have lost the power of speech.

'You were involved in this?' I probe.

'I admit to nothing – did anyone hear of me admitting anything? No, madam, indeed not. I am merely informing you of certain facts I have been furnished with, via first-person eyewitness accounts.'

'You mean, by Pip?'

'Pip and others.'

He proceeds to tell the most extraordinary tale involving a convict who returned from the colonies where he had apparently been transported many years earlier. Goodness knows what terrible crime he committed to be given that sentence; just thinking about it makes me shudder. Pip had been attempting to smuggle out this Transporter, one Abel Magwitch, before authorities realised he was back in the country – for, of course, Magwitch contravened the law the moment he came back from Australia and set foot on English soil. Magwitch had once been a lackey of Compeyson's, no less. Somehow, Compeyson got wind of his return, and decided to bring him to justice. Why? Because

Magwitch stopped Compeyson from escaping the Hulks many years ago, on our very marsh one Christmas Eve. That news gives me pause – they must have been the convicts I had encountered as a child, when trying to run away.

To think I had met the man who had cast such a shadow over not only Mother's life but mine!

The next confrontation between the two criminals happened recently. With the help of Pip, this Magwitch person had been trying to leave the country on a small rowboat with a view to hailing a steamer as it headed for the open sea. At the last minute, Compeyson and some officers had tried to apprehend them. Magwitch, who sounds a desperate fellow, had launched himself at Compeyson and the two tumbled into the water. They had been sucked into the steamer's great paddle wheel, both receiving terrible injuries.

'This was four days ago, and Compeyson was found just this morning. His body was in a state, apparently, and he could only be identified by his clothing and the papers in his pockets, but I have been informed there is no doubt. Everard Compeyson is dead.'

Still Mother says nothing. I study her keenly. There are no signs of an attack of the vapours. Her eyes are set on a far distant point and she seems not to see or hear.

'Why were Compeyson and this Magwitch such mortal enemies?' I wonder aloud.

'Thieves have no loyalty,' Jaggers replies.

'And how on earth did Pip become embroiled with these awful creatures?'

'I really couldn't say.' That is Jaggers-speak for 'I know but don't want to divulge'. A thought occurs: the last time Pip visited he mentioned that he now knows the identity of his benefactor, and the source of his great expectations. Could it be that for some reason this criminal, Magwitch, has been sending Pip money? But why? I squirrel the idea away and promise to look into it at a later date.

'Pip must be quite shaken up by his involvement in all this,' I muse instead. 'He is still injured from rescuing Mother, is he not?'

Jaggers rises up on his toes, his boots creaking in agreement with my supposition. 'He has, I concede, had a time of it. For only two days before he made his ill-thought-out attempt to leave the country with a criminal, he was attacked and held prisoner by Dolge Orlick – you may remember him as the fellow who guarded the gate and premises here for a short time some years ago.'

Oh, I definitely remember him. My dealings with him have been more recent than that...

Mother stirs from her stupor. 'Is Pip all right?'

'He is. He was rescued by the butcher's boy and Herbert Pocket. Though of course he went from one disaster straight into another with this other convict.'

Fancy Pip, the most gentle of souls, being mixed up with such ruffians. I will write to him and enquire about his health. On behalf of Mother, of course.

She puts a tremulous hand out and touches Jaggers to bring his attention back to her. 'He is dead? Compeyson is dead?'

Poor Mother, she doesn't seem able to accept that her nemesis is no more. Jaggers takes his hand away and starts to scrape under his nails.

'He is, Miss Havisham. That he is.'

She nods. A smile – an actual smile – spreads across her face.

'I shall look forward to seeing him in hell when my time comes, for there can be no heaven for me. If there is any justice I shall be appointed his torturer.'

Chapter Sixty-Two

NOW

SATIS HOUSE, 1835

Mr Jaggers swiftly deals with Mother's changes to her will. Then she asks for the curtains to be drawn, for although she now enjoys the light she feels more comfortable in darkness. He obeys, and I prepare to follow him once he leaves the room, so that I can ask about my marriage situation. Mother stops us.

'There is another reason I asked you here, Mr Jaggers,' she says.

My sharp look would cut paper. She has given no hint there is anything on her mind.

'It's Estella. Mr Drummle has proved himself not up to the task of being a good husband, and I wish her to be extricated from the marriage. Please arrange it.'

That familiar command is in her voice. It has been missing in recent weeks.

'No.' Jaggers goes to stand in front of the fire, which has a metal guard around it for safety. He puts one foot up onto the seat of a chair and leans an elbow on his thigh, staring us down as if daring us to argue. Jaggers is even more used to being in charge than Mother.

'You disappoint me. A man of your reputation is capable of anything,' she says.

'My record speaks for itself. If it is possible within the realms of the law, then I succeed. The limit is the law, you see, not I.'

Nausea sweeps through me. I pick up my knitting to hide my discomfort. 'Could I simply divorce him?'

'Expensive, scandalous, and even worse it is almost impossible to prove wrongdoing on the husband's part. The evidence must be extreme and overwhelming, and even then it is unlikely to sway a judge to take a woman's side should her husband not agree to it.'

Ruin versus a lifetime with Bentley. As a scandalously divorced woman I could live here in Satis House, taking up Mother's place after she is gone, and let life pass me by while I rot alongside the bricks and mortar, undisturbed and unlamented.

Tempting but…

The darkness seems to inhale me, leaving no air for me to breath. No, this cannot be my best-case scenario.

Besides, it is likely my petition for divorce would be unsuccessful, for there is no evidence of what he has done. I can't – won't – ask Yvette to help me, for it would put her and the other revolutionaries in danger. So, I'd still be ruined, but have to live with Bentley, who will make my life ten times worse for making us the talk of the town in our unsuccessful divorce proceedings. In that scenario, my greatest hope would be that he killed me quickly. He will never be so kind as to end my suffering swiftly, though; instead he will visit me every night and make me relive my nightmares, I'm sure.

My knitting is trembling so visibly that I put it down in case anyone notices. I will not admit my fear. I refuse to acknowledge how what this man has done stalks my waking thoughts and is relived every night in my dreams.

Mother clenches a fist and beats it against her breast. 'Bentley Drummle is cast from the same mould as Arthur and Everard Compeyson. I will not allow him to ruin my daughter's life.' Each word accompanied by a hollow thud. 'Can my will be written in such a way as to leave everything to Estella, and her only?'

'You cannot now that she is married.'

Her hands rise to her hair. She clutches at it.

'Mother, stay calm.' I feel her frustration, though. Society is a fool. What can be the possible purpose of making it almost impossible for women to escape a brutal marriage?

'There can be no bending or breaking of the law in my presence,' Jaggers says sternly. His eyes don't move from hers. 'I don't wish to know about such things. If Estella were to take reams of your money now and invest it in portable property, for example – expensive rings, brooches, anything that is small and easy to move – and then deliberately "lost" them somewhere that her husband could never find, then I would not wish to know anything about it, for I would have to advise that such actions are questionable legally. None of this is any of my business.'

It seems a spending spree is called for. Then, perhaps, I can run from my fate...

Mr Jaggers is staying the night at Satis House. He and I dine together (Mother still does not like to eat in front of anyone but me), the two of us sitting at one end of the naked table that for so many years held the wedding banquet. My stalking fear makes it impossible to swallow a morsel. Afterwards, we play cards, while Mother stays in her room sleeping. Finally, I start knitting, while he drinks a glass of red wine. He offers me one but my stomach is too curdled by the thought of my future sentence with Bentley. Our silence is comfortable, though, for although I respect Mr Jaggers I do not fear him as others do.

'I have told Pip about your marriage.'

His words make me start. They fill the hush and seem to hang between us, accusing me.

I pick up a dropped stitch and carry on knitting, finishing the row.

Jaggers breaks the silence again. 'Indeed, I offered him an opinion, though one based on years of experience of seeing people at their darkest.'

'We all know your expertise in that matter,' I agree. 'The evidence on the subject is overwhelming.'

The gentle clack of my needles is the only sound for some time.

'Are you going to share your words with me?' I ask at last.

'I will, since it is about you. I told him that your marriage will be an unhappy one, and a violent one.'

Saliva fills my mouth, fear flooding every sense. My bruises have gone but my ribs still pain me and make me gasp sometimes, and a man as sharp as my lawyer friend will not have missed that.

The pattern instructions in my 'Knitting Teacher's Assistant' pamphlet are harder to see through misty eyes.

'I know men like Bentley Drummle. If it's a battle of strength, then he will win. But...' His pause is long, and calculated to make me look at him. He continues only when I do so. 'But if it is a match of cunning, you will win. You are far cleverer than your husband, Estella – and the brain rarely loses.'

His stare would be impenetrable to most, but I have known him all my life. I nod. Pain shoots across my ribs, taunting me. *What use is cunning when he can do to me what Orlick did to Mrs Gargery*, it asks.

Fear freezes my words in my throat. I can't reply.

Yet there is a spark, deep inside me that refuses to be blown out. Instead, it glows all the brighter in the growing storm, building to a fire...

I will not let fear win. I will not accept my fate meekly. I will not run. Jaggers is right: my husband has bested my body only. I can use my mind to get out of this. But how?

Chapter Sixty-Three

THEN

LONDON, 1833

There are some people who are drawn to each other, without logic, without reason. Bentley was unlike the other moths who were drawn to my flame; he kept just enough distance not to get his wings singed. It made me notice him. It made me *keep* noticing him. While others fluttered around, pulling ever closer, Bentley stared from across the room, a smirk of superior amusement on his face, whistling as if he didn't have a care in the world. The whistling annoyed me. It was rude and unnecessary, and made me confused because it was so at odds with the intense way he watched my every move like a lion sizing up a tiger.

I vowed to ignore him because his presence only caused irritation for me.

He wasn't even handsome. He was naturally stocky, and had the beginnings of a paunch and redness of pallor that hinted at overindulgence in food and drink – but it was his arrogance that made him unattractive. The constant proud tilt to his jaw caused him to look at the world at a permanent angle. His clothes were expensive but he was careless with them to the point of excess: wine stains all over his hand-embroidered waistcoat, a jagged tear in his silk shirt, he didn't care. He seemed to go out of his way to spoil what was beautiful. His hair was always messy and it occurred to me that to always be so very disarranged meant that it must in fact be carefully arranged that way. Why? It irked me so that I wanted to march over and demand to know why he felt himself above such basic manners as brushing one's hair and not whistling in company.

I was definitely going to ignore him.

The more I watched, through careful glances, the more I noticed. He seemed to repel and draw people to him all at once, as if they knew him to be dangerous but couldn't help themselves. Sometimes he was surrounded by a fawning pack of other young men his age, all rich and eager and braying with laughter at his every carefully dropped word; other times he only had to give them a look to send them scuttling.

This made me all the more curious. They found him odious and yet couldn't keep away from him, in fact they seemed desperate to curry favour. It didn't seem possible. But then I remembered another predator from my youth.

Back on the marshes or hiding in the long grasses of the garden at Satis House, I had often seen weasels hunting. At first glance their sausage bodies and short legs were a comical combination, but they were fierce, lightning fast and tenacious, and I'd seen them take down rabbits far bigger than themselves within a heartbeat, then drag them away to feast upon. For this reason of course, as soon as a rabbit sees one, it bolts in fear and the chase is on. But the weasel sometimes does a curious thing: it dances. The rabbit or mouse seems so surprised that it stops, despite itself, to watch. The weasel leaps acrobatically, shakes and somersaults and twirls about, seemingly dancing for the joy of it, but it is a dance of death, for all the time it is slowly moving closer and its prey is stepping closer, too. They are drawn to each other. And then the weasel is so close that its prey can feel its fur ruffled by the breeze the movement is kicking up, but still they don't move, unable to take their eyes from the thing that they know can kill them, but which is acting in such an uncharacteristic way.

And then the weasel strikes. The dance of death's final bloody steps have been taken.

Bentley was like the dancing weasel, dazzling his prey to come closer, fascinated despite themselves.

Then I realised something else. I was a dancing weasel, too.

Like all sensible apex predators, we avoided one another for a long time while simultaneously keeping a wary eye on each other. But one day at a ball, after staring long and hard, he pushed himself away from the pillar he'd been leaning against and walked across the room. A hot knife through butter, he slid through the men gathered around me begging for their names to go on my dance card, and ridiculously held out his hand as if to rescue me.

He didn't utter a word, just looked at me.

I found myself taking it.

The dance of death had begun.

Bentley may have looked like a toad, but he was surprisingly elegant as we waltzed. Around and around we swirled, until I was so disorientated that the room blurred and only we existed.

Still he hadn't spoken to me. I was not going to break the ice.

'That's a very nice dress you're wearing,' he said suddenly, in a slightly gruff manner.

I thanked him.

'Unusual colour. Not many could pull that... brightness off.'

That pause...

The compliment discombobulated me. Was my magenta gown too bright? I had wondered that myself but had been pleased to be one of the first to wear the latest dye innovation.

On we swirled.

'Your cravat is very... ornate.' I replied. My pause deliberate.

He threw his head back and laughed. After that he told me a little bit about himself, and of course, dropped in the fact that he was almost a baronet, if only seven people ahead of him were to die. It was mentioned with a casual air but it was clear that it meant to impress.

I did not bother pretending to be impressed. Please. I was being pursued by lords.

At the end of the dance, he took my hand and kissed it, of course, like they all always did. He looked deep into my eyes. A heartbeat, two, three passed.

This is the declaration of how beautiful I am, I thought, *how wonderful I am and how he desires to spend more time with me. As per usual.*

Finally, he spoke. 'Do you like France?'

'I lived there for several years. They have beautiful cuisine.'

'Uh-huh. I thought so.'

'Do you spend a lot of time over there?'

'Yes.'

I was left confused for a moment, wondering where the conversation was going. If indeed it was going anywhere.

'Yes, I thought I could detect a hint of garlic on your breath.'

With that he kissed my hand and walked away, leaving me mortified. Nobody else had mentioned it. Why hadn't anybody else mentioned it?

I left the ball early. At my lodgings I immediately loaded my toothbrush up with as much powder as it could hold and scrubbed vigorously. Finally, satisfied, I rang for my maid.

'Would you like a new dress? You may have this one, if you like.'

She was effusive in her thanks. As she held it up against herself, beaming, I was pleased. It was far too bright. How common and vulgar.

Bentley hadn't used those words, but I felt in my bones that my second-class blood was there for all to see, showing out despite my breeding, whenever I let my guard down.

Time passed, each day identical to the last. My movements could be tracked by the broken men I left behind me like a trail of breadcrumbs in a forest. If there was a big, bad wolf, it was me. All the men vying for my hand fell away one by one. The only person who was rejected and remained (for Pip only spoke in hints and never actually asked for my hand) was Bentley Drummle.

The first time he proposed to me, he spoke nonsense about hearts and flowers and romance, which was so fake that I laughed – actually laughed – and had to turn my head away.

'If you're going to lie, why not promise me the moon, too? Or as many diamonds as there are stars in the sky.' I smiled, hiding most of my amusement behind my fan but fooling no one.

'Young lady, I am a catch. I may become Sir Bentley Drummle one day,' he blustered. How quickly he caught himself, though, and instead threw back his head and gave that great, barking laugh of his that spoke of sharp teeth and snapping jaws. 'Lord! You won't be taken in as easily as the rest of your simpering sex, will you? I shall have to get up early in the morning to catch you.'

'Mr Drummle, you would have to stay up all night long to be early enough for that feat.'

He laughed again and nodded. Challenge accepted. Then asked me to dance. His name was next on my card, so I felt obliged to accept. I was taken aback by how well he had taken my rejection. I braced myself for honeyed words of persuasion, or perhaps bitterness and recriminations, for I had experienced those and everything in between. One young man (I want to say Henry or Hugo, or possibly Hector. I'm almost certain it began with an H) had even threatened to end his life if he couldn't have me. To my knowledge, his family had whisked him away to their country pile, where his nerves were nursed by a kindly second cousin of a quiet and calm disposition, whom he eventually married, and they never again entered London.

Bentley was a different animal, however. He simply made polite conversation as if he had never proposed. Long afterward I found myself chewing my lip trying to understand, but finally shrugged and realised that as he had not meant a single word he had said, of course he had not cared a jot at the refusal.

Still, I found it… unsettling… that he had taken my rejection so well when others had been almost destroyed by it. I pondered the puzzle of Bentley Drummle often.

Bentley continued to attend all the social gatherings, and acted as if nothing had changed between us for several months. He still skulked nearby, a lion frightening off rivals to his pride, or stared at me from across the room as if he was Franz Mesmer. Sometimes he would dance with me, though, speaking in that authoritative way of his that was clearly used to having every word obeyed. Nothing changed between us. That was the curious thing.

I admired his resilience, if nothing else.

Something about his unflappability made me start taking note of what he said at the social events. I told myself that it was because he wasn't interested in fawning over me like other men were and telling lies to ingratiate themselves. He told the truth, and saw me for who I truly was. If my hair looked a bit strange at the back, or the cut of my dress didn't flatter my figure as much as it could, he informed me. When he said something nice, it felt like a real achievement, and so it meant something to me. Although, he would quite often comment in a way that felt like a compliment but also had me blinking rapidly. Something about his directness both hurt and appealed.

I told myself it was grounding; that I needed someone in my life who saw me for me, without my pedestal. What rot. Now, I see that he was taking advantage of insecurities that already existed. The reason why his critical words resonated wasn't because he spoke the truth, but because he echoed my inner fears. Some people have that ability to see somebody and just know where their vulnerabilities lie, and Bentley was just such a man.

Without realising it, I was becoming a fish who enjoyed the deliciously painful tug of the hook in my mouth that reeled me ever closer to being landed.

Chapter Sixty-Four

THEN

SATIS HOUSE, 1834

'Remind me, Estella, who was the fellow who sent you that ruby necklace?' Mother's voice quivered with pride. 'No expense spared, only the very best for this beauty, you know, Pip. They all fall over themselves to turn her head, but she is far above them all. Aren't you, Estella?'

All I could bring myself to do was to incline my head slightly, then turn away to stare at the fire.

Pip often escorted me on my regular visits home from London society to see Mother, acting as a chaperone to keep me safe during my travels as it was frowned upon by society for me to travel alone.

We three sat by the fire and Mother clutched my hand, as usual, and demanded I retell tales already recounted in my letters to her. She wanted me to relive triumphs and thus hurt Pip.

Her love was as suffocating as a blanket tangled about me and over my head, and I longed to throw it off. Along with many other things, it was getting harder lately to put up with.

Unable to get a response from me, she continued to bait our guest. I watched her huge shadow on the ceiling as it swooped over him.

'How does she use you, Pip?' she asked in a stage whisper. From the corner of my eye I spied him glance at me, embarrassed. It was exasperating and unseemly behaviour from Mother. Pip did so much for us, had proved himself to be more like family – in the truest sense, not like the Pockets. How I wished she would stop baiting him and leave him alone. I gently extracted my hand from her iron grip and as she tried to tease confessions of admiration for me from Pip, I slid my arm out, which had been drawn through hers.

'What!' she shouted at me.

'Sorry, I am tired and just wanted to shift position, that is all.'

'More like you're tired of me. Such ingratitude!' She struck the floor with her walking stick. 'How can you be so stone-hearted to one who raised you and fed you with the bleeding remnants of my heart until you grew into a strong, fine lady?'

'There's no ingratitude. I know I owe everything to you. All that is good, all that is bad, all that I am is because of you. If you see what you do not like in the creature you created, who is to blame for it?'

Pip shifted uncomfortably, not knowing where to look. He opted for staring at the only other animate thing in the house – the flickering fire. Mother turned to him in wild appeal.

'You see how I love her. You know the jealous, burning love I have bathed her in. Yet I receive nothing in return.'

This was too much.

'Everything I do is for you. My whole life has been devoted to your wants, needs and visions; all has been sacrificed on the altar of your making. Do not accuse me of lacking in love for you. But if I can't show it, it is because I have learned too well the lessons you drilled into me from the moment I first sat on that stool at your feet.'

'So imperious, so contemptuous,' moaned Mother, pushing away her grey hair with both hands.

'At your behest. You have schooled me, and rewarded me for excelling.'

Mother swayed in her seat, holding her head in her hands as if it may explode from pain. The frenzies were something I had known all my life, and the only way to deal with them was to stay totally calm and emotionless.

'You taught me that the giving and receiving of love is a terrible thing that will hurt,' I tried to explain. 'You raised me to be incapable of it, Mother; therefore, though I feel for you more than anyone else in this world, it is only as deeply as I have been made capable of doing *by you.*'

She gave a low moan and slid to the floor among the dust. Pip made a movement with his hand to catch my eye and I nodded. He slipped from the room.

I stood up and went over to Mother.

'My life is not a jewel on the table for you to pick up when you desire, then return to the exact same, dust-filled place,' I hissed. She cowered from me. 'You barely eat, because I am the tasty morsel from which you gain all sustenance. Beware that you don't devour me completely.'

The mewling cry of a helpless child escaped her lips. How my cold heart hated her at that moment. I could have comforted and calmed her in my old way, but I was exhausted by her clinging to me like the strands of a sticky web. There wasn't a single part of me that hadn't been given over to her and her whims, and still it wasn't enough. I turned on my heel and walked from the room.

My steps were as fast as my mind as I stalked furiously along the High Street, running through – and from – that argument with Mother. The summer sun made me squint, adding to my angry frown.

On the other side of the road, coming towards me, was Biddy. She and Pip had become friends at school; were they still? I wondered how much Pip had to do with her now that he had outgrown this town and become, for want of a better word, a snob, since becoming a gentleman. He never spoke of her any more, but the memory of how his eyes had softened when her name was on his lips, and how my stomach had soured as a result, returned to me; and so I found myself studying her.

She had grown into a pretty young woman, a few years older than I. She was shorter than I, too. My glance deepened. Her head was bent to the ground, the picture of humility, and little wisps of fair hair escaped from beneath her old-fashioned mob cap and caught the sun so that she appeared almost to have an angelic glow. She looked exactly the kind of person Pip should be in love with, if his head hadn't been turned by Satis House.

I was about to look away and walk on, when I noticed she was biting her lip as if something was troubling her. Every few steps, she glanced over her shoulder. Finally, she turned about-face, her hands balled up in fists as she clenched the material of her skirts.

The person walking a few feet behind her slouched up. I would have known that hulking, skulking gait anywhere. Dolge Orlick.

But it was unlike any Orlick I had seen before, for this one widened his mouth in a terrifying semblance of a smile and seemed to, well, caper, if such a description can be applied to someone so incapable of the deed. As he approached her he went onto his toes and staggered about in a bent-knee, jaunty way, his head at an angle. At first I thought he must be having some kind of attack, but, no, I realised with fascinated horror, it was worse than that.

He was flirting.

Biddy didn't know what to do. While her brave feet stood fast, her body was a reed in the wind, leaning away every time he danced near and swaying back only when he drew away.

'Please, leave me alone,' she begged. I was too far away to hear her, but could divine the words from her lips and bearing. For all she was common-born she was too polite to raise her voice and cause a commotion which could reflect badly upon her.

'Burn me if that'll happen,' bellowed Orlick. He danced on. Perhaps he thought he was a weasel doing the dance of death. He was more like a charging elephant. 'Garn, smile! You look prettier when you haven't that sourpuss pout. Come closer and let me make you grin from ear to ear.'

Biddy's voice remained low but she seemed determined even in her fear. She spoke again, trying to appeal to a kindness a man like him did not possess.

'Dance with me!' he said. Catching her hand and putting his arm about her waist, he twirled with her. 'We could dance a lifetime, me 'n' thee. I like to think of the ways I could make 'ee jig in private, all out a breath like. You'd like that, I can tell. You'd pretend you didn't, all coy at first, I know what you ladies are, but you'd soon show your true self along me.'

She pummelled his chest. I took a step forward, enraged. The butcher, Mr Trabb, appeared at his shop door, apron bloodied, hands on hips, and looked at the show.

'What's going on here? This man upsetting you, Biddy?' he asked.

Orlick growled but let her go. She hurried past her rescuer and into Trabb's shop without saying a word. Her flushed cheeks and reddened nose spoke of threatening tears. The butcher took a step forward into the street.

'Blood and bone, I'll set my cap at whosoever I want,' Orlick growled.

'Not if she don't want it.'

Orlick stepped closer to him, pulling his great fists up his body as if they weighed heavier than the forge hammers. They were huge, his knuckles wide and flat. If the butcher was intimidated it didn't show. He folded his bulky arms and eyeballed Orlick.

In the window appeared Biddy's pale face. The former gatekeeper looked at her. Thought. Then stretched his body and yawned.

'You want to watch yourself with a temper like that,' he told Trabb. 'Get you into trouble one day, it will. Good job I'm a peaceable man myself.'

He walked away and calm was once more restored to the High Street.

That incident between Biddy and Orlick stayed with me as I took care of some errands, informing Pumblechook of a rent rise for his corn chandler shop, and buying some new knitting needles and yarn for myself. Who did Orlick think he was to treat women thus? What he had said to Biddy was disgusting, no wonder she had felt threatened: his meaning had been obvious. He was a danger – look what he had done to Mrs Gargery. Biddy could be next. Although he wanted a relationship with her now, how long would it be before he grew angry with her for not choosing him?

My knife, the one cleverly concealed in a fan, was in my pocket. As I walked towards home I rubbed my fingers over the guard to soothe my distracted thoughts – when who should stumble into view but Orlick. If he'd been the worse for drink during his encounter with Biddy, he was positively bory-eyed now. He rolled along the pavement and out into the marsh, following the path only approximately. He growled and muttered at the dark clouds gathering above and sometimes sang fragments of an unrecognisable tune. He swore at tufts of grass that tried to trip him up, and bushes that leapt in front of him to snag his clothes, and even a cow got a telling-off for looking at him askance and 'asking for trouble'.

I followed at a good distance, my anger and knife giving me courage.

Chapter Sixty-Five

THEN

FARMER RIPLEY'S BARN, 1834

Why I was following Orlick I couldn't say. There was little thought other than that of a hunter seeing the irresistible sight of injured prey. There was no logic. Instead, an inescapable instinct seemed to take control of me.

Orlick finally reached his destination. The barn belonged to a farmer named Ripley, who was a tenant of Mother's, so what was Orlick doing in there?

I crept forward. Then changed my mind and angled my approach towards the side of the barn, to lessen the chances of being seen. I tried to find a handy crack in the wooden boards to press my eye to, but Ripley took good care of this building. I sidled around to the door, which Orlick had left wide open despite the growing chill in the air, presumably too drunk to even notice. If I peered around to look inside, he would see me instantly, silhouetted against the daylight, and the thought made my heart ratchet up in pace, though not in an unpleasant way. My quarry was cornered but dangerous and I still had no idea what my plan was. Perhaps I should just walk away.

A strange sound started up. Like the bass buzz of a thousand bumble-bees, followed by a sort of strangled choke for breath and a long, rasping sigh. It came again. Only on the third hearing did I realise what it was: snoring.

It presented an interesting opportunity.

Lifting up my skirts so they didn't brush the ground and alert him to my approach, I stepped into the barn. It took a moment for my eyes to adjust to the dark interior before I spotted the body collapsed onto a pile of hay.

An opportunity indeed, but what to do with it?

I found a clump of dirt so dried and hardened that it was like a stone, then hid behind more hay. Popped up and lobbed the stone. It bounced off Orlick's forehead into the straw. I almost giggled. His snoring stopped. And started again. His eyes had not opened. He was utterly intoxicated.

Feeling safe now, I cast around the barn trying to think of what to do. Orlick was huge, strong and violent, and I was no match for such a foe physically. But when it came to wits I outmatched him easily.

I thought of Biddy and the fear in her eyes as he'd pawed at her and made lewd suggestions. Biddy was nothing to me, why should I put myself in danger for her? But it wasn't about her; it was about him. A man thinking he could do whatever he wanted, whenever he wanted. Who saw women as nothing more than someone to obey him and never answer back; to do what he willed, and then accept being cast aside. He had killed a woman whose only crime had been to fearlessly stand up to him.

How many other women had he hurt?

He needed to be punished.

All Mother's words about men rushed to my head so they pounded like blood in my ears.

Hurt them before they hurt you…

Take their power and use it against them…

Destroy them…

I stood over the helpless drunk, the knife in my hand, my head and heart thrumming so that I could no longer think. It would be so easy to end his life. No one would be worse off for his loss, and some would be left far better off. My feet moved forward seemingly of their own volition and—

I forced myself to step away and breathe. What was wrong with me? How could these thoughts enter my head even for a moment?

Spotting some rope hanging coiled from a hook, I had an idea.

Sidling around Orlick's prone body, which was covered with a scattering of hay, I took the coil of rope down from the hook, and looked at him again. He was still snoring, though it was lighter now than before. I prodded him gently with my foot, ready to run. He didn't notice, still passed out from all the alcohol he'd drunk before and after that encounter on the High Street with Biddy. Thinking again about the casual way he'd threatened and cajoled her nudged the devil in me into action. Sliding the knife into my pocket freed my hands so I could lift his arm – by God, it was heavy. He didn't react in any way, though, and one wrist was gently but swiftly bound. I lifted his other, concentrating on keeping my movements gentle.

Something had changed. Something I couldn't quite discern didn't feel right. I glanced up at his face. He was still out of it. I shifted my grip on the rope and got back to work.

Huge fingers encased my wrists. With a cry of horror, I tried to jump back but was caged. Orlick was awake – of course, that's what I'd noticed without realising: he'd stopped snoring when he was pretending to be asleep. He pulled me to him so our faces were inches from each other, and pulled a slow, horrible smile. His breath made me want to pass out, the alcohol fumes were so strong.

'What do we have here? Does the fine lady fancy a bit of rough with old Orlick? I can give you what you need.'

He kissed me roughly. I bit down on his lip, tasting blood. With a shout, he lashed out, sluggish with booze. I dodged and rolled, jumped up again, but although I was faster and smaller than he, he was used to brawling. My tight corset and the weight of seven petticoats encumbered me. It was an uneven match, for sure. Another heavy blow; this time it landed. Within seconds he had floored me, his weight rolled on top of me.

I kicked and yelled and struggled with all my might. Nothing shifted him. His lips were all over my face, his hands pawing at my clothes. My mind abandoned me and there was only fear. All I could do was lash out and try to reach the knife in my pocket. Almost there. No, I had to pull away to stop Orlick getting hold of my hands. Once he did that I'd be helpless. I tried again. His hip was in the way. Panic overwhelmed me.

The darkness of the barn seemed to engulf me until it disappeared. Flashes of Mrs Gargery; she was all I could see. *The sharp crack of Orlick's blow. Her skull opening. The thump of her body hitting the floor. The pool of blood in which she lay growing slowly bigger, her head reflected in its gloss. Gasping, gasping, gasping for breath, her fingers twitching as if to catch the vitality escaping her.*

'The harder you fight, the more fun to be had when I conquer you,' said Orlick. His words cut through, snapping me from panic to focus. He'd got my hands over my head and was leaning up on his elbows to leer down at me, smug in his victory.

Now!

I brought my knee up sharp between his legs. He let go my wrists as he curled up on himself like a cooked shrimp and I lashed out, landing a lucky blow to his Adam's apple. He fell onto me, winded. The breath knocked from my own lungs, and pain fired through my ribs, but I pushed at his dead weight. Somehow, I rolled him off me, got to my knees, gasping. Couldn't stand yet, still fighting for breath, but I had more than him, for now. Thinking fast, I whipped out the knife – and shoved it between his legs where he lay, stopping short of stabbing him.

He shrank away, as he fought for breath. Unable to speak, all he could do was look at me, knowing that for the time being the mouse had bested the cat.

It was my turn to smile. I pressed the knife into the cloth. He whimpered.

'If you move an inch against me – as much as a hair's breadth towards me in violence – I'll turn you into a eunuch. Do you understand?'

He growled but nodded.

'I know who you are, Dolge Orlick, but most importantly I know *what* you are. I saw what you did to the blacksmith's wife, now lying cold in the ground thanks to you.'

His eyes tightened.

'That's right. I could see you dangle from the gibbet for what you've done. And if you ever bother Biddy, or me, or any other woman, that's exactly what will happen.'

It suddenly occurred to me that this was an utterly stupid threat which only served to put me in danger from him in the future. The first thing he'd want to do was eliminate me, thus ensuring the secrets I knew could never be revealed. I thought fast.

'People I trust hold a sworn written statement from me.' Jaggers, I suddenly thought; I could do exactly that with him, if I ever got out of the barn in one piece. 'He's been instructed to release this information to the authorities if anything happens to me in the future. I'm keeping quiet for now, but only if you leave all women alone, including Biddy.'

He growled.

'Or maybe I'll just cut your balls off now? What do you think? Hmm?' A little extra pressure and the cloth gave beneath the blade.

Orlick's only move was a deep swallow.

'Can you read and write?' I asked. He looked confused but shook his head. 'Very well. I'm going to hold out a blank piece of paper and at the bottom I want you to make your sign. Later I shall write out your confession to the crime against Mrs Gargery, and it shall appear as if you have signed it. Another little safeguard, see, which will stay with the lawyer friend I have.'

'Jaggers.' Fear and venom was behind that single word.

'Of course; I forgot momentarily that you know him.'

Just like Mother, I always had a notebook and pencil on a chain around my neck. It was the one she'd given me when I started running errands for her, and was handy for jotting down thoughts and ideas that may come to me out of the blue. On a page of that book, Orlick drew what looked like a T but what I took to be a great forge hammer.

All that remained was for me to leave. Orlick was watching my every move, though. The second his manhood was no longer near steel, he might just be stupid enough to kill me and damn the consequences. The rope still dangled from one of his wrists. I nodded towards an upright beam. Once he had shuffled so he was seated with his back to it, I bade him throw the rope behind it and himself then I picked up the end and ran around the beam several times, pinning his arms to his sides and tying him in place.

'Well, this was fun, but it's time for me to head homewards, Orlick. Don't forget, keep away from me and all other women or you will end up dancing not with Biddy but at the end of a short rope over a long drop.'

Stepping from the darkness of the barn into the bright sunshine seemed shocking, reminding me of my first years at Satis House. There was a spring in my step and a song in my heart the like of which I hadn't felt since my days in Paris. I was alive again.

Even in my triumph it was obvious to me that I'd acted impulsively and almost paid a terrible price.

But you didn't. And it was fun, a quieter voice in my head seemed to say. *Now THAT is power over a man – and far more exhilarating than a silly little refusal of marriage.*

The more I thought about it the more my pleasure shrank, though. What had I been thinking, to put myself in such danger? And as for threatening him with a knife that way... Yes, he had deserved it, but surely I hadn't meant to make good on my threat? No. Of course not. I'd never have hurt him, I couldn't hurt anyone.

Definitely not, I told myself. The idea was shocking.

Everything had been Orlick's fault, anyway. Damn the man. I had returned from France a lady, accepting my fate with quiet dignity – or at least, embracing the lie determined to make it the truth. Yet there, in that barn, was evidence that I would always have that evil in me which the Pockets, for all their faults, must have somehow been able to spot. Which the girls at the boarding school had noticed and rejected me for.

I pulled back my shoulders as Madame Flaubert had taught me, rectified my posture, and glided away. I would try harder. I would suppress the anger.

Somehow.

Only now, looking back across the years, do I see that I failed to see the most important thing about the entire encounter, for hindsight is always a sharper lens through which to look. I may not have believed I would butcher Orlick's manhood – but he had. That murderous thug who had lived an entire life of violence had not moved at all, had not tried to overpower me. He knew what I was capable of before even I did.

Orlick was the first to recognise me for what I was: a kindred spirit.

Chapter Sixty-Six

NOW

SATIS HOUSE, 1835

There's someone to see you, Mrs Drummle. I know you said you weren't to be disturbed by anyone, but he is most insistent.' Lydia dances from one foot to the other.

Bentley. It has to be. He's come at last from Paris, determined to return me to our nightmare honeymoon. I try to stand but my legs are suddenly too weak.

But Lydia shakes her head. 'He says he was sent by Mr Drummle, though.'

Ah, a show of power by my husband. I am not even worth dealing with directly, instead he thinks he can click his fingers and I'll come running.

I put down my knitting and walk from Mother's bedroom.

'Be careful,' she calls after me.

My legs feel strange and wobbly, like a newborn lamb taking its first steps. A deep breath and I force myself to stand straighter.

Shoulders back, head up, Estella.

I walk into the reception room and there is Joseph, Bentley's trusted servant. He stands when he sees me, hat tucked neatly under his arm.

'Mrs Drummle, forgive the intrusion, but I wanted to give you an update on what I've discovered about Camilla Pocket.'

My lips part in confusion I'm not convinced I hide. Joseph ploughs on.

'I found nothing of interest about Mrs Pocket herself, but her husband Mr Raymond Pocket is another thing, entirely. He has quite the reputation among certain circles for loving a game of cards, and has run up considerable debts. His luck ebbs and flows, but he is generally in debt to various...' He trails off, searching for the right word. '...insalubrious types.' He misinterprets my befuddlement. 'Crooks and card sharps and the like,' he expands.

Oh! I had completely forgotten about the conversation Bentley and I had at our wedding – several lifetimes ago, it now feels. He had suggested he get Joseph to investigate Camilla to see why she hated me so much, insisting there was probably a secret there. It seems he was right. Camilla's desperation to get her hands on more money is almost certainly driven by the desire to wipe out her husband's debts. Who knows, perhaps they are often under threat of violence from the people they owe. Knowing she is struggling to deal with the repercussions of a man's bad decisions puts her in a different light. It almost makes me feel sorry for her. But trying to kill me when I was a child, simply to solve her problems, was unforgiveable. Even now, I fear that she and Sarah might try to move against me again once Mother is gone – but that problem is many years away, thank goodness.

The main question haunting me currently though is: why is Joseph telling me all this?

Has Bentley not informed anyone that we're estranged? Perhaps he is ashamed of his actions. Or is allowing Joseph to come to me with this information his way of subtly saying: *I know where you are and I'm in no hurry to get to you – yet.*

'Thank you, Joseph. This is enlightening. You've done well. Did Mr Drummle send any message with you?'

'He is still in France, ma'am.'

'Of course. Of course...'

We exchange a look. There is the strangest sensation Joseph is trying to weigh me up as much as I'm trying to appraise him. To what purpose? Surely not to aid me against his master? I should dismiss him. Yet, perhaps there's more to glean from him. I realise I'm chewing the inside of my cheek and stop immediately.

'It's, er, very interesting, in fact, what you've discovered. I always thought Camilla was the force behind their actions, never imagined Raymond – dull as he is – would have any exciting secrets. A gambler. Appearances can be deceiving, can't they?'

I'm desperately trying to reach for a subtext he will understand, and can't quite grasp it.

'Everyone has their secrets,' he replies. Each word seems deliberate. Perhaps it is my imagination. 'Not everyone is as lucky as Mr Raymond Pocket to have such loyalty, though.'

Is that a criticism of me? Or a hint that he is not as dutiful to Bentley as he should be?

'Oh? Well, not everyone deserves it. I'm certainly not sure he does,' I reply, biting back a snap.

He cocks his head on one side and gives me a long look before answering. 'Appearances can be deceiving, as you said. Those that seem to display the staunchest devotion can often lie at the heart of someone's undoing. That is, if the person deserves to be taken down for some reason.' He leans forward, conspiratorial, and thoroughly unservant-like. 'It can be useful, sometimes, seeming steadfast while plotting someone's downfall, for example. And we all have our personal limits on what we will put up with.' He straightens up. 'Perhaps Mrs Camilla Pocket is of that belief. Of course, this is only conjecture on my part.'

'This has been most illuminating, Joseph. Thank you for your report. I trust that one day I will win your loyalty, and perhaps even eclipse that which you give my husband.'

We both laugh lightly. There is no mistaking the understanding we have reached.

Joseph doesn't approve of Bentley's actions – whether against me or involving something else, I can't be certain right now. Until I can be sure I won't be speaking more openly to him. Subtext will suffice. Can someone who switches allegiance from their master who pays their wages, to another person, really be trusted?

However, an allegiance with a man skilled at digging out information on anyone and everyone could be very handy in my coming war against my husband.

I spend the evening with Mother, playing Beggar My Neighbour; me in the armchair and she in her bed, while we talk. Her cheeks are pink with health since she has started taking the air, although she still isn't walking as much as she should.

'You acted perfectly,' Mother says after I have told her in full about the conversation with Joseph. 'Not too trusting, but enough to bring him to you if he really is tired of Drummle's ways. He could be very useful. Ah-ha, an ace!'

'If he could spy for me, tell me what Bentley is up to,' I reply, laying down four cards.

Mother is already reaching to scoop them up before I've put the fourth down. Her hands sparkle, for she has taken to wearing her rings again now her hands are healed, and her necklaces. It had worried me that she might be sliding back into her old ways, but she seemed to read my mind and explained that she missed the feel of them, but did not miss her wedding dress at all. She told me that now Compeyson had left this earth she felt no desire to wear her old gown, even if it weren't burned to cinders.

I playfully flap her hand out of the way. 'Not so fast, I have a knave. And... ah, I win the cards.'

We start a new game, and again take turns to put down cards between us.

'So what will you do next?' she asks.

'With your permission, I should like to start buying jewellery, as Mr Jaggers suggested.'

'I'll arrange for a lump sum to be withdrawn from the bank for you. There's five hundred pounds in that box over there, so start with that.'

'Not the safest of hiding places, Mother, but yes, I'll take it with thanks. I may invest some – no, Mother, you've only put down two cards and a king is three. What was I saying? Yes, I may invest some in bribing Joseph.'

'Careful you don't insult him. If he is transferring his allegiance to you because of his scruples, it might be damaging to offer him a reward.'

'How many scruples can he have when his job is to investigate others and find their secrets? Oh, you're out of cards – I win.'

'Again.' Mother yawns. 'Time to retire. I might take a little laudanum, tonight, to help me sleep.'

'Oh? Is everything all right?'

We've been reducing the amount she uses for a couple of weeks now, and she hasn't taken any at night for three days.

'Just a pain in my leg, that's all.'

She shows me only after being nagged. The skin is still pink but is healing well – far better than we had dared to hope. Her left calf does look a little red and swollen, though. It's hot against my fingertips.

'We'll call the doctor if it's still like this tomorrow. Better safe than sorry,' I say.

'If it's warm tomorrow I have a mind to sit outside,' says Mother. Her voice is carefully casual, as if this were not the first time in more than a score of years since she set foot past the walls of the manor house. 'We could visit Aurora's resting place, perhaps.'

'Well, it is Good Friday tomorrow, so let's hope for fair weather,' I say, keeping my voice equally as light. 'We should see some butterflies if we're outside.'

'And smell some blossom. You know, now Everard is dead, I feel different, somehow. Better. I'll never be a gad-about-town, for there is no desire in me to go beyond the boundaries of the grounds here, but there is no harm in the daylight and natural world.'

She drinks down her draught of rhubarb water and laudanum, and I kiss her on the cheek.

'You've been a wonderful nursemaid, far better than I deserve,' she says.

'Who decides which person is deserving?'

We chuckle and say our goodnights, but as I close the door, Mother tries to have the last word.

'I love you, Estella.'

'I love you, too, Mother. Now go to sleep!'

Chapter Sixty-Seven

THEN

SATIS HOUSE, 1834

lthough I did not fully realise the importance of my encounter with Orlick, I knew it was evidence of something wrong within me. For all my ice-queen act, that impetuous fire from the years prior to Paris was evidently still burning. It disturbed me that it had leaked through and influenced my behaviour, and I started to fear it might happen again. I couldn't help but feel the strain of living a lie was exacerbating my problems. As much as I tried to only act and think and feel the way Mother instructed, I was not a piece of machinery. Never being allowed to be my true self, and keeping my emotions at bay, was becoming an increasing struggle. Frustration and anger were once again turning into mercurial, volcanic behaviour, and that simply could not be allowed, for it would destroy all chance of a future for myself. I would end up in an asylum.

As summer greens were replaced by autumn's furnace of colours, I continued to ponder. Something needed to change in my life, that much was obvious. But how? Mother still wanted me to break men's hearts and wreak her revenge, but realistically how much longer could I do that for?

I must choose a different life. One for myself. It was time for me to have a serious talk with Mother. As soon as I arrived at Satis House, she seemed to sense there was an ulterior motive for my appearance, for she watched me through half-closed eyes reminiscent of the snakes I had seen on a visit to London Zoological Gardens.

'Do you remember once, many years ago, I asked you about the possibility of reopening the brewery?' I began. Her eyes grew more hooded. 'You were right, of course, to refuse me – I was not ready then for such a huge undertaking.'

She nodded, rested her chin on her hands, atop her cane. 'Go on, go on. Speak what is in your heart, and do not attempt to butter me up.'

'Very well. I am ready, now. Mother, I am desperate for the chance to use my brain. You raised me to abhor men and I do! That is precisely why I do not desire a traditional life, but instead want to forge my own way.'

Her head reared up, the cane lifted... cracked down with a storm of dust. 'Never! Never will those doors open again. All these years of pretending to do my will when all the time you are as self-serving as those vipers, the Pockets.'

'Mother—'

'Oh, that I should live to see this day!'

'You've lived because of me. I have tended to you. I have fulfilled your every cruel whim. You live through me, but you will not do this one thing for me? Please, Mother, I can't keep living this life, it is killing me, I... I'm begging you.'

The candlelight made her eyes glitter. 'You think me old and feeble and foolish, that you can wheedle your way around me so artlessly. Child, I survived the greatest liar there has ever been; do you think I can't see that you only pretend to care for me so that you can steal everything I have?'

'What do you have, Mother? A dwindling fortune? A house that is rotting around you? A heart so shrivelled that it resembles prey the spiders have sucked dry of all blood?' I took a deep breath. 'I don't want to argue with you. Please, I am asking you... This would be the perfect solution. I could stay here with you – just think, we could be together. I'd never want to marry, the business would be more than enough for me – it's all I desire. To make something of myself, to have independence, to be useful.'

That familiar moan, starting low and building, made me close my eyes in despair.

'We could be together,' I tried again.

'Never! Never!' She shook her head, beat herself with her frail fists. 'Never! Never!'

It was no use.

Mother had stopped me from reopening the brewery, but she would not stop me from having agency over my life. There was only one alternative open to all ladies if working was barred to us. Marriage. It didn't seem feasible for me, though. I could not love someone, I was no longer capable of it. Nor did I wish to tie myself to someone who loved me, for I'd only make them miserable, and couldn't even enjoy it because where was the fun in torturing just one person for the rest of my days?

There was one final possibility, however...

Sunlight streamed through French doors, which had been thrown open to admit the fresh autumn air. Bentley and I sat on the patio, on cane furniture recently bought by Mrs Brandley. Bentley's eyes ran over my face, and his smile was full of appreciation at what he saw.

'Lord, but you really are the most beautiful creature. You know' – he shifted closer. Was he going to try to kiss me? – 'you have one eye slightly smaller than the other. It's most curious.'

I moved away abruptly and laughed, while planning to spend some time before a looking glass, studying my wonkiness.

'Don't be ashamed. It's a compliment. No one else but I would notice, I'm sure, because they don't study you as I do. I see you, Estella Havisham. Your imperfections make you all the more attractive to me.' He took my hand. 'Estella, marry me. Marry me and together we will build a future that will make everyone jealous.'

A sound came from inside the room of a page turning. Mrs Brandley and Miss Lucy were sitting chaperoning us and ostentatiously not listening to our conversation.

'How?' I tried for dismissive curiosity – a tough one to hit.

'I want a career in politics; one day I will be prime minister of this land, and that's only the beginning – the true benefits come afterwards.

Think of the business opportunities, the profits to be had from such prestige. By my side I need someone with beauty but also brains; that person is you.'

My chin raised in appraisal. 'You don't speak of love or hearts and flowers.'

'To you? Of course not. I know you better: I speak of power-sharing.'

Power-sharing. Now that did snag at my heart appealingly. 'So what you propose is not marriage but a business arrangement?'

'More a marriage that benefits both parties.'

'Let me speak frankly, Mr Drummle: I'm not interested in sharing a marriage bed with anyone, nor in producing children. Any woman who does that immediately loses all sovereignty over herself, and I'm not fool enough to do so.'

He pouted, considering. Finally he nodded. 'You wish for all business? Very well. Accept my proposal and there won't be a single person who won't look at us and feel envy. We will be the talk of the town. We will hold all of London in our thrall, Estella. Everyone will want to be like us. And then – then it will be the whole damned country who will be under our influence. Lord, together, nothing can stop us.'

'You really want a partner? You will listen to my ideas and give them as much weight as your own?'

'Of course. We are nothing if not honest with one another, Estella; it is something I value and sense you do, too.'

What he said appealed. As an unmarried woman there were few options available, even with the Havisham wealth behind me. Marriage would open doors, allowing me to go through society free of the shackles of constant attention and flirtation from those who wished to trap me.

'None of this ridiculous hand-holding,' I said, and withdrew from his grasp. 'Tell me your business plans and I shall see if they sound enticing to me.'

He spoke of being prime minister, of sweeping to victory with me by his side. Of me building a separate 'court' which would provide a base of influence more subtle than his. I would be the power behind the government, I realised, and he would be the figurehead. He would deal with running the country while I wooed contacts who could allow us to invest in upcoming industries and factories. I'd finally become the businesswoman I had dreamed of being. My place would be unique among women.

Bentley might be odious, but I knew exactly what to expect from him, knew how to handle him. He would never be disappointed in me nor I him, for our expectations were cerebral not emotional.

This was also an opportunity to please Mother. After all, I'd be marrying one of the worst men on the marriage circuit, which would break no end of hearts all at once.

This way, though, instead of being trapped in wedlock, I'd be in control. I'd never have to feel; instead I could remain a cold, unfeeling, untouchable creature.

A new chapter was opening with no change required on my part. It sounded perfect. Although I did decide on one alteration – it was time to stop carrying weapons and embrace the life of a society lady once and for all. The old, unpredictable, scary me would be left in the past; it was time to embrace my bold new future.

'You make a good case,' I said. 'Very well, I agree.'

'Perfect.' He smiled, showing his teeth.

The wind shifted slightly, bringing with it fresh promise of ice, and so we went inside to celebrate.

Mrs Brandley was effusive in her congratulations. Miss Lucy gave me a curious look.

'You know he's a lazy, vazey hang-in-chains. Don't you? A total lobcock,' she whispered.

I was starting to like her.

When I told Mother of my impending marriage her hysteria lasted a full two days.

Chapter Sixty-Eight

THEN

SATIS HOUSE, 1834

From the moment of my engagement I was in a state of both excitement and dread. The main source of my dread was not the marriage itself, which I felt sure was a necessary and prudent move. Nor was it Mother's histrionics. It was all about Pip's reaction.

My stomach churned so much it could have made butter from milk. Like Camilla, I found myself taking ginger. Like Mother, I was tempted to pace the corridors in the small hours of the night. I knitted in frenzied fashion, with stockings growing at alarming speed as my needles clacked in time with my whirling mind.

The moment of dread finally arrived a handful of days after my engagement. We were in the dressing room, and I was sitting on a cushion at Mother's feet, knitting to hide my agitation, when Pip swept in. His eyes were fever-bright, cheeks red, and there was such an air about him as I had never seen before. Mother and I exchanged a look, wondering what had caused such high emotion, for my engagement had not yet been announced so it could not be that.

My heart was wild at the thought of telling him. Why? Why did Pip bring out such strange, strong emotions in me? How was it possible to feel so protected yet so vulnerable around him? Why did my skin warm at his touch but also get goosebumps? Why was there the sensation of comfort that reminded me of a cat stretching before a fire and made me smile like a simpering fool?

Why did I want to be a better person in his company?

In order to hide my silly emotions, there was only one thing to do. Act indifferent.

'What wind blows you here?' asked Mother.

Pip replied that he'd gone to Richmond yesterday and, after discovering I was here, had followed me. I didn't look up, just kept my needles moving.

He sat down at the dressing table. 'I am as unhappy as you can ever have meant me to be,' he declared to Mother. Then he launched into a meandering explanation as to why. It seemed he had discovered that his benefactor was not her, as he had always foolishly assumed. So, that was his complaint. It had been cruel of Mother to lead him on in his misapprehension, and she'd only done it to annoy the Pockets – and this Pip had finally realised.

'You made your own snares,' she replied. 'I never made mine.'

Knit one, purl one, knit one, purl one. My fingers never faltered, but my mind lingered on her words. Mother had made a snare of me and done everything in her power to lure Pip's neck into the loop that was choking the life from him. To claim otherwise was either lying to herself or him.

Still my fingers moved smoothly.

'You led me on,' he said. 'Was that kind?'

'Why should I be kind when no kindness was ever given me?' she demanded. The sharp crack of her cane connected with the floor. I glanced at her, surprised – the accusation seemed to have hit home, and I wondered why. Guilt?

There was only one way this could go. Pip, for the first time in his life, would surely grow angry. He had been used and manipulated since boyhood. An innocent child brought here to play on the whim of an unhinged woman; ritually humiliated and used as a whetstone for me to sharpen my skills in cruelty; misled into thinking what little good fortune had come his way was down to Mother purely so she could make the Pockets jealous; and always, always encouraged to love me at all cost, no matter how much it pained him. No wonder he tugged and railed against the snare that held him fast even as it bit deeper.

But instead of bitterness, he simply begged a favour of Mother not for himself but for his dear friend Herbert, with whom he had once fought over me. Several years ago, when Pip first came into his fortune, he had, without his friend's knowledge, set up an annual payment to further Herbert's career.

'For reasons I cannot go into, I'm losing my patronage and won't be able to continue doing this. He is a good, hard-working man who has never tried to profit from being your relative. Please, I beg you, take over this secret payment.'

So even as his world fell apart, his thoughts were not for himself.

'Estella,' he said finally. His voice trembled. 'You know I love you.'

Knit one, purl one, knit one, purl one. I glanced from my work and met his eyes. Took in his devastation. Saw the burning desire that brightened his cheeks. I came to the end of my row and started a new one, keeping the yarn's tension safe between my fingers.

'I've loved you from the first moment I saw you, and love you still more now. I'm not fool enough to think I'll ever call you mine, especially now that it seems I am about to become very poor again—'

What was happening in his life? Why were his prospects being pulled from under him so suddenly? I did not ask, my concentration bent on the jumper. I needed to start decreasing the stitches to shape the neckline, so mustn't lose count.

'It would have been cruel of Miss Havisham to use me so, had she thought about the impact it had on me. But I suspect that she was so busy enduring her own pain that she never truly considered the pain she inflicted.'

Decrease the row by two either side...

'All this talk of love and pain is unnecessary,' I said. 'What people think is love is really an image in their minds of someone they imagine. Those people don't really exist. You don't really love me; you love an ideal you've created of me. Mother created such an ideal with Compeyson, for otherwise she would have seen him for what he really was, not the courtly dream she had woven.'

I did it with Yvette, otherwise she never would have blinded me to her false ways, I added silently.

He said nothing.

'Pip, you blame Mother, but I warned you – repeatedly – to take care around me, that I don't reciprocate your feelings, that I am incapable of love. The happy ending you wrote for us was only ever in your dreams.'

'It cannot be true,' he begged. 'You're too young, too beautiful, to be so hardened. It's against nature.'

'It is my nature. This is how I was made, Pip; how I was forged. You are the only person I've tried to warn and save from heartbreak,

because you do mean something to me… but not in the way you want.'
I turned the row.

'You love Bentley Drummle that way?'

Finally, my fingers stilled as annoyance rose. 'You aren't listening.
I've said time and again that I can't love; why won't you believe me?'

'I know he is here in town, pursuing you.'

'We are to be married.'

Pip crumbled then. He covered his face with his hands and cried.
Actually cried. Mother's face, always pale, turned a ghastly shade of
grey. After several moments Pip was able to speak again.

'Don't throw your life away on him. He is the worst of men. Miss
Havisham gives you to him only to hurt those men who love you.
Even if you don't want me, at least choose a husband who will make
you happy and love you all your life.'

'Mother hasn't chosen him, I have. Preparations are already in place
for the wedding.'

'You choose to fling yourself away on this brute?'

'Better I "fling myself away" on a man who loves me and then realises
I can never feel the same way? But we have talked enough; there is
nothing left to say.'

'Please—'

'It is done. You'll forget about me in a week.'

He took my hand. Tears fell onto it. 'Never. You've been my every
thought since I was a child. You're in everything I see, all I hear, you
shape my hopes and dreams.' He raised my hand to his lips so fervently.
'May God forgive you for making this mistake, Estella.'

After Pip had fled from the room, Mother did not speak, did not move.
She sat with her hand over her heart, seemingly holding it in place in
case it spilled forth. I set my knitting down and stood, stepping from
the circle of light cast by the fire and the candles in the wall sconces,
and into the twilight of the room.

'Pip is right.' Mother's voice cut through the deadened atmosphere. 'Do not marry Bentley. You… you deserve to have someone who loves you, who stands by your side always and looks after you—'

'It's a little late for such talk,' I scoffed. 'You know he'll be arriving any moment. We're spending the evening putting the final touches to the wedding plans – or had you conveniently forgotten?'

'He will hurt you. A man like that is only out for himself. Why have you chosen to bind yourself to the worst man you could find?'

'Because it is what you trained me for.' My voice rose. I clenched my fists and opened them again slowly, bringing my voice down. 'Did you think I could go on like this forever? I am sick of my life. Pip has gone; good, he has taken my past with me. Now I am stepping into the future with Bentley. Yes, it's without love, but it's also without confusion and lies. There is honesty between us and shared visions for the future.'

Mother shrank into herself, her fingers trembling over her heart.

'It seems to me, Mother, that you want me to stay in the darkness with you – but I choose the light. There is a world out there that I'm going to embrace. I might not be happy, but at least I won't be damned miserable, brooding over missed opportunities and slowly decaying into nothingness.'

In my bedroom, I calmly set my knitting bag upon my bed and pulled out my work, tugging it here and there into shape. Yes, it was coming on nicely… damn, there was a hole. Right by the neck, where it was obvious. Right where Pip had told me he loved me.

I held it against my face, the wool so soft. My fingers sank into it. I pulled. The yarn bit into my skin, harder, harder, then parted softly as I tore it to pieces.

With a yell I swung my arms wildly. Swept everything from my dressing table with a cry. Items bounced across the floor. A crystal perfume bottle from Paris. A daisy chain Pip helped me pick that long, hot summer when I was twelve, which I'd pressed. My favourite fan, the knife flying from its hiding place.

I had broken Pip's heart. Shattered it into pieces. I knew the pain I had inflicted, for I had suffered it myself. But I'd done it for his sake. If I'd accepted his love it would only have meant worse hurt waiting for him in the years to come, when he realised my soul was emptier than a desert.

I dried my tears and set everything right. My decision was made. Bentley and I suited each other.

That was the fiction I told myself. It seemed that for all my years of bitter experience, I was still that child reading fairy tales in the library.

Chapter Sixty-Nine

NOW

SATIS HOUSE, 1835

Sleeping in my own bed is far more comfortable than the cot beside Mother, but it's only been a handful of nights since I moved back to my room and it's not been enough to get me used to being without her. Being alone is... not pleasant. Last night, while drifting into sleep, there was a tapping at my window. It was Bentley, come to taunt me. I was up in an instant, letter opener in hand as the closest thing I could find to a weapon. Staring out at the moonlit ruins of the gardens, overgrown bushes morphed into that dangerous man, laughing at me in the wind. The tap, tap, tap came again, right against the window—

It was just the branches of a tree. Nothing more.

But it was a reminder. However much time was left, eventually he would come for me. And when he did, what then?

There was no more sleep for me that night. As a result, I am up and back in Mother's room at sunrise.

The church bells are ringing as I ease the door gently open, for today is Good Friday. The curtains are drawn, the room dark, but the darkness is my old friend and I move across the room as sure-footed as if a candle is in my hand.

Then pause. That sound – Mother is panting like a dog in the midsummer sun. A bad dream, no doubt. I strike a lucifer, the white flare blinding against the gloom, and light a candle.

'Estella.' Mother can barely get my name out. She starts coughing. Sweat beads on her face. 'C-ca-can't... breathe...'

'I'm here. Everything will be fine.' I take her hand while with the other I almost yank the bell pull from the wall. Lydia arrives swiftly. 'Send for the doctor immediately.'

Mother's panting is getting faster. There's a frenzy to it; a desperation that fills me with dread. Her eyes start to roll.

'Mother! No, stay with me! The doctor is on his way.'

Pant, pant, pant…

'When you get better, think of all the things we can do together. I don't care what Bentley says, I'll never leave your side again.'

Her eyes are back on mine. Bulging wide in effort.

'That's it. Breathe with me. Nice and slow, in… out… in… out.' She tries but it's no use. What can I do? How can I help? Would more laudanum aid her?

Her hand squeezes mine. Back arches from the bed. Head digs into the pillows.

Flops down again.

'Mother!'

Silence.

'No! No, please.'

Her hand slides from mine. I pick it up. It drops again. The same thing keeps happening.

'Hold my hand. Come on, grip it. No, you-you – hold my hand. You have to hold it.'

Her chest isn't rising and falling. Her eyes are glassy.

'Don't leave me. Please, you can't leave me. We've only just become friends… I need you.'

I climb onto the bed beside her and curl my head onto her chest. There's no heartbeat.

'Mother, I love you. Please come back.'

That's how the doctor finds me when he arrives. Whether he came quickly or slowly, I have no idea. He tries to peel me from Mother's body. I cling to it, wailing; other hands join his to pull me gently but without argument.

This won't do. I need to get control over myself. I smooth my hair, my clothes, try to stand like the woman who puts fear into men's heart and not like a fool with tears making her cheeks sore.

'She was well last night, why has this happened now?' I demand.

The ice in her heart had finally melted – toward me, anyway. This had been the start of a new understanding between us.

'These things, ah-hem, come out of the blue sometimes.'

'No. She was getting better. She'd fought through everything that could have killed her; there was no sign of infection. She had a little pain in her calf last night, that's all.'

We could have lived happily in this house. We could have returned it all to the light, and been content together, independent from men.

'Describe it.' His voice is sharp and most unlike his usual tone.

I explain last night's symptoms. He ponders the ceiling before speaking.

'It's possible there was an occlusion of the vein by blood clot. They are sometimes fatal, and your adoptive mother was in frail health already. And of course you ladies are the weaker sex, you have not the strength of men to fight off such things.' He trails off delicately.

My legs seem to work on their own. I turn and walk from the room. One foot in front of the other, somehow.

Mother is dead. We finally had a natural mother-daughter relationship. We should have had years together…

I sway. Put a steadying hand out into the pitch blackness and rest it against the corridor wall.

And a smile spreads.

She's in hell now, with Everard Compeyson, just as she wants. No doubt she's already setting to her vocation of torture with something red-hot and scalpel sharp.

Mother's funeral dawns, sharp with a late spring frost. It melts in the rising sun, creating a mist that hangs low in the air, clinging to the headstones in the graveyard and creeping across the vast, flat marsh.

Although Mrs Brandley asked to come, as well as Mr Jaggers, I didn't want anyone there. Pip did not contact me. Lydia is waiting back at the house, as instructed. There is only me to listen to the vicar's sonorous voice, as monotonous as the drone of the lone bumblebee that visits a posy of flowers left on a nearby grave.

A sod of earth, a soft *thwump*, and the ceremony is over.

Wiping my hands on my handkerchief, I turn and walk from the cemetery. A figure is hovering, almost hidden behind a broad yew tree. My stomach drops. Bentley? No, it's a woman who steps onto the path in front of me.

Recognition makes my slowing heart speed again.

'What are you doing here, Yvette?'

'When are you going to accept that I will always be here for you, whenever you need me?'

'No, no one is ever there for me, truly. We are all of us on our own. Everyone always lets me down. Even you did, although you made it up to me by saving me from Bentley, so... you owe me nothing.'

'This isn't about debts. After seeing you again, I've forgiven you for not waiting for me, and... don't you know how I feel about you?'

I shove my soil-smeared handkerchief into my reticule, and start to walk away. She catches my arm. Her skin is so warm against the inside of my wrist. I soften, then remember. 'What do you mean, *you* forgive *me* for not waiting?'

'The past doesn't matter. Look at me and you'll know the truth.'

'You think my mother's funeral is the best moment for this? Leave me, Yvette.'

'I love you, Estella, and I came here to tell you that. There was no chance to before...' She hurries to catch me up as I stalk away. 'Let me say my piece.'

I don't slow. 'There was a time I was ready to give up everything for you and run away, but I'm not interested in your love any more.'

'The morning that we were meant to run away together I got word that my brother had been arrested for being a revolutionary. The little bit of money I'd kept back from selling that ring of my aunt's? I used it all to bribe Gérard's guards and free him – to fail would have cost him his life. That's why I didn't go with you.'

I stop. She hadn't abandoned me all those years ago? 'You could have told me in the note. Why should I believe you now? It's convenient, a thief turning up as I come into a fortune.'

'Please. There was no opportunity for me to tell you; everything was happening so fast that morning. I had to find the right people to bribe to save my brother's life, get the money needed, make sure it all happened; and all the time knowing you were waiting for me. I couldn't commit that information to paper – what if it had fallen into the wrong hands? It could have been used against him, me, even you. All I could do was scribble those few words. By the time I looked for you, you'd fled to England. You didn't even reply to my letter. How easily you abandoned me.'

My hands are on my hips, I open my mouth to argue…

Her excuse does make sense.

'Huh,' is all I can manage. She smiles. How well she can read me.

'Ever since then Gérard has been living in hiding, continuing his revolutionary work. And I have joined him. I have realised I cannot sit idly by any more, accepting the inequalities that pervade society, and choosing to take only for myself. Those who can take a stand for others must do so.'

She checks over her shoulder. There is no one in sight to overhear us.

'Did you ever wonder how I found you again, and came to your aid? It was not coincidence, it was fate. The man who has made my brother's life a misery, who has hounded him and been determined to see him behind bars, is Jean-François Dupont. Gérard was arrested because he was planning to kill Dupont, for he is guilty of so many crimes against the poor, owns factories that keep people working in slave-like conditions, creates legislation that means they have no chance of escaping that life ever, starves his staff and beats them.

'Gérard… he was desperate and acted foolishly. He was going to shoot Dupont, but changed his mind at the last moment. But the evidence of his plans was enough to have him thrown in jail. As if he could ever hurt anyone, he lacks the killer instinct. You know what he put in his note to me? "Sometimes we cannot give in to our desires". He is always so…' She taps her forehead. '…in his head.'

Sometimes we cannot give in to our desires. That phrase pulls a memory from the back of my mind. He and I in the parlour, waiting for Yvette to finish work. He had used those words and I had assumed he was talking about the love his sister and I shared. All along he had been trying to seek my opinion on his murderous thoughts.

Yvette continues: 'We keep an eye on Dupont through a network of spies, and when we discovered certain plans he shared with his English cousin, this Bentley Drummle, we decided to spy on him, too, if we got the chance. His Parisian honeymoon was the perfect opportunity, so I got a job in the household. Imagine my surprise at seeing who his new wife was. Still, I kept myself hidden and followed you both.'

Another memory. The shadowy figure I'd spotted several times when we first arrived in Paris, and the constant sense of being watched – it had been Yvette.

I am still, so very still, not knowing what to say or think or—

'You are hiding yourself again, just like you did when I first met you,' Yvette says. 'The mask is on and no workings show on your face, no emotions, no thoughts. You are a careful blank, but I know you. I know the fire that burns beneath your skin. Estella, run away with me now. There is nothing to stop us. We can go where Drummle will never find us.'

Tempting. So tempting.

'He would hunt me down to the ends of the earth rather than let me go again.'

'Let him. You have seen the friends I have, they are everywhere. We can bring down the aristocracy and create a world of equality together. Just think of it! There are riots coming and change will once again sweep France, bringing a new, better regime. And you and I will be at its head.'

I think about it. But not for long. My time for happily ever after ended on that French pavement years ago, when a hastily written note broke my heart.

'I am not the person you fell in love with, who loved you. I was a different woman before Bentley – someone who could have changed and lived and grown to be like other people, perhaps. What he did... it has altered me profoundly. Much as I'd like to go back in time, what was broken can't be mended.'

There is sadness to my words, but no internal struggle. I tried love and it didn't work out; I tried a marriage of business and it was a disaster. I don't know what is next for me, but it's time to move forward into it.

'Estella, I know you still love me—'

'Not enough,' I whisper. 'This is my decision: to reject love. I'm sorry you've made a wasted journey but… I do want to say thank you. I'll always treasure that time in Paris. Goodbye, Yvette.'

Back at Satis House, I pull off my bonnet and sit in the inky-dark dressing room. I am alone. Mother has not gone, though. I feel her presence in every fluttering flame and dancing shadow, in each plume of dust stirred by my steps; with every draught she seems to breathe. Last night I dreamed of being hugged by her. Muscles relaxed, breathing was easier, comfort surrounded me. When I woke my pillow was damp.

There is no one left on earth to love me or protect me. Perhaps Pip – but only perhaps. He is a unique creature, unlike anyone else I've ever come across, and my regret at letting him go is deep. It's too late for that, though.

Never one to let people in at the best of times, now, in the worst of times, I have shut down my emotions and am hiding in numbness. It's not much of a plan against my devil of a husband. There's been no time to hide any fortune from Bentley: he will get his hands on everything, and gleefully waste each halfpenny in front of me.

A fat-backed spider scurries over the back of my hand, resting on the arm of Mother's chair – mine now. They look so delicate with their long legs, so easy to kill. They lure their prey to them, and their prey only realises when it is too late that they have walked into an invisible trap. Just as they are struck with deadly speed and precision.

I will draw inspiration from them. I will prove Mr Jaggers right. I will best Bentley.

Lydia shocks me from my reveries.

'Begging your pardon, but you have a caller. Mr—'

'Lord! There's no need to announce me. She knows her master, don't you, Estella?'

Chapter Seventy

NOW

SATIS HOUSE, 1835

That voice. It catapults me back in time. *Pain. Terror. Helplessness. Smashing glass. Torn body. Broken spirit.*

I thought I was further down the road of recovery than this; that I was stronger. But I'm scared. I'm *shaking*. Words dry up in my mouth as I face my husband, the man who almost killed me, for the first time since my escape.

'So your mother is dead, eh? Condolences and all that. We'll put this place up for auction, sell off the contents; I've already put things into motion so you don't need to worry your little head about it.'

Bentley's hulking body turns to diminutive Lydia, who has reached an age where she shrinks more with each passing year. He shoves his hat, coat and gloves at her to take away. 'Consider this notice, with immediate effect. I want you off the premises by the end of the day. Let the others know, too, eh?'

She holds her apron to her face, visibly keeping her sobs in check as she scurries from the room clutching Bentley's paraphernalia. Still I can't speak or move. All my confidence has gone like smoke up the chimney. I grip my knitting to me as a comfort blanket, feeling the fine silk yarn and the scarlet beading I've put in place, along with the almost pin-slender bone knitting needles. I concentrate on the feel of them to keep me calm. Remember how I tried to get Mother to breathe slowly, and attempt to mimic it. I'm only marginally more successful than she had been.

Bentley steps towards me. My grip tightens on the needles. The ball of yarn falls to the floor and rolls towards him. He picks it up, amusement playing across his toad features.

'Yours, I believe. For now.'

He reaches out. I flinch. He chuckles.

'You're not going to make me have to do something we both regret now, are you?' he asks, voice so low it seems to vibrate through my body.

He runs his forefinger along my jaw and it is all I can do to swallow.

I want to kill him. I want to punish him the way Mother is punishing Compeyson in hell. I fantasise about wreaking terrible revenge on this devil for what he has put me through. My body trembles, pulled taut to snapping point with the urge to take the knitting needle and ram it into his ice-blue iris. He's so strong, though, so fast. I don't think I can do it.

I think of the spiders. I remember Jaggers' words to me: '*If it's a battle of strength, then he will win. But if it is a match of cunning, you will win.*'

How can I beat my husband when he is so much stronger than me?

Then I think of Mother. Of how laudanum helped contain her pain. It makes me realise there might be another option open to me.

An oblivion courtesy of drugs. I need not feel anything.

Through sleepy, half-open eyes I watch the dust floating in the air being hit by sunbeams that make them sparkle. A slow, wide smile stretches across my face and I try to reach out to touch the magic. Bentley has my arms pinned down. There's a tiny spark of fear and panic, but it's suffocated by euphoria. Whatever he does can't hurt me, I'm invulnerable, because – my goodness, I'm floating underwater, so heavy, so supported, and everything is blue here, apart from high above me the sunlight cuts through the surface, and I'm sinking down, down, down into my new home, so does that mean I'm a mermaid now...?

In hindsight, I probably didn't need to take quite so much of Mother's laudanum. A drop or two would have sufficed, but my haste made my hand slip and an opinion of 'the more the merrier' prevailed.

Now the happiness and indestructibility I felt thanks to the opiate have all but disappeared, replaced by shame at giving Bentley my body. There was no choice, though. It is enshrined in law as his absolute right to demand 'marital relations' with his wife, and if I did not resist there was a chance my beating would be less severe.

With or without the violence, I could not have endured the marriage bed without the laudanum.

A tear almost escapes, but I wipe it away and recoil from my hand which smells of *him*. My whole body does. I want to scrub myself clean.

'Estella, where are you? I want breakfast.'

Adjusting my collar over the red handprint circling my neck, I perfect a winning smile in the mirror before emerging from the dressing room.

'Here I am, husband.' My voice is husky, as if I have a cold coming.

'Lord, you made me jump. Are you trying to kill me from fright? What's to eat?'

'I'll ring for Lydia—'

'Servants are all gone. I got rid of them last night, remember?'

Of course. The summary dismissal of the loyal men and women who had been there my entire life had hurt so much I'd blocked it out.

Bentley is giving a cruel smile. 'You'll have to make something, Cinderella. You think that you're too good to be my wife. Well, this is what you're worth: to cook my food and clean my boots, that is all – and you're damned lucky to have that much. Unlike mine, your blood is not noble. You are a nothing, a nobody, and now you don't even have the protection of your weird mother. So what are you going to cook me? Chop-chop.'

My mind speeds. 'I've never cooked in my life—'

'Better learn, then. Or I can teach you lessons in something else, the choice is yours.' Those cold eyes, that thick-lipped sneer. Suddenly, he throws his head back and laughs. 'Lord! You took me seriously. Honestly, you're so gullible, Estella.'

He decides we should breakfast at the Blue Boar. He is mercurial during the brief carriage ride there, seeming to enjoy toying with me. The only thing that gives me strength to suffer it is the bottle of laudanum nestling in a discreet pocket in my skirts, ready for use should I need it. I don't want to take more but I will if I have to...

'I'm only having a bit of fun,' he says as we approach the entrance of the establishment. 'Can't you take a joke? Come on, smile, we're on honeymoon.'

With that the door swings open for us, held by a boy in a uniform with shining buttons and boots. Fawners appear and ingratiate themselves to the happy couple: the almost baronet and his fine new wife.

Once seated at our table, Bentley orders eggs, sausage, bacon, mushrooms, tomatoes and more for us both. I can't eat that much. Swallowing anything will hurt. I start to protest.

'Let me spoil you,' he says, in a way that sounds like a threat.

While waiting for the food to arrive, he announces a need to relieve himself and leaves the table. Now I'm alone it is so tempting to dose myself with more tincture, so that I might escape this vile reality. But the food arrives faster than expected. Knowing how Bentley loves his salt and pepper, I season it for him, adding a little extra for good luck. Goodness knows I need all the luck I can get right now. But we must make our own fortune, rather than trust to providence, and with that thought at the forefront of my mind, I lift the lid of the coffee pot to check on the contents. Swirl it around and smell its aroma.

Perfect. Bentley will be in good spirits after this feast.

'This tastes strange,' he complains after several mouthfuls. 'I'm sending it back.'

'Please don't, it's my fault. I was just trying to be a good wife by seasoning it for you, so if it's wrong then I apologise.'

He glowers. Then smiles and chomps another mouthful. 'You're learning. I'll make a wife out of you yet, with a bit of training.'

Another mouthful. My eyes can't leave his lips and the churning chewing.

'Are you not eating?' he asks.

'If you don't mind,' I say meekly. 'All I want is water. I seem to have picked up a sore throat from somewhere.'

'Lord! You better not be contagious,' he replies. He gives a little giggle.

The thought of catching a throttled throat from me doesn't put him off eating and drinking as if it is his last meal.

Next time he looks at me his pupils are tiny pinpoints in his mean eyes, but he gives a great laugh. He's enjoying himself; that's excellent.

Another mouthful and he's slurring his words.

His eyelids are drooping.

The knife and fork fall from his grasp with a clang that makes others look up from their breakfasting. I pick them up and hand them back. They drop into my waiting palm, so I give him a good draught of coffee instead, guiding it to his lips.

He sways in his chair and falls to one side onto the floor. My shriek catches the attention of anyone not already looking. The manager hurries over.

'Oh! Sir, my husband seems to have been taken ill. Could you help me get him into our carriage?'

With effusive thanks, while clearly and valiantly fighting off an attack of the vapours, I oversee things and soon Bentley is safely inside our transport. His driver gives me a curious look.

'We must head for home with all haste,' I order.

A crack of the whip and the sound of pounding hooves fills the air. We are heading for London and my new life.

Chapter Seventy-One

NOW

BENTLEY'S LONDON RESIDENCE, 1835

For the entire journey to London Bentley sleeps, his chest rising and falling so shallowly I'm concerned for his health. I find a mirror and hold it to his face; it mists with his breath.

Good. It would be most annoying to kill him accidentally, after all the effort of stopping myself from stabbing him when he first arrived.

As I asserted previously, I am not a monster.

Now there are independent witnesses who would, I'm sure, corroborate that my husband was suddenly taken ill, and that I was most distraught at the sight.

The previous night, voluntarily putting my head into the lion's mouth as it were, had been the hardest thing I've ever done. Try as I might to think of other ways, I came up with nothing else that would put my husband off his guard as much as my meekly submitting to him as if defeated. The only way to get through the disgusting act of our joining had been by drugging myself. As grotesque as it was, as much as it would stay with me for life, even through the laudanum haze, my plan had worked because afterwards Bentley felt he had the upper hand.

Before dosing myself, I'd been sure to seek out Lydia and thrust some money into her hand.

'Distribute this among the staff, and don't stint on your own reward,' I'd urged.

They had lost their jobs because of Bentley, but at least they would receive severance pay thanks to the £500 in that old jewellery box Mother had pointed out to me the night before her death. There had been no time for me to spend it, and with Bentley around there would be no opportunity. The servants deserved what I gave them – especially Lydia.

With the house empty, my husband had demanded his marital rights. There was no other choice open to me if I wanted to live, and so I had taken the black drops.

The following morning was the part of my plan that was left entirely to chance. All I could do was keep the laudanum with me and hope there would be an opportunity to dose him – and if not him, then myself. He'd gone to relieve himself at the Blue Boar, and his food arrived unexpectedly swiftly, so I'd taken the gift providence had sent… and poured almost the entire remains of the bottle of laudanum into his coffee pot, with the few drops left sprinkled over his food as an extra seasoning.

Thank goodness it had worked.

Both the worst and best thing about Bentley is his immense stupidity and arrogance. Even when he thought the food tasted odd, he didn't suspect I was acting against him. Arrogance is such a blinker – I should know, it brought about my own downfall, for I badly underestimated my husband's flaws before marrying him.

Now I am in Bentley's London home – our home. Joseph and others help to convey him to our bedroom.

'Should I call for a surgeon?' he asks. His breath comes hard between each word, for Bentley is a heavy fellow.

Joseph, Joseph, Joseph, I cannot make up my mind about you.

Can I trust him or not? Talking in subtext is all well and good, but sometimes things must be plainly spoken, and there is far too much at stake for me to take the gamble.

I consider tipping him, handsomely, for his hard work in carrying my great lump of a husband to bed, but fear that might raise suspicion rather than dampen it. Instead I lean forward so that my hair tickles his face, and I sense him breathing in my aroma.

Another one falling under my spell.

'I would never admit this to anyone else, but I feel I can trust you...
can't I?'

I widen my eyes and bite my bottom lip. Then pull back. Having
him desire me is one thing, but I don't want him to act on it.

He leans forward ever so slightly to hear my next words.

'Mr Drummle has not been at all himself since our marriage.' We
exchange a meaningful look that conveys that we both know Bentley
has been precisely and perfectly himself. 'I'm ashamed to admit it but
he's been drinking since the moment he woke this morning. He'll be
fine in a couple of hours when he's slept it off.'

Joseph nods in sympathy at this new black mark against his master.

'There is something Mr Drummle and I need you to do for us,
though. An assignment. We need you to find out more about Camilla
and Raymond. Who exactly do they owe money to, that kind of thing
– obviously, you know more than I about such matters. He says you're
to take as long as you want. All expenses are covered.'

He looks doubtful. 'Perhaps I should wait until Mr Drummle has
awakened.'

I bite my lip and nod. 'Of course. Although... well, you know what
he will be like if you've wasted time. He might be furious. But you
know him better than I.'

How quickly men accept that women have been cowed. It takes
nothing for Joseph to accept my new meek personality, deferring to
him in all things.

Thankfully, he agrees and leaves the house forthwith.

The rest of the servants are, for now, easily handled as I insist they
leave their master's care to me, his devoted new wife. They do as they
are told, of course.

Finally, I have some breathing space. How long it will last is another
matter...

It's been a month now since I settled into my city house. It really is quite
luxurious and I'm putting my own touches here and there to make it

more homely. Mother's dressing table has been transported here, and looking in the mirror makes me feel connected to her again. I feel she is looking back at me, approving of every decision made since her death. Sending me her best from purgatory.

Beside me the fire crackles approval.

'*Never trust.*'

'*Break men's hearts.*'

'*Make them pay.*'

Echoing my husband's actions, all the old staff have been replaced. It's not unheard of for a new bride to want to have a fresh start when she takes over the running of the household, and so the decision has raised no eyebrows.

I am inspired also by my time as a young girl in Paris, by Yvette. She taught me the power of perception; that as long as one is seen to be fitting in with society and following its expectations – being a good little girl, for all intents and purposes – then nobody takes any notice of women. This is how I intend to get exactly what I want: the freedom of being a married woman, with none of the pesky drawbacks. I welcome the invisibility society gifts me thanks to the magic gold band on the fourth finger of my left hand.

No one suspects a well-mannered, beautiful (I know it is considered vain to say such things about oneself, but why dissemble and demur?), respectful newlywed of having her husband locked up in a bedroom.

Bentley is so dosed up he's incapable of doing anything more than nodding his head, giggling occasionally, and dribbling. Thank goodness laudanum is easily available from shops, and is used by all from teething babies to women with painful monthly courses, so no one questions why I need so much of it. For now, my husband's withdrawal from society has been accepted as us enjoying blissful newlywed life. Another solution may be called for later, but for the time being it's enough to keep people away.

The new servants understand that he has health problems, and are paid generously for their discretion. I hope they earn their fee.

Joseph may require more careful handling, but for now he is happy to spend time and money away from his odious master. Meantime, I can finally grieve for Mother properly.

Mr Jaggers was right, as ever. I could have killed Bentley quite happily, but this way is far better. Instead of embracing the violence that sometimes lurks inside me, I've turned my back on it and have gained the upper hand through cunning not strength. At last, I can relax.

London's yellow glow from the gas lamps reaches up toward the indigo sky and spills down puddles of light across pavements. All is hustle and bustle even as evening falls. I breathe in the sounds and smells, and relax into the anonymity of city life where people don't meet one another's eye or take note of a neighbour's actions. I'm starting to fall in love with the capital.

I've just been to visit Lucy Brandley. Miss Lucy and I have formed an unlikely friendship. I'm teaching her how to knit, after her mother challenged me, saying it was impossible (she had tried for many years and given up).

Lucy lacks the will rather than the ability, seeing making garments as 'women's work' when what she wishes to do is use her formidable brain to become a surgeon. As I explained the rudiments of knitting, we talked about perceptions, and I informed her of my theory that sometimes in order to do what one *wants* one must *appear* to be doing what society expects. She saw the merits of this and in an afternoon grasped the basics of casting on and casting off, and knit one, purl one. She quickly grew the scarlet yarn I'd brought with me into the makings of a scarf.

She's a funny thing, loves her books, has no interest at all in fashion. Laughed, in fact, at my beautiful new dress, which rather hurt my feelings as I am rather proud of it. The modiste made it from the very latest Parisian patterns, and the huge hat is equally fashionable.

'How on earth can you move in that get-up?' she asked.

I drew myself up for a haughty retort – and found myself instead giggling, too.

'They're the latest sleeves, although they are large even for my liking. The new look is to pair them with a dropped shoulder hem like this. It does rather inhibit movement.'

We laughed as I tried to lift my arms above my head.

'A lady only needs to be able to lift a cup of tea to her lips,' I joked.

'If a gust of wind comes along you'll take off with those sleeves, they're like sails. Not to mention that gigantic bonnet.'

Somehow it was hard to take offence at Miss Lucy, because she was not being mean, she is genuinely confused by fashion. A pleasant afternoon was spent talking, knitting and laughing.

Although I left the Brandley house rather later than anticipated I've enjoyed the walk home so far. The pressure to have a constant chaperone is less now that I am a married woman, so although Mrs Brandley looked slightly shocked when I said I'd be walking, she did not insist on calling a hansom cab as it was daylight. Walking is the best way of piecing the city together as a whole and learning its personality. I pass flower sellers on street corners, match sellers, all manner of vendors, but now that it is getting dark they are disappearing.

Still, home is close by, so I feel no fear. There's an optimism for the future that I haven't felt before. I can make friends, visit people, have a normal life (or as normal as possible with a drug-addled husband under my control). Just look at me!

Another couple of streets, and I am surprised to see it has got dark early thanks to storm clouds gathering. It starts to rain. I badly underestimated how long the journey would take.

I'm passing an alleyway and hurry by – but hear something. A scuffle. I pause, listen.

Grunting, gasping.

I peer into the darkness, knitting bag clutched before me. The alley is between the main street's gas lamps and down it is impenetrable darkness.

A shriek. High-pitched and quickly cut off.

The sound of a woman in trouble.

Chapter Seventy-Two

NOW

LONDON, 1835

My feet are moving before my brain can catch up. Slowly, slowly, slowly edging into the deepening grey, ears impatient, straining. There's hardly any noise, just scuffling sounds, but my animal instincts know there's danger. There's a smell in the air, one I know all too well.

Maleness.

The smell brings the memories of Bentley and Paris and...

A waterfall of remembrance drags me over the edge, tumbling, helpless, breathless, to smash me on the rocks of my mind's memento mori.

The human part of me wants to run away and hide.

The animal wants to attack. The part of me that's been honed from childhood and forged in the white heat of Mother's hatred, the part hammered and shaped with constant blows of orders.

Ignore your feelings. Ignore your humanity and your emotions, and do what it takes to protect women and hurt men, because that's what you were put on this earth for.

My knife is out of my knitting bag and in my hands. I'm moving forward, full of crusading purpose. I will stop this man, I will save this woman.

Because he is Bentley and she is me.

Every man is him. Every woman is me.

My eyes are adjusting. I can see shapes. In the dim light are two people, wrestling. A large shadow and a slender one.

'Think you can turn me down and get away with it?' A man's voice. Coarse, with a twang of a Midlands accent. 'I love you, Bessie, and I will have you.'

The woman's bright white eyes bulge with fear in the darkness as he throws her to the floor. His slab of a back is to me; he is oblivious of my existence, intent only on what will happen next.

I know what's going to happen. I remember it happening to me.

I'll kill him.

I'm running now, skirts rustling like an angry wind through trees. My arm lifts to bring the knife slamming down into his neck with all my might behind it—

That's the intention. But my arms won't rise, not high enough. My fashionable sleeves stop me.

He's heard, of course he's heard my approach. Turns. Squints at the bizarre sight of me.

He sees the knife – twists… It slides off his jacket, barely nicking the heavy woollen material. Iron fingers close over my wrist, a vice squeezing until my bones almost bend. I let the blade drop. A slap across my face has me dropping to the filthy cobbles, slick with rain.

Something flashes past my face. Pain detonates through my stomach. Another kick has me coughing, retching.

The woman is shouting for help. At the end of the alley comes an answering shout in a deep male voice: 'Is everything all right down there?'

We're saved!

'Don't get involved, Stanley. If they sell their bodies, what do they expect?' says a woman's voice, so sharp it cuts through the air. 'Turn to God!' she calls down the alley, and then they are gone.

There's no help coming.

There's only me.

There's only ever been me.

Where's the knife? I can't see it. Does he have it? Must find the knife.

My knitting bag is lying nearby, the blood-red ball of yarn unravelling across the cobbles, looking grey in the barely-there light. I roll towards it, coughing, gasping, able to move only because the man has turned towards his first victim again. I pick up a knitting needle. It's very long, but not sharp.

With enough force, it might inflict an injury.

There's fire in my lungs, molten lava in my blood, pounding in my head. No one will ever hurt me again. I can see Bentley's face before me, not my assailant's. This time I will fight to the death.

A vicious upward stab at his stomach. It meets no resistance. I've missed him. Hands are on me. The knitting needle is prised from my grip.

'No!'

The woman screams, but I make no sound, just a silent parting of my lips in shock as I feel the full force of a blow that sends me tumbling all the way across to the other side of the alley. I hit the wall and slide down, winded. Can't get my breath. Lungs won't inflate.

The woman is fighting for me. She's pummelling the man's back. It won't do any good, she's far too weak, and he doesn't even slow as his hands sink into my hair and he pulls me up by it. The woman is an annoying fly to be swatted away; a backhanded slap has her sagging to the floor, but she doesn't fall all the way, instead hangs there on her knees, and he seems to be pulled backwards, off balance momentarily. I can't make sense of it, then realise what has happened: her hand is entangled in the long scarf he's wearing.

The scarf...

Breath coming back to me, I grab the other end of it and bear down. Weighed down by us both, he falls. I'm ready, scrambling forward, looping it about his neck more securely, bracing my feet.

'Pull with all your might,' I gasp.

We're in a tug of war. Life is the prize. Tighter and tighter the knitted wool stretches. The man bucks and leaps like a salmon swimming upriver. He scratches and kicks and flails. Blows land. I feel nothing.

At last he passes out.

The woman looks at me, panting hard. Says nothing.

'Go. Run,' I say.

'Is he alive?'

'His chest is rising and falling, sec.'

'I'll fetch help—'

'More trouble than it's worth. Go, and never speak of this to anyone.'

'But what about when he—'

'You think a man would admit to being bested by two women? He won't talk about this; he'll never trouble you again. Now go, before he wakes.'

'I… thank you. If it hadn't been for you…' She doesn't finish, just limps away as quickly as she can, and doesn't look back.

When I'm sure she has gone and that no one else is going to peer down the alley, I kneel over this man. Something unfamiliar is singing through me. Making me feel like I could fly, like I'm invincible, a goddess.

Someone with the power over life and death.

I shift behind him, so that his head lolls into my lap. He is out cold as I stroke a finger down his cheek and unwind the scarf from about him.

I take both ends of it and wrap them around my wrists, lift his body slightly so that my knees are braced against his back, replace the scarf about his neck, then bow backwards with my full weight.

He cannot fight back. It doesn't stop me. Nor does pity, for I have none.

He would have raped and murdered that woman he professed to love. He would have killed me for trying to stop him.

The scarf digs into my flesh because I'm pulling so hard. Around the inside of my head circles the shrapnel of my childhood bedtime stories.

'*Wound them.*'

'*Make men destroy themselves with their desire for you.*'

'*Avenge all women who have been left broken by the unfair sex.*'

My straining effort makes his booted feet dance against cobbles.

There's an infinitesimal shift in the body. His life escaping him.

He is gone.

My breath blows hard as a blacksmith's bellows as I stand. I look down at my throbbing hands. It's as if they belong to someone else.

This alley is dark, so dark, as dark as my soul, but still there is just enough light for me to see that my hands are stained with something sticky. My blood. In this half-light they look slate-grey but I imagine them as the colour of the half-finished shawl I have been knitting, the vibrant wool lying unspooled somewhere nearby, across the filthy cobbles. Just an hour ago Miss Lucy and I were innocently crafting together, now...

Beneath the blood veneer are cuts and open wounds where my knuckles have split on impact. An experimental try at gently opening and closing my hands to ease muscles cramped from the effort of strangulation makes me suck in my breath, short and sharp. A smell reminiscent of a butcher's shop hits my nostrils, mixed with the rank tang of urine, and the freshness of petrichor.

In that first surge of action the pain was blotted out. Now it is rushing in, along with...

I need to stop these ridiculous thoughts and try to find out where all the blood is coming from.

I hold my hands out and take a little shuffle backwards, trying to get away from them and the truth they spell out in violent vermillion. My stomach heaves. I hurriedly wipe my hands on my clothes – and they find something unexpected. My fingers explore. There is something protruding from my bodice. Something long and thin and cold to touch and... realisation dawns.

It is a knitting needle. My own knitting needle.

My heart, which had been slowing, speeds up painfully again, and as I pull the homely weapon out my breathing comes in gasping huffs that refuse to be controlled. My new corset has saved me, I realise. The needle was rammed home with such force that it could have killed me had it not hit the whalebone and slid harmlessly to one side, sticking not in my flesh but my clothing.

Murder, I think. *How did it come to this? That I should do such a thing!*

Terror, anger, regret, guilt...

They aren't the emotions singing through me. No, it is joy. Absently, I lick my lips. A metallic tang of blood spreads across my tongue as my thoughts start to shout.

Murder! It was always going to come to this!

Tears fall: happiness and relief forming a river down my cheeks. Slowly, I fold down onto the damp cobbles and curl up, red hands over my head, trying to quiet myself when all I want to do is scream my elation at finally accepting my fate.

This won't do. I must pull myself together or someone will discover me beside a cooling dead body. I scrabble on the ground and gather up my sodden belongings along with my thoughts.

Smoothing my hair, I try to put my huge bonnet back on, but it's too battered. Instead I pull up the hood of my cloak, and arrange it to hide the worst of my wounds. Stand in the onyx alleyway for a moment longer. Take a breath, and walk from black to grey to the soft halos cast by gas lamps. Normality. The busy crowds bustling around swallow me without a second glance; for I am an invisible woman. No one realises my truth.

My name is Estella; it means 'star'. I was, I believe, named in the hope I would be a light to guide my adoptive mother out of the emotional blackness that enveloped her. Instead, I have become something far darker than any night. Every moment in my life has brought me to here, every decision made by others on my behalf, even the times I've tried to escape destiny by acting in the opposite manner have somehow turned me around to this end. I have been manipulated, used, smashed, misunderstood, judged, loved, and feared. I've tried to please my mother, society, my husband… But the battle inside me is over, at last, and I accept everything about myself.

I am a woman in a man's world.

I am a weapon.

I am complete.

And I will kill any man I come across who hurts women.

A Letter from Barbara

Listen to two people describe an event and they are never identical. From the wording used, to the points emphasised, there are always differences, and even details such as the time or what someone said – even who said it – may be disagreed over.

This book is no different. It is not a retelling of *Great Expectations*, but it does include some familiar scenes that also take place in Pip's story – and that is the key, for *Great Expectations* is all from Pip's point of view. This book is all through Estella's eyes, and just as in real life, the two characters may sometimes disagree as to the details, the time, the place, the exact wording of speech. If *Estella's Revenge* were to be fitted over a map of *Great Expectations* there would be meeting points but it would not identically trace its outline. How can it? Therefore, I have not tried to replicate Pip's voice, nor Dickens' unique style, because all I would produce would be a weak echo. Instead, I have tried to capture the spirit and pay homage, while creating something distinct and unique – just like Estella herself.

I have been fascinated by Estella for years. From the first time I read *Great Expectations* I wanted to know more about this enigmatic character whom Dickens gave such a poignant character arc as she paid a terrible price for her pride and cold heart, but ultimately became a better person for it. It was in many ways a moral lesson typical of Victorian times. Yet Estella's acceptance of her violent husband and her life lessons didn't sit quite right with me, and there was a paragraph (spoken by Mr Jaggers about Estella's marriage to the violent Bentley Drummle) that made me wonder if Dickens had secretly agreed with me.

> *"The stronger will win in the end, but the stronger has to be found first... he may possibly get strength on his side; if it should be a*

question of intellect, he certainly will not... may the question of supremacy be settled to the lady's satisfaction!"

Over the years, with every reading of *Great Expectations*, my fascination with Estella grew. Here was a character who had been raised in darkness and told daily to never love, never trust, and to break men's hearts as soon as she was old enough to. Imagine the psychological damage that would have on a child – and the adult she would grow into. And so, through the gaps in *Great Expectations*, Estella's story began to grow in my mind. The more I researched and followed breadcrumbs left by Dickens, the more I realised my ideas for her fitted inside Pip's world beautifully; and the more I loved this strong yet vulnerable and completely damaged woman.

I do hope you enjoyed reading *Estella's Revenge* as much as I adored writing it. You can find out more about me and my books, and the next instalment in Estella's journey, by visiting my website or following me on social media.

www.barbaracopperthwaite.com
x: www.twitter.com/BCopperthwait
Instagram: www.instagram.com/barbaracopperthwaite
Facebook: www.facebook.com/AuthorBarbaraCopperthwaite
Bluesky: www.bsky.app/profile/authorbarbara.bsky.social

Acknowledgements

Without the incredible writing of Charles Dickens, who created in *Great Expectations* a timeless classic that I have read countless times (seriously, I have no idea how often I've read it since that first time aged fifteen) there would be no *Estella's Revenge*. My biggest debt of gratitude must therefore go to him.

When I began writing *Estella's Revenge*, it was a passion project that was never meant to go out into the world, but as it started to come together I knew I couldn't keep her to myself. Who could I trust with a book that meant so much to me, though? I allowed myself to fantasise about my ideal publisher and the word that came to me again and again was 'passionate' – I wanted someone who was as passionate about Estella as I was, who had total belief in her and wanted only the best. Top of my list? Keshini Naidoo at Hera.

I'm so grateful to Keshini and my wonderful editor, Jennie Ayres, who together have been Estella's biggest cheerleaders. From the very first Zoom meeting it was clear we all shared the same vision and ambitions for Estella, and every step of the way they have not only met all my wildest hopes but surpassed them. The entire team at Hera has blown me away with their enthusiasm. Jennie, special thanks to you for your kindness, patience, brilliant suggestions and for always pushing for Estella to be the best she can be. Also, Ross Dickinson, your work as copy editor was forensic – and your enthusiastic notes made my day. Thank you!

But every journey starts with a first step, and I wouldn't have had the courage to start exploring Estella's story (and keep going with it) if it had not been for the incomparable Sophie Hannah and her amazing Dream Author coaching programme. It has truly changed my life. I'm so grateful to Sophie – and also my fellow Dream Authors! Sarah Clayton is a fellow DA, and a fabulous coach in her own right. When I doubted I'd ever get Estella finished, she kept me going.

The members of The Savvy Writers' Snug have also been invaluable, offering support and advice.

Thank you to The Heath Bookshop, which provided a friendly, welcoming, book-filled space for me to write when I needed a break from working at home. It's become my favourite place to be!

Huge thanks to my lovely friends Shell Baker and Emmi Ketley, for always being there for me, and Anna Mansell, for listening to the rants, the tears, the fears, and the cheers! Julieanne Caie, my scientist friend and voice of logic, you've not only been a great support but the breaks in Tynemouth have healed my soul and inspired me.

My family deserve an award for always answering random questions at the drop of a hat – thank you Rona, Ellen and my best friend, Mom. Special mention to my big brother, Rory. And then there's Nan, whom this book is dedicated to. She passed away many years ago, but is always in my thoughts. She always offered up better endings to every film we watched together – I think I got my storytelling skills from her.

And if I really were to hand out awards, the biggest and shiniest would have to go to my partner, Paul, who understands when I disappear into a make-believe world for hours on end, who listens as I talk endlessly about the 1800s and plot ideas and characters and that I'm a bit parched so could I have a cup of fruit tea, please, and… It's not easy living with a writer, I'd imagine, but he never lets it show. Thank you for all your amazing support and belief in me even when I don't have any in myself. Big thanks to my dogs Buddy and Scamp, for the love and licks, and the gentle reminders that I need to get away from my desk and walk you guys.

And finally, my biggest thanks to you, my readers. Thank you so much for choosing *Estella's Revenge*! I'd love to hear your thoughts so do get in touch on social media or leave reviews wherever you can. I can't wait to share the next instalment of Estella's adventures with you!

Barbara Havelocke